SUBSUMPTION

CHOICE IS EVERYTHING

LUCIANO W. PESCI

First Edition. Copyright © 2020 by Somnio

Cover design by Rafael Andres

Edited by Lindsay Egginton

Published by Somnio

299 S Main Street, Suite 1300

Salt Lake City, UT 84111

lucianopesci.com

Ordering Information:

Quantity sales. Special discounts are available on quantity purchases by corporations, associations, and others. For details, contact the publisher at the address above.

Printed in the United States of America.

ISBN 978-1-7356190-3-3

❄ Created with Vellum

To everyone who believes in the Light.

CONTENTS

PART I

PARALLAX

SATURDAY, JULY 23, +1 NE

1

DEAD MAN WALKING

[Sequence ID# 928] [Data Begins]

T he last thing he remembered was finally breaking free from the suffocating confines of the putrid bathroom. His next challenge was shuffling through the dimly lit plane without bumping the shoulders of passengers sleeping in aisle seats. He was the only person still awake. The low hum of the cabin was hypnotizing, but the air was uncomfortably warm and smelled of stale sweat. Everything about the plane looked well past its expiration date. *Having this many people in such a small space is unnatural*, Marcus thought, jostling by incapacitated row-mates to his window seat. Instability replaced his sense of calm, as if the floor would drop from beneath him.

He took a deep breath to center himself, but before he could exhale, or fasten his seatbelt, one of the plane's alarms blared. The wall beside him ripped away, sucking him into the nighttime abyss. The whole incident happened twice: instantly and in slow motion, with both versions fading to black. At thirty-five thousand feet, there was a third of the normal oxygen, and Marcus lost consciousness moments after the plane tore apart. He fell until he was below the Death Zone, the boundary where human brains can stay awake. As his vision came back into focus, Marcus found himself tumbling alone through the darkness. An arc of golden light stretched across the horizon, separating the endless water below from the infinite space above. The sky was clear in every direction, and the moon's reflection danced across the purple sea in a long silver beam cut by isolated mountain islands.

Despite the present circumstances, Marcus felt peaceful. *This was a nice place to die*, he thought. As a child, someone told him that fear of death would shut down his brain, but his mind was sharper than ever. Time had slowed to a crawl. Each passing second was like a century. His life didn't flash before him in a series of visuals; instead, it engaged all of his senses. He remembered the feeling of his mother's embrace and the rosemary scent of her shampoo. He felt the earth under his bare feet as he explored the mountains with his father. Although his mind didn't remain on any memory for more than an instant, each immersed him.

How ironic, Marcus thought. Years ago, he'd read a *Popular Mechanics* article about consciously falling from an airplane that broke apart mid-air. He only remembered fragments of the story, including it was worse to hit water than concrete because it swallows you up even if you survive the impact, which a surprising number of people do. There was nothing but sea below. Marcus knew he had zero chance. He wasn't sure how much time was left, which liberated him from obsessing over the exact moment of his end. For now, he could enjoy being alive surrounded by unbounded beauty.

His mind wandered to the other passengers. He'd been the first one to board and avoided eye contact with the parade of first-world refugees carrying a hodgepodge of personal belongings to their temporary seats. If he'd known they were destined to die together, he'd have behaved differently. As Marcus contemplated the meaning of their shared fate, a massive explosion illuminated the night; it was the plane. The force was powerful enough to shove him across the sky, momentarily warming his exposed skin. He was naked, stripped of his clothing by the air rushing around him. As the orange ball of fire disappeared in his peripheral vision, the chill of the wind returned. Flickering scraps of metal, cloth, and plastic littered the air like confetti. It was all that remained of the other passengers. His heart ached for them, but he still had time to enjoy these fleeting moments of life, and a final wave of joy washed over him.

[Sequence ID# 928] [Data Ends]

Marcus woke up next to five members of the Cohort, three more than when he'd started the Sequence. Like the two that'd preceded them, all were holding uncharacteristically still. The large elliptical space was dark, and the low hum of the Liberty Bell provided a sense of momentary comfort. He searched his memory for any hint of what he'd just done, but drew an expected blank. His head, chest, and stomach were burning with pain. *This had to be the peak of his anxiety*, Marcus thought. *It felt like waking from a nightmare as a child, when fear, uncertainty, and doubt heighten the senses.*

He descended to the iron-red floor and shuffled toward his locker to remove the EXO. A note in the locker room invited him to party with the rest of his Cohort. From his conversation with Brad that morning, Marcus knew their time as a team was running out, but he had no idea they'd completed their final Sequence together. Antony was waiting, and since family came first for Marcus, he left the Lab without saying goodbye.

It was a hot July night, and the ground radiated as he walked off the University campus. The smell of barbecues and fire pits permeated the air, along with the muffled sounds of music. Thick grey clouds blanketed the sky now, and humidity magnified the orange sun as it slipped behind the mountains. *The world seemed stable, even if he was on edge. The peace was temporary since the fireworks would begin any moment. Utah was celebrating.*

He couldn't shake the uneasiness. Despite taking his recent drama into account, this was worse than usual. In an attempt at self-distraction, Marcus checked his phone, but the plan backfired spectacularly. There was a bombardment of encrypted messages about the end of the world from Jordan, a threatening email from Dianna cc'ing her lawyer, a dozen missed calls from Antony, and a single text from Monica. He cleared the other notifications and read Monica's message:

> *IMS. Plz stop ignorin me. I luv u. Don't end things like this. Just talk 2 me. :-(*

Marcus stopped and took a series of slow, deep breaths. Though the words didn't change, each reread caused a flood of different emotions to course through his veins. It'd been an intense four months. *For such a short amount of time, it felt like an eternity.* The shriek of fireworks caused him to jump out of his skin. As he regained his composure, his phone rang, triggering a memory of the choices that brought him to this moment …

PART II

SELECTION

TUESDAY, MARCH 15, +1 NE

2

FEDERATION CONSPIRACY THEORIES

Marcus was torn from his dream by the deafening shrill of the alarm clock. Its evil red glow flashed 08:38 as the sun peaked the ridgeline of the eastern mountains and poured into his small upper-floor bedroom. He'd slept through its repeated warnings after a restless night and now was late for class. He leaped out of bed and rushed to the bathroom mirror to complete his daily affirmation. This ritual influenced the outcome of a normal day for Marcus, but today it was critical: he was meeting his first Federation alien after class. Marcus squeezed a lucky coin in his right hand while he stared at the fear written across his face and spoke aloud:

I'm the man in the mirror. Better today than I was yesterday. And because today I may die, I'll use this opportunity at life to improve myself and help those around me. I'll stay calm and only focus on things I can control. I will not fear. No matter what I face, I'll face it from a place of peace and love. I'm capable of this. I'm the man in the mirror.

Marcus was just over six feet tall with slightly curled dark brown hair, broad shoulders, thick eyebrows, long eyelashes, and the olive complexion of his Italian mother. He had a strong square jawline, an enchanting smile, and hazel eyes that seemed to change color depending on his mood or clothing. Marcus threw on yesterday's black shirt and jeans before bolting down the tight old staircase, through the large kitchen, and out the side door. He could either walk the uphill length of campus to class in twenty-seven minutes or run it in thirteen. Today he'd have to run.

As he burst into the classroom, his momentum brought the instruction to a momentary standstill. All eyes were on him. There were twelve other students in his Federation Acculturation and Cooperation Tract (FACT), a higher education alternative setup after First Contact by the Federation to train Praetors, human emissaries working with the aliens to integrate worlds. These classes were small to foster personal relationships between students and their teachers and ran in tandem with the standard university system.

Marcus's FACT teacher was Bill, an older guy in body only, well over six feet tall with a silver ponytail and matching beard. He sported round glasses and dressed like he was on eternal vacation. A deep voice completed his towering presence, yet he was the most affable person Marcus had ever met. Bill instilled confidence in his students that no matter what they faced, he'd be there for each of them.

"Thank you for joining us!" Bill said with his characteristically large smile.

"Sorry," was all Marcus could muster between gasps for air.

"We've been talking about choice following Disclosure. Your abrupt appearance is apropos."

Bill was one of several Connectors hired by the Federation to teach FACT at universities around the world and was fluent in five core pillars of knowledge: art, hard science, history, mathematics, and social science. What set Connectors apart from professors of the old ivory tower ideology was their creative spark, an ability to find unexpected links between these five disciplines and fold that knowledge into one engrossing educational experience. Bill, like other Connectors, was accused of being a Shadow, a derogatory term for aliens masquerading as humans. Accusations persisted because the Federation looked and acted like people. This wasn't because God made universal beings in humanity's image, but rather a result of the Federation's cloaking technology easily manipulating the five human senses, leaving the mystery of Bill's identity unsolved.

"As I was saying," Bill continued while Marcus found his seat in the second row, "when First Contact took place on New Year's Day last year, we were hit with a wave of revelations. Overnight, we learned we weren't alone in the universe, and humanity was facing an imminent invasion from an unseen third group, the Confederation. The choice presented to us was either voluntarily integrate into the Federation's universal society or reject their offer of alliance and face the Confederation on our own."

"It's way too convenient there's one sensible choice in that situation," said Ameda, the class's sole black student and esteemed local rap icon. He played up this identity with horizontal tram lines shaved into his short hair, gold-framed glasses, and throwback M.C. Hammer-esque clothing.

"The Confederation threat to conquer and enslave us exists regardless," Bill said, pressing the tops of his hands against his lower back, interlacing his fingers, and twiddling his thumbs skyward while pacing. This stance reminded Marcus of kings and generals depicted in history books, and it signaled that Bill was in a state of deep contemplation.

"Assuming they're real," Ameda scoffed. "There's no proof beyond the Federation's word. The only firm detail they've shared is that the Confederation is human."

"That's a valid concern. Scrutiny of the Federation's claims, omissions, and actions is healthy," Bill replied.

"Do you think the Federation made it up?" Marcus asked Ameda. "If so, why? To what end?"

"What about world domination?" Ameda answered.

"In the fifteen months since the Federation arrived, they've been peaceful," Marcus countered. "They've never shown any desire for conquest or—"

"Minus North Korea," Ameda interjected.

"The exception that proves the rule," said Quinn, the class's ROTC soldier and unapologetic Irish loud mouth. "They brought that on themselves by preemptively attacking the Federation. Every other nation was smart enough to sign their peace treaty. The Federation did what humans have never been able to on their own: end state-level conflict. Attacking another nation means attacking the Federation, and no one wants to end up like North Korea."

"Right," Marcus said. "Everywhere you look, there's evidence the Federation is helping us."

"I don't buy it." Ameda turned around to face Marcus with his next challenge. "Your best friend is notorious for exposing all the ways the Federation could threaten us."

Marcus scanned the class for Jordan, but he was MIA. Ameda was correct; no one else on Earth knew more about Federation conspiracy theories than Jordan. Marcus's favorite theory claimed Buddhists could see through the Federation's cloak from a sixth sense developed through meditation.

"And Jordan's not the only one," Ameda continued. "Last month when we all went to hear that guest lecturer from George Mason—"

"Dr. Bryan Caplan," Lindsay clarified. She was an older student with big hazel-green eyes and brighter red hair than Quinn. She was Bill's teaching assistant, tasked with remembering such details.

"His survey data showed that 97 percent of intellectuals in the United States were suspicious about the promise of Federation integration and the benefits of free-exchange with them," Ameda continued, "assuming we don't collapse on our own from downward harmonization first."

"He also said those intellectuals were wrong," Quinn pushed back.

"Then why is the Federation isolating exchange to universities and advisory relationships at the Black Market? Just open the flood gates if the economic impact is gonna be so great for us."

"Project Noble is doing that," Marcus insisted. "Universities and classes like ours are ground zero for the transition. And Caplan, like anyone willing to point out the positive aspects of the Federation's presence, has been opposed, sometimes violently, by people screaming they're 'invaders' and 'occupiers' despite—"

"Jordan uses those terms. All the time," Ameda preempted.

Marcus knew he was right. Whispers made it clear the class was forming factions in the debate.

"Why universities?" Quinn asked Bill.

"According to the Federation, it's for their diversity. Universities represent a natural microcosm of humanity where people of different backgrounds and beliefs converge to learn. There's another point worth considering, Confederation and inter-state conflict aside: the Federation arrived at the height of our social instability. But, as the actions of some Coalition members prove, they still haven't eliminated inter-personal conflict like what Caplan and others are subjected to. Murders, and suicides for that matter, have continued at varying levels since disclosure."

"Wait, the Coalition, or the Confederation?" asked Ameda.

"It's easy to confuse the two, but I'm talking about the Coalition now. The fight against integration with the Federation's universal society unifies their loosely affiliated human organizations."

"That doesn't necessarily make them pro-Confederation," Ameda replied.

"Objectively speaking, their behavior benefits the Confederation —assuming they exist."

"Two things," Marcus jumped back into the discussion. "First, my girlfriend, Dianna, is a therapist for the Coalition at their Salt Lake clinic. She helps people with real problems, so it's not like they're a mindless monolithic mob, even though I believe they're wrong about the Federation. Second, the spike of murders and suicides after the Federation's Disclosure is down to pre-arrival levels, and in most places are now lower."

"Most of those deaths were religiously motivated," Bill explained. "If you look at the demographic patterns, it was disproportion-ately older uneducated people driving the trend. You kids don't appreciate how some people fear change since your generation is used to constantly adapting to new choices. The Federation's arrival challenged entire world-views, many of which go back thousands of years. Something as simple as the New Era calendar proved too much for a few people. They couldn't handle starting over at zero, with years before being negative values and those after being positive. Suicide and violence are predictable human responses to situations of uncertainty, but they are, like every-thing else, an individual choice."

"Why didn't the government just cover up the Federation's arrival?" asked Quinn. "They could've chosen to integrate without any of us knowing and told us after it was done."

"Could they have?" Bill challenged. "I know a lifetime of main-stream media has implanted the idea that an all-powerful govern-ment could sweep something like this under the rug with a few Black Suits, but the Federation went to the public with their Disclosure, person-by-person, simultaneously across the globe. Governments didn't have the option to cover it up. The only choice available was how we individually reacted. A few people went on murdering sprees, and a few more chose to kill them-selves. Everybody else adapted because people had already accepted alien contact as a matter of 'when,' not 'if.' The better question is why that was the case."

"Pop culture," said Lindsay.

"Definitely!" Bill answered enthusiastically. "That played a powerful role in preparing the public for the Federation's arrival, but what else?"

"Education?" asked Quinn.

"In what way?" Bill asked.

"When you're educated, it's easier to know when people are fucking with you," Quinn replied.

The class erupted into laughter.

"That's undoubtedly a benefit of education," said Bill. "But is that it? How does being educated translate to the mostly peaceful transition we saw?"

The class found itself collectively quiet.

"I'm glad our topic for the week sparked such a lively debate! I want to end our thesis day by telling you the tale of Buridan's ass."

"Nice," muttered Quinn, triggering another round of laughter.

"It's a paradox with roots back to Aristotle." Bill paced slowly through the wide symmetrical rows of seats. "The most popular version features a donkey. This animal is equally hungry and thirsty. To his left is food and to his right is water. Since he's a lazy ass, he'll go to whichever of the two options is closest. He swings his head back and forth to decide which life-saving sustenance is closer, but by chance, they happen to be an equal distance apart. Can you guess what happens?"

"The donkey dies," Marcus said.

"Correct, though I doubt you actually guessed it."

"My mom used to say I'd die like Buridan's ass when I'd take too long picking candy at the store."

Bill laughed from his belly before taking a deep breath and resuming. "Okay. Good. What do you and the ass have in common?"

"We both can make a choice," Marcus answered.

"Exactly," Bill replied. "You have the free will to make choices nobody else can make for you. You, me, us. We have more choices available than any generation that's ever lived. Said another way: we have more free will than our ancestors."

"With what?" asked Ameda.

"Your education, job, where to live, who to marry, which god to worship. Whether to believe the Federation's claims that the

Confederation is out there waiting for the right moment to pounce on Earth."

Another long silence began.

"Your tranquility tells me you appreciate the gravity of our thesis for this week, the ideas of individual choice and free will. Tomorrow, during our antithesis class, we'll attack these ideas with everything we've got. On Friday, we'll synthesize our knowledge and come to a consensus. Are there any other questions before we call it a day?"

"I can't believe this is the case," said Lindsay, "but I don't think we've discussed who came up with their names, the Federation and Confederation."

Bill chuckled. "I'm not sure. However, I doubt it was the Federation. I'd be shocked if they'd seen *Star Trek* before reaching Earth. There are uncanny similarities between our new alien allies and those depicted in science fiction stories, but that's a discussion about the genre for another day."

"Why are the names backward?" asked Ameda.

"What do you mean?" Bill probed.

"By definition," Ameda explained, "a Federation is involuntary, and a Confederation is voluntary. But the Federation is about voluntary choice, while the Confederation is about force."

"And yet," Bill said with a smile, "the side we choose is up to us. See you all tomorrow."

Marcus emerged from class into the unexpected warmth of the morning sun. It felt incredible on his skin. It'd been a dark, dry winter, with March roaring in like a lion. Trees were blooming, and everything felt alive as he slowly trekked across campus to meet his first, undisputed, alien. He'd gone less than a hundred feet when Velia, another student from Bill's class, caught up with him.

"Marcus, hold up. That was a pretty heated debate today. I thought you made some great points!"

"Thanks," Marcus replied curtly. He was ambivalent toward Velia because she seemed to spend more time watching him than paying attention to the actual lectures. She was a foot shorter than Marcus with deep brown eyes and wild curly brown hair that spilled past her shoulders. She had an athletic build and a friendly smile, but Marcus couldn't pinpoint the reason she made him nervous. Her incessant questioning and unavailing chitchat didn't help.

"Where are you headed? Want to cerebrate on the weekly topic?" Velia was referring to the required self-study time, a core part of FACT class.

"I can't today. I'm on my way to Carlson Hall."

"Really?" Velia paused, standing in place, then ran to catch up to him again.

He hadn't considered the consequences of sharing details about his interview with the Federation researcher. Since Velia knew about Project Noble from FACT, he didn't hesitate.

"You were invited to Selection?" she asked.

"I was."

"When? And how? That sounds so interesting! I'd love to know what goes on in the Lab."

"Yesterday at the Pi Day celebration. Federation Scouts dressed like Albert Einstein were—"

"Why?"

"Why what?"

"Why were they dressed like Einstein?" Velia clarified.

"Pi Day is also his birthday."

"How old would he have been?"

"I don't know," Marcus snapped. "Want me to Google that for you?"

"No need. Why'd the Scouts invite you?"

"They had a virtual reality game set up and—"

"What was the game about?" Velia's eyes widened.

"It was a first-person shooter against drones. I'm not trying to be rude, but I was planning to go over interview questions in my head on the way. If you don't mind?"

"Make sure to prepare an answer about what your biggest weakness is. It always seems to come up."

"Thanks. Enjoy the rest of your day."

"You too ...," she said with a look of unjustified abandonment. "Good luck!"

The damage was done, and Marcus spent the rest of his walk preoccupied with the guilt of being an ass to Velia.

Mesmerized by the magnitude of this moment, Marcus paced outside the Lab. Carlson Hall was a literal stone and mortar enigma of the Federation. Unlike the other schools with FACT, the University of Utah was unique for hosting the only Federation research Lab on Earth. People called it Utah's Area 51, the birthplace of a new wave of alien technology. Except here, the aliens were undoubtedly in charge. The real purpose of the Federation's Lab was known only through the Objective Statement for Project Noble:

For the cause of cooperation toward mutual progress. All exchanges will be individual, voluntary, and tied to commerce, education, or research through social experiments aimed at understanding the human Form to assist in the integration of worlds.

Marcus circled the building multiple times. Carlson Hall had an S-shaped layout, like the *Tetris* piece he hated getting as a kid. Its three stories looked tiny next to Rice Eccles Stadium, home of the Utes football team. Ute meant "land of the sun," but another possible translation was "people of the mountain." The name was taken from a local tribe displaced during Manifest Destiny. As Marcus stood in the stadium's shadow, he wondered if the Sabines, a people who suffered an identical fate during the expansion of the Roman Republic, saw their name used at Roman arenas. Marcus grew up immersed in history; his father had been a professor of Classics at the University of Utah and had an office in Carlson Hall.

Despite its historical importance as the first female dormitory on campus, and former home of the school's history department, the building was torn down a few years before the Federation's arrival to expand the neighboring law school; society needed more people to throw its stones. As part of the University's agreement following First Contact, the law school was later moved to a smaller footprint next door so the Federation could rebuild Carlson Hall, a feat accomplished during a single evening.

Marcus's mind was swimming as he approached a nondescript brown metal door facing the back-alley loading dock. This is where the Scouts told him to go. He was growing increasingly nervous, and began to mentally recite what he knew to avoid focusing on the unknowns. *Through that door was an interview with a Federation Shadow. This was the first step in Selection for the Cohort, an elite group of humans engaged in the Federation's social experiments as part of Project Noble.*

Marcus timidly touched the door's handle, pausing to take a deep breath before pulling it open.

3

CLOSE ENCOUNTER OF THE ACADEMIC KIND

Marcus was met by a disappointingly average academic office decorated with large oriental rugs, overstuffed leather sofas, and antique tables crowned with colorful Tiffany lamps. Tall frosted glass windows lined the western wall, and the tart scent of lemon wood polish permeated the air. An enormous mahogany desk, like the surrounding shelves, was overflowing with books. Despite everything having a rich golden hue, it felt welcoming. The room was empty of people or aliens. Beyond the sofas was a massive black door. Compared to the rest of the room's decor, it didn't seem to match.

Whenever Marcus encountered something this out of place, he'd involuntarily sing a song line from *Sesame Street*: "one of these things is not like the others." He hummed as he crept toward the door. He could see it consisted of two distinct parts: a wide arched frame built from dozens of tiny honeycombs and a pitch-black material where an entry should be. There was no handle. When he pushed on the solid surface, his hands slid away like they'd glided across ice before colliding into the soft, pliable frame.

"Welcome, Marcus," a booming voice said.

Marcus felt like his heart might burst from shock. The Federation researcher was standing beyond the couches. "I'm Brad. Nice to meet you."

Marcus stood frozen in place.

"Want to sit?" Brad gestured toward the overstuffed seats.

Marcus remained unmoved. Brad closed the gap between them, getting so close Marcus could taste the Shadow's breath.

"Are you okay?" Brad stared Marcus square in the eyes.

Marcus could only nod.

"Are you high right now?" Brad whispered.

"I'm, uh … no. I'm sorry, I'm just … I'm nervous." Marcus was starstruck by the fact that Brad was an actual star person. He cleared his throat. "Where would you … I mean which—where should I sit?"

"Wherever looks comfortable. And relax, I was trying to lighten the mood." Brad came alive with laughter, sitting on one of the couches. "This isn't the Olympics, so doping won't disqualify you. Come take a load off. Did you just come from class?"

"Yes." Marcus felt accomplished for answering so decisively as he sat opposite Brad. He was finally calm enough to assess the situation. Brad looked normal. He was a few inches under six feet with a dad bod. He appeared to be in his early forties, was balding, and wore thick black-framed glasses that magnified his grey eyes. He sported a big smile, and as Marcus could tell, he had a dry sense of humor. Brad held a leather-bound notebook emblazoned with the Federation's blue-and-gold logo featuring a bird of war in profile with wings extended. *It looked Roman*, Marcus thought.

"How rude of me. Do you want anything to drink?" Brad asked. "We've got every type of water under the sun or milk … Mountain Dew … crab juice?"

Marcus knew the reference from an episode of *the Simpsons*, but was so shocked a Shadow would say something like that he didn't respond.

"Not a *Simpsons* fan? Was that before your time?"

"I thought that's what you were referring to. … Yes, I'm a fan … this is … so weird." Marcus was losing his cool again. "May I ask you something?"

Brad laughed. "Of course. Anything. Just stop talking to me like I'm your superior or this meeting will be short and boring. What's your question?"

"Do you have a last name?"

"Nope. Just Brad. Like Madonna or Beyoncé."

"Why are you wearing a white lab coat?"

"Now, that's an interesting question!" Brad leaned forward. "The simple answer is it's comfortable, versatile, and I make it look good. But the real answer is I'm signaling my quality and trustworthiness through something you already associate with those things."

"A doctor's lab coat?"

"Exactly. You know, nobody has ever asked me that question before. Enough about me, we're here to talk about you. What do you think about me?"

"You're a … an … alien?" Marcus felt strange hearing himself say the word out loud.

Brad grinned from ear to ear. "Yes. Yes, I am. I won't make any *E.T.* jokes, so don't ask. Unless you're tipping, then I accept all major credit cards and crypto."

Marcus was baffled by such an extraordinary event happening in such an ordinary way. He was raised on movies where aliens were larger than life, fearless, and intimidating. Brad was none of these.

"So tell me about yourself, I'm dying to know everything about you," Brad probed.

"I'm nineteen. I grew up in Utah, but I'm not Mormon. This is my second semester as a sophomore—"

"You're in Bill's FACT class, right?"

"I am. You know Bill?"

"We go way back." Brad's eyes sparkled. "I assume you're planning to become a Praetor with the Federation post-graduation from Bill's class then?"

"That's my hope," Marcus said with a nod. "The idea of being an intermediary for humanity as we integrate into your galactic civilization is incredibly exciting to me."

"Would you say it's your *pothos*?"

"That means deepest desire, right?"

"Yes," Brad confirmed.

"It's definitely in the top three at the moment."

"Let's back up for a second. What motivates Marcus Adams to wake up every morning? What's the single most important thing in your life right now?"

Marcus didn't hesitate, "My family."

"Interesting. Who does that include?"

"My brother Antony, my girlfriend Dianna, and my best friend Jordan. We live together."

"All four of you?"

"No, sorry. Just me and Jordan. We have a house a few blocks from here. Dianna has her own apartment on the other side of campus, up by the hospital, and my brother's house is thirty minutes south of here in Lehi."

"I didn't mean to make assumptions, but this is Utah." Brad winked. "Tell me about each of them."

"Jordan's been my best friend since I was six. He's also in Bill's FACT class, but he doesn't want to become a Praetor. He enrolled to keep an eye on me and 'understand the enemy' as he put it. Antony is my older brother by nineteen years. He runs a data company and isn't married. I started dating Dianna during my first semester just before you, I mean the Federation, arrived."

"You've been dating for … eighteen months?"

Marcus knew what Brad was hinting at. "It's complicated."

"Your Form's relationships invariably are."

"We … well, specifically I, didn't plan to take things this slow. It's just how this is playing out."

"Why?" asked Brad.

"I don't know if there's one reason. Things changed after the Federation arrived."

"Tell me more …"

"To put it in terms you'd understand, our relationship is like a supernova. It started with a passionate, instantaneously explosive moment. It's been nebulous ever since. I think we have a strong enough bond that we'll be pulled back together to recreate something radiant, instead of fading into the cold vacuum of interstellar space."

"You should've been a poet," Brad smiled. "Have you told your family you're here today?"

"No, none of them know."

"Hypothetically, if I offered you a spot in Selection, how would each of them react to the news?"

"Antony would be excited for me. For sure. Jordan and Dianna think you're the devil, so that'd be a tougher sell. Again, not that *you* are the devil—"

"I get it," Brad replied. "So why are you here? What do you hope to get by joining the Cohort?"

"I want to protect my family from being enslaved by the Confederation. I believe I can do that with you, through Project Noble."

"What about the rest of your family, beyond Jordan, Dianna, and Antony?"

Marcus's stomach sunk. He hadn't prepared an answer to this question, and an awkward silence began. As second after uncomfortable second passed, Brad smiled with ease; he clearly knew about Marcus's parents but wasn't going to be the first to say anything.

"As of yesterday," Marcus said after a long pause, "both of my parents have been dead for a decade."

"You're an orphan?"

"Yes."

Brad's growing smile felt inappropriate. "Tell me about them."

"My father's family was Scottish and English. He can trace his lineage to the Samuel line of the colonial Adams family. My mother was Italian, and both of her parents were immigrants."

"You're using an awful lot of past tense," Brad replied.

"Antony is my only living blood relative."

"Tell me what your biggest weakness is."

Marcus couldn't believe this question came up and cursed himself for not heeding Velia's advice.

"Need a moment to think it over?" Brad asked.

"I've had a hard time controlling my emotions. Mostly when I was younger."

"Which ones? That's a pretty broad list."

Marcus rubbed the outline of his lucky coin through the pocket of his pants. "Anger, to the point of blinding rage. I saw a few therapists before I learned it was all stemming from a fear of losing the people closest to me, especially my immediate family."

"Because of your parents?"

"One of the earliest memories I have is my maternal grandmother's wake. It got worse after a cluster of deaths among the kids from my school. But it went off the rails after my parents died."

"But you've learned to control it?"

"I don't slip into a debilitating depression like I used to. The therapists called it learned helplessness. I feel like I've overcome that part," Marcus said confidently.

"Is that why you carry a Memento Mori coin everywhere you go?"

Marcus was shocked by Brad's insider knowledge. Before he could answer, the Federation researcher responded, "Denim isn't a barrier to my vision. I gave you an ocular patdown and clocked it in your pocket before you sat down."

"My final therapist gave it to me," Marcus retrieved it. "He taught me about Stoicism and these coins."

"I'm a Stoic at heart myself. That's a significant part of their tradition." Brad took his glasses off and rubbed the bridge of his nose before placing them back on his face. "Marcus, my man, I'm officially offering you a position in Selection."

Marcus was overflowing with enthusiasm when Brad cut him down. "Before you answer, you need to be clear about what this means. So listen carefully. Once you accept the position in Selection, you'll begin a series of social experiments called Sequences. The Cohort nicknamed this Subsumption. Everything your five senses tell you will lead to the false conclusion that it's real. In some Sequences, you'll be yourself: Marcus Adams, the devastatingly handsome FACT student orphan. In others, you'll be a completely different person. The needs of the experiment will determine your identity. Every Sequence will test you mentally, physically, and emotionally. You'll never be hurt or harmed in any real way, and when it's over, you'll wake up feeling like you took a nap with no memory of what took place. The data collected during these experiments will be the sole property of the Federation."

"What's the point of your research?"

"I'm focused on 'big ideas' like how your Form makes choices, the effects of fear and joy, or the acceptance of failure, stuff like that. Your data, along with the rest of the Cohort's, will be used in Project Noble to understand your Form as we integrate worlds. It's incredibly important work."

"How often will I have to do a Sequence?"

"During Selection, it'll be every day, including the weekend. If you miss a session for any reason, you'll be unceremoniously canned. But Selection is more than Sequences. Throughout all of this, you have to keep up with the rest of your life. Family, school, being a model citizen. All of it."

"Okay," Marcus echoed his earlier enthusiasm.

"If you survive Selection, then you can join the Cohort and determine your own schedule."

"How often do the other Cohort members do Sequences? And how many of them are there?"

"There are eleven active members. Seven others have been redacted."

"What does redacted mean?"

"They quit, and for the record, the rumor we ate them is false," Brad smirked. "On average, the active members are here a couple of times a week, and some come every day. But until you're through Selection, you'll have no overlap with them in the Lab. It'll just be you and me."

"Is this a lifetime commitment?"

"You're asking me to predict the future?" Brad's eyes widened. "That depends on you. This is all voluntary. You can redact yourself at any time for any reason. And we don't expect you to work for free. Each Cohort member receives their quota of Tek in exchange for the time they log in the Lab."

Marcus had never used Tek. However, he had a general sense of what it was: a one-way version of the Federation's cloaking technology that let a user manipulate their perceptions, but not those of others. Although it was literally honeycomb-shaped, Tek was a figurative black box, the size of a postage stamp, and just as thin. It never had to be charged, made no noise, and had no wires. It was lighter than paper, equally pliable, and completely indestructible. Users wore Tek like a nicotine patch. It turned on when you thought about wanting to use it, and turned itself off when you were done. Even though no one knew how Tek worked, no one cared. It did what they desired before they had to ask, which is why it'd become one of the most high-demand products in the world.

"What do people use Tek for?" Marcus asked.

"There are two primary buckets of utilization if you want a simplifying metaphor," Brad replied. "The first bucket holds all the Tek features related to SIMs—"

"Those are fake worlds, right?"

"Sort of. SIMs are micro-worlds the user explores in the same detail as their daily life. They're a simpler version of the immersive experience technology used in the Lab for Sequences, but your Form makes the SIMs for either personal or mass consumption."

"How?"

"You lay back somewhere, get comfortable, call up the SIM with your Tek, close your eyes, and experience a turnkey reality. It's an out of body experience inside your brain."

"I should have been clearer. I meant, how are the SIMs made?"

"My bad," Brad said. "Tek can record your life in real-time to create a SIM, a process your Form calls Netting, which makes it the ultimate memento since you can relive an experience in perfect detail."

"Like a snapshot of life?"

"Exactly. Couples can experience the excitement of their honeymoon again, families can relive their favorite milestones, or mourners can revisit the final rites of a loved one on an anniversary. You can also live-stream your point of view. Periscope Parents—"

"What's that?"

"A name your Form gave to the guardians who check on their kids through the child's eyes using Tek."

"Creepy ..."

"Your media loves that feature too. They use it all the time, and it's revolutionized reality television."

"My brother said Tek is killing the media industry."

"Murdering it in broad daylight in front of its family. The old guard corporations are, anyway. They're being displaced by a boom of individual SIMatographers who make Contrived Nets that let you live a scripted story instead of watching it. But it doesn't look like it'll kill your adult entertainment industry, those people are resilient. They've unilaterally determined every media format since at least VHS by adapting and growing, Tek is no exception. They've pioneered a slew of new uses for it, all in true first-person," Brad winked again.

"Is that the only way to create a SIM?"

"No. You can mine your brain for memories of past experiences, a process called Derivative Ghosting."

"I could relive anything from my life?" asked Marcus.

"If you can remember something, it can be cataloged and stored for future use. You could relive a moment from your childhood or hold your parents again. Think of it like New Era scrapbooking. The quality isn't the same as something you'd record in real-time with Netting, since memories are subject to the retrograde of your brain, but they're much better than a faded photo or shaky video."

"Can those files be shared too?"

"Yes. Which is why the criminal justice system loves Tek; the days of lying to judge and jury are over."

Marcus's mind raced through all the possibilities.

Brad set his notebook down on the coffee table between them. "The second bucket for Tek's utilization has nothing to do with SIMs. It's about how you interact with the world around you, known as Complementing. This feature allows you to filter reality as you experience it."

"Filter which parts?"

"Anything that affects your five senses. You can't change physical realities, just how you perceive them."

"I don't understand," said Marcus.

"If you live in a one-bedroom apartment, you can experience it as a palace if you don't try to walk through any walls. Bland food can taste like the finest dining and music can stream to your brain wherever you go, without bothering your neighbors. Complementing with Tek is the zenith of individualistic expression, a world for one where every detail is tailored to your preferences. Some of your Form use it as a daily enhancer, while others use it to live another life altogether."

Marcus said nothing, so Brad continued with his list. "Tek can also translate languages instantly, a feature called Babbling. It breaks down one of the last dividing lines among the versions of your Form."

"Why is Tek my compensation for Subsumption?"

"Technically speaking, there's nothing else on Earth as valuable per ounce than Tek."

Marcus was feeling more relaxed and sat forward to match Brad's posture. "Tek manipulates reality?"

"Your personal reality, yes. And your Form can't get enough of it, which brings us back to you, your role in this Lab, and why your compensation is with Tek. Global demand is being supplied entirely by the active members of the Cohort. If you pass Selection, you'll be joining this elite group and can reap the financial benefits of that privileged position by supplying Tek to the market."

"If I pass."

"Correct, and I'm sure you've already heard our failure rate is nearly 100 percent."

"What happens if I fail?"

"At the highest level, the fate of the universe is put in jeopardy. But on a more personal level, you'll sink your Form's chance at integration, leaving them vulnerable to the Confederation. You came here because you want to stop that from happening, and you're wise for it. One way or another, war is coming. The better we understand you as a representative of your Form, the more we can help you protect yourselves from the jaws of Confederation wolves."

"Why you do care?" Marcus asked. "What's in it for the Federation?"

"That's a cynical question," Brad scoffed. "In a word, the fate of the universe hinges on your Form … what you do will determine whether we all survive."

Marcus paused. "When will the war take place?"

"I wish I knew. Things are in motion, so soon. The Confederation has amassed forces near Proxima Centauri and can travel nearly the speed of light. They're only ever five years away."

"Five years is a long time," Marcus replied.

"In universal terms, it's less than the blink of an eye. Time is not on our side. Integration with the Federation involves three distinct milestones. M1, the first and most important, will be reached when I complete my work and fully understand your Form. Your Form will reach M2 once Earth has transitioned socially, economically, and politically to a full member of the Federation. And M3 will be reached when your Form's battle readiness is deemed sufficient to face the Confederation. That's substantial ground to cover in five years, assuming they start their journey tomorrow."

"From Proxima Centauri?"

"Correct," Brad replied.

"Is their home planet in that system?"

"No, they occupy two planets in the Vega system."

"Vega?"

"Asimov and Sagan were prophets," Brad chuckled before getting serious again. "The Confederation also has a special forces unit called the Black Star Hunters based in the Sirius system."

"Where did the Confederation come from?"

Brad fiddled with the lapels of his lab coat. "They were part of the Federation. Until the Schism."

"What's that?"

"A separation that's proven to be irreparable so far."

Marcus slumped back into his seat.

"I realize this is like drinking from a firehose, but there's one last point to discuss. I don't expect you to keep the details about what you do at the Lab secret, but for your protection, you should limit it to those you can trust. There are plenty of people who don't like the Federation or the work we're doing. You don't want to become a lightning rod for their irrational animus."

"The Coalition?"

"Among others. Making it into the Cohort is like winning the lottery. You can't begin to anticipate who will emerge to get something from you if they knew."

"What stops people from camping out across the street and watching who comes and goes?"

"The Pomerium. It's an extension of our cloaking technology. Any would-be paparazzi only see a boring old building, meaning you can circle it with immunity from prying eyes." Brad smiled larger than usual. "So there's my disclosure. Take a walk and think about it. If you want to start Selection, be here tonight at 8:00 and we'll jam."

Marcus was ready. This was what he wanted. He started to commit on the spot, but Brad stopped him. "Take some time and pull a Ben Franklin on this decision."

"Money?" Marcus was confused.

"Benjamin Franklin developed a method for listing the pros and cons when weighing any decision, an idea he got from the philosopher Plato. If it worked for them, it could work for you. You need to fully understand this choice because no one else can make it for you. You're alone in this." Brad stood up and extended his hand. "It was nice to meet you, Marcus. Thanks for stopping by."

PART III

TOTAL AWARENESS IS PARANOIA

TUESDAY, MARCH 15, +1 NE

4

POST OFFER SHOCK SYNDROME

Brad's warning replayed inside Marcus's mind as he stood outside the Lab, reflecting on the last half hour; Subsumption sounded great, but Brad was insistent about taking time to consider the choice. Marcus began his mental pros and cons list, but his stomach groaned, demanding attention. He hadn't eaten yet today. This afternoon he'd attend a symposium on Rome that marked the Ides of March, having been one of the lucky students to win a lottery seat to the blockbuster event. Since that was hours away, Marcus headed home for food and the inevitable confrontation with Jordan about Brad's offer to start Selection.

Jordan was loyal. He'd broken his father's heart by passing on legacy admission to Stanford after Marcus's last-minute acceptance to the University of Utah. Though not blood-related, they were brothers in every other way. Fate brought them together when Marcus's family moved to the mountain town of Sundance, where Jordan was living a rich-kid lifestyle: surrounded by material abundance but suffering a scarcity of supervision and emotional support. Jordan's parents were bound to their careers by golden chains, so he finally found the home he wished for with Marcus's family.

Jordan was a few inches shorter than Marcus, overweight from an excessive drinking habit, and had an abnormally thick beard for a nineteen-year-old. Tattoos of cartoonish bees covered his left forearm, along with the phrase "paranoia is total awareness," and he sported piercings in his ears and left eyebrow. He believed society peaked in the 1980s and dressed like a character from the decade's seminal sci-fi movie *Weird Science*. To the rest of the world, Jordan was known as the EDM prodigy DJ Beez Nutz, making him a bonafide celebrity on campus. He was a master of manipulation, a skill he paired with a passion for public speaking to spread Federation conspiracy theories. This was an echo effect of his childhood trauma, having spent most nights alone listening to the paranormal-themed radio talk show, *Coast to Coast AM*.

Jordan funneled the public's distrust of the Federation into his Lyceum, an online group of armchair sleuths dedicated to exposing the alien race's "true intentions." Individuals of all identities and intellectual abilities converged on the Lyceum to discuss theories ranging from historical alien visitation to manipulation of human genetics, lost civilizations like Atlantis, and stargates. The most popular theory, offered by Jordan himself, claimed the Federation was gathering data in anticipation of a global attack on humanity. Debates were vicious, protracted, and hilarious. Whenever *The Onion* ran out of new content, Marcus would visit Jordan's site and laugh at how people behave when given a modicum of anonymity.

Marcus knew his friend was crazy but wrote the behavior off as a consequence of Jordan's proclivity to constantly, chemically, alter his own consciousness. He accomplished this through a mix of cannabis and alcohol, but sometimes included mushrooms, MDMA, and DMT. He claimed to own the only surviving copy of

Polybius, the mythical 1980s arcade game, which he'd purchased off the dark web for its supposed ties to the CIA's MKUltra program. Marcus only played the game once; the hallucination-inducing movements, colors, and sounds were too overwhelming.

Jordan justified his perpetual mental modification as a fast pass to the flow state, the alleged source of his creativity, citing the same pattern in other famous writers, artists, and leaders. He'd learned his favorite mind-altering trick from surrealist painter Salvador Dali, who would fall asleep holding a large metal key above a plate on the floor. As he passed into the dream realm, he awoke to the clatter of the key striking the plate, and would then furiously create his art. Jordan built a similar system using biometric data to jolt him from bed so he could make music or muse about the threat of a Federation apocalypse.

Marcus entered the side door of their house the same moment one of Jordan's randos ran past him, shoes in hand. She had jet black hair and equally dark eyes. Bright red lips contrasted against her pale skin, and earlobes full of piercings complemented the rest of her almond-shaped face. A curvy body hid beneath the oversized acid-wash denim jacket she was wearing. Jordan was sitting at the kitchen counter and forced words through a mouthful of food, "Welcome home, bro."

"Was that Bonnie from FACT?"

"That girl is straight-up wild. We did this whole Bonnie and Clyde roleplaying thing. She should get an Oscar, that's all I'm saying. But yes, she's in the brainwashing class with us. How was it this morning? We decided to have a dual cerebrate session instead." Milk dribbled from the sides of his mouth as he grinned. "You hungry?"

"That looks like you're eating a bowl of Oreos—"

"Plus, heavy cream. The breakfast of champions."

"I'll pass. Class was good. We talked about the Confederation."

"That's some Project Blue Beam bullshit," Jordan growled, referencing *the* cornerstone upon which his Federation conspiracies were built.

"And you're our Serge Monast. When will the earthquakes start? I want to get that in my calendar."

"Laugh all you want, dude. The holographic shitshow started the second the Federation showed up. Do you need me to get an updated body count for you? Mark my words: Tek is the gateway for their telepathic communication. How do you not see these parallels?"

"Personally, I'm excited about the rapture of when we'll all get lifted into the sky. That's on deck, right?"

Jordan turned his focus to scraping the bottom of his bowl. "So ... where've you been? Class ended an hour ago."

"I was at Carlson Hall."

Jordan, still chewing, stood up and moved closer to Marcus. "What?"

"I was at the Federation Lab, interviewing for Selection into their research Cohort."

"Wow ... I'm surprised to see you alive. How'd you manage to escape the 9th circle of hell?" Jordan massaged Marcus's stomach. "Or did they just rape you and lay their alien eggs in your abdomen?"

"It was disappointingly normal. Even the researcher, Brad, was anticlimactic. You'd walk past him in public and never know he's not a human."

"Everything looks normal so you don't question the abnormal shit they're doing in there. Seriously, I don't understand how someone as smart as you can't see this for what it is. They're like Rome two thousand years ago, not rocking the boat by changing anything after they take over so everyone believes things are okay. It's an elaborate form of population control. Maybe you don't remember all the stories your father told us, but I still do."

Marcus refused to take the bait, so Jordan changed tactics. "Did Brad say you're the Quiznos Cadillac?"

"You've lost me. I don't get the reference."

"It's from *Dune*, dude. The chosen one. The 'Kwisatz Haderach.' If you're going to cavort with those invaders, you should brush up on what other humans have predicted they'd be like."

"I don't think they're giant sandworms, I mean I can't say for sure, but Brad fit in the building—"

"I'm talking about understanding their motives. The hidden things they want but aren't telling us."

"Seemed aboveboard to me. I'm pretty sure I'll go back tonight. I've been offered a spot in Selection."

Marcus forced a moment of silence as he forged through the confines of their fridge. The small space smelt of rotting produce. When he reemerged, Jordan was right next to him. "I think you're making the single BIGGEST mistake of your life if you go back there. You'll regret this. I promise. Why do you think they pay people so much with something you can't get anywhere else in the world?"

"Don't do the rhetorical question thing. Out with it. We both know you're going to say it anyway."

"Those Cohort WHORES," Jordan shouted, swinging his still-clenched spoon toward campus, "have to be distracted from the obvious truth."

"Which is what today? I haven't been online yet."

"The same thing it was yesterday, and the day before, and the day before that—they're supplying intimate knowledge of how we work so the Federation can destroy us with the least effort."

"Brad didn't look like a conqueror to me."

"They're bigger, stronger, and faster. They can't be stopped. We've already been conquered, Marcus, now it's a matter of what they choose to do with us. And you want to be a part of that? Why? What could you possibly get out of this? It's not like you need the money …"

Only someone with such intimate knowledge was capable of a comment that hurtful, Marcus thought. "I want to do my part to protect humanity from the Confederation. I'm doing this for all of us. Even for you."

"Thank you, Jesus!" Jordan cackled. "You'll have to keep secrets from me. This won't be like middle school when you stole that guitar from music class. This time, if you talk, you'll put everyone in danger." Jordan was referring to the Lyceum's theory about an enforced code of silence, an omertà, among Cohort members, since none had talked to the press and no one knew their real identities. "Do you think you can keep a secret like that from me?" Jordan whimpered.

"Like you don't have any secrets of your own."

"False equivalency. Don't bring me into this. It's about the choices you're making. Right now. You have no idea what really happens in that Lab. And when you find out, you won't be able to tell me."

"That's not true. Brad said I could tell whoever I want. I just need to be selective about it."

"I will have to expose you. You know that right."

"No, you won't," Marcus said confidently. "You're talking from a place of anger."

"What about Dianna? Have you told her yet?" Jordan obsessively stroked his beard.

Marcus hesitated with an answer.

"Right. Aboveboard my ass! You didn't tell either of us because you're lying to yourself."

"Thanks for the free therapy," Marcus mocked.

"You have to tell her. You owe it to her. And she won't react well to this."

"Let me worry about *my* girlfriend. You're inventing problems based purely on assumptions."

"What the fuck does that mean?" asked Jordan.

"You still haven't explained why the Federation, with the infinite power you say they have, hasn't destroyed or enslaved us." Marcus clarified.

"Yet!"

"Right … yet …"

"Tek is their version of a scouting party. Look at its acronym: Telekinetic Electromagnetic Kapture."

"That's an urban myth. Billions of people use it every day, and nothing has happened to them."

"YET! None of them has the slightest idea what's going on."

"Do you know something billions of other people don't?" Marcus said, squinting at Jordan.

"People stopped paying attention long ago. They couldn't keep up with the pace of technology: printed organs, water captured from thin air, asteroid mining, self-driving cars, robot baristas, and sexbots. It was overwhelming. Then along comes Tek. Perfect timing. What are the odds? People were craving the next great product and had zero interest in understanding how it works."

"They're busy enjoying life. That's a bad thing?"

"There's an infinite number of ways Tek can exploit people. So yes, it's a terrible thing. Those nitwits are wrong, and so are you for getting involved without understanding what's going on."

"What am I missing? We sit in the same class. I read what you read. I know what you know."

"No, you only know the official script and the partial evidence to support it, because that's what you want to believe. It's confirmation bias, bro. Don't be blind to what you can't see."

"You say that all the time, but I still don't understand what it means."

"It means that until a few hundred years ago, we didn't know colorblindness existed. A FEW HUNDRED YEARS! What makes you think we've figured out all the possible ways the Federation could exploit us with Tek?" Jordan noticed his hyper-cadence, pausing to regain his composure. "Imagine what life was like for some nineteen-year-old kid like us when Copernicus overturned thousands of years of established 'facts' by saying the Earth wasn't the center of the universe. That's how much things have changed because of the Federation, even if it all still looks normal on the surface. Truth doesn't change, Marcus. It's our understanding that does. No matter how much we know, it's incomplete."

"This is different."

"Oh, really? How?" Jordan challenged.

"Copernicus had evidence. What's yours?"

"For starters, my intuition. But since that isn't enough for you here's more evidence: a few of the conspirators at Lyceum have been trying to figure out how Tek works by scanning and hacking it—"

"And who are these people? Do you trust them?"

"The main hacker is the same guy who made your fake ID, and that's been working fine for you ... right?"

Marcus had no reply.

"Every time they try to break into the Tek, they get sick. Instantly," Jordan continued. "I'm not talking about a virus on their computer. I'm talking about their actual physical bodies. They don't have to be using Tek when it happens. It doesn't even matter if they're on the other side of the planet from the device. The instant they start, they feel physically ill, and the second they stop, it ends. How is that possible? Do you remember hearing anything about this from Bill? I don't. So no, you don't know the truth or everything I know, which is why you're blind to the fact that you're walking into a lion's den by getting this close to the Federation. And even if you don't mean to, dude, you're showing them how to destroy us."

It was an impressive speech, but Marcus was unmoved. Sensing his attempt had failed, Jordan reverted to reverse psychology. "Okay. Whatever. I've said my piece. You can't say someone didn't warn you. If you want to be the Federation's hammer against humanity, that's your choice, but I think you're fucking retarded for it. Now if you'll excuse me, I need some rest—I pulled an all-nighter."

Jordan strutted defiantly across the kitchen and descended to his basement sanctuary. He'd get high, bathe himself in his music, and troll online about the impending doom. When it was clear this attempt had failed, he'd move to other tactics, all of them ultimately ending with an apology and reconciliation. Jordan would never give up on his brother.

5

KILLING TIME

The anticipation of today's meeting with Brad kept him up most of the night before. The fight with Jordan hadn't helped his energy levels either. But there was work to do, so he retired upstairs to study. Marcus's room was tiny, designed long ago for people significantly smaller than him; his twin bed and antique workspace took up all the available space. The Cedar of Lebanon desk was one of Marcus's most prized possessions, a bequest from his grandmother Beatrice, who the brothers lovingly called "Nonna." She'd brought the wooden artifact back to the United States as a child. Everything about the piece felt important. As he spread his homework out across the surface, he could hear his father's voice say, "Man needs a system. No matter how flawed, a man with a system will always beat a man without one."

Despite his system and an equally studious work ethic, fatigue won the war. He woke hours later to the muffled vibrations of Jordan's music. He didn't remember dreaming. Marcus felt terrible after naps, and this was no exception. Fear of having missed symposium seized him, but he saw there was still time to make it. Marcus grabbed his tablet and started toward the Carolyn Tanner Irish Humanities building at the heart of campus. It was a long walk across the same path he'd traversed twice today, but his slower pace was pleasant; it provided a moment for continued reflection on Brad's offer.

The history department relocated to the Tanner building from Carlson Hall in -13 NE, a few years before his father's death. Marcus had vivid memories of visiting for the first time. It felt hollow compared to Carlson Hall. Most of the offices were empty because, unlike the law school, the humanities had been shedding staff since the Soviet Union launched Sputnik in -64 NE. Since then, the disciplines of war won the public's hearts and minds; society was too busy blazing a path toward its future to look back on where it had been. Regardless, Marcus's father had been one of the last great historians of that earlier era.

Everything changed with the Federation's arrival. They were mesmerized by stories of humanity's past, especially the ancient world, and particularly Rome. Since historians had a monopoly on this knowledge, they became the new global elite overnight. The professor leading today's symposium, Luke Kelly, was a prime example of this meteoric rise in social status. He frequently joked about having gone from reading Latin and playing Xbox one day to acting as a consigliere to the Federation the next. Luke had a thin frame bordering on frail, a mouth full of snarled teeth, and one lazy eye. Regardless, he was a fountain of energy serving as a world-class lecturer, the curator of ancient antiquities at the Utah Museum of Fine Arts, and one of the few humans who could get private meetings with the Federation, no questions asked. He was a bigger celebrity than Jordan, but Marcus knew Luke before he was cool, as Antony's mentor and their father's most beloved graduate student, their mother excluded.

Marcus weaved his way through the Tanner building's crowded lobby and past the IKEA style furniture to an Italian deli counter.

Caputo's was the social focal point for the entire building, and Marcus regularly stopped here for coffee when he was able to attend symposiums. With drink and tablet in hand, he took a seat in the building's auditorium at the end of a row.

Luke adopted his mentor's style, honoring the original meaning of the word "history" by telling everything as a story. Supported through a host of sponsorships, Luke had crafted an immersive multimedia experience, which included the most advanced Tek complement for viewers at home or in the audience. All of this made Luke's symposium the highest-rated live program in the world, surpassing the Black Market fights broadcasted from Nerio.

Luke's narrative was captivating, moving fluidly through political and military history, then to social and economic life before covering art and culture. All the stories Luke told, like Marcus's father before him, were also useful. *He would have made a great Connector*, Marcus thought. The room went dark, and screams of excitement cut across the auditorium's silence.

"Good afternoon," Luke said over the roar of music. Images of Rome scrolled across electronic surfaces surrounding the entire lecture hall.

"Welcome, welcome, hi everyone," Luke paced the stage like a rock star to the continued cheers of the crowd, "thank you, thank you."

Symposium felt more like a concert than an academic lecture. It would've been impossible to describe this situation to someone even a year earlier; they wouldn't have believed history could impact people like this.

"Thank you," Luke said one last time as the room quieted. "The topic for today's symposium is the Crisis of the Third Century, a fifty-year period of chaos within the Roman Empire. As we talk, I want you to imagine what it was like to live in a world experiencing repeated economic depressions. A world where money was so worthless, it couldn't buy life-sustaining grain. Where plague and unending civil war chewed through the citizenry while elites spent their time vying for power instead of using it to society's benefit."

Marcus imagined a world like the one Luke described. It sent chills up his spine.

"The fact that today's symposium falls on the Ides of March is as poetic as it is prophetic for modern society. With Caesar's murder on this day, two thousand and sixty-six years ago, the Roman Republic ended. Forever. While the Roman Empire that replaced it would expand and continue for hundreds of years, the centralization of power from the People into the hands of a single ruler proved incapable of solving the social rot that'd taken hold of one of the world's first known superpowers. And home to sixty-five million people, or one of five humans living on Earth at the time."

Luke paused dramatically. "Caesar's death, while not a direct part of the Third Century Crisis, was a sign of what was to come hundreds of years later, after the assassination of Emperor Severus Alexander. For the next half-century, Rome would have as many emperors as it had in the previous two hundred and fifty years. These individuals were known as 'Barrack Emperors' because their power resided in the control of armies whose fighting destroyed critical infrastructure, opened the borders to foreign invasion, and created conditions for plague and famine to ravage the Roman population. All of this gave support to the saying that 'soldiers starve last.' "

Uncomfortable laughter rippled across the crowd.

"This instability collapsed the global economy, and for the first time in seven hundred years, the city of Rome had to fortify itself behind a new set of walls. While this stop-gap measure had few pros, it created a wide range of new and unexpected cons—"

Luke's comment reminded Marcus: *pros and cons*. He'd almost forgotten Brad's direction and pulled out his tablet. The task proved to be an intellectual tractor beam; despite his love for Luke and today's topic, he spent the rest of the symposium working on his list. The final score was twenty pros to fifteen cons. He'd return to Brad's Lab tonight.

Marcus looked up in time to catch Luke's closing remarks, "Even though Emperor Aurelian, under the banner of his personal god Sol Invictus, finally reunited the fractured empire, it wouldn't last. Subsequent emperors redivided Rome into eastern and western portions. When the western half fell in -1545 NE, it plunged much of the world into a thousand years of comparable darkness as important knowledge of engineering, art, and science collapsed. This is a period you know as the Middle Ages, or Dark Ages, under the control of another centralized power, the Catholic Church. It wouldn't be until the Renaissance that this lost knowledge was reborn, priming the progress that brings us together today."

Luke's silence signaled the end to the audience, and the crowd climbed to their feet in jubilation as music blasted through the auditorium. *The energy was electrifying*, Marcus thought as he cheered.

"Quiet down, please. Thank you … shhhhhhhhhhh," said Luke. "A happy Ides to each of you. Remember that right now halfway across the world in the eternal city of Rome there are people leaving flowers for a man, a 'tyrant,' whose death by political frenemies in a knife-free zone shaped who we are today, and where we choose to go next."

Marcus's father used to say this every March 15th, so he knew the next line before Luke said it. "So … ask what you are doing with your life that the world will remember thousands of years from now."

Marcus loved hearing a piece of his father live on through Luke.

It was almost 3:15 p.m. when Marcus walked out of the Tanner building. He had hours to burn before returning to Brad's Lab. He didn't want to go home and risk another skirmish with Jordan; his mind was made about joining the Cohort. As penance for his earlier failure, he headed to the library to study. The Marriott Library was named after J. Willard Marriott, the Mormon business magnate whose hotels scattered the planet. In -52 NE, he'd donated a million dollars to the library. In return, the library renamed itself. The building was retrofitted to withstand an earthquake, a necessary upgrade since the University sat directly atop a major fault line. The library's renovation wasn't just structural. It also included an Automated Retrieval Center, the ARC, capable of handling three times as many books as existed in the Library of Alexandria.

The Marriott Library was mostly empty. Officially the school canceled Spring Break because of the looming Confederation threat, yet students were still off unofficially celebrating. Marcus found a quiet corner and settled in. But his mind wandered to the Federation, to Brad, to the Lab, and what tonight would be like. He turned eighteen the day the Federation arrived, which made him feel personally connected to them. Safe even. But the idea of starting Selection was making his stomach turn; he couldn't shake Jordan's warnings. Leaning on his Stoic training, Marcus was able to focus on his studies. The next time he looked up, it was 6:28 p.m. He couldn't do another minute in the books.

It was a short walk to the Student Union, where Marcus headed straight for its arcade. He came here for *Lethal Enforcers*, the first-person police shooter game he'd grown up playing at home on Antony's Sega CD. Tek had destroyed the gaming industry too.

Few people wanted to play something with their hands when they could actually live it. Arcades like this still littered the landscape because it was cheaper to keep them running than remove the machines. But their status was self-evident, tucked into a back corner beyond a sea of dusty billiards tables. This space, like the library, was empty and smelled pungently of stale popcorn and industrial-grade carpet cleaner.

Marcus pulled the game's light gun from the holster, dropped in a quarter, and slapped the large red start button. He wasn't sure if he was playing for entertainment value or nostalgia.

"Mind if I join?" said Velia.

Marcus was surprised to see her. She'd appeared out of thin air. "Not at all. Jump in."

"How'd your interview go?"

Marcus hesitated after Brad's warning, but Velia already knew so he didn't see the harm. "It was good. They offered me a spot. I start tonight."

"Congratulations," Velia exclaimed, gunning down every single bad guy on the screen.

"Thanks … I'm sorry for how I acted earlier."

"What do you mean?" feigned Velia.

"It was rude to cut our conversation short. I don't know much about you or anyone else in FACT."

"Other than Jordan."

"Obviously."

"What would you like to know?"

Marcus was struggling to keep up with Velia's skyrocketing score. "The usual. How old are you?"

"How old do you think I am?"

"If I had to guess, I'd say … twenty-one?"

"You nailed it. That's incredible!"

"You're wise beyond your years."

"How's that?" Velia was noticeably nervous.

"You were right about the biggest weakness question."

Velia took a break from blasting criminals to throw Marcus an easy smile.

"Are you from Utah?" Marcus was checking off question boxes like this was a Census survey.

"No, I grew up outside of Portland. Then I bounced around for a while."

"How'd you end up here?"

"My mom was from Utah. But the scholarships are why I came here. What about you?"

"Born and raised," Marcus proclaimed.

"Are you Mormon?" Now it was Velia's turn to whittle down the boxes to put Marcus in.

"No. I was raised Catholic."

"With the last name Adams?"

"My father was Anglican but converted for my mother when they got married."

"Do you still go to church?"

"No. I was never that religious to begin with."

"Me neither," Velia declared.

Marcus died multiple times, but Velia was still playing on her first quarter. "You're good at this."

"I've been playing video games for a *very* long time," she commented.

As he bent over to feed the machine another chunk of alloyed metals, Marcus's eye was drawn to the pattern of black stars sketched up both of her arms. There were three distinct shapes, each based on a pentagram modified by adding two or three additional points. The trio of shapes repeated in varying sizes, and all were solid black except for a single five-pointed star on the inside of her right forearm. It was, by and large, the biggest on either of her appendages. "I like your tattoos."

"Thanks," Velia replied, noticing his fixation on the unfilled pentagram. "It's a work in progress. I love them, but it's an expensive hobby. I have to earn each one. Do you have any?"

"No, needles make me nervous."

"Me too, actually."

"Jordan's got a ton of tattoos. I've gone with him a few times for moral support. Honestly, I don't think I could tolerate that level of pain."

"It's addictive," Velia said with a wide grin. "A serious rush."

The conversation dipped as she propelled them into game stages Marcus had never reached. It was fun being lost in the moment with someone free of ulterior motives. Then he saw the time. "Shit!"

"What's up?" Velia looked at Marcus while continuing her devastating gunfire.

"I've got to go. They told me if I miss a session, I'll be fired. Thanks for the game. It was fun."

"Yeah, it was. Good luck."

Marcus was already on his way when his gut stopped him. He raced back to Velia's side. "One more thing," Marcus said sheepishly, "the Federation researcher told me to be careful about who I tell. About Selection, that is. I'm sorry to ask, but can you keep this between the two of us?"

"Absolutely." Velia locked eyes with Marcus. "You can trust me to keep a secret."

"Thanks. Have fun with the rest of the game."

The sun was setting as Marcus ran across campus, arriving at Carlson Hall right at 8:00 p.m. This time, he opened the door to Brad's Lab with confidence.

6

GO TOWARD THE LIGHT

"Marcuuuussss," Brad welcomed with the intonation of a Vegas casino greeter. "Good to see you again, brother. Let's get started."

"Do I need to sign something first?"

"A line on a fancy-looking piece of paper doesn't make your commitment more meaningful. You're here. You've made your choice."

Marcus had questions, but Brad stopped him. "We could spend all night talking about Subsumption, or you can answer everything firsthand by experiencing it. What do you want to do?"

"Let's get started."

Brad moved toward the mystery door beyond the couches. "After you, good sir."

"I just walk through?" Marcus was skeptical, seeing up close that the door was still solid black.

"Yup. Just like in *Stargate*, but without all that gratuitous CGI."

Marcus took a deep breath and closed his eyes. His forward momentum was abruptly halted by the slippery solid surface, tripping up the rest of his body and causing him to stumble to the floor.

"Oh my gosh! I'm sorry," Brad said through heavy laughter, extending a hand to help Marcus up. "I didn't think you'd fall. I couldn't resist an opportunity to lessen the tension. I hope you're not hurt?"

Marcus rubbed his face and wiggled his nose. "I'm fine."

The pain vanished as Brad activated the door. "Now you can walk through."

Marcus was disappointed as he stepped across the threshold. There was no roller coaster ride through a wormhole, no blur of stars and colors as they zipped by at warp speed. It felt like crossing between any two spaces. But as he entered the cavernous locker room, he realized this wasn't the normal world anymore; the elliptical area was way too big to fit inside Carlson Hall.

"Where are we?" Marcus turned to Brad.

"The locker room of the Cohort."

"Is this still Earth?"

"Haha! Yes. You're still inside Carlson Hall."

Marcus looked around in astonishment. "There's no way."

"Unlike your Form's nineteenth-century doctors, I am not blowing smoke up your butt."

"How is this possible?"

"We're better at feng shui than you."

The walls looked exactly like the honeycomb scales of the door-frame, but ten times the size. Everything had a silver shine to it. Abstract patterns of color and texture rolled across the room's vast surfaces at varying speeds. Marcus visually swept the space, attempting to take it all in. His attention stopped on a series of doors with a name and number inscribed on each. The first one caught his eye:

01. MONICA

Marcus loved that name. There were no visible light sources anywhere in the room, yet her door and everything in the locker room was perfectly lit. The floor matched the silver color and texture of the walls, while a star show slowly traversed the ceiling.

"Take it all in," Brad was extra enthusiastic, "this moment marks the beginning of your Selection."

"How long does it usually take?"

"In most cases, a month or two, but one of your Form finished in just over a week. Step through that door and change," Brad pointed to the far side of the room to a portal marked 'proxy.' "That'll take you to your locker. From there, just follow directions to get placed into your EXO."

"Placed?" Marcus balked. "By who?"

"Someone who can keep a secret."

"And what's an EXO?"

"The suit you'll wear during the Sequences."

Marcus's heart was pounding. As he approached the door, he hesitated, turning back to find that Brad had vanished. The only way out now was to quit. He wasn't ready for that, so he moved forward. The instant his body was through the locker door, it congealed into a solid wall behind him. He was alone in a narrow but brightly lit bronze-colored room made of more honeycombs, unsure what to do next.

"Well, what are you waiting for? Dinner and a movie? You have to earn that around here. Strip," said Brad.

Marcus turned around, like a dog chasing its tail in an attempt to find the source of Brad's voice.

"Stop spinning, I'm not in the room," Brad replied through more laughter. "I should've told you we will communicate like this."

"How am I hearing you? It doesn't sound like anything I've ever heard. Where are the speakers?"

"We don't have to vibrate the air between us when we can vibrate your jaw bone and accomplish the same result with higher fidelity. Think of it as a perfect phone call, straight to the brain."

"No one else can hear you?"

"Nope. To an outsider, you look like a crazy person, spinning in place and talking to yourself."

One of Jordan's conspiracies claimed cases of schizophrenia had skyrocketed after the Federation's arrival. At this moment, Marcus wondered if this technology might explain that trend.

"It doesn't," Brad preempted the thought. "We don't come into someone's head uninvited."

"You can hear my inner thoughts?"

"Yes. I'm reading your brain and all of your body vitals too. But don't worry, I won't bootleg the footage. I'll give you some privacy to suit up."

Marcus undressed and placed his items on the shelves and hooks of the locker wall. The room was cold in nothing but his birthday gear. Glowing arrows on the floor pointed toward an octagon enclosure that was all frames, with no walls or roof. He stood still until a soft voice encouraged him.

"Welcome, Marcus. I'm Hi!-D, your digital assistant. It is my job to see you to and from the Experimental Chamber, but I can also answer any questions you might have."

Marcus looked around the small space but didn't see her either.

"Nice to see you again. In-person that is," Marcus said. "Well, not really in person, but you know what I mean."

Hi!-D appeared in front of him. "Excuse my physical absence. I thought you might prefer privacy."

He was intimately familiar with Hi!-D from his Disclosure Moment and the Federation's Public Service Announcements. She was an artificial intelligence, a digital imposter, rendered to appear as a woman in her early thirties with pale skin and hair that was literally luminescent. Patterns of blonde, red, and orange highlights continuously flowed like fire from her scalp down to her shoulders. She had piercing hazel eyes, bright red lips outlining her perfect teeth, and a polished British accent.

"Are you here as my assistant or my chaperone?" Marcus's oscillating voice betrayed his anxiety.

"I'd like to think of myself not unlike a Hellenistic house slave or a Victorian-era butler, a source of deep wisdom and experience, not just someone to assist in the menial task of keeping you alive. With our formalities now out of the way, please step into the octagon so we can fit you with an EXO."

The arrows on the floor continued to beckon him forward. Once he stepped through the side of the octagon closest to him, Marcus was sprayed from head to toe in a flexible black substance. It was constructed of the same material as the locker room but was so light and airy that he worried he was still naked. The suit didn't obstruct any of his senses; his fingertips felt every grain of detail through the material, his vision was crystal clear, his hearing was crisp, and the air felt fresh with each breath. Marcus didn't like this feeling. It reminded him of getting numbed out and watching a nurse drive an IV into his arm without feeling it. The arrows reappeared and pointed to a door on the far side of the octagon where his locker had been.

"Please step through," Hi!-D requested. "This is your big moment."

As he moved past the doorframe, a deep soothing hum replaced the silence of his locker. Across the floor, far from where he was standing, a thin column of light illuminated a giant iron-red honeycomb panel.

"Marcus … Maaaarrccuussss," said Brad in an angelic voice, "move toward the liiiight."

Marcus wasn't in a playful mood yet and stood still without replying.

"Just move forward, the rest is taken care of," Brad explained.

Marcus navigated the dark abyss to reach the comfort provided by the sole source of light.

"Selection, like your work in the Cohort, should you survive, will consist of Sequences. These are social experiments, meaning we control every detail of the world around you. You'll never be in danger. In fact, during these experiments, you'll have zero physical contact with real persons, places, or things of any type. During this initial phase of Selection, you'll have memories of the experiments, which allows us to collect accurate data about your choices with minimal fear while balancing the need to help you adjust to the newness of it all. If you continue to progress, we'll move into Stealth Mode, where you'll have zero memories to ensure your experience in one experiment doesn't bias your future Sequences. It's our way of sampling with replacement."

"WHERE AM I AND WHAT AM I WEARING?"

"You don't need to shout. This is a highly-advanced communication system, not walkie-talkies from your childhood. You're in the Experimental Chamber in Carlson Hall, at the University of Utah in Salt Lake City, on planet Earth. You're currently standing in the southern wing of the building inside the Liberty Bell, as the Cohort calls it. You've never left the building and never will during a session. Ever. You're wearing a suit made of spider silk, goat milk, and honey."

"Milk and honey?"

"And spider silk. It's a fascinating substance because it's extraordinarily strong and astoundingly flexible—a testament to the hundreds of millions of years of R&D it underwent to reach this point. We mix genes from honeybees and spiders, put that code into the milk genes of goats, and BAM, an abundant, organic-based wonder material."

"It's a liquid?"

"It starts as a liquid, straight from the goat's teat, but with an appropriate bacterial agent, it can be shaped into anything of any solidness. We call it Organics."

"Bacteria?" Marcus said incredulously, looking himself over.

"The construction crew of the future, hard-working and easy to collaborate with because they inevitably take the path of least resistance. The honeycomb maximizes structural strength with minimal material. It's a highly efficient design. Do you have any other questions before we start?"

After a moment of nothing, Brad replied, "No? Great! Here we go."

The room illuminated to reveal Marcus was standing in another immense ellipse. Unlike the locker room, this one was covered in iron-red panels, but these were the largest he'd seen in the Lab. Without warning, the ground fell from beneath Marcus's feet. It wasn't like floating in the Peter Pan sort of way. Instead, it felt like falling into the sky. He groaned from the sensation.

"Interesting, isn't it? We can tweak the gravity field to balance you wherever we want in the room."

"Why do I have to be up here?" Marcus protested.

"Your body lives everything you do in the Sequence, though we can turn you into a vegetable for specific experiments if necessary. Plus, having you isolated in the air guarantees you won't get injured on our watch."

"Why does this feel familiar?"

"It does?"

"Yes. Like a dream I had as a kid where I'd fly around the school-yard over everyone's heads."

"Interesting. I hesitate to use this word for fear of what it may conjure in your pop culture-saturated brain, but our initial phase of research will be 'exploratory' in nature."

"How so?"

"We assess your physical and mental developmental stages to calibrate future Sequences around your capabilities and limitations."

"How many Sequences does it take to calibrate someone?" Marcus asked.

"I'm predicting you'll be faster than most, but a dozen or more is common. Now, if you don't have additional questions, and I can tell from your brain data you don't, let's get this show on the road."

7

TAKE 3 SEQUENCES AND CALL IN THE MORNING

[Calibration ID #0] [Training Data Begins]

W hat happened next transcended dreams, fantasies, or memories; it was like suddenly changing the channel on life. In the blink of an eye, Marcus was standing in a moonlit meadow. The outline of mountain peaks towered over him while a shadow rolled across the landscape before dissolving. He peered down at his body, and the suit was gone, replaced by the outfit he'd left in his locker. Marcus was astounded by the ethereal scene and reminded himself this was all fake, though it was difficult to be sure. A soft breeze blew as he took in the panoramic view. Thousands of stars glimmered above him; *the sky hadn't looked this empty since the Federation arrived*. He was isolated, feeling like there wasn't another person anywhere in the world. Marcus closed his eyes, turned his head upward, took a big breath in through his nose, and exhaled through his mouth. The damp air even tasted real.

[Calibration ID #0] [Training Data Ends]

When he opened his eyes, he was back in the Liberty Bell, hovering.

Brad was ecstatic. "Perfect!"

Marcus couldn't think of anything in particular that he'd done, but before he could speak, Brad continued, "We lose a lot of people at this point. They can't handle knowing it isn't real and mentally melt. You did more than you realize. Now, as my grandmother says, drink while the water's running!"

[Calibration ID #1] [Training Data Begins]

In another instant, Marcus found himself struggling to balance on a thin log forty feet above a small river of raging whitewater. Terror seized him as he sized up the situation. *There's no way the log can hold this much weight,* Marcus thought. The roar of the river echoed through the surrounding pine-topped ravine at a deafening volume. His arms stretched skyward, holding an equally parsimonious set of branches at their terminus.

"The goal is to get to the other side using your desire not to fall," Brad coached.

That desire was proving powerful since Marcus had a genuine fear of heights. Even though he'd grown up at a ski resort, he shied away from similar situations because the fear made it difficult to breathe. He remembered laughing during scenes like this in a movie when a protagonist would recite some mantra to calm down, but now Marcus locked onto something his therapist, Garett, taught him: just keep breathing. He recited this as he let go of the branches and began teetering across the log.

His movements were small at first, each inch having to be won in an intense struggle of balance over fear, but soon he picked up the pace. He realized that with only a few key muscles and steady airflow, he had superior control and more focus. As he neared the other side, Marcus was momentarily distracted and lost his footing. He grabbed desperately at the thin log but missed it. He was falling fast. Marcus closed his eyes and waited for the inevitable, but it never came.

[Calibration ID #1] [Training Data Ends]

[Calibration ID #2] [Training Data Begins]

When he braved to look again, he was standing alone at a gun range. "Welcome to weapons training!" Brad proclaimed.

This was going to be easier than the log, Marcus said to himself. Like most of his generation, he was familiar with guns from *Lethal Enforcer*-type video games. But he had the additional benefit of growing up in a home where real firearms were readily available.

"This exercise will test your physical, emotional, and mental capabilities," said Brad. "Pick any weapon from the wall, load it, then put two rounds on the target."

Downrange was a cardboard silhouette, an effigy of evil. As Marcus scanned the selection of weapons, he found a highly-customized AR-15; it resembled one his father had owned. This weapon was the civilian variant of the military power horse, and it was Marcus's favorite because it had a different personality than other guns. He inspected the rifle, checking it was on safe and unloaded with an empty chamber, all without placing his finger on the trigger or pointing the barrel at anything he didn't plan to destroy.

Once he knew the weapon was safe, he took his position at the end of the firing lane, loaded a magazine, and chambered a round. Marcus knew what to do next: square up to the target, scan the foreground and background to ensure it was clear to engage, raise the weapon to shoulder height, press his face against the stock, and align his sights on the enemy. "If you're to this point," Marcus could hear his father saying, "you better mean it." The warning was for a good reason; once he disengaged the safety, only five pounds of trigger-pressure separated life from death.

Marcus took a deep breath and squeezed the trigger during a lull in his exhale. When the gun fired, a wave of pure power pulsed through his body. The surrounding air was violently pushed away, and adrenaline surged through his veins, temporarily distracting him from the ringing pain in his ears. He'd been so focused on the weapon he forgot to wear hearing protection. Marcus engaged the safety and set the rifle down with the business end facing the target. He'd made a perfect headshot.

He reviewed the remaining cache of weapons, realizing why he'd failed to remember ear and eye protection: there wasn't any available. Knowing he was ill-prepared made his second shot difficult since his mind and body would anticipate the coming chaos. The trigger would drop the hammer, driving the firing pin into the primer, starting a fire inside the brass casing and forcing the bullet down the rifling of the barrel as the round propelled toward its final destination. Understanding these details did nothing to help him keep calm—it was mind over matter now.

He lifted the rifle again and took a series of even deeper breaths, disengaged the safety, and, ignoring what was to come in favor of what was immediately before him, pulled the trigger. The resulting force was even more painful, and Brad made it worse by screaming like a rabid sports fan. "BOOOOOOOOM!"

Marcus put the gun on safe again and stared at the silhouette. The two rounds were on top of each other, the modern equivalent of Robin Hood splitting an arrow with another arrow.

[Calibration ID #2] [Training Data Ends]

The gun range dissolved around him, exposing the iron-red glow of the Experimental Chamber. The change of station from one world to the next was becoming more disjointed with each jump between Sequences.

"Still doing great. Your data looks equally awesome. Up for more?" Brad asked.

"Yes."

"Want to level up?"

"Sure."

"Attaboy! Quick note, this next Sequence might feel like living inside of a moving blur."

"Like a dream?" Marcus asked.

"Possibly. You'll be someone else with recollections of other people, places, situations, and skills. It will feel very familiar and very, very real. That's intentional since we're using some of your own memories to create the setting of the Sequence. But you might also remember who you are and your real-life memories, causing your brain to fight itself. This is a transitionary experience to test if you're ready for Stealth Mode."

"Realer than the last few?"

"Immeasurably. For the majority of your Form, this experience feels so real it completely distracts from actual reality and dissolves your identity momentarily."

"Am I going to remember this one?"

"Just like the last. For this one, you'll be driving up Provo Canyon—"

"Toward the dam?"

"No, you'll be driving to the Sundance Ski Resort."

Marcus had done this thousands of times. *This would be cake*, he thought.

"Pump the hubris-brakes. There's a catch. It's set in 1985, and you'll be in a VW Beetle that's already archaic by that year."

"Okay."

"With no power steering."

"I can handle it," Marcus assured.

"In a snowstorm."

The details of this memory weren't immediately familiar to Marcus, but the set and setting meant it couldn't have been one of his own lived experiences.

"Here we go," said Brad.

[Calibration ID #3] [Training Data Begins]

The last thing Marcus remembered, he'd just passed Bridal Veil Falls; in the early morning light, he couldn't tell if it was still frozen enough for ice climbing. *Either way, that'll have to wait for another day*, Marcus thought while gripping his steering wheel. The old car struggled on the slushy two-lane mountain highway, but it had survived the worst of the winter. This spring storm was unexceptional. He was finishing his first season as a lift operator at the ski resort, a job he loved because it took him into this canyon six days a week. It also meant he could get stuck in his car, so he'd converted the backseat into a bedroom. The front trunk was equally cram-packed with his outdoor gear.

Once summer arrived, he'd finish training as a paramedic and spend all his free time fishing in the river that ran parallel to the road. The most popular spot, and one frequented by other fisher-men, was a blind curve just coming into view. As the road did a set of preemptive zigzagging, he slammed on the brakes to avoid hitting a line of cars parked in the middle of the road. In addition to killer fishing, this was an accident hot spot. A group of two dozen people stood in the road beyond the vehicles. Marcus stepped out of his car, slipping on the slushy snow before falling flat on his face. He was unhurt and cautiously made his way to the crowd; everyone was inspecting the empty bend in the road.

"What are we looking at?" Marcus asked a man whose face silently screamed of shock.

He didn't answer.

"Everyone needs to get out of the road. Even this early in the morning, there's going to be down-canyon traffic from the dam," Marcus warned. "The second a vehicle comes around that bend, we're dead meat."

The crowd ignored him.

"Hello?" Marcus persisted.

Someone finally responded, "There was an accident around the corner."

"Is someone helping them?" Marcus asked.

He was met by renewed silence. He scanned the bystanders, which included some of his coworkers.

"Has anyone gone for help?" Marcus was losing patience.

No one said a thing.

"If anyone has a CB radio, call for help." Marcus jogged back to his car, where he found his girlfriend and coworker, Beth, had just arrived. "Why's traffic stopped? Another accident? They need to tunnel through the mountain already. I hope someone just slid out, and it's not more serious."

Marcus dove into his trunk and retrieved a small first-aid kit. "I don't know. No one's helping, so I'm going to see what I can do. Wanna come?"

"Absolutely."

The pair pushed past the crowd and rounded the blind spot to find a scene of pure horror. A semi traveling up-canyon had struck an International Scout, a Jeep competitor designed for rough roads. The head-on collision threw the Scout backward onto the steep mountainside shoulder and sent the semi into the river where it sat perfectly upright, water racing beneath it. The driver was standing on his roof and waved frantically to Marcus and Beth. The smell of gas and blood was overwhelming. Flames burned in patches across the slushy ground making for surreal surroundings.

In the middle of the road laid a decapitated woman and what Marcus presumed were her two children. Both boys appeared to be alive and barely moving. They ran to the older of the two since he was closest. The boy looked to be about eight years old and was slipping in and out of consciousness. He was surrounded by a dark halo of blood, while more surged from his forehead. As Marcus repositioned him to apply a compress to control the bleeding, he discovered another gushing wound on the back of the boy's head. He covered both sides with his hands and gently squeezed, causing the child to lurch.

Marcus could feel the problem and motioned for Beth to come closer so he could whisper, "There's a big rock embedded in the middle of his forehead. I need to distribute pressure around the wound, and this compress is already soaked. In the backseat of my car are clothes, pillows, and a blanket. Grab as much as you can. Once we get this kid in better shape, we'll check on his younger brother."

Beth departed, and Marcus felt deep gratitude for having such a reliable partner in this moment of crisis. He turned back to the child and started talking in an attempt to keep him awake. "It's just you and me now, kid. Can you hear me?"

The child was motionless again.

"Kid, can you hear me? Wake up, kid. Come on."

The moments dragged on, and doubt in his ability to save the child was building. "Please, God, don't let this kid die on me. KID, WAKE UP! Just for a second. Tell me your name so I don't have to keep calling you kid. Come on, wake up."

Marcus saw movement in his peripheral vision. The truck driver emerged from the icy river and rushed toward Marcus to offer assistance. "Put me to work."

"Did you call for help from your radio?"

"I couldn't. Everything in the cab got fried when I hit the river. Has anyone gone for help yet? It's forty-five minutes each way."

"We don't know. How long ago did this happen?"

"I'm not sure to tell you the truth. Could've been twenty minutes? Ten maybe? I can't be positive."

"What's your name?"

"Jerry."

"Hi, Jerry. I'm Marcus. My girlfriend, Beth, just went to get more supplies. I've got this kid as best I can, his brother is over—"

Before he could finish, the younger child shrieked at the sight of his headless mother.

"I'm on it, boss." Jerry ran to cover the mother's body with his jacket and removed his shirt to conceal her head. He turned the child around to stare out at the river then shouted back at

Marcus, "It's a miracle, but he's fine. I can't find a scratch on him."

Beth appeared around the corner with an older woman and a young man; she'd motivated the crowd in a way Marcus couldn't, and another wave of gratitude came over him. Beth distributed blankets to Jerry and the young child, while the woman and his coworker helped Marcus get the older brother's head resting on a towel atop a pillow.

"I'm Marcus, you've met Beth, and that's Jerry. What are your names?"

"I'm Margaret."

"I'm Kyle."

"Kyle, can you hold this other pillow on his forehead? You have to make a gap between your hands because there's a rock in there, and you don't want to push it. You have to go around it. Okay?"

"Roger Roger."

"Margaret," Marcus said, "will you keep talking to Kyle and this kid? Keep them up and focused. I'm going to go check the car."

"I can do that," she replied.

Marcus grabbed his first-aid kit and started climbing the snow-bank toward the Scout. The front was smashed in like an accordion. When he reached the vehicle, he could see the father was pinned to his seat by the dash. It had crushed his ribs. Blood was oozing from his mouth as he murmured incoherently. Marcus couldn't do anything for internal injuries and moved on to the back of the vehicle where two more older boys sat, dazed. They were covered in scratches from broken glass but otherwise looked to be fine.

"Can either of you hear me?"

"Yes," the oldest of the two answered. "Where's the rest of our family?"

Marcus turned around to direct him to the carnage on the road, but the vehicle's slanted position hid the sad scene below. Triage dictated news of their mother would wait until they were both stabilized. "Do either of you hurt anywhere on your body?"

"No," the boys said simultaneously.

"I need you to stay here, okay? There's burning gas all over down there. Stay with your dad and keep him up and talking. Help is on the way."

Marcus slid down the slope and ran to Beth and Jerry, who'd moved the younger boy to his brother's side by Margaret and Kyle. The pillow under the boy's head had already gone from white to crimson.

"There are two more boys and one adult in the vehicle. The boys are fine, but their father is critical."

The small child began sobbing again.

"Keep talking to your brother, sweetheart," said Margaret.

"I'm going to find out if help is on the way," Marcus explained. "If I don't immediately come back, it means I went for it myself. Can I take your car? You blocked me in."

"Definitely. The keys are in it," replied Beth.

As Marcus rounded the blind spot, the crowd recoiled at the sight of his blood-covered body.

"Has anyone gone for help?"

"N ... n ... no," stuttered a trembling young woman.

Without another word, Marcus departed. Sitting in Beth's car, he had a literal life or death decision to make: go up or down? The distance up the canyon was half as long, ski patrol would have more medical supplies, and he could call for help from the resort's phone. That was the best option.

Marcus weaved around the stopped traffic, past the gawking crowd, and through the accident site, waving to the unexpected A-Team that fate had created. The resort was up a narrow pine-filled fork off the main canyon. What had been slush at lower altitude was now pure ice. Beth's car was older than his, and her bald tires caused him to slide uncontrollably across both lanes of the road. More than once, the car came to a halt then went backward. He doubted his directional decision, but after fifteen minutes, he finally reached the resort and burst into the lobby.

"Who's on ski patrol?"

"Carl," responded a bellhop. "What the hell happened to you? Are you okay?"

"Get him down here right now. Tell him to bring his medkit. There's been an accident in the canyon at the river bend below the North Fork junction. One person is dead, and two are critical."

"I'll call an ambulance," offered the manager from behind the welcome desk.

The next five minutes felt like an eternity as Marcus warmed himself in front of the lobby's fire, hypnotized by its dancing flames. His mind kept replaying the scene of the accident and the way fire burned on the snow. *He never imagined something like that was possible.* Bouts of crying intermixed with anger at the tragedy he'd witnessed. His mental wandering was interrupted by Carl's arrival. "You rang?"

"Can I explain on the way?" asked Marcus. "And can you drive?"

"Rock and roll," was all Carl replied.

[Calibration ID #3] [Training Data Ends]

Marcus snapped back to reality in the Liberty Bell. He felt horrible. His stomach was tense, his heart was pounding, and his head ached, but he was ready for another Sequence.

"Glad to see you found yourself again," Brad said casually as Marcus descended to the floor. "Great work today. Let's call it a night."

"We're done?" Marcus protested.

"We identified your developmental stages. The exploratory phase is complete. That was exponentially faster than I expected. You should be happy!" Brad knew what Marcus was stewing over and appeared in person. "I know you're feeling a lot of confusing emotions, but being able to turn this off is a big part of what separates those who make it into the Cohort from everyone else. Remind yourself that none of what happened was real, like a dream. It's behind you. From now on, you'll be in Stealth Mode so you won't have to cope with memories like this. Go relax for a few minutes. I'll meet you in my office."

After cooling down in his locker, Marcus found Brad waiting on an office couch. He did a double-take at the grandfather clock in the corner. "How is it almost midnight? That felt like an hour, maybe ..."

"Time is subjective in the Sequences," Brad replied. "Within limits."

"What limits?"

"Your body has a good sense of its own rhythm. We can only trick it for so long."

"Long like hours, or long like years?"

"Bioindividuality means the answer depends on the person. Some people immediately reject the experiment. For others, it'd take a lifetime to wake up. Go home and get some sleep." Brad opened the Lab door. "Tomorrow will be very different. How about 3:30 p.m., right after your class?"

Marcus agreed and set out, unsettled, into the darkness.

PART IV

PUBLIC SERVICE ANNOUNCEMENTS

WEDNESDAY, MARCH 16, +1 NE

8

THE TREK

He collapsed onto his bed. Marcus had never been this tired in his whole life. Even as the physical symptoms faded, he couldn't tune out the Sequence. His phone lit up the dark room. It was Dianna:

Coffee? Fine Arts Museum? Noon?

Her laconic text message signaled she was upset. The new day had just begun, and he was already exhausted by it. Marcus agreed to her terms and fell asleep, rolling out of bed eleven hours later. The house was eerily silent. No music. No clanging in the kitchen. No giggling randos. No Jordan. Marcus showered, grabbed his lucky coin, and headed for the museum without completing his daily affirmation. He needed to arrive early, since that was safer than being late with Dianna, a standard she didn't necessarily hold herself to. Antony said this tardiness was passive-aggressive behavior, but Marcus assumed the best in people and believed Dianna was too busy for her own life.

Marcus usually walked everywhere, but he still felt fatigued and jumped on the light rail at the stadium. As the train climbed campus, the Wasatch Mountains loomed in the distance. He loved living here surrounded by these sentries; their omnipresence made the world feel finite. They were also practical, approximating the cardinal directions, though no one used them for that anymore since they had the Public Service Announcement display instead. This curved screen was a gift of the Federation, visible high in the sky from any angle, any time of day, and any kind of weather. It was always there and, like Tek, customized the information it projected for each viewer.

By default, the PSA screen showed the time, date, temperature, and geographical orientation. It also shared news, weather alerts, 'this day in history' facts, and displayed the current milestone status of Project Noble. However, it's most important feature was providing closed captions for the Federation's Public Service Announcements. Hi!-D, the same Federation emissary from Brad's Lab, presented every PSA. Everyone in the world knew who she was because she'd delivered their individual Disclosure Moments. Jordan was convinced the PSAs were part of the Federation's propaganda machine. But since they only played in public spaces and their messages were clichés, like inspirational posters, Marcus didn't buy into this conspiracy theory.

It was a short distance from the light rail to the Utah Museum of Fine Arts, taking him past the indoor arena where his brother gave the commencement speech fourteen years earlier. It'd been a proud day for their family, but it was the first milestone without his grandmother, Beatrice. She was a benefactor of the Museum, and Marcus's mother honored that legacy by serving on the institution's board until her own death. Antony even completed an internship at the Museum under Luke Kelly, displaying glass objects from the ancient world. The first time Marcus explored his brother's exhibit, he questioned if his own possessions would be on display to the public thousands of years in the future.

Marcus took a seat at one of the UMFA's many patio tables. This would be the place, at high noon, like the cowboys of Utah's past. Clouds covered much of the sky, but the sun periodically peeked through to offer transient warmth. As he settled in, Hi!-D appeared in the sky to deliver a Public Service Announcement. Her slightly translucent hologram occupied the space below the PSA screen down to the horizon. She looked like a god projected across the atmosphere:

> "Good afternoon, citizens, and welcome to another wonderful day! As you go about your to-do's, remember that we depend on one another. Too often, we allow fear and uncertainty to drive a wedge between us. So today, set aside your doubts and do something unexpectedly kind for a stranger. Trust them. They may just return the favor. Because together, we're stronger."

It was noon.

Marcus sat like patience on a monument. From his available historical information, he had no way of predicting how late Dianna would be. She was in the final phase of her PhD, working long hours collecting data at the local Coalition clinic for her dissertation. She was an emerging academic star, having coined the term PASS, Post-Arrival Stress Syndrome, to describe the litany of afflictions she observed doing field research. Dianna was the most ambitious person Marcus knew, other than his brother Antony, and he loved that about her.

She was deeply passionate about her work and its potential to shape public policy, particularly for kids. Occasionally this bled into their relationship, and she'd treat Marcus like a child. Their seven-year age gap didn't help, but that was less of a problem than their political differences. Marcus learned early that feigned capitulation was a better strategy than debate. Dianna was an articulate ideologue who shared Jordan's gift for oration, making her an intellectual force to be reckoned with.

Despite the many qualities she had in her favor, Dianna was prone to deep bouts of insecurity, which manifested as paranoia or rage. Marcus believed it stemmed from her adolescent obesity. She'd shed the physical weight by embracing extreme exercise and breaking her mother's food conditioning, but deep down, she still carried the psychological weight of a fat kid. This made Dianna human nitroglycerin, prone to explosions of emotion given the slightest shock.

Marcus viewed her shortcomings as a reflection of his own. This mutual vulnerability formed the foundation of their bond, which could be wondrous. Real magic happened whenever they sat together in silence. The feeling reminded him of how Mormons described the Holy Ghost, a cosmic bolt of lightning racing up the spine and out every extremity. It was pure, pleasurable energy unlike anything else in his life and, these moments, as infrequent as they were, made the hardships seem trivial. Marcus appreciated they were both works in progress and knew they were capable of more together than on their own.

Marcus failed to notice Dianna casting a shadow over him upon her arrival. "Earth to Marcus."

He acknowledged her with a smile. "Hi."

"May I sit?"

"Of course, that one's for you." Marcus gestured toward the empty chair across the table.

Dianna was beautiful in a classical way, with long straight blonde hair and elegant legs and arms. She was curvy for an avid runner, with a soft face, full lips, large deep brown eyes, and a nose that testified to her Greek lineage. Her smile was magnetic, and she could melt Marcus with it when she wished to.

"Where have you been the last two days?" she interrogated. "You completely dropped off the radar."

"The usual places: class, home with Jordan … the library … you know?" Marcus wasn't ready to bring up Selection. Not yet.

"No, I don't know, that's why I'm asking. It was incredibly inconsiderate of you. I couldn't focus on anything else. I would be working or studying and suddenly have these horrible visions of you with some other girl, or lying dead somewhere."

Marcus took no solace in the order of her fears. "I was a call or message away."

"I worked a thirty-six-hour shift, slept for a few hours, and have been studying since I texted you last night. I don't have the time or desire to chase down my boyfriend like a bounty hunter. This week is hard enough for me, and I don't need the added stress of worrying about your wellbeing."

"Why's this week hard for you?"

"Are you serious?" Dianna's face displayed her pain and disgust. "We talked about this. Last year. Same week even."

Marcus vaguely remembered a conversation about her twin brother, but in general, Dianna was opaque about her family background. Without hard facts to hold on to, it was easy for him to forget. The only things he knew for certain were her mother had been a single parent, and her brother died when they were kids. He guessed this involved the latter, "About Apollo?"

"Yes. This week brings up anniversary reactions for me. I don't need you piling on more trauma."

"I'm sorry. I'm here now, want to talk about it?"

"No, Marcus. I don't need you to solve my problems. I just don't want you to create new ones."

"Want a drink?" Marcus hoped coffee could secure the peace.

"Sure." Dianna grabbed her purse. "I'll have—"

"I got it." Marcus knew she'd refuse, but offered anyway.

Dianna handed him five dollars. "Black, smallest they have."

Marcus stood in line at the museum's café, thinking about ways to break the news about Selection. None of them felt right. He could see Dianna studying through the windows, highlighter in hand, intent on conquering whatever block of knowledge was before her. She paused to pull out a chair for an elderly woman making her way toward the patio. Dianna's desire to help those who couldn't help themselves was another characteristic Marcus loved about her. It reminded him of his mother.

He returned to their table with the peace offering and exact change. Dianna gently rubbed the top of his thigh when he sat down. "I'm sorry I get worried. I'm anxious in general right now. It's been so bad this week. You're the only thing in this world that makes me feel safe. I promised myself I'd never be this dependent on anyone, but I can't help it. Don't break my heart by disappearing, okay?"

"Okay."

"Promise it will never happen again, and we can move on."

"I said okay."

"That isn't a promise."

"I promise."

Dianna's petting intensified. "It doesn't feel like we've had any time together lately."

"We haven't. Too bad we have class."

"I don't. Blow off your responsibilities and take me to your place." Dianna bit her lip.

Marcus hesitated; Brad was clear about maintaining his academic performance as part of Selection. Plus, he enjoyed class.

Dianna was unrelenting, "I need to feel you, Marcus. The touch of our lips, your breath on my neck, your hands running up and down my skin … I need to know you still belong to me."

The temptation was too much for him. "Let's go."

"Not yet. Finish your coffee," Dianna said, grinning. "The anticipation is the best part. Tell me about your night? What did you do? Where were you?"

She wasn't going to move on after all. Marcus recognized this moment for what it was and instead chose to lie. "Home. I was thinking about my parents mostly, looking at old family photos and stuff."

"I forgot this is a hard time of year for both of us. I'm sorry, sweetheart."

"You can't let grief get you down. Life goes on."

"Being Stoic about your pain only makes it worse. God, I am so sick of hearing about that bullshit."

Marcus was confused by her comment. "What?"

"Never mind," Dianna dismissed.

"I don't understand. What bullshit?"

"You sounded like a man from my dissertation committee just now. I'm sorry for snapping. He and I don't get along."

"Don't you pick the people on your committee?"

"It doesn't work like that," Dianna cackled at his naivete. "I'm required to have one tenured faculty member from outside my department. He's a close colleague with the chair of my committee. They work together in the neuropsych ward at the hospital. Since I didn't have any other options, I got stuck with him."

"What was his comment?"

"It wasn't a comment. It was a criticism. And a baseless one."

"What did he say?"

"That my literature review is too narrow since it only draws on modern sources, biasing both my theoretical model and empirical conclusions. He said I should look at Stoicism specifically, but that's old school trash. No real intellectual takes those ideas seriously. My PASS model is cutting-edge since it's based on actual data. I've seen the suffering these kids deal with daily. They don't know how to cope with the stress the Federation causes. The ramblings of racist old white men thousands of years ago offer no insight into this problem. His criticism is baseless, and his Stoicism angle is useless."

Dianna didn't know about Marcus's coin or his daily affirmation. He'd hidden both from her, but couldn't help feeling like she was talking about him. "Can he kill your dissertation?"

"No, but he can delay it another year."

"Seems trivial in the big scheme of things, no?"

"My program only offers four years of funding," Dianna was getting aggressive again. "A delay means I have to come up with tuition. I realize you don't understand that kind of stress, but for the rest of us, money is a big deal."

Dianna had been living on her own since the day she turned eighteen. Her humble financial situation was another source of their conflict: she resented Marcus for coming from wealth. Before he could respond, fate forced their conversation in a different direction. Dianna checked her phone, twirling a lock of hair while turning red with rage.

"What is it?" Marcus inquired.

"A text. From Jordan."

Marcus's heart stopped; he knew what would happen next.

"Read it," Dianna demanded:

What do you think about our boy getting into bed with the invaders?

"What the hell is he talking about, Marcus?"

"I can explain," he paused to pick his next words.

"Now!" Dianna was boiling over.

"I was invited to join the Federation's Cohort."

"Invited?"

"Yes."

"You're going to turn it down, right?"

"I already started. I was there last night … I lied."

"You son of a bitch!" Dianna's elevated voice drew the attention of everyone on the patio.

"I was going to tell you, but you said this week was already hard, and I hesitated. I'm—"

"GOD! You're like one of the kids from the clinic. This is just another impulsive decision."

"That's unfair and you know it."

"Why are you doing this? You're already rich!"

"It's not about money."

"So you're doing charity work? For aliens? Do you even hear how absurd this conversation is? You are literally surrendering yourself to these—things, Shadows, whatever. Don't you understand how this looks? If anyone at the Coalition finds out I'm dating a Federation collaborator, do you think they'll let me finish my research? You're jeopardizing everything for both of us. If not for money, then what? The thrill? Like your brother? That's it, isn't it? You want to do dangerous things like your brother. Well, the next step in emulating him, just so we're both clear, is to be with a different woman every week. Which is it, Marcus? The thrill or the women?"

"It's neither of those. I'm doing this for us, for our future. To save us from the Confederation."

"I don't need to be saved, Marcus! How many times do I have to repeat myself? It's the Federation that's the threat! Right here, right now."

"You don't know what goes on in the Lab, but I do," Marcus tried to de-escalate. "I was there. I experienced it firsthand. I can tell you what the Federation is like ... what their research is like."

"I don't want to know about those occupiers! I don't even want to be having this conversation! Ughhh! I can't believe how selfish you're being. They've brainwashed you, and there's no point continuing this conversation. Your lack of judgment is shocking after everything Jordan's told you."

Marcus didn't agree about the risk and remained unmoved like when dealing with Jordan.

"Right. Stay silent. What else can you do? Life isn't a game, Marcus, you shouldn't gamble with it like your brother does. You are so lucky, do you realize that? And you're risking it all by getting into bed with the Federation. I knew something was wrong last night, that's why I texted you. I could feel it. So let me share some of those feelings with you now. When you enter into a committed relationship, like the one I thought we had, you lose the luxury of making decisions on your own. What you do impacts me." Dianna violently shoved her things back into her purse. "This isn't how you treat someone you love! I'm leaving now, but not because I want to. I'm leaving because you don't care about anyone, including yourself. Mark my words, you are making the biggest mistake of your life."

"It could be worse, right? I could be seeing another girl ... or dead." Marcus felt good repeating the alternatives in Dianna's original order.

"WHAT A WASTE OF MY TIME!" Dianna shouted as she stormed off.

Everyone on the patio avoided eye contact with Marcus as he sat alone.

9

FEAR, UNCERTAINTY, DOUBT

Marcus was the first to arrive at class. He mentally replayed his argument with Dianna, trying to identify what he could've done differently. As the classroom filled with students, each sat silently immersed in their own world. Jordan was MIA again. A few students were sporting Tek on the insides of their wrists. This placement was less popular than concealing it beneath clothing but more common than wearing it in the center of the forehead, a practice propagated by the myth it amplified Tek. *Whatever their reality looked like*, Marcus thought, *it couldn't compare to Brad's Lab last night.*

Everyone's attention converged as Bill entered. "Welcome to another day on the right side of the grass!"

"What does that mean?" Jack asked. He was the class's resident expert on data and a British citizen with no discernible accent. He had a pale complexion, sandy blonde hair, a short beard that accentuated his long neck, and a thin physique.

"You're alive. Or you'd be on the other side of the grass."

A few of the students giggled at this explanation.

"Today we'll make like sophists and formulate an antithesis argument," Bill paced the room, "by attacking yesterday's idea that we have free will to make choices. We'll explore the belief that any attempt to exert free will is like swimming against a raging river, one that drowns you without ever noticing. We'll start at the macro level, with a topic as massive as the Confederation, and end at the micro-level with the tiny threat of toxoplasmosis."

"The parasite?" asked Jack.

"Exactly!" Bill affirmed. "Since we're going to criticize the notion of free will, let's agree on a definition first. Who has one?"

"Free will is how we push back on the universe," said Ameda.

"I love it," Bill perked up. "Let's run with that. But you're wrong. Right? The universe has already been predetermined."

"I don't think so," Ameda responded.

"You're mostly alone in that belief," Bill countered. "Whether it's called luck, fate, destiny, or randomness, the majority of people believe their path is determined. Are they wrong? And before you answer, consider this: if we take the entire history of the universe and condense it down to a single 'Cosmic Year,' a metaphor used by Carl Sagan, our solar system didn't form until late August. Dinosaurs lived a whole five days, from December 25th to December 30th, and primates like us showed up on December 31st, just after two in the afternoon. The pyramids were constructed twelve seconds before midnight, and the modern world has existed for the literal last second."

"Whoa," said Che. Though his immigrant parents named him after the nefarious Communist, he typically sided with the capitalist faction of the class. He had a smile that lit up the room, the body of a classical statue, golden brown skin, and short curly black hair. After Jordan, he was Marcus's favorite classmate.

"Damn right," Bill smirked. "Let's take this time metaphor further. If we represent the history of known human civilization, the ten thousand years since the Younger Dryas cataclysm, as twenty-four hours, then your life fills the final eleven seconds."

"How long would our life be on the cosmic clock?" asked Che.

"Ten thousand times faster than a blink of the eye."

"Will that change thanks to the Federation?" asked Marcus.

Like he'd been waiting in the shadows for the word to be spoken, Jordan unexpectedly arrived.

"Mr. Kilravock," Bill welcomed, "we've missed you. I assume you've been busy cerebrating?"

Marcus caught Jordan and Bonnie exchange smiles as his friend settled at the back of class, far from his usual seat next to Marcus; this slight was intentional.

"Definitely," Bill said to Marcus before interlacing his fingers and twiddling his thumbs. "Assuming we don't all die during a Confederation invasion first, I bet humans live much longer thanks to Federation knowledge. But that doesn't change how tiny the window is for our existence, and this is where all choice happens as we currently understand it. Even if you're capable of making a choice right now, 99.98% of existence has already led to this moment. Some call that pure determinism."

"Isn't that predestination?" asked Jack.

"It has many names," Bill replied.

"Yesterday you told us we could choose our job or who we marry," Lindsay challenged, "and that's all true. We can."

"Let's assume I was previously correct, and we can choose those things. We can only marry from among a subset of the living, and the job we work has to exist unless we're going to create it. Even then, we're still locked-in by existing technology."

"What does that mean?" asked Ameda.

"Technological lock-in, or path dependency, means the decisions of our ancestors, whatever their motivation, determine the choices we face today. If that's true, do we have free will?"

"Isn't technology proof we can change the universe like Ameda said?" Marcus asked. "Human history has been defined by our ability to push back on nature and create a new world. It was hard work accomplished through calculated, correct choices."

"The current state of our technology is incapable of stopping the Confederation. Just like we can't go back in time and kill baby Hitler or stop an asteroid from hitting Earth tomorrow, those events determine the world we face today, choices be damned."

"We could stop an asteroid," Quinn boasted.

"I doubt Bruce Willis can save us," Bill beamed, "and fifty years ago, the answer would've been an indisputable negatory. Roger Roger?"

"Doesn't that support the idea that through choices, we can shape our future world?" asked Sukanksha. Su was a soft-spoken international student from India whose brilliance matched her beauty. She had welcoming brown eyes, dark hair, and an alluring smile. She was always the first person to pair up with Marcus during group assignments.

"For the sake of argument, let's say we could pull it off. As impressive as that might be to us, do you think the Confederation, or the Federation for that matter, would share our sense of accomplishment given their technological superiority? We simply cannot stop either force on our own. It's not a choice we have available to make, and probably never will."

"We can choose to work with the Federation," Marcus replied.

"I don't think it's fair to call that a choice," Jordan retorted.

"I agree," said Ameda.

"Let's avoid a turf war on that point, gentleman. Instead, answer this," Bill posed the question to Marcus, "you mentioned nature. Which do you believe is more powerful, nature or nurture?"

Marcus took the bait, "Probably nature."

"Why?" Bill asked.

"I've seen it in action in my brother's chocolate lab. She's the quietest dog you've ever met until she rides in a car, then she goes crazy. Like, absolutely nuts, whining and barking until you let her out to run alongside the vehicle like a wolf in the pack. She couldn't be happier when she does it. She comes alive. It's pure instinct. It may be deep down, but it's still in there. It's just her nature."

"Excellent example," Bill exclaimed. "And isn't that an argument in favor of a deterministic nature? Since she can't change what she is deep down?"

Marcus realized the booby trap he'd stepped into.

"That was the argument for eugenics," said Bill. "Generations of scientists tried to use the technology of their day to steer our nature in a new direction. But it's been a failure. In the case of your brother's pet, a force it couldn't stop changed it into a dog in appearance only. Deep down, the wolf is still in there. This animal had no say either way. That's doubly deterministic, isn't it?"

"Wasn't eugenics pseudoscience?" asked Che.

"The jury is still out. Our DNA contains the collective history of billions of years on this planet, and we still don't understand how it all works. That means every theory to this point, and any choices made based on those theories, was incomplete, and the causal relationships were uncertain, even if occasionally predictive. Believing that because humans can make a chocolate lab, we've therefore figured everything out about genetics, is definitely wrong."

"Imperfect information is the real problem then?" asked Su.

"That's an important limitation. Human knowledge is finite, meaning we can never know everything that affects a situation. So any choice we make, like tinkering with genes, is done under uncertainty. How can we have free will if we're only guessing? The fact we know so little should give us pause. And, to make matters worse, technological empowerment is also breeding doubt these days."

"Deep fakes?" said Jack.

"That's one worthwhile example."

"I don't know what that is," admitted Che.

Several of the other students nodded in agreement.

"AI-generated falsehoods," Jack explained. "It can be audio, video, or any other digital format. The artificial intelligence uses past examples to create a fake alternative future. They're getting so good it's almost impossible to tell what's real anymore."

"In such a situation," Bill posited, "where you can be tricked into believing something that's false, do you still have free will? Now let's go a step deeper, pun intended. What about mind control?"

"Like HAARP?" Jordan asked excitedly.

"What's HAARP?" Lindsay responded.

"The High-Frequency Active Auroral Research Program," Jordan explained. "It's electromagnetic warfare our government has waged against the public for decades. They can implant ideas and emotions in people's minds with ELFs."

"Santa's little helpers?" Quinn mocked.

"No. ELFs, as in extremely low frequencies. They can even use the technology to kill."

Quinn led a chorus of sighs and snickers at Jordan's claim of conspiracy.

"This university did research for the Air Force to show how much electromagnetic energy is needed to destroy people's internal organs. Educate yourself."

"It's interesting you bring up HAARP," said Bill. "I know from conversations with the Federation that they believe programs like HAARP are the result of the Confederation's longstanding, albeit clandestine, involvement in human affairs. They use fear to create a crisis of confidence, then offer the only solution. That way, we'll beg to be saved, and they can do whatever they want with us."

Marcus observed Velia stroking one forearm with the index and middle fingers of her other hand.

"Bullshit!" Jordan shouted. "That's deflection. Pay no attention to the actual aliens here now, right? It couldn't be them, no! It's gotta be some other, still unseen and unproven, alien threat?"

"HAARP was running long before the Federation arrived," Marcus challenged.

"How do we know they weren't working with the government before Disclosure? Whistleblowers claimed a project was in the works several decades before their arrival. Anyone else catch today's PSA? That kind of space show is straight out of Project

Blue Beam's playbook. The Federation is out in the open now, so the logical assumption is that it's been them all along."

"Let's bring this back down to Earth and talk about other, proven, forms of mind control," said Bill. "Namely, toxoplasmosis. This parasite can permanently change the fear instinct in mice so they'll get eaten by a cat."

"Why does it do that?" asked Su.

"The parasite only reproduces inside a cat's digestive system. This strategy helped it become one of the world's most common parasites. So here we have an example of something microscopic that can alter the ability of a bigger animal to make choices."

"But that's just for pussies," Quinn declared.

"It's also in humans, and it's linked with severe changes in behavior—"

"Like what?" Jack interrupted.

"Schizophrenia, for starters, but suicide and other risky behaviors also show a strong correlation," Bill stated. "To emphasize this point again, if something as small as a parasite can control us, do we have free will? And this is a detectable force. What if there are other unknowable forces at work?"

"What about the Oversoul?" asked Lindsay.

Bill smiled from ear to ear. "You read my mind better than one of Jordan's government agents! We studied Ralph Waldo Emerson a few weeks back during our discussion of Transcendentalism in Antebellum America. What if Emerson was right, and we're all part of a larger collective soul that manifests in clusters of individuals who keep reincarnating to learn and bridge a Great Divide together? The 'Over-soul,' as he called it. Do you have the choice to come back to this world? Did you choose this life, or was it chosen for you? How would those things impact your perception of free will?"

"Why don't we remember it then?" asked Che.

"Countless ancient myths explain this. The one you're probably most familiar with is the idea of drinking from the river Lethe, which you might know as the waters of oblivion, not to be confused with the Tom Cruise sci-fi film of the same name. If we want to get crazier than a Scientologist here, what if astrology has a mechanism we don't understand? Are there deterministic qualities to your nature given when and where you were conceived in the larger universal spacial sense? Johannes Kepler, the famed astronomer, believed this to be true. If he was right, how would that affect the existence of free will?"

"What a mind trip," Su said somberly.

"Many of those same ancient cultures believed that fear limits our ability to reach higher levels of consciousness. Entire sets of choices that require a calm mental state could be out of our reach, whether the fear originates from a microscopic parasite, a government gone awry, or an alien threat."

"That seems pretty far-fetched," Ameda added.

"ABSOLUTELY!" Bill shouted at full volume, startling everyone. "See how you feel right now? The anxiety and cloudiness? Fear, uncertainty, and doubt are the ultimate tools of control. When people believe there's no way out, they tear themselves and each other apart."

"But fear keeps us alive," Quinn challenged.

"Does it? Do you feel capable of responding rationally right now?"

"Of course I—" Quinn was overpowered by the earsplitting blast of an air horn, which Bill materialized with the mystique of a magician, sending the class's hearts racing again.

"HOW BOUT NOW!" Bill screamed.

Quinn struggled to respond.

"Do you know how to survive an encounter with a bear?" Bill asked calmly.

"What?" Quinn was still consumed by shock.

"How do you survive coming face-to-face with a bear? The spoiler is that you can't let fear guide your choices. You have to stay calm and assess the bear's mental state. Specifically, whether the bear is in a defensive or offensive mode. For the former, you must squash any notion that you're a threat, and for the latter, you need to show that you're ready to fight. That's your free will in a single constrained moment. Regardless of where the bear's mind is at, if you succumb to fear and run, the bear ends up with a tasty treat."

Bill's joke landed, and the class's collective spirit climbed. Bill continued playing devil's advocate, driving home the idea that choice was an illusion by invoking limits to human cognition from injuries, mental illness, chemical impairment, and the beliefs of past eras involving demons and witches.

Marcus's mind started wandering to the thought of his next Sequence. According to Brad, like the souls from Bill's system of reincarnation, Marcus wouldn't have any memories of tonight's experience. The idea resurfaced emotions of last night, and his heart started palpating. Anxiety must've been painted across his face because Bill snapped him back to the present, "You feeling okay, Marcus?"

"What? Yes, sorry … I was just lost in thought."

"You look worried," Bill said, genuinely concerned.

"It's nothing, but thanks."

"This is probably a good place to end. To recap our antithesis argument, if you have free will, which is debatable on the deterministic nature of cosmic time alone, the choices available for you might be trivial in nature. Thanks to imperfect information, the chances of successfully shaping your interaction with the universe are basically zero. You're just a scared primate, driven by uncertainty, and possibly paralyzed by fear-inducing parasites as small as toxoplasmosis or as large as the Confederation. Cerebrate on that. I'll see you all Friday."

10

BACK IN BED WITH BRAD

J ordan approached Marcus as the other students deserted the classroom. "Can we walk and talk?"

Marcus nodded, and the pair headed into the sunlight; the heavy cloud cover had mostly cleared.

"Look, dude, I'm a big enough man to admit when I've been acting aggressively. I trust you to watch out for yourself. I know you think you're doing the right thing. Even if I don't share your feelings about the Federation, I'm here for you … I'm sorry I bailed yesterday."

Marcus predicted this reconciliation, but Jordan's interference with Dianna was unexpected. "What about the text?"

"Which one?"

"To my girlfriend," Marcus clarified. "You broke the news before I had a chance and—"

"I assumed you told her. It'd been like twenty-four hours."

"Assuming isn't the same as knowing."

"You're right. What happened?"

"What do you think? She went nuclear and stormed out."

"Are you guys done for?" Jordan asked, his eyes widening.

"I don't know. She reached a new level of rage, that's for sure."

"I didn't mean to force the issue," Jordan justified, "but how did you expect her to react? You know how she feels about the Federation. If you believe you can change that, you're delusional."

"I don't agree," Marcus protested.

"I love you, bro, but you'll be forced to choose. Dianna won't be second fiddle to the Federation."

Marcus wasn't prepared to accept that truth or his role in creating this situation and lashed out. "I appreciate the advice, but your interference inflamed things. The reality is, you might have already chosen for me."

"I'm sorry, that wasn't my intention. We both care about you. A lot. That's why I reached out to her. I didn't know it'd blow up like this … I'd rather die than see you two split up."

Marcus was sure of Jordan's sincerity. "I know. I appreciate the apology and accept it. Where you headed?"

"Home. You?"

"In that direction."

"You're going to the Lab?" Jordan inquired.

"Yes."

Jordan said nothing, so Marcus spoke, "I finished the exploratory phase ahead of schedule. This afternoon I'm starting a new type of Sequence."

"What's that?"

"The name for their social experiments."

Jordan's paranoia got the better of him, and he changed topics. But when Carlson Hall came into view, he couldn't contain his curiosity. "What were the Sequences like?"

"The Cohort calls it Subsumption. It's another reality. I don't know how else to describe it. It completely engulfs you, like the best virtual reality game you can imagine. It's real as this moment right now. There's no way to tell the difference."

"Did you feel everything?"

"Yes. And I remember everything like it actually happened. Though, that won't be the case today."

"What did you have to do? In the experiments?"

"Are we off the record?" Marcus teased.

Jordan's slumping shoulders couldn't mask the impact of this comment on his sense of loyalty. "If you tell me to keep a secret, I will."

"Yesterday, you threatened to expose me ..."

"Scouts honor," Jordan held three fingers up.

"I shot a gun. In another, I crossed a ravine, and in one, I was standing alone in the mountains at night." Marcus omitted the car crash. He wasn't ready to revisit that memory.

Jordan continued questioning, but quickly realized he was talking to the trees, turning around to see what had grabbed Marcus's attention. Hecate was cresting over the western mountains. No matter how many times they'd seen this, it was still amazing. In sci-fi stories, aliens arrived in aerodynamic starships, but the Federation didn't do that; they appeared with a planet.

Hecate was perfectly pale blue and the size of Jupiter. It had a single blemish resembling the Great Dark Spot of Neptune, and the entire planet crackled with an electric layer of Auroras. Four moons of differing colors orbited the Federation planet, and when the whole entourage was visible, it occupied an enormous portion of Earth's empyrean.

Like most objects in the solar system, Hecate had a prograde orbit, but its faster velocity made it one of the few celestial objects to rise in the west and set in the east, completing a single revolution around the Earth every thirteen hours. And because Hecate was 500,000 miles away, not much further than the average apogee of the moon, it caused dramatic eclipses. These lasted just over half an hour, during which time the sun's rays were concentrated into eight pillars of light that shot from behind Hecate like spokes on a wheel.

The Federation's home planet made a transit of the sun roughly every eight hours somewhere in the world, and given its current position on the horizon, the next eclipse would happen in a few hours over Salt Lake. Scientists didn't debate the effects of periodically diminished light on the planet anymore. Instead, they focused their pedantic panic on Hecate's gravitational impact. Yet, time and tides continued to wait for no one, so the human math was missing something.

"Shadows may walk around looking like us, but they're alien in every sense of the word," Jordan softly spoke as they watched the planet rise. "The Federation has, what, a billion years of evolution on us? The movies of our youth lied to us, man. We have zero chance against them. Look at what happened to North Korea— there one minute, gone the next. That's the war of our future, Marcus. No explosions, no heroic overcoming of unbeatable odds. Just inexistence. How do we fight that?"

"Maybe we don't have to since this isn't a fight," Marcus said and turned to face Jordan. "I realize how hard it is for you to be supportive of me. Of this. I don't know how to explain it, but Selection feels like what I'm supposed to do. Like everything lined up so I could be here for this moment, in this place. I feel it in my bones. Thanks for trusting me."

"And I feel like the reincarnation of Cassandra of Troy, screaming that Hecate is the Federation's Trojan Horse, but you won't listen. My gut tells me this is the beginning of the end, but I've said my piece and will respect your choice. I hope you'll reciprocate and respect mine to bitch about it."

It was an equitable solution, and the two of them hugged before Marcus walked into the Lab.

Brad hailed Marcus's return, "Hello, Earthling! How was class?"

"Good. I'm ready to get started." Marcus motioned toward the locker room door.

"In a minute," Brad sat on the couch. "Let's pregame first. I want to get your thoughts about last night."

Marcus sat across from him. "It was intense, but I've been so wrapped up in the rest of my life, I haven't had time to process it."

"I've never had a proxy say the first time slipped their mind!"

"I slept in, had a huge fight with Dianna, went to class, and I just finished making up with Jordan about starting Selection."

"Sounds like you're getting it from all sides. Who's madder?"

"Dianna. Without a doubt."

"Do you want to share the details?"

"How honest can I be here?" Marcus asked.

"I've never been frocked, but I'll be your priest."

After a moment of reflection, Marcus dove in, "I was waiting for the right way to tell her about Selection, but I hesitated, then I lied. She found out anyway, which made things way worse."

"Dishonesty does that."

"That's not very priestly of you," Marcus said defensively.

"Then I'll be your Huckleberry instead."

"She doesn't make it easy to be honest. That's not an excuse, it's just part of the equation. If I told her outright, she still would've written off Selection as an impulsive catastrophe of a decision."

"Was it?" asked Brad.

"No. She associates impulsivity with my brother, and to say they don't get along would be an understatement. Anything I do that reminds her of him causes me problems."

"What's the association in this instance?"

"It's a long story …," Marcus cautioned.

"I have all the time in the world," Brad relaxed into his seat.

"We met because she was the teaching assistant for my intro to psychology class. It was my first semester at the University, and I was part of a mock focus group she led with a dozen other students. I asked her out a week later, and we had an instant connection. A few weeks after that, she came to me crying and said we had to file a disclosure form with her department because TA's aren't supposed to engage in romantic relationships with students."

"Did she know the rule before you got involved?"

"Probably. Either way, her supervisor told us to put things on hold until the end of the semester, but I dropped the class the next day. She was furious that I didn't talk to her about it first. I thought I was doing the right thing. I took a big hit to my GPA so we could be together. She interpreted it as an impulsive decision and blamed my brother's bad example. Things were never the same. Then you showed up, and it got worse, but you know that part already."

"So Selection brought back old feelings for her?"

"I guess," Marcus pondered. "But describing my choice to join Selection as impulsive is false. I know she's afraid of the Federation and is angry I didn't ask her permission. She can be controlling. She'd try to direct the oceans if it was possible."

"We can do that." Brad was coolly confident.

"Do what?"

"Move an ocean. It's not that hard."

Marcus sat in awe of the omission.

"She's a psychologist then?" Brad perked up.

"Almost. She's studying to be one."

"What's her field of specialization?"

"Developmental psychology," Marcus answered.

"She helps kids?"

"Mostly."

"Interesting …"

"Why's that?" Marcus asked.

"You get a bigger bang for your buck if you help someone when they're young. It's like shooting an arrow: the further away your target is, the more precise you have to be from the beginning. It's particularly true with psychology. The word combines two Greek roots meaning the study of the soul. It's influential work."

"That's ironic," Marcus laughed.

"In what way?"

"Because Dianna doesn't believe the soul exists."

"Do you think you'll be able to make amends with her like you have with Jordan?" Brad asked.

"Maybe. She's much, much madder."

"They usually are."

"They?"

"Mating partners," Brad clarified. "They worry about what happens here. It's natural since this isn't a desk job."

"We're not mating, or at least we haven't yet."

"But you're hoping to?"

"I want to, but I'm not like my brother. It takes a lot for me to jump into bed with someone. I need to know there's a future in it for me. I want a family more than a fling."

"And you think you can have that with Dianna?"

"I hope so. After our fight, the chances are lower."

"I'm sorry to hear that," Brad consoled. "Given what I know about your Form, concern can be a good sign of deeper attachments. Do you know what Dianna wants, long term?"

"Deep down, I think she wants a family too. It's hard to tell because she holds everything close to the chest. I know she never had a healthy family dynamic growing up. I think that's why she's attracted to developmental psychology since she gets to live vicariously through the people she helps. But when it comes to our relationship, the future isn't as encouraging, even if we patch things up."

"Can you be more specific?" Brad asked.

"Whenever things are progressing, we seem to have a serious fight. We always make up, but at best, we get back to where we were. I have a hard time saying goodbye to anyone, especially Dianna, and sometimes it feels like she uses that to keep us in the same place."

"Uses it how?"

"Antony says she's a 'bait and switch bitch,' because when I've made the mental decision to move on, she does a one-eighty and is super affectionate. It'll be wonderful for a while, and then we plateau again. It's like we're in a feedback loop, and nothing I try breaks us out of it. But I love her, so I give it another shot. I think she feels the same way."

"Selection is voluntary," Brad reminded Marcus. "You could quit and break the cycle."

"I joined Selection to protect her and the rest of my family from the Confederation. I'm not going anywhere."

"Godspeed navigating that emotional minefield. Never surrender the high ground," Brad smiled. "Let's switch gears. Is there anything else you'd like to talk about before we get started?"

"There is, but it'd be personal. For you."

"I give as good as I get."

"Is the human image you're using a translation of you, or is it like a mask you picked out and put on?"

Brad allowed a moment to pass, "Every identity is the result of choice. You may not be paying attention, or understand it in the process because it happens slowly over the course of your entire life, but this identity is as real for me as yours is for you."

Marcus was accustomed to Brad's humor, so the depth of what he said took him by surprise.

"Anything else?" Brad asked.

"Yeah. Is Hecate a ship or a real planet? Is it natural or something you built, like a Death Star, if you know what that is?"

"Everyone knows about the Death Star," Brad smirked. "Hecate is our home in the same way Earth is yours. We're just mobile. It's our American Express, and we don't leave home without it."

"The planet looks like it's all oceans. Where do you live?"

"Inside the eye of the storm."

"The dark spot thing?"

"Yup. It's larger than the Great Dark Spot on Neptune and, not to humblebrag, it moves ten times faster."

"How fast?"

"Fifteen thousand miles per hour."

"How do you survive then?"

"My mother used to say there's no such thing as bad weather, just poor preparation."

"Utah must feel peaceful in comparison."

"I'm not going to lie," Brad leaned forward, "I love it here."

"What's your favorite part?"

"The geology. Your state is home to three geographical provinces. All of them are fascinating and unique. One happens to be my favorite spot on your entire planet."

"Which one?"

"The Rocky Mountains. They are AMAZING!"

"Really?"

"Are you calling John Denver a liar?" Brad challenged. "But seriously, if I weren't here right now, I'd be out exploring the Uintas."

Marcus was skeptical. "You're a hiker?"

"What, the mountains aren't big enough for both of us?"

"No, I just never considered what aliens do on their day off," Marcus explained. "I grew up hiking in those mountains. My family went to Red Castle every few years to fish the lakes."

"I know that area well. It's near Kings Peak."

"The one and only," Marcus replied.

"Have you ever climbed it?"

"No. I've seen it from a distance. I think it'd be awesome to summit one day if I could conquer my fear of heights. I got vertigo just listening to my brother's description of scaling it."

"Second by second, time is running out," Brad coaxed.

"What are the other two provinces? I live here and don't even know what they are."

"Shame!" Brad scowled. "The Colorado Plateau to the south, with one of the highest concentrations of National Parks and hydrocarbons on your planet. And the Great Basin, the desert stretching from here to Reno. All three provinces converge around the Salt Lake Valley. It's a unique place, and like I said, I love it here."

The locker room door activated; it was time.

"Suit up," Brad said, "then head to the Experimental Chamber."

Marcus walked into the locker room with a mission, pausing to look at Monica's glowing door again. There was something magnetic about her name.

11

KINGS PEAK

"**W**elcome back," Hi!-D greeted Marcus in the locker room this time.

All at once, the space morphed into an alpine wilderness. The fake environment projected across every surface transfixed his attention; it even smelt like real pine trees.

"Would you like a different environment, or maybe an experience? A scene from a book? Or immersive art?"

"I don't know what you mean," Marcus admitted.

"The room can respond to your thoughts. If you want to view something, it will come on. If you want a chair in a different location, it will move for you. The room is a great mind reader."

"Thanks for the tutorial, maybe next time." Marcus moved on to his locker, donned his EXO, and entered the Liberty Bell; the space didn't feel like an abyss anymore. As he started to float, Brad began another direct-to-brain broadcast.

"Just like before, you'll never be in any physical danger. That said, today will be different because we're going into Stealth Mode, meaning I won't talk to you, and you won't remember any of it."

"If I can't remember what happens, how will I get better at the Sequences? How do I improve?"

"Subsumption isn't about your personal growth—you have a real-life for that," Brad explained. "This research is about getting data to understand who you are as a singular exemplar of your Form. Sequences are a close variation of your life because they're meant to test you as an individual. You're the only one who can be you. Some of the details will vary, but the sum total of your experiences to this point have already shaped who you are, straying too far from that core identity results in biased data."

"Biased?"

"In the most illustrious deeds," Brad said dramatically, "there is not always a manifestation of virtue or vice, nay, a slight thing like a phrase or a jest often makes a greater revelation of character than battles when thousands fall ..."

"I recognize that," Marcus searched his memory.

"It's from Plutarch's *Life of Alexander the Great*. But in all seriousness, there are dimensions about who you are that, when manipulated, turn the data into stochastic noise. You can't be a poor child of a third-world nation or a one-legged middle-aged lesbian, because your mind knows it isn't your actual identity. It's like hitting the reset button—you'd spend the entire time trying to reorientate yourself. Since we can't watch you forever, we opt for going an inch wide and a mile deep over the alternatives. To put this in terms you'd understand, this isn't *Quantum Leap*, but if you pass Selection, I'll happily be the AL to your Sam for Halloween."

"Bring a real-life Ziggy, and you've got a deal," Marcus bantered. It was one of Antony's favorite shows, and Marcus was raised watching reruns.

"Do you have any other questions?"

Nope, thought Marcus. *This comms system was convenient, even if it was rather invasive.* The thought of having no memories of what was about to happen made Marcus gleefully anxious, like on the final ascent of a roller coaster, sure of his safety in the face of guaranteed danger.

Brad counted down for him, "Three ... two ... one ..."

[Sequence ID# 396] [Data Begins]

The last thing he remembered they'd just reached the top of Anderson Pass, a fourteen-hundred-foot climb marking a high-point in the seventy-eight miles of the Highline Trail. "I don't know if we should still try to summit," Marcus wheezed. The air was getting colder and thinner. He was making the attempt with a mountaineering friend from work. Tim was an expert in the backcountry, which meant he could be dangerous from bouts of conditioned hubris. The final mile to the summit would be their eleventh of the day, but they only had three hours of sunlight left.

"What?" Tim asked, as if he'd been ignoring Marcus.

"I think we need to turn back. We aren't going to make the summit before sunset. We can't navigate this place in the dark."

"We'll be fine. It won't require ropes. Plus, we have headlamps. We haven't come this far to only get this far," Tim insisted.

The trail's switchbacks looked more intimidating from the top, and they'd have to go back this way to reach their camp. Rain was common this time of year, especially in the early evening, but they'd stayed dry so far, and the good weather looked like it would hold. *Still*, Marcus thought, *everything was taking much longer than either of them expected.* He ignored his intuition. "Okay, let's move."

A mile to their south was the 13,518-foot Kings Peak, the highest point in Utah, and the ninety-third highest in North America. It was a stunning place. The terrain was marked by dramatic peaks with razor-thin ridges separated by fish-packed basin lakes and rivers. It'd taken seven hundred million years for this quartzite, shale, and slate stone to end up beneath their feet.

Despite being a hundred miles east of Salt Lake City, this was the literal definition of nowhere. Anderson Pass was above the timberline, the demarcation where trees stop growing, so the area resembled a moonscape. But in the valley below, twenty-foot Rocky Mountain Firs swayed like soft green grass, breaking up the tan color characterizing the rest of the landscape.

"Stay close," Tim strapped on their pack and led the way.

Their initial ascent followed the ridgeline heading south along a thousand-foot drop on one side. Movement was slow here because every step had to be earned by testing the balance of individual rocks. Any slip could trigger a slide that'd bury or kill someone below, but they hadn't seen another soul in two days. *Worst case, it'd just be the two of them that died*, Marcus thought to himself.

There was no single path to the summit, and small cairns were scattered everywhere, indicating the direction past travelers had attempted. Whether they were lighthouses or roadside memorials was inconclusive from a distance; false horizons abounded. After a tough thirty minutes, they'd gone a third of a mile, and Marcus expressed his concern again. "We're moving too slow. We won't make the summit for an hour at this pace, so we'll be coming down in the dark. It's time to accept reality and turn back."

"If I had a baby carrier, I'd throw you in it. Stop wasting time talking and keep moving."

Everything Marcus knew, everything he felt, was questioning this wisdom. He wasn't going to split from Tim; you didn't do that in a place like this. Whatever happened, they'd be safer together.

"If you get us killed, I'm going to kill you," Marcus mocked.

The pace picked up slightly now that he'd accepted the impossibility of calling it off. It was an amazing landscape. Some stones were the size of refrigerators, cars, or small houses, while others were the size of a football. The randomness of the rockslide formed more than a few patterns resembling Stonehenge. The emotional toll of passing one false horizon after another was at its breaking point when, finally, the summit emerged.

Spirits were on fire as the two raced to the top. Determination had paid off. They'd made it. The wind was so intense that Marcus worried he'd be blown from the ridge. He crouched to reduce his profile as he approached the edge, sitting down and sliding the final few inches while the sun doused him in welcoming warmth. This summit resembled a place where gods would've convened. A broad, flat stone led right to the edge of a two-thousand-foot drop overlooking the world. His stomach cramped at the thought of falling, but Marcus swung his legs over the edge and leaned forward to peer between them. Everything he could see, in every direction, was down. He knew he was baiting fate, but it was a rush to be this close to death.

"Wasn't this worth it?" Tim asked, standing aside Marcus.

"Absolutely."

The entire Yellowstone Creek Basin was below them, bathed in autumn's golden sunset. It was one of the most beautiful places in the Uintas, conveniently located below Utah's highest peak.

"Told you," said Tim.

His boastfulness gave Marcus no comfort. They had just over an hour to get off this ridge and back down Anderson Pass before running out of sunlight. Marcus took a long last look, knowing this moment could never be replicated. It was peaceful.

"Ready for the rock scramble of death?" Tim laughed.

Going down a mountain is usually faster thanks to gravity, but not here. Every step required more effort than during their ascent. They'd entered a de facto competition to see who could find the fastest path back, resulting in widely separated positions on the rockslide. The contest shaved twenty minutes off their return, leaving thirty minutes to descend Anderson Pass. The sun's final rays of the day washed the neutral-colored rocks in a deep red, transforming the area into a Martian landscape. The moon hovered above the summit now, and for the first time during their three-day trip, clouds were forming around them.

"We need to go," Marcus pointed toward the growing threat.

They only had a daypack with them, which Tim carried, having left the majority of their gear at basecamp below Smiths Fork Pass. But they'd packed essentials: water, a water purifier, Tri-O-Plex bars, a first-aid kit, hats, gloves, waterproof shells, head-lamps, wet fire tablets, waterproof matches, a butane lighter, a Smith & Wesson .40 caliber handgun, and an early generation monochrome GPS unit to log their path back to camp.

As they reached the basin floor, the sun's glow was gone.

"Here," Tim handed Marcus a headlamp.

"Where's the GPS?"

"In my pocket," Tim replied.

"Can I have it? I want to look at the trail."

It was Marcus's turn to lead now. The return to camp would take them three miles southwest, through forests and meadows along more of the Highline Trail, then three miles northwest to the base of Smiths Fork Pass. Marcus knew from geometry and common sense it'd be shorter to head northwest, but this was impossible. Yellowstone Creek Basin was shaped like a T-Rex footprint, with Anderson Pass at the tip of one outside toe and their camp at the tip of the other.

In the daylight, their trail had been easy to see, but in the moonlit pine forest, the glow from their headlamps proved insufficient. After a few hundred yards, it was clear they'd be dependent on the GPS. Marcus looked at his watch again. Everything was taking too long. All conversation had ceased; they were tired and on a mission. As the far edge of the pine forest came into view, Marcus turned around to ask for his jacket. Tim had been within six feet for most of the day, but now he was gone.

Marcus frantically scanned the surroundings, his headlamp following his frenzied focus. He covered the light, hoping to spot the beam from Tim's in the distance, but there was nothing.

"TIM?" shouted Marcus.

There was no reply.

He had no idea when they'd separated, and he anxiously debated staying put or following the GPS breadcrumbs back to camp. Panic morphed into paralyzing fear. He'd only felt this one other time in life: as a child, lost in a department store. It'd been fifteen years since that moment, but now he was reliving that same type of terror in perfect detail.

Marcus screamed into the silence, "TIM ... IF THIS IS A JOKE IT ISN'T FUNNY ANYMORE!"

Marcus stood waiting for a reply, but none came.

The clouds were beginning to cover the moon. It was about to get even darker. He calmed down enough to listen to his intuition, which told him to move but not which direction to pick. He ran back to Anderson Pass, retracing their steps. The last time he remembered seeing Tim, they passed a small creek on the other side of the forest. Marcus was exhausted and hated traversing this ground for a third time today, but his adrenaline was in the driver's seat. As he approached the creek, he covered his head-lamp; total darkness engulfed him.

This scrambled search continued until he was standing at the base of the pass. Tim was gone. For the first time in his life, Marcus realized what it meant to be totally alone, an isolated individual in the world, and he hated it. Marcus's mind raced down a darker path than the environment around him. Depression took over. Tim had everything except the GPS and Marcus's headlamp. There was nowhere else to go. He turned back toward camp.

They'd been above ten thousand feet the entire day, and the inevitable consequences of high altitude combined with fatigue took their toll. He felt weak, his stomach was uneasy, and a major headache had started. It was altitude sickness, and he needed to reach lower ground before it got worse.

Everything was becoming dreamy when he sensed someone breathing down his neck. Marcus whipped around, stumbling from the fear, but no one was there. He covered his headlamp again but saw nothing. *It must've been his imagination,* Marcus told himself. The GPS showed lower ground was in the forest near the creek, so he headed there as quickly as his battered body could carry him.

Marcus collapsed beside the water, kneeling to submerge his mouth. It tasted wonderful. After a few minutes of sitting with the light off, his headache mostly subsided. He was getting comfortable being alone, having proved by necessity that he could handle it. Camp was uphill from here, but their tent was the only other place they both knew. It was the logical place to go. He submerged his face again, drinking as much water as his stomach could carry. As Marcus stood, flames of pain shot up his legs. His feet were tired of being the middleman between him and the earth. His initial pace was slow, but as numbness set in, he found a rhythm, finally emerging from the forest.

To his north, standing at eleven-thousand feet, was Smiths Fork Pass. It was a long gradual ascent in wide-open terrain, but his next obstacle made itself known head-on: high winds. The air was freezing as it raced over the ridge and into the basin, opposing Marcus's advance, and giving his headache a second life. He didn't make it far before hitting the wall, a phenomenon familiar to marathon runners when their liver and muscles deplete all possible reserves of glycogen, the human body's gasoline.

Marcus couldn't take another step. It didn't come on gradually; it happened instantly, forcing him to sit in the face of unrelenting wind. He'd been still for less than a minute when his headlamp cut out. Without it, he couldn't see the monochrome screen of his GPS. The anxiety of the situation was too much, and he vomited uncontrollably. All the water in his stomach returned to the Earth.

Marcus wiped his mouth and fiddled with his non-functional light. He had no spare. It was with Tim, wherever he was. As another wave of terror seized him, he recalled something his mother said after his department store scare: "If you let go of fear, you'll find your way home." Marcus's trip down memory lane was interrupted by more vomiting. He knew he couldn't continue like this, so he stood, bearing the pain, and started up the hill to camp.

Marcus's eyes had fully adjusted to the dark, and he could see surprisingly far now, which is how he caught a glance of something darting across the trail ahead of him.

"Tim ...?"

Marcus didn't know what it was, but it'd been large and fast. He was hesitant to walk that direction, but that's where the path would take him. After a few steps, he saw movement out of his peripheral vision and turned to face whatever was out there. Again he saw and heard nothing. Hallucinations were possible with extreme altitude sickness, and he questioned if this was even real. The air was so thin that Marcus gasped for each breath. The wind was getting worse, which made him concerned about their tent, and he still felt the urge to throw up. He tilted his head upward, placing his hands on the back of his neck to muster the energy to continue.

There was a small break in the clouds, allowing him to see the stars. They were brighter here, far away from the urban glow. This light had traveled infinite distances to be with him, yet their mutual moment was short-lived. As he stared skyward, he noticed two beings, one standing on either side of him. Whatever they were, each was yards away, holding perfectly still. He was unsure what to do, so he did nothing. His breathing was shallow, and his heart was pounding. He thought about running, he thought about holding still forever, but the list of options was short. He lowered his head and got a better view of the creatures, which looked like wolves. *They weren't indigenous to this area anymore.*

Marcus peeked over his right shoulder, finally seeing the indisputable outline of a large fuzzy animal. He didn't need to corroborate the thing to his left was also a wolf, because they both began to growl in a low evil tone. Instinct gripped him. Marcus ran. He had no idea what was happening behind him, but every molecule in his body propelled him forward. He continued up the trail until he collapsed, turning to discover nothing was chasing him. He scanned the distance for movement and listened intensely, but there was nothing out there. He was alone. As he threw up again, he convinced himself the wolves were apparitions.

Despite the pain of standing, his headache, the broken headlamp, the useless GPS, the constant vomiting, Tim, the wind, and the phantom wolves, Marcus kept moving. Hours later, he could see the ridgeline of Smiths Fork Pass, which meant he was close. They'd set up camp near a small pond below the ridge, hoping it'd provide cover from the wind in the otherwise barren basin. Marcus located the pond and circled it, but his fears were realized after rounding it a second time. No Tim. No tent. He broke down again, his crying interrupted by bouts of vomiting. The last place they both knew about was the car, but that was eighteen-miles away at the China Meadows trailhead.

The thought of making that journey crushed Marcus. He curled up at the base of the ridge to avoid the frigid wind. *How had he allowed it to get to this? He should've insisted on going back when they reached the top of Anderson Pass. He knew better. This was his fault, even if Tim wouldn't listen.* Marcus's internal dialog was spiraling out of control. As he lay there, surrounded by darkness, he remembered something else: the car keys were in the tent. Marcus giggled deliriously—his night wasn't remotely close to being over. He picked himself up and followed the ridge. If Tim wasn't at the car with the keys, it'd be another twenty-seven miles back to civilization.

[Sequence ID# 396] [Data Ends]

Marcus woke up in the Liberty Bell. He searched his memory for anything between Brad's countdown and the present moment, but there was nothing. He felt horrible, worse than after any of the previous calibration Sequences. His entire body ached. Both his stomach and chest were heavy, like being crushed under the weight of overfilled sandbags.

"Excellent!" Brad said directly to Marcus's brain. "You make a habit of this, and you'll sail through Selection. I'll meet you in the locker room in ten."

Marcus moped back to the octagon in his locker. *This sucked*, he thought, while removing his EXO.

Brad was waiting in the locker room as promised. "Congratulations, you did great."

"My chest feels like I've been running sprints in a gas mask."

"Really? Maybe it was too much for one day. You were in there for almost three hours. Go home and rest. Noon tomorrow?"

"Okay."

"By the way," Brad explained as they entered his office, "after the Sequences you're welcome to hang out, but I won't make an appearance. Shut off the lights if you're the last one out."

Marcus didn't understand how the lights functioned, let alone how to turn them off.

PART V

A MILLION LITTLE STARS

WEDNESDAY, MARCH 16, +1 NE

12

SHOUT AND CHEER, ANTONY'S HERE!

Marcus walked out of the Lab and into the soft light of the early evening hour. He could smell the spring blossoms after their afternoon of sunbathing. The air was hot now, a sign of the erratic weather Jordan and his Lyceum co-conspirators blamed on Hecate. The Federation denied involvement, and Marcus believed them; if they could move a planet, they must know what they're doing.

His phone vibrated. Antony was calling.

"Hey," Marcus began, "I was going to—"

"Where are you?" Antony interrupted.

"Walking home from campus. Why?"

"I'm standing outside your house."

"So go inside. I'll be there in two minutes."

"No one's here. And if I wanted to be inside, I would be. Time is money!" Antony echoed their mother when she was in a hurry.

Despite being nineteen years older than Marcus, and part of the allegedly apathetic Millennial generation, Antony was a poster child of success. He'd graduated in five years with a double major in economics and computer science, along with an MBA, but dropped out of law school after their parents' death to assume the role of legal guardian for Marcus.

Antony's academic achievements carried into the private sector. He was a thought leader in Data Science and prided himself in putting the "sexy" into what Harvard Business Review called 'the sexiest job of the twenty-first century.' Through innate talent and an unrivaled work ethic, Antony became a begrudgingly respected businessman—people either loved or hated him, but none denied his brilliance.

His relationships with Dianna and Jordan were examples of this polarizing pattern. Antony had never married or even dated seriously. He was a remorseless playboy, and Dianna despised him for it. But Antony and Jordan bonded through similar tastes in music, a mutual love of drugs, and a shared fascination with extreme sporting. Antony was as much a fill-in father-figure to Jordan as he was for Marcus, promising to take both on a Grand Tour adventure following their sophomore year of college, mere months away. In return, Jordan supplied Antony with cannabis grown in and around his parent's perennially empty mountain home.

Jordan wasn't alone in his admiration of Antony. All 1,617 Companions of Antony's firm were intensely loyal. He'd adopted their title from Alexander the Great's shock unit because, like their ancient equivalent, they had the business world under siege. Fast Company characterized Antony as a modern King Midas, and the millennial Henry Ford since everything he touched turned to gold. But the comparison went further: they also claimed he was crazy.

Marcus felt this was a bunk equivalency since Ford captured his friend Thomas Edison's last breath in a test tube to preserve his soul for reanimation. People thought Antony was nuts because he kept giving away all of his money. The first time he liquidated his wealth, the media wrote it off as a publicity stunt, but when he did it every year after that, they said he was madder than a hatter.

Dianna wasn't alone in her enmity toward Antony, and the other haters similarly focused on his offensive use of language. This was a machination motivated by his personal heroes, which he collectively called his guardians. The most important of these were Trey Parker and Matt Stone, the creators of *South Park, Team America,* and *The Book of Mormon Musical,* who Antony asserted were the greatest satirists of any generation.

Antony also idolized Tyler Durden, the mythical soap-maker-turned-leader of Project Mayhem, for combining two of his personal passions: civil disobedience and fighting. Their maternal grandfather, Cristiano, had taught Antony to box. This eventually led him to another fighting system, Krav Maga, for its simple, effective, and vicious tactics. These attributes resonated with Antony, who lived the Heroic Code tattooed across his back: "no friend served me, and no enemy wronged me, who I haven't fully repaid."

The last of Antony's guardians, and the one that provided his professional persona, was Ari Gold, HBO's pseudo-fictional Hollywood agent. Antony was quick to compliment and slow to criticize if the person showed merit. Otherwise, he was ruthless. He loved being unpredictable and mastered the art of practical jokes on his family. Like Gold, Antony dressed to impress, ensuring he was never not the best-looking person in the room.

As Marcus approached his house, he could see Antony leaning against his Tesla in a three-piece suit; he'd come straight from work. Both brothers inherited the soft Italian beauty of their mother, with an olive complexion, dark hair, and deep brown eyes. Antony was a half-foot shorter than Marcus, but just as handsome and more magnetic. He had *arete* and *auctoritas*, both words from their father's vocabulary, meaning he had the "It Factor."

Antony noticed Marcus's approach and offered his standard salutation, "SHOUT AND CHEER, ANTONY'S HERE!"

"It's good to see you," Marcus replied.

"Is this my brother? Who's now a member of the world elite?" Antony extended his arms, and in a dramatic tone, continued his cry to the sky. "IS THIS MY BLOOD, working with the Federation as a representative for ALL OF HUMANITY TO SAVE THE WORLD?" Antony was being dramatic but genuine.

As the brothers embraced, Antony squeezed him harder than a python. "Congratulations, I'm VERY proud of you. You honor our family name."

"How'd you hear?"

"A little birdie told me," replied Antony, which was code for Jordan.

Marcus had to set the record straight, "Thanks, but I'm not a member of the Cohort yet. I have to survive Selection first."

Antony leaned back with meme-worthy disbelief. "We don't give up, Marcus. Ever. If you don't make it this round, you can try again. *Sempre avanti.*" His brother had invoked their family's favorite dictum: "always forward."

"That's not how it works. I only get one shot."

"Then don't fuck it up. The fate of the universe is at stake."

"What are you doing here?" Marcus inquired.

Antony huddled in close like he was about to say something inappropriate. "Want to see me fight?"

"Where? At Krav?"

"No. The Black Market. At Nerio."

Marcus was stunned. Nothing Antony said was adding up. He'd never done a public fight, ever, and now he was making his début on the world's premier fighting circuit? Marcus hadn't been to the Black Market, but he knew these fights were as intense as they come. "When? Why?"

"Tonight. Because it's time to find out if my training's been a good investment."

Today was a day of many firsts. "Okay, give me five to drop off my stuff."

"No time, I need to get there to register."

"I want to tell Jordan first."

"No one's home, I told you that. We need to go. Now," Antony said through a frustrated smile.

"I have to change! Five minutes." Marcus wouldn't be deterred.

While picking clothes, he tried to call Dianna, but the ringing went to voicemail; she wasn't ready to talk. Putting her out of mind for the night, Marcus pocketed his lucky coin and returned to find Antony sitting in his car, raring to go.

"You'll be late for your own funeral."

Marcus grinned. "Thankfully, that won't be a problem for *me*."

Antony's Tesla was a gift from Elon Musk for solving one of the visionary's Starlink satellite constellation data problems when no one else on Earth could. The seat belt alarm kept dinging. His brother refused to wear it, believing mandatory belt laws increased auto-related fatalities, since drivers felt safer, took greater risks, and ended up killing more pedestrians. It was one of the many data-backed examples Antony invoked about government rule-making run amuck.

The alarm wasn't stronger than Antony's conviction, but it broke Marcus's. "Can we please turn up the music so I don't have to listen to that noise the whole way?"

"Just block it out."

"I can't."

"If you don't control your mind, Marcus, who does?"

"I'm not in the mood for one of your philosophical lessons tonight. I need to relax. Please?"

Antony turned up the music as the singer belted a lyric about humanity having one foot on the moon and one in the cave. The song reminded Marcus of another family dictum: "from the stable to the stars." As they wound down the hill from campus, the Wells Fargo Center was towering in the distance. This building was home to Nerio, one of the four Black Market sectors, and where Antony's world would collide with his opponent's.

Salt Lake was the biggest metropolitan area in the Great Basin, and sociologists described it as having dual identities: the Angel and the Beehive. The Angel was exemplified by the city's Temple, once the largest structure in the Big Field, the original name Mormon settlers gave to the valley. During the last century, the state's pro-business policies gave preeminence to the Beehive, the symbol of industriousness. Today, Utah was home to thousands of tech companies, earning the nickname Silicon Slopes.

Salt Lake was also home to major financial institutions, all of which hired Antony for his ability to predict their future with data. These transplants competed against Utah's original moneylender, the formerly Mormon-Church owned Zions Bancorp. But Salt Lake was a pioneer of another financial institution, the Industrial Bank, and Antony's Companions were at the vanguard of assisting these alternatives to traditional banking.

Marcus dialed down the music. "How's work?"

"Eighty percent bliss, twenty percent getting rammed in the ass by a government cactus. If you want to relax, don't get me started."

"That bad?"

"If there was ever a blatant use of bureaucracy as one group's hammer, this is it."

"So what you're saying," Marcus asked, "is you're their nail?"

"There's never been a single industrial bank failure in this state, but every alphabet agency is trying to regulate them out of existence or force them to fit into the mold the Darrow family has crafted. It won't work. They function on different principles."

"Like?"

"The first industrial banks loaned money based on personal recommendations, not collateral. That's radically different."

"People used to care about their reputation."

"A person is only as good as their word, Marcus."

"How does the Darrow family fit in?"

"You don't build a banking monopoly without scratching the balls of government. Benedict Darrow's family knows how to play the game."

"Lobbying?"

"That's the PR version. Real power comes from hiring former regulators to win government bids and avoid compliance costs."

"That's got to be illegal." Marcus's naivete was showing.

"Nope. It happens so much that it's got a name: regulatory capture. And the Darrow family are the Jackson 5 of it. Without fail, when our paths cross, Benedict is sitting on the same side of the table as the government agents. They're his hammer."

"And you have to work with him?"

"Dealing with the Darrows is an inevitability, their hands are in everything. Pharmaceuticals, shipping, media, financial institutions. That's the thing about money, Marcus—once you have it, it's infinitely easier to make more. But Tek-Mart took it to a whole new level for Benedict."

"Will we see it?" Marcus was noticeably excited.

"You can't enter the Black Market without walking right by it."

"Can I ask you something … since you work with the government so much?"

"Anything," Antony assured.

"Do you think they've been conspiring with the Federation … even before everyone's Disclosure Moment?"

"Jordan's in your head about Selection."

"We talked about it in class today. Bill challenged Jordan's claim that the Federation is responsible for all the social instability, but he didn't deny it's happening. He agreed it's real."

"Who does Bill think is behind it then?"

"The Confederation," answered Marcus. "He said they've been inciting fear through government and media for a very long time."

"Deep state," Antony muttered, as if to himself.

"What?"

"I don't know who's ultimately pulling the strings, but I have zero doubt it's going on," Antony explained. "That's what power does. It sows dissent, envy, and hate. It divides and conquers to keep expanding. Everywhere and always."

Marcus was silent.

"Are you doubting your decision to start Selection because you're worried Jordan is right and it's the Federation's fault?"

"He never shuts up." Marcus laughed nervously.

"What is your intuition telling you?"

"… That the Federation is the key to our survival."

"Then let go of fear and trust yourself," Antony encouraged.

"Speaking of fear," Marcus pivoted, "are you nervous? About fighting?"

"No."

"How long have you been planning this?"

"A couple months, why?" Antony asked.

"I'm trying to figure out if this was one of your impulsive decisions."

"They're instantaneous decisions, and this one was carefully crafted."

"What's going through your head right now?"

"Something Dad said. He told me not to be a punk. That I should never look for a fight, but if one found me, I needed to be the person to end it."

"He told me that too," Marcus empathized.

"When?"

"After I got in a fight at elementary school."

"Right." Antony roared with laughter. "It isn't often that a kindergartener bashes another kid's head into a wall. I was standing in line to get my graduation gown when Dad called and told me about it. Didn't you become friends with that kid?"

"For a minute, but then we moved to Sundance."

"Do you even remember why you were fighting?"

"Every single detail, up until I blacked out. Remember the summer we went to San Francisco?"

"I can still smell the fried food mixing with the stench of sea lions on that pier," Antony reminisced.

"Pier 39," Marcus clarified. "I had a rock collection from the Exploratorium I brought for show and tell. When I got off the bus, this kid smacked it out of my hands. I remember watching it shatter and getting angry. He kept laughing at me, calling me names. I snapped, going into blackout mode from pure rage. I remember the blood running down his forehead and nose when I woke up from it. He was a textbook bully and got what he deserved."

"You don't have to convince me, *sic semper tyrannis*."

"What made you think about Dad right now?"

Antony was somber. "Mom and dad have been on my mind all week."

"Me too. I don't think tonight is what he meant."

"I know," Antony said with conviction, "the person I'll face wants to be there. Just like me."

"Have you been to a Black Market fight?"

"Not in person." Antony stopped the car at Main and East Broadway. The Wells Fargo Center stood like a sentinel over them. Frenzied anti-Federation protesters choked the sidewalks surrounding the building. Despite sharing the same enemy as Jordan, even he thought these people were zealots. The Coalition bussed protesters in, since the Mormon Church's official policy was cooperation with the Federation, making local outrage talent scarce.

Marcus loved reading protesters' signs. As they waited for the light to change, he indulged:

The Federation Is The Devil!

PSAs Are The Tool Of The Occupiers!

The Federation Is Hitler Reincarnated

Tek = Mark of the Beast = 666

JUSTICE FINDS ALL FEDERATION ALLIES!!!

"Hey, that one's talking about you," said Antony.

"How do we get up there? To Nerio?"

"Everyone has to go through the Black Market."

"How? The Black Market is a mile from here."

"In your mind's eye," Antony explained, "picture the old Gateway Mall. Remember the clock tower by the splash pad fountain?"

"Yeah."

"At the base of the tower is a door. It takes you to the rooftop club exactly four hundred and twenty-two feet above us." Antony pointed skyward.

"So ... you've been there?" asked Marcus.

"No. I've been to the other three sectors of the Black Market, but never stepped foot in Nerio. This will be a first for both of us."

The light changed, and Antony burned rubber, sending a toxic blue cloud wafting over the mob of Coalition protestors.

13

SPEAK OF THE (TEK-MART) DEVIL

Like with Carlson Hall, the world knew the story of how the Gateway Mall survived America's retail apocalypse to become the Black Market. The Gateway was teetering on bankruptcy when the Federation offered to purchase it the day after arrival. But today it was the only shopping center of its kind and tourists poured in from every part of the planet to enjoy the alien-owned bazaar.

"What's it like?" Marcus asked as their commute continued.

"In a few minutes, you can answer that yourself."

"Are all the stores run by Shadows?"

"I'm sure some are, but you're misunderstanding things," Antony explained. "The property itself is the only part that's owned by the Federation. The businesses have human proprietors. I guess some could be Shadows in disguise, but I know for a fact that meat bags like you and me run a few."

"Which ones?" Marcus asked.

"Tek-Mart is the big dog. But the former head of security from my office owns a 3D-printed gun shop in the Pontus sector and he's 100% patriotic human."

"Tony?" Marcus asked.

"The man. The myth," Antony affirmed.

"How can his shop stay open when they're doing illegal stuff?"

"It isn't illegal at the Black Market. Their treaty with national governments recognizes land held by the Federation or its citizens as sovereign territory—like a privately owned embassy. No one can shut it down. And since Federation citizenship is available through a vending machine in the Ignus sector, no one will bother you after you leave."

"Seems like the Coalition would harass people who've visited, even if the governments won't."

"Any incident involving a Federation citizen, like being assaulted, is adjudicated through a Federation court. And they're notoriously harsh on the guilty and false accusers alike. Plus, the Coalition would have to identify you first, which is hard since you can get there from the safety of your living room."

"Really? How?"

"What is this, twenty questions?" Antony teased. "If you win a pass in the daily lottery, you set a time and location for a portal to pick you up, then just walk through into the Terra sector. The same portal takes you home when you're ready, so no one has to know you were ever there."

"Did you win one? A pass for today?"

"No."

"I don't understand."

"There's a loophole."

"There always is with you," Marcus murmured.

"Employees and owners of Black Market businesses get a Fast Pass. I'm a partner in Tony's gun shop, and since I bought you some shares too, we can both come and go as we please."

"If the portal takes us there, why are we driving?"

"Cause fuck the Coalition. I won't be intimidated by those lunatics. I want them to see me walk in. You're welcome to cover your face if you're worried about those fascist paparazzi."

Antony pulled into the valet parking, and the brothers stepped from the vehicle. The Black Market looked like any commercial center from the outside, a mix of stucco, brick, and glass facades, surrounded by concrete paths cut by a decorative tree or two. More Coalition protesters stood across the street, screaming the same messages as their comrades outside the Wells Fargo Center.

Antony faced them, middle fingers to the air. "All this animus reminds me, how's Queen Kos handling your new social status?"

"She's not answering my calls since I told her about Selection."

"If you want my brotherly advice, stop giving your power to her by thinking about it. Put it behind you and live it up tonight … because there will be plenty of worthy temptations," Antony winked. He grabbed a bag from his trunk and charged into the Black Market.

Everything in the open-air mall was oversaturated. Colors were brighter, richer, and warmer. The air was crisp and pleasant smelling, and the happy sounds of people echoed everywhere. Upon inspection, Marcus could tell the surfaces were made of the same Organics material from Brad's Lab. The whole place had a nice atmosphere; vibrant and alive compared to its outer facade.

People continuously poured through portals surrounding the promenade. Holographic signage was everywhere, competing for people's attention. Marcus was struck by how orderly the Black Market was. This wasn't the dark, dangerous place he'd pictured; it looked like Vegas on performance-enhancing drugs, but cleaner.

"It feels balanced here," Marcus said softly.

"It's always seventy-two degrees."

"Always?"

"It was like this on opening day in the dead of winter."

"How do people start a business here?" asked Marcus.

"The Federation offered allotments through a lottery before the Black Market opened. Anyone could enter, but only once, and it had to be done in person."

"I remember that now, Jordan said it was a scam to identify people. He was just ramping up his conspiracy theories back then."

"Registration exploded," Antony replied.

"So these are all the winners?"

"Some people sold their spots. I know Benedict Darrow got six allotments by paying homeless people to register their names for him."

"He bought their claim if they won?"

"What he bought was a turnkey empire," Antony clarified.

"Meaning?"

"Two weeks after arrival, Tek-Mart opened for business."

"On your birthday?" Marcus asked.

"*Our* birthday. Benedict is six years older than me."

"That's a clever way to get allotments," Marcus admitted.

"That's the thing, Benedict isn't a clever guy. His whole life he's followed a script, the same one every Darrow has before him."

"He must've figured something out," Marcus added. "Tek-Mart turned him into the world's first trillionaire."

"Because he's got a monopoly on the supply of Tek. Take that away, and he'd be one Trojan Horse peddling island among a sea of taxless competitors."

"There's no tax here?"

"Duty-free zone, dude," Antony exclaimed. "There's only one regulation the Federation enforces: everything here is voluntary."

"That's shockingly vague," said Marcus.

"Once you crossed that invisible line in the sand, the one demarcating the human world from the Federation's, everything you knew went out the window. People can't pour in like a bunch of Gauls and take over by force. It's impossible."

Marcus recognized the protective technology from his first meeting with Brad. "It's called a Pomerium, the same thing surrounds the Federation's research Lab."

"I'm jack's complete lack of surprise," Antony answered. "The Coalition calls it the Zion Curtain."

"What stops them from stealing or killing once they're inside?"

"I'll show you." Antony took a swing at Marcus, who fell to the floor, attempting to avoid his abrupt aggression. Antony was locked in place, conscious but unable to strike. "It's impossible. I can't force something on you. It has to be voluntary."

"Got it," Marcus stood up. "It's Libertarian Disneyland."

Antony regained self-control before continuing, "People get along here."

"Obviously."

"It's not just because they can't hit each other. Businesses who serve the same kind of customers consolidated into the four sectors, so if you're looking for a fight, like me, there's a place for that, and we don't have to bother the nice families at the non-pasteurized ice-cream shop in the Ignus sector."

"Which sector is this?"

"Terra. We need to get going."

In front of them was a white stream of light resembling silk and fire, elevating people to the next level of the promenade.

"What's up there?" asked Marcus.

"Tek-Mart and a sky bridge to the Black Market. It's our route to Nerio," Antony stepped into the stream.

Marcus followed. The silken light lifted him smoothly to the second level. Before him was a large section of ground enclosed by a glowing white circle. In this boundary, people were experiencing nature in perfect virtual reality, in full view of the large crowd queued below Tek-Mart's imposing logo: TM™.

"What is this thing?"

"Terra's Cycle. Every sector has one."

"Benedict understands the location, location, location mantra," Marcus said.

"He used all six allotments to get this space."

"Anyone can come here? To the Black Market?"

"There's a short blacklist of rabble-rousers," Antony explained, "but for the rest of humanity, it's just one lottery away. Let's keep moving."

"Wait, I want to try the Cycle."

"We don't have time." Antony gestured toward another white stream of light acting as a sky bridge to the heart of the mall.

"ANTHONY? ANTHONY ADAMS!"

Antony recognized the voice and the intentional mispronunciation of his name. The brothers turned to see Benedict Darrow coming out of Tek-Mart with a group of sycophants hot on his heels.

"Anthony, I knew that was you! Didn't I call it?" Benedict turned to his eagerly nodding entourage.

"Hey, BeneDICK," Antony offered his typical retort. "I'd say it's a surprise to see you here, but you do own the place."

Benedict was about the same height as Marcus, but with the lean frame of a marathon runner. His chiseled jawline gave him a hyper-masculine aura, but there was something off about his smile; the perfect teeth couldn't mask a feeling of complete untrustworthiness.

"Who's your handsome companion?" asked Benedict.

"This is my brother Marcus."

Benedict squeezed Marcus's hand like he was trying to juice it. "Your brother already knows my crew, but this is Chet, Thad, and Toby," Benedict waved haphazardly at the middle-age men standing behind him before pointing precisely, "and that lovely lady is my sister, Hannah, and her six-year-old son, Lucius."

Marcus made the rounds, again getting strength tested by each handshake before turning to Hannah, whose grip stayed securely on Lucius's shoulders. She had long brown hair, a shy smile, rotund figure, and wasn't much taller than her son, whose eyes burned with determination uncharacteristic for his age.

"Hi Lucius, I'm Marcus." Even the kid tried to crush his hand.

"What brings the Adams family to our market?" asked Benedict.

"I'm looking for a fight." Antony smirked.

"Did you hear the good news? We'll be working together again, this time on the One Identity project. Your algorithm, my databases. The perfect pairing."

"I did. Congratulations. Hey, thanks for the stop and chat, really. But I've got a fight to win."

"Break a leg. Or good luck. I'm not sure what you're supposed to say before a battle."

Antony pushed on Marcus's back, driving him toward the transport stream.

"You weren't too patronizing," Marcus encouraged.

"Like Mom said, don't let someone else's bad behavior change you."

"His sister and nephew seem nice."

"She's awesome. It just takes a bit for her to open up. I suspect she's the silent brains behind Benedict's surge of success. The Darrows are the modern Medici family, but without the good parts like funding art or investing in the community. That kid doesn't stand a chance growing up in Rich Uncle Pennybags's shadow."

"What do the other three guys do?"

"His boogle of weasels? They feed Benedict's ego and have a collective IQ of under sixty-nine. Toby is the worst of them."

"Which one was he?" Marcus asked.

"The fat Viking-looking one with the beard. He's the archetypal beta-male, groveling at Benedict's feet while ruling the rest of the crew like a tyrant. He never skips an opportunity to describe himself as a natural-born leader, despite lacking the requisite qualities. You know, if you hadn't delayed us multiple times tonight, we would've missed them, so thank you."

"I'm happy to help where I can."

Antony turned and tousled Marcus's hair.

14

FOREIGN SECTORS

The second the brothers stepped from the transport stream, a saleswoman from Build-or-Buy Baby, the Market's family planning business, made a bee-line for them. Antony did a double take at his brother, "The stores here employ Drummers like this lady. They'll try to make a personal connection with casual conversation that turns into a sales pitch. Don't talk to them. Ever. And for the love of everything, keep moving."

"The boys are out tonight!" Their silence only increased her insistence, "Where are you going? Don't be like that. We can talk."

Marcus found ignoring her harder than blocking out Antony's seatbelt alarm and cracked, "Nerio."

"Thrill seekers, huh? You know, that's one of the characteristics we screen the kids for, before placing them in our pageants."

"Child pageantry?"

"An American tradition! We have different Origin Leagues for the kids. If you're looking to pick one up and think you can pass our rigorous background checks, here's today's schedule," she said, handing Marcus a flyer.

"What are Origin Leagues?" he asked.

"We keep the kids in groups based on where they came from, so they can relate to one another until they're adopted. Our Second Chance kids are abortion transfers, the Hard Knocks were all abandoned, and the CRISPR Kids are built from scratch. It's never too early to become a guardian to one of these great kiddos."

The moment she cut off the conversation, another female Drummer took her place. "Instead of building a kid, which will be a lifetime of work, why not build your perfect partner? At Twin Flame, we're pioneering the field of personalization dev."

"Development of what?"

"You tell us what you want in a partner, and we create three Allies."

"Allies?"

"It's short for Alliances. We create three for you."

"Meaning people?"

"Humans only," said the woman, smiling. "We get them to adulthood, then host a pairing ceremony where the four of you decide what happens next. You're not limited to one. We're predicting a 90% match rate when our first batch comes of age."

The woman's pitch was interrupted by a male Drummer, "Why play genetic Russian roulette, stick with what you know. At Carnate, we'll bring back a lost loved one using their DNA."

"I didn't think to bring that with me tonight." Marcus patted his pant pockets.

"If it's a genetic relative, we can get the data from your blood."

Marcus regretted opening Pandora's box; a mob of Drummers now trailed Antony and Marcus as they traversed the sector.

"Why waste your love on a person," said another female Drummer. "What you need is a pet tiger."

Marcus stopped moving to listen to her pitch.

"At Eye of the Tiger, we modify big cats to live as your pet."

"No. Way."

"Yes way. And don't worry. Statistically, our tigers are safer than having a gun in the home or driving without a seatbelt."

Antony grabbed Marcus by the arm and dragged him away. "I have to register. That's why we're here. Don't stop moving."

"Fine," Marcus fretted. "These shops are doing advanced stuff to say they're all run by humans."

"That's because of FTAP."

"Which is?"

"The Federation Technology Accelerator Program, it's similar to what venture capitalists do to ensure a return on their investment."

"So the Federation is invested in these shops?"

"They don't have any ownership," Antony clarified. "They're interested in helping humanity further its own technological progress through innovation. Anyone with a store in the Black Market has access to FTAP's advisors. They can pick the Federation's brain."

Marcus scanned the rest of the sector as he was towed along. "What's Reminiscent?"

"It sells replicas of old discontinued toys."

"Wait, like stuff from our childhood?" Marcus asked. "No chance we can stop there?"

"None!" Antony's frustration boiled over. Their path was blocked by a crowd surrounding the sector's vending machines.

"These are popular."

"Each sector has them. I've never understood why people love buying things from a machine. Even the Romans loved doing it."

"The Romans had vending machines?" Marcus was skeptical.

"Yeah, in Alexandria," said Antony. "For selling holy water."

"What's in these?"

"Marriage licenses and divorce papers."

A golden sky-bridge carried the brothers over a farmers market on the lower level cross streets.

"You hungry?"

"No," Antony answered.

"Where does this food come from? It smells incredible."

"From Federation citizen farms."

"Why's this transport golden, but the other one was white?"

"We're switching sectors. Each has a unique color matching one of Hecate's four moons. Terra is white. Pontus is gold."

On the far side of the transport, everyone sported bathing suits. "Why's everyone here dressed like we're at the beach?" asked Marcus.

"Because we are. Pontus is the fitness center of the Market and has the biggest Cycle, an underground beach wrapped by a circle like the one at Terra, except this one's golden and way larger."

"Have you been there?"

"No. I hear it's just like the real thing, with open sky above and endless waves below. But here cute little animals swim up to be petted."

Pontus feels like the large manipulated spaces in Brad's Lab, Marcus thought. Everything was bigger in this sector, and signage for a store called Biohacked caught his attention. It promised physical perfection through steroid gyms, genetic interventionism, and extreme plastic surgery that included skin and hair color changes. Immediately next door was Guinea Pig, an experimental medical facility claiming to add decades to life through radical procedures.

There were fewer Drummers here, but one tried his hand with Antony, "You gentlemen interested in an adventure?"

Antony said nothing.

"Did one of the pet tigers from Terra get your tongue?" asked the man as he paced alongside them.

"We're in a hurry," said Marcus.

"If you don't already know, at Vicarious Adventures, you can live weeks of vacation in just a few minutes. Let me paint this picture for the two of you—we walk into one of our large rooms and the lights dim, the temperature is comfortable, and there's no noise. Absolutely none. You lie back, I flip on the Tek, and you share an adventure better than the real deal. A minute later, you're back on your way. What d'you say?"

Neither responded, so the man returned to his storefront.

"Vicarious Adventure is an example of a Tek-Stack business," Antony explained. "They couldn't exist without the Federation's technology."

"What's Set & Setting?" Marcus asked, looking ahead in the sector.

"Spiritual guidance with the assistance of psychedelics." Antony slowed his pace. "Jeraldine owns it."

"Who?" Marcus inquired.

"Mom's friend. Garett's wife. Remember?"

Antony was referring to the only therapist who'd broken through to Marcus during his troubled youth. "I sort of remember her. I think we only met once."

"Makes sense. We'd see them at church, but by the time you came along, Mom and Dad weren't nearly as devoted to regular attendance. She's incredible. Come back some time," Antony offered.

"Sounds like her store would appeal more to Jordan. He'd never come here."

"He might for that," Antony said, pointing to Immutable, an extreme piercing and tattoo shop.

"Am I seeing things, or do those people glow," asked Marcus.

"Your eyes don't lie. They use radioactive metal ink."

"What the hell ..."

"They claim it's safe, but check back in a few decades, then I'll believe it. The ink is activated with a low-grade electrical signal."

"They can turn off their tattoos?"

"Living light bulbs," said Antony as the brothers approached another vending machine bottleneck at the end of Pontus.

"What's in these? This crowd's twice as big."

"Body parts."

"Body parts?" Marcus parroted.

"Yes. Body parts. They're mostly 3D-printed, but if you need a kidney, there's a button for that. And Guinea Pig will put it in for you."

Ignus was the final of the three sectors located at the Gateway Mall, and the penultimate one before Nerio. A red transport stream lowered them to a giant circular space surrounded by storefronts. The entire place glowed red and was covered in fire pits scattered among sections of green grass. The sector name was inspired by its Cycle, the Inferno Fountain. This was the first thing a visitor saw entering the sector, and even Antony paused to watch people run unscathed through its flows of liquid fire. As they stood in awe, a server approached with large skewers of meat.

"Greetings from your friends at Indulgence, the Market's best bistro. Would either of you like to sample our panda steak?"

Antony tossed a piece into his mouth. "It's delicious."

"Is it really panda?" Marcus waved the food away.

"Bamboo fed. If panda isn't your taste, we offer lion, horse, giraffe, gorilla, sea turtle, or a dozen other exotic delicacies. All raised on sustainable, free-range ranches. Everything's to die for."

Antony took a second sample and pushed Marcus in the direction of Nerio.

"I thought you didn't have an appetite," Marcus mocked.

"Never pass up a free meal," Antony smirked, "especially when you're hungry."

"I don't trust samples," Marcus justified.

"You never turn them down at Costco."

"Costco doesn't serve endangered species."

"If they're being raised sustainably," said Antony, "then by definition, they aren't endangered."

"Why's a restaurant handing out samples?"

"The law of reciprocity, they give you something small, and you feel obligated to buy something bigger. The drug dealers at Nerio are the same way: the first one's always free."

"What's BFAD?" Marcus pointed at a shop that surpassed even Tek-Mart's size.

"Bitch for a Day. You can buy people there."

"Slaves?"

"More like indentured servants with unbreakable contracts binding all the parties to their agreement. It's voluntary."

"Is that the Depot?" Marcus motioned toward another building on the far side of the sector.

"Yup. Oldest building in the Black Market, it was built when the transcontinental rail came to town."

"What does it do now?"

"The Soap Box. It's part comedy club, part town hall."

"I can't picture that," said Marcus.

"When you can't hit someone to shut them up, they don't hold anything back. The Soap Box gives those people a place to bloom. It's hilarious. It's also home to the sector's vending machines."

"What do they sell?"

"Federation citizenship," Antony said, "which is free."

Marcus scanned the other storefronts of the sector. Crystal Ball financial services shared walls with a Cuban cigar shop called Twain's and an antique store selling mummified bodies and dinosaur fossils called Golden Age. Level Up advertised advanced degrees that could be earned with Tek in months instead of years, and Utterly was the non-pasteurized dairy shop Antony invoked earlier. One store made Marcus burst with laughter. "Naked Ape?"

"Panda fur won't go to waste. Indulgence also owns the Naked Ape."

"This place isn't at all what I was expecting." Marcus gazed one final time at the Inferno Fountain.

"What'd you imagine?"

"I don't know … I didn't expect it to be this familiar. Or safe."

"People need a place like this, where they can be themselves. Things aren't always illegal because they're dangerous. Sometimes they're dangerous because they're illegal. The Coalition spreads a lot of disinformation about this place. Especially about Ignus."

"Why?" asked Marcus.

"They associate fire with more sinister conspiracies."

"It's mesmerizing."

"Fire is humanity's first great technology. 'Ignite' is one of the oldest words we know of. You can seemingly trace it back to when the whole world spoke the same language."

"I remember Dad talking about that."

"The Coalition isn't the only group that hates this place."

"Jordan and the Lyceum?"

"Yes, but no. I was talking about organized criminals. Customers won't deal with a cartel when the Black Market has low-interest financing, customer service, and guaranteed safety. Let's move. The door to Nerio is over there."

Antony led them to the base of Ignus's clock tower. A large door-less entrance was framed by fluted stone columns supporting an eighties-style neon sign with the club's name. There were no bouncers, no velvet ropes, and no lines despite being the club's sole access point. Beyond the entrance, at the far end of an empty corridor, was a solid black door identical to the one in Brad's office.

As Marcus and Antony approached, the door activated, allowing a symphony of music and light to flood in around them. Their first glimpse of Nerio was intoxicating, drawing them across the threshold, and instantly onto the roof of the Wells Fargo Center. The edges of the club were outlined in the blue glow of the sector's Cycle. A giant similarly colored circle occupied most of the trapezoidal-shaped roof, holding hundreds of dancing people inside it. The noxious scent of equal parts perfume and cologne mixed into one powerful olfactory cocktail.

"Do all the sectors have a Cycle in a Cycle like this?" Marcus shouted over the music.

"No. Nerio is the only one completely within its own Cycle," Antony shouted back. "That inner ring is where the fights happen, and it doubles as the dance floor."

Free-floating honeycomb platforms followed the curve of the Cycle over the linear edges of the roof with matching azure glowing outlines. The view from Nerio was dazzling. The city surrounded them on every side as the sun slipped behind the Oquirrh Mountains to the west, revealing the pastel indigo and purple twilight sky. Marcus was glad he'd stepped up his wardrobe; well-dressed people were everywhere. A significant number of them wore masks. Some concealed their entire face, others only the upper half.

"Why are they disguising their identities?" Marcus shouted.

"The fights are broadcasted live," Antony shouted back. "Registration's downstairs. Stay close."

Antony maneuvered around people and furniture before reaching the roof's edge. Steps jettisoned into the open air, descending three stories along the face of the skyscraper. Each individual stair was made of a transparent panel, only visible from its glowing edges; the stairs didn't connect anywhere to the building, and there were no handrails. Vertigo paralyzed Marcus as his brother dropped over the edge.

Antony noticed he was alone and turned back to offer fraternal encouragement, "You need to relax."

"That is SUCH useless advice!" Marcus barked.

"Do you remember the stairs in Cape Cod?"

"Are you seriously comparing a four hundred foot drop onto concrete with Nonna's open-riser stairs?"

"You're scared about falling, like when you were a kid, and you thought it was possible to slip through the gap between stairs, right?"

"I want to hit you so badly right now." Marcus grit his teeth.

"Just like at Nonna's, you won't fall." Antony leaped like a BASE jumper into the open air above the plaza.

Marcus's heart plummeted into his stomach, but his fear changed to confusion at what he was seeing; Antony was hovering above the urban expanse.

"It's intense. You should try."

"I'll take your word for it," Marcus said as he cautiously stepped forward.

Antony levitated back to the stairs, leading the way to a long, and equally transparent, sky platform that entered the side of the building through a glowing blue arch. They were met by a three-story open space resembling something between a bar and Wall Street's trading floor. Screens endlessly scrolled statistics while inebriated individuals paced from place to place, many clenching lit cigars or steaming pipes in their mouths.

"What is this?" Marcus was dumbstruck.

"The Betting House. It's the adult swim of the Black Market, serving more marginalized tastes. Fight Registration's in the back."

"Drugs?" Marcus replied.

"Plus gambling, sex, and violence, including leaked *Call of Duty* type military training SIMs. It's also ground zero for xTek."

"What's xTek?"

"Tek with a parental warning sticker. People trade their files through these Voyeur Pods," Antony slapped the top of a device resembling Jordan's sensory deprivation tank. "They're the sector's equivalent of vending machines. It's the closest thing we have to the Federation's cloaking. When you get in, you can be whoever you want while interacting with other Voyeurgers. The networked pods are scattered all over the sector."

"So you don't know who you're trading with?"

"Guy Incognito." Antony surged onward, opening a gap between them, which was filled by a female Drummer.

"Are you terminally ill or burned-out on life?"

"No," replied Marcus.

"Well, if you find yourself in that place, keep us in mind. We provide a most blissful passing."

Marcus stopped moving. "What?"

"Legacy Keepers is a full-service euthanasia and posthumous identity manager."

"Suicide?"

The woman handed Marcus a colorful brochure featuring smiling faces. "We serve elderly couples, those with a terminal illness, and anyone else seeking dignity in passing."

Marcus stood silently.

"Are you worried about the costs?" She continued. "Because you're a healthy enough young man, and through our partnership with Nudge, the body part reseller here in the Black Market, we can get you advanced payment, which will more than offset the financial costs. There's usually enough left over to throw one hell of a party."

"To celebrate what?"

"Your ascension to the other side, of course."

"You mean my death?" Marcus countered.

"Yes. It's our most popular option. Everyone loves it! Then each year following your ascension, we send a holographic telegram of you to your loved ones. That way, your memory continues to live on."

"I think I'm good, thanks."

The saleswoman pressed a hand into Marcus's chest. "We also offer an insurance option. You pay a modest amount monthly, and after five years, if you develop an irreversible infirmity or lose the zest for life, you're covered. If that's not your thing, our stasis service allows your head to be cryogenically preserved, so it can be transplanted to a different body once the technology matures … in case it's the present world that's got you down."

Marcus couldn't see Antony anymore. He pushed past the pie-eyed people to find his brother at a kiosk surrounded by another sapphire circle.

"Glad you could make it," Antony said, stepping into the ring.

15

IN IT FOR THE KILL

"**W**elcome to Fight Registration," Hi!-D said in her smooth accent. "Are you both here to fight?"

"Just me," Antony answered.

Without further formalities, Hi!-D launched into a series of questions, "How many rounds would you like in your fight this evening?"

"Three."

"And what length?"

"Five minutes each."

"Single combatant or multiple attackers?"

"I'm a one-on-one kind of guy." Antony grinned.

"Good to know. Do you have specific opponent demographics in mind? Gender, age, ethnicity, income, religious affiliation."

"Affirmative: male, thirty-two, German, upper-middle-class, Lutheran."

"What about your opponent's psychographics?"

"A fan of *ABBA*."

"Noted. What fighting class would you prefer?"

"Heavyweight."

Marcus was shocked by how quickly Antony's answers were coming. There was no hesitation. The Q&A with Hi!-D continued for a few more minutes, but Marcus was distracted by the fact Antony was anything but a heavyweight.

"Last question. Would you like to fight to submission or death?"

"Death," Antony said with conviction.

Marcus's stomach dropped harder than before. "What, ANTONY! This is ridic—"

"Shhh," Antony silenced him with a piercing glance.

"What are these questions for?" Marcus asked.

"Once I know your brother's preferences, I can find him an opponent."

"Then what?" Marcus probed.

"Once a match is made, I notify each fighter of their ratio, which is a measure of the predicted physical advantage or disadvantage each faces in the match. Then, they have fifteen minutes to confirm."

"What if he refuses?"

"If either fighter declines, or if time passes before both confirm, the match dissolves, and I try to find your brother another fight."

"What stops fighters from hanging outside registration and figuring out each other's ratios?" Marcus inquired.

"Beyond the circle you're standing in," Hi!-D motioned toward the floor, "no one can see or hear you. To them, you're an imperceptible muted blur."

"Like the cone of silence?" Antony laughed.

"Exactly!" Hi!-D replied before turning back to Marcus. "Does that answer your question?"

"But whatever fight you find for him right now, it'll be to the death?"

"It can be, though, it's more common for fighters to show mercy in victory. Actual death happens much less than you might expect."

Hi!-D's clarification didn't make Marcus feel better.

"Well, gentlemen, I have everything I need. I'll come find you when I have a fight."

A door adjacent to Fight Registration took them back to the rooftop club. People were laughing, smiling, and patiently waiting for violence to erupt. Antony found a couch overlooking the fight floor and settled in, completely calm. He was named after their father's favorite Roman, Marc Antony, because he was a survivor. When Marcus was born nineteen years later, their father thought it'd be hilarious to complete the homage. Their shared name proved an apt omen of the brothers' bond, raised to believe nothing came before family.

"Why'd you answer heavyweight?" Marcus asked.

"Trust me."

"And death?"

"Are you short on faith today, or what? I told you, I've got a plan!" Antony smiled.

Marcus knew he was manipulating something. This was the same smile he had when convincing a teenage Marcus to approach random people's houses for food; if the homeowner questioned anything, he'd say it was for a scavenger hunt and ask for an unrelated second item, usually a coin from before World War II. But this wasn't a middle-class neighborhood full of Good Samaritans. The House were pros at spotting scams.

They didn't have to wait long before Hi!-D appeared, sitting beside Marcus to face Antony. "I have a fight for you. Your ratio is two, so whatever you think you're capable of, I predict you'll have to work twice as hard to win. Would you like time—"

"I accept," said Antony. "I'll place ten million on myself."

This was another way the Pomerium divided worlds: here, fighters could be beneficiaries of their own athletic efforts.

"Fantastic, gentlemen. I'll only return if the fight has been dissolved and I find another match for you. Before I go, there's one last detail to sort out. Would you like to fix your bet or let it float?"

"Float."

For someone who'd never fought here, Antony was sure familiar with every part of this process.

"Fantastic. If I don't see you again, best of luck."

Once Hi!-D disappeared, Marcus renewed his inquisition, "What does it mean to float?"

"My bet is benchmarked to whatever ratio the Betting House comes up with, and not the two-to-one Hi!-D predicted—assuming the fight happens. The House only sees confirmed fights."

"I don't understand the difference."

"The ratio Hi!-D calculated is based on her own assessment, but once the fight is public, the people at the House see the details about the fighters. Then they determine their ratio. Fixing means I take Hi!-D's ratio, floating means I take what the House offers. I'm pretty disappointed though."

"Why?" Marcus asked.

"I was expecting a seven from Hi!-D." Antony leaned forward before continuing, "I've been money-balling this place, and the reigning champ, Zedd. He's been undefeated for the last thirteen months, and I've been mining him for data the entire time. That's why I entered heavyweight. That's why I said *ABBA* and death. It's also why we came on a Wednesday night. Those factors are predictive of Zedd. I entered them to maximize my chances of fighting him."

Marcus retrieved his Memento Mori and fiddled with it before asking the obvious, "Why would you want to fight him? Especially for your first fight?"

"First *public* fight, there's a big difference," Antony replied. "I didn't just study Zedd. I had to learn the whole registration process too. Especially how answering questions in different ways determined what other questions would be asked."

"How'd you do that when you can't listen to anyone else's registration?"

"I paid people to fight. At first, they reported back with the questions she asked. Then, I had them answer in specific ways to see if new questions were proposed. Finally, I figured out how each answer correlated with fights Hi!-D offered, and with fights that happened. It sounds harder than it was."

"Where'd you find people to pay ... to fight?"

"The first few were guys I knew, but once word got out about my sponsorship, fighters flocked to me. A lot of them work with me and want to fight. Getting paid for it was a bonus in their eyes."

Marcus was impressed, even for Antony.

"But you don't think it worked? Since your ratio was lower?"

"We'll see. In a few minutes, we'll see." Antony laid his head back on the couch and closed his eyes. "*Si vis pacem, para bellum.*"

Antony's legs weren't incessantly bouncing like usual, which meant he was either nervous or in a true state of pre-fight nirvana, thought Marcus. Antony had never lost at anything in all his life, or at least that's how it seemed. But the threat of losing was greater than zero since Antony was fighting someone significantly larger who ruled undefeated on the world's toughest fight circuit.

When Nerio erupted in exultation, it was clear Antony's cleverness paid off. Hovering over the fight floor was the terse notice:

Zedd vs. Antony

The ratio against Antony climbed: two, three, five, eight, thirteen —then rapidly accelerated onward. Both combatants had five minutes to report to the fight floor, which was now awash with highlights of the Champ's past battles playing in perfect three-dimensional detail. A holographic panel, led by commentator and comedic podcaster, Joe Rogan, skewered Antony for pulling another publicity stunt.

"Who are they?" Marcus shouted over the noise.

"The Peanut Gallery, expert voices from the Betting House. I have to change," Antony roared.

Each corner of the roof's trapezoidal shape functioned as a private lounge, utilizing the same cloaking trick as Hi!-D's registration booth. Only fighters could enter these lounges, with the southern one being strictly reserved for the reigning champion.

Marcus stood alone in the club. The city's glitter matched the shimmer of the stars above, amplifying Nerio's supernatural feel. The beauty of the crowd was well above average, but one unmasked woman monopolized his gaze. She was orbited by people vying for attention, but stood apart, confident and proud, with high cheekbones, sun-kissed skin, long black hair, and hourglass curves screaming of seduction. She caught him staring and stared straight back with her deep green eyes. Marcus was startled by Antony's hand on his shoulder.

"I'm supposed to be the nervous one." Antony was barefoot and shirtless, wearing only gym shorts.

Marcus deflected, "Are you … uh … anxious?"

"A little. What matters is channeling it into a win."

Nerio reached new hysteria as Zedd emerged from his lounge. Antony shouted over the Champ's fight song, "Is it just me, or is Zedd a gay name?"

Antony spoke without his filter, but it was the kind of name an end-of-level boss from *Lethal Enforcers* would have. As the Champ walked confidently onto the fight floor, his title seemed fitting. Zedd was a monster. He paced along the blue circle while stats hovering above his head gave Marcus's fear numerical support: he was eighty-six pounds heavier and nine inches taller than Antony. The fight would be three five-minute rounds, though no one had made it past the second against him.

Despite being pure violence, many rituals and ceremonies surround fighting, including playing each contender's fight song. As Zedd's music faded, it was Antony's turn to shine. The silence of the club was broken by "Tip Your Bartender," his favorite Glassjaw song. Hearing the heavy guitar accompanied by red-hot vocals gave Marcus chills. Antony said if he ever charged into war, this would be his soundtrack. Now Marcus understood why. It was raw power, like having his knees scraped to the bone by a cheese grater.

When a fight starts, no one sits—it's too intoxicating. Everything you know as a logical person tells you fighting is a waste, that it's causing suffering and physical damage, but it's impossible to look away. People compare it to watching a train wreck, though it's much more hypnotizing since it involves humans. Marcus was captivated by the violence about to unfold. The Romans had taken it to another level with their arenas, and before the Federation arrived Hollywood, had gone even further by mastering realism through illusion. Violence was a constant across cultures and generations. Humanity needed it, and this crowd was no exception. Everyone stood silently, waiting for the carnage to commence.

As soon as they touched hands, Zedd rushed at Antony, unleashing a volley of strikes to the head. These movements were matched by an explosion of sound and light in the club, fed by the crowd's energy. Unlike the graceful fights of pop culture, real fights happen in chaotic bursts because fighting is exhausting. Strikes don't come in constant fluid arcs; they explode from unexpected angles. Marcus watched helplessly as Antony fell back, covering his head to absorb the strikes with his arms.

Zedd broke off the assault and stepped back to catch his breath. Antony retaliated by attempting a kick at the Champ's groin; he'd transformed, like flipping on a switch, pacing with the confidence of a lion. But it was such a physical reach that Zedd easily redirected, absorbed, or blocked everything. Antony kept up the pressure, striking at the Champ's legs and denying him even a moment of rest.

The first round ended without Antony making a meaningful hit, but he was still standing. As he approached the edge of the fight floor, blood was streaming down his face. "Head wounds bleed a lot, but if you're able to hold a conversation, then it's just an inconvenience." Antony smiled, the whites of his teeth contrasted with the blood filling his mouth. "Before you say anything, wait one more round. Then you can tell me whatever's on your mind. One round! Okay?" asked Antony.

"One round," Marcus reluctantly agreed.

There was nowhere to sit, so Antony drank water waiting on the sideline and spat blood before heading back out. He rolled his neck and flexed all the muscles of his upper body, drawing Marcus's attention to his brother's back tattoo; from a distance the text outline of the Heroic Code resembled a bird of war, similar in spirit to the *Aquila*, the Roman battle symbol. As the opponents tapped hands again, Zedd repeated his earlier tactic, rushing on Antony, but this time the fight went to the floor. Antony crunched his entire upper body, tucked his chin into his chest, and brought his hands to his face to protect what mattered. Zedd held nothing back, striking at Antony's head, ribs, and abdomen until he managed to roll out from under the Champ, pushing himself up and away from the ground fight.

The intensity of the audience dipped as the fighters stood apart, facing one another. Zedd charged at Antony with a flying cross punch, nicknamed the superman for its gravity-defying brutality. As he made contact, the energy of the spectators shook the entire club. Antony responded with a kick to Zedd's head, his first solid strike so far, but the Champ countered with a front kick to Antony's chest, sending him across the ring to collide with an invisible rope surrounding the fight floor.

The club surged in waves of noise and light as Antony tried to run out the clock, moving constantly while throwing a rapid series of low kicks to the outside of the Champ's legs in an attempt to exploit a weakness of the human body; a large nerve running up the outside of the thigh. Zedd responded, turning his threatened leg out each time to absorb the strike with his shins. It wasn't an optimal outcome, but it was better than letting the nerve get crushed. Zedd's size was becoming a liability and Antony was moving at twice his speed. With each strike to the legs, he made it harder for the Champ to keep up and counter-strike. Zedd was noticeably fatigued as the second round ended.

Antony gasped for air. "What happens next is uncharted territory."

"Congrats. If your plan was to show how many times you can get hit and stay standing, it's going marvelously," said Marcus.

"Have you ever wondered why they call a square boxing mat a ring?" Antony mused.

"That's not top of mind, no. What's your plan for dealing with Zedd? He's gonna be pissed you've made it to a third round. How are you going to stop him from killing you now?"

"He swings hard, I'll give him that," Antony admitted, "I'll just have to swing smarter."

"What?"

"Pavlov my dear brother. Pavlov."

"What the hell does that mean?"

"Exactly," Antony smiled as he bounced his way back to the center of the fight floor.

Zedd and Antony stood facing each other for the final time. Rage seethed from the Champ's face as he extended an arm. Antony kept bouncing in place, tapping hands before dropping to the floor and delivering an L-kick that finally destroyed the thigh nerve Zedd had previously protected. The Champ stumbled but didn't fall, delivering a barrage of strikes to Antony's whole body.

Antony pivoted away from Zedd and returned to his earlier approach of throwing leg strikes over and over. The crushed nerve was making it hard for Zedd to respond to the attacks because it meant placing all his weight on the destroyed leg. Antony kicked at the other leg, but before the Champ could place his functional foot forward, Antony swept it, sending Zedd off-balance head first, a moment Antony exploited by delivering a knee to the Champ's undefended face.

Antony had been fighting a war of attrition, holding out for a single advantage, which Zedd just gave him. Fights usually end with one person balled-up on the ground, arms covering their face while their opponent strikes without opposition, but this was an exception. Zedd had been knocked out cold and the club was silent. There was a new champion of Nerio.

Antony stood alone in the ring, extending his arm like a Roman emperor to the stunned crowd, giving the thumbs up. He planned to be a merciful ruler.

"Victory, Antony Adams, by knockout," Hi!-D's voice said over the tail end of Antony's fight song. For the first time that night even the Peanut Gallery was speechless. As he faced Marcus it was clear this had bordered on a Pyrrhic victory; Antony was covered in blood and sweat.

Marcus offered a hand, but Antony refused, "They have to see me do this myself." Antony moved through the whispering spectators to the Champion's Lounge, where Hi!-D was waiting.

"An impressive show, absolutely brilliant! Would you like me to keep your name in the fight pool for the evening?"

"No, please." Antony didn't have anything left.

"Very well," Hi!-D said enthusiastically. "Your float was twenty-one which brings your winnings to two-hundred and ten million. Would you like to convert that to crypto, or open a house account?"

"A crypto card would be great," Antony said.

"Of course. Will you both be staying to dance?"

"Yes," Antony insisted before turning to Marcus. "Go have fun. I need to piece myself back together. It'll take a while. I'll find you when I'm ready."

"Are you sure you want to be alone?" Marcus asked.

"I'm standing, so I'm fine. Seriously … go find Mrs. Adams."

"Right then," said Hi!-D. "I'll be back with your crypto card shortly. In the meantime, do enjoy everything Nerio has to offer."

16

SWIMMING IN STARS

The fight floor had absorbed the blood and sweat before filling with dancing people. Patterns of color rolled across the club in sync to the music, and the vibration from the bass could be felt resonating through everything. As the song changed, Marcus was met by one of the most beautiful sights he'd ever seen: a million little stars swirling over and around everyone as they danced.

"I imagine that's what a galaxy looks like to a god, do you agree?" said a seemingly familiar female voice; it was deeper than Hi!-D's or Dianna's, confident and feminine. Marcus turned to see the woman he'd locked eyes with earlier, and he came alive again.

"It's incredible."

"Can I buy you a drink?" she asked.

"I'm not of age."

"You aren't in Utah anymore, Toto. Let me guess what you like—sex on the beach? No, wait, vodka and Red Bull?"

"Glenlivet, double, on the rocks."

"My kind of man," she smiled.

Instantly, a blue orb arrived with their beverages.

"This is like something out of a sci-fi movie, right? Enjoy it, because tomorrow, you'll be annoyed by how inconvenient the rest of the world feels," she said, raising her glass. "Cheers."

As they sipped their drinks, she looked Marcus over. "That was an impressive feat from your friend. No one thought it could be done, and, no offense, definitely not by someone his size."

"He's my brother," Marcus said with pride.

"I know everyone that comes through Nerio by name, and I know who your brother is, but you're a mystery. On behalf of the Nerio family, welcome to the party." She grabbed his hand and began shaking it. Her soft skin and long nails felt amazing. He worried she could feel his heart pounding through his fingertips, and broke contact, turning again to face the star-clad dance floor.

"It's even better inside," she explained. "It feels like the environment is giving you a big warm hug."

"How does it change like that?"

"The DJ controls it. The music, lights, and simulation. All of it."

Marcus didn't see a DJ or a booth. "From where?"

"It's not a single person. Everyone's the DJ." She grabbed his hand again, pulling him toward the dance floor. "It's hard to explain—you have to experience it."

As they crossed the blue line of the Cycle, the environment immersed all of his senses. Marcus was a great dancer, a skill he'd inherited from his grandfather. She moved gracefully despite her stilettos, occasionally pressing her body against his, and continued to gaze into his eyes. Neither said a word while they danced. Marcus felt connected to her; she was strangely familiar. As a slower song started, she broke their silence, "Fate is warning you."

"How's that?"

"This song is called 'Evil Beauty.' It's one of my favorites." She placed her arms around his neck. "Music speaks truth when you need it most. This song has to be an omen."

"You don't look evil to me."

"What about beautiful?"

Without another word, she kissed him. They were surrounded by people, but they'd left the world behind.

As she ended their embrace, the enigmatic woman renewed her warning, "Your aura is on fire right now. It's a sign of our connection."

"You can see it?" asked Marcus.

"Yes. And it's magnificent."

New Ageism wasn't new for Marcus, so he didn't falter.

"I have another skill, but it scares people."

"What is it?"

"I can see the future."

"And?"

"You're going to fall hard for me."

"Impressive." Marcus maintained eye contact.

"I know you. I don't *know* you in the traditional sense, but I can tell we've met before," she placed her hand on his heart, "in past lives. I feel like I've been waiting for you a long time … that we're reincarnated lovers kept apart by fate, who've finally found one another again."

Marcus wasn't sure what was more hypnotizing, this woman or their experience. It didn't matter; he'd given himself to the moment. "Want another drink?"

"Lead the way," she replied.

As they crossed over the glowing blue line, Marcus felt the dance floor's connection fade. In its place, a milder form of his post-Sequence sickness set in, and he heaved over, placing both hands on his stomach.

"Are you okay?" she asked.

"Yeah. I'm a little dizzy. It's been a crazy day. I haven't eaten, so the drink must be hitting me."

Marcus soldiered on. He had no idea what time it was, and he didn't care about food. He just wanted to stay with her for as long as possible. They found an empty couch near Antony's lounge and settled in to talk. The conversation came easily, like between old friends reunited after years of separation. She wasn't the same woman who'd sized him up earlier; she'd let down her guard. She asked an endless stream of questions, the majority were generic chitchat, but they went really deep on Marcus's goals with school, the importance of family to him, and what Antony was like. Despite intimate feelings toward this woman, Marcus never mentioned Selection or Dianna.

"Speak of the devil," she said as the new champion returned.

"I see you've found some fun," Antony struggled to say through a locked jaw. His face was comically swollen.

"I'm sorry to end here, but we're leaving," said Marcus. Her look of dissatisfaction forced him to explain, "I wish I could stay, but he needs help getting home."

"I completely understand. It's fine. He looks horrible, by the way." She hesitated, adding, "Maybe I'll see you again?"

"Definitely. There's a long list of people who want to punch Antony in the face. We'll be here. A lot."

"Bye." She wiggled her fingers daintily.

Marcus realized they hadn't exchanged names. She'd felt so familiar that he never thought to ask.

"Did you have a good time?" Antony inquired.

Marcus wanted to avoid that conversation. "You took forever. It's been like six hours."

"I patched myself up and fell asleep in the ice bath. Then I watched the fight."

"Your fight was less than twenty minutes."

"I watched it a few times." Antony was a complete mess. His suit wasn't tucked in, his tie was missing, and pale skin-toned Band-Aids stood out over his black and blue face.

"You sure you're okay? She's right, you look terrible."

"The only way I could be better is if there were two of me, then I could love that much more of myself. Can I crash at your place?"

"Of course. I'll drive."

Marcus grabbed the gym bag and they moved toward a one-way portal promising to transport them to the valet. Before they could enter, another female voice cut through the chatter of the club, "Hey, Marcus! Marcus Adams!" It was Velia. She frolicked toward the brothers with faultless enthusiasm.

"Hey … I'm surprised to see you," said Marcus.

"God, I love fights! I won a standby lottery pass. I'll be telling people about tonight for the rest of my life!"

"That's what she said," Antony murmured.

Velia smiled, then waited for an introduction.

The realization hit Marcus. "Sorry. Velia, this is my brother—"

"Antony Rex!" Velia exclaimed.

"What?" the brothers said synchronously.

"That's what people in the club are calling him." Velia looked around the room as if she'd been elected to speak on their behalf.

"Antony, this is Velia. She's in my FACT class."

"Nice to meet you." Antony felt like he recognized the girl, but couldn't place her face, and offered his bandaged hand instead. Velia pushed past it and hugged him like a fangirl, causing Antony to groan from the unintended pain before she abruptly let go.

"Are you guys leaving?" Velia probed.

"Yeah," Marcus replied, "it's been a long, hard—"

"That's what she said," Velia interjected, laughing with Antony. "I just wanted to come and pay my respects to the Champ! It was nice meeting you, Antony. See you Friday, Marcus."

The brothers passed through the portal. While waiting for Antony's car, a dark-eyed woman approached, donning one of Tek-Mart's pure white uniforms.

"Excuse me," Antony said, startling her.

She was in her late thirties with a shy smile. Antony's battered appearance was making her nervous. "Sorry, I didn't mean to scare you. Do you work at Tek-Mart?" Antony ask in a softer tone.

She said nothing.

"Hand her the crypto card," Antony instructed Marcus. "It's in the outer pocket of my bag."

There was an unanticipated language barrier, so the woman put a piece of Tek on her wrist to communicate; she could understand them, but her words still came out in Russian. When she realized what was happening, she tried to refuse. Antony explained how he won the money, and through tears of joy she embraced him, reviving his pain, and praised the act of generosity.

"This puts you under an obligation," Antony told her. "You have to use the money to help others too. No one else can do it for you. It's on you now."

The woman walked away from Tek-Mart.

"She has no idea how much money is waiting for her." Marcus helped Antony into the passenger seat of his car. "Not the amount, but she understood the impact. Benedict doesn't even pay Tek-Mart employees a subsistence wage. It has to be a second or third job."

Marcus held Antony's door open. "I've heard, and tomorrow there'll be ten more people waiting to take the job she gave up."

"Imagine great-grandma like that, an immigrant woman cleaning office buildings at night for next to nothing and rolling cigars during the day just because she didn't have options. Never forget where you come from, Marcus. Collect people, not things—those who know you, owe you, and love you."

By the time Marcus walked around to the driver's side of the Tesla, Antony had fallen asleep, head resting against the passenger window. Marcus pulled away from the valet at the

Gateway Mall and briefly gazed at the Wells Fargo Center in the distance. He could still feel the mystery woman's magnetism; she'd imprinted herself on him.

It was 3:11 a.m. when Marcus pulled into his driveway and parked behind the house. Antony was still sleeping, so Marcus broke into song, "Ohhhhh! How I hate to get up in the morning, Ohhhhh! How I'd love to remain in bed!"

"Shut. Up," Antony barked without opening his eyes.

Marcus continued belting the Irving Berlin song, a favorite tactic of their father's when he wanted to wake them, "You've got to get up, you've got to get up, you've got to get up this morning!"

Antony was unbroken.

"We're home," Marcus said, gently placing a hand on his brother's shoulder.

PART VI

95% CONFIDENCE

THURSDAY, MARCH 17, +1 NE

17

APOPHIS FABLES

Marcus woke with a vicious hangover, still wearing the same clothes from last night. He'd meet Brad soon. The comfort of his room was replaced by dread, like something terrible was coming. He rose from bed, palmed his coin, and began his daily affirmation:

I'm the man in the mirror. Better today than I was yesterday. And because today I may die, I'll use this opportunity at life to improve myself and help those around me. I'll stay calm and only focus on things I can control. I will not fear. No matter what I face, I'll face it from a place of peace and love. I'm capable of this. I'm the man in the mirror.

Marcus wandered the house, but Antony was gone. He could hear Jordan's music blasting from the basement—his "do not disturb" sign. Marcus felt guilty about kissing the woman from Nerio and checked his phone, but there was nothing from Dianna, so he scrolled through old voice messages to find one in particular: the last he'd received from his parents. His eyes welled up while it played; this was an important anchor holding the family's memory together.

Marcus left home and was hustling toward Carlson Hall when Hi!-D's sky-hologram delivered a PSA:

> "Good afternoon, citizens, and welcome to another wonderful day! Each of us is bombarded by criticism. Whether it's constructive is entirely on you. Can you separate fact from fiction? Can you identify parts that are false and ignore them, while acknowledging hard truths? This takes confidence in yourself and your judgment. So today, listen to your gut. Then tomorrow, verify you were right. Because together, we're unstoppable."

It was noon.

Brad was reading at his desk. "Looking sharp as obsidian! Want some water? You've been going at a serious pace."

"How can you tell?" Marcus inspected himself.

"You're wearing the same clothes. Your blood alcohol is elevated, and your sweat is full of androstadienone, indicating a sexual encounter. And you reek of aggression."

"I watched my brother's fight and danced with a woman at Nerio. But I changed after our session yesterday ..."

"I'm always watching." Brad smiled. "Plus, I saw coverage of Antony's upset over Zedd. You were in the background, looking almost as handsome as me. By combining all this data, I reached my original conclusion: you're dehydrated. Here. Drink up."

"I'm impressed."

"Feel free to throw money," Brad said. "Let's pregame."

"What were you reading?"

"A commentary on the trial of Socrates, and why your Form requires a scapegoat when things fall apart. Whether it's witches, werewolves, or philosophers, someone pays the social debt."

Marcus sipped on his water. "Light reading."

"Funny, I might use that. Know the story?"

"My dad quoted Federalist Paper fifty-five all the time."

"Had every Athenian been a Socrates," Brad belted, "every Athenian assembly would still have been a mob."

"He usually invoked that quote on Black Friday."

"Your Form's tendency toward mob mentality is fascinating. It's why we showed ourselves to you individually during the Disclosure Moment—to minimize the 'freak out' factor."

"It worked for me."

"What was your moment like?" Brad adjusted his glasses and sat forward.

"Jordan, Antony, and I were partying to celebrate our birthdays and New Year's Eve. I drank too much, and then someone moved me to my room. I woke up with Hi!-D at the end of my bed, convinced it was a dream. I didn't feel fear. I thought it was awesome this was all happening on my birthday."

"It wasn't a coincidence. We picked a moment the world was celebratory. Speaking of things worth celebrating, ready to work?"

"Sure."

"You know the drill."

Marcus gazed at Monica's door as he walked the locker room. *Antony was right ... he wouldn't fail.* Hi!-D was missing as he moved through his locker, to the octagon, and on to the Liberty Bell.

"You've transformed," Brad echoed in Marcus's head. "Your brain waves are calm, your heart rate's normal, your blood pressure's fine, and all electrical signals are stable. On paper, you couldn't be sexier."

"I'm getting used to it. This reminds me, I got sick after the last Sequence, but you said I wouldn't feel anything."

"Have you experienced residual memories of the Sequence?"

"No."

"Inexplicable flashbacks, nightmares, and or day terrors?"

"None."

"How long did it last?"

"Maybe thirty minutes? It was strongest right after the Sequence, but it faded."

"We'll run Stealth Mode again and see if we can monitor the feeling," Brad said. "But to warn you, today is going to push you. Hard. I'm predicting this will be the most important Sequence of your Selection."

[Sequence ID# 417] [Data Begins]

The last thing he remembered was the look of horror on Monica's face as the MP's explained his right to remain silent from behind the barrel of their guns. She'd had a bad feeling about today, but Marcus didn't listen to her or to his own intuition. He desperately wanted to believe his social exile was coming to an end. But hope had been replaced by rage. Now his blood was boiling. He knew Dianna abused her power to orchestrate all of this. She'd been calculating her moves for a while, down to the fake "emergency" she used to lure them to her office at the Planetary Defense Force headquarters. And because Dianna was a spiteful person, she ensured Monica was by Marcus's side to hear the charge sheet being preferred against him at this moment.

"How is this legal?" Monica protested. "He's a civilian. You don't have authority anymore."

"There is clear and convincing evidence Marcus committed his crimes while enlisted in my unit," Dianna snapped back. "He will be prosecuted under the Uniform Code of Military Justice. I will only say this next part once: stay calm and cooperate so there's no need to use force."

"A court-martial?" Marcus was incredulous. "You're serious?"

"As a heart attack," Dianna replied while dressing him down, "the PDF doesn't take lightly subversion, the corruption of its cadets, or the loss of innocent lives. Since you pose a clear flight risk and will undoubtedly continue your crimes if free, you're being taken into custody now to await trial."

"Fuck you," Marcus replied coldly.

"You're nothing if not predictable," she seethed, turning away. "TAKE HIM!" Dianna barked at the MPs, who seized him by the arms. Marcus had no intention of resisting; it'd only give her more ammunition for this witch hunt. As he was being hand-cuffed, Monica started crying.

"MARCUS!" was all she could shout in anguish.

"FIND ANTONY," Marcus shouted back while being whisked from the room.

"I know this is hard to hear," Dianna patronized to Monica, "but your husband is a traitor. He hurt all of us, especially me after all the years of mentorship I gave him. Somewhere along the way, he became lost and we paid a heavy price for it. He'll answer for what he's said and done. I'm telling you this as a longtime friend who has your best interests at heart: get a lawyer, not just for Marcus but for you too. You need to distance yourself from him starting now."

"Just because you believe your own fairytale, that doesn't mean the rest of us do too. We're ready to fight you to the bitter end." Monica stormed out of Dianna's quarters.

The moment Marcus was out of sight from Dianna and Monica, the MPs placed a hood on his head. Despite being deprived of vision, he could tell they'd moved him to the backseat of a large vehicle; he could smell the leather interior and feel the wobble of its precarious center of gravity as they drove around for hours. When the momentum stopped, Marcus was ripped from the vehicle, hastily escorted indoors, and pushed onto a squeaky metal chair in an otherwise silent room. Hands ran over his legs, arms, and chest, attaching cables to his body. When the hood was finally removed, he found himself sitting in an empty warehouse, beneath the only light in the entire space, connected to a lie-detector-type machine. The smell of dust and wet concrete was overpowering. A thick strap across the back of his neck tightened, forcing his face forward until his chin rested in a mount, his retinas aligning with an eye scanner. The final step involved placing an EEG cap on his head.

"I hope you'll tell the truth," Dianna said from behind him. Being unable to turn and face her added to the humiliation. After hours of interrogation, ranging from canned questions to establish a baseline, to accusations meant to rattle his emotional cage, the polygraph technician read the results: Marcus was deceptive.

"THIS IS FUCKING RIDICULOUS," Marcus roared. "I'M NOT DECEPTIVE AND I'M NOT LYING! YOU KNOW THIS IS BULL-SHIT! I'LL FUCKING RUIN YOU FOR THIS!"

His struggling provided the excuse the MPs had been waiting for, and they beat him mercilessly. Repeated strikes came to his back, kidneys, and ribs, but one to the head turned the lights off.

When he woke up, he was alone on the cold floor of a small cell built into the corner of an empty concrete basement. The massive room was interrupted only by the bars of his prison and large cylindrical support columns. The smell from a filthy privy bucket mixed with the stench of mildew in the air. He'd been forcibly changed into a black jumpsuit while unconscious. A constant humming hour after hour drove Marcus toward madness. It never changed pitch even slightly and never paused. It was a relentless reminder of his unchangeable situation.

He'd fallen asleep again, resting long enough to reach the slow-wave stage of sleep but not long enough for dreams to begin, when a familiar voice woke him, "Marcus! Look at me if you can hear me."

His brother's voice triggered immediate waves of grief and relief; he wept hysterically.

"How'd it get to this? Who kicked your ass?"

"The military police," Marcus choked back snot and tears, "right after the polygraph."

"Why in the world did you agree to take that? Did you think it'd clear you? Because it never does."

"THEY MADE ME!"

"Take a deep breath."

"They strapped me to a table by the neck like a dog, okay?"

"Street justice. They reserve the worst for deserters," said Antony. "I wouldn't be surprised if Dianna included that charge to try and get you killed in the system on the way to trial. In the grand scheme of things, the polygraph is the least of our problems. Do you understand the charges against you?"

"Not really. The MPs read them at my arrest, but I was so upset I could barely keep breathing."

"Didn't you sign your charge sheet, in front of Dianna and another officer?"

"Never happened."

"This could be good for us. I'll do some digging. Until then, let me tell you what you're facing. Article 85 is the desertion charge, Article 107 is making false official statements, but the big one is Article 94 for mutiny, qualifying you for the death penalty. They have a list of credible witnesses, your personnel records from the PDF including all your communications, and decades of crazy shit you've said in public, plus the classified data you leaked."

"Dianna's said that data is fake at least a million times. How could it be evidence now?"

"Let's avoid exaggerations. They only need to show that you thought it was real to prove it fits the bigger pattern of Marcus Adams, Menace to Society. They're also saying you hacked the NostRa mission and crashed the probe into the asteroid."

"Dianna is setting me up. I didn't hack anything. I used her credentials to log into the mission VPN after she axed me. That was my mission and my moment after a lifetime of work. She was trying to take it from me. I wanted to watch it in real-time."

"They're saying you stole her credentials."

"I guessed them. Her password was 12345."

"That's the stupidest combination I've ever heard in my life! It's the kind of thing an idiot would have on his luggage. ..." Antony was quoting a movie line from their childhood, but Marcus was so caught up in the current moment the joke failed to register.

"I'm giving it to you straight because you're my little brother and I love you," Antony was serious. "You might be in checkmate. A military trial is far from a fair shake. Everything is stacked against you. And that's under normal operating conditions. Virtually everyone alive hates you, and since Dianna is the head of the PDF, she's the ultimate convening authority over your case."

"She'll be my judge?"

"No. She had the power to investigate you, to pick your charges, and to ensure you face trial, but she won't preside over you in the courtroom. Your case has already been referred to a judge, some guy named Jordan Kilravock."

"Never heard of him."

"Dianna also had the authority to pick your trial prosecution. You'll recognize the old gang: Benedict Darrow, Chet, Thad, and that little bitch, Toby."

"Wonderful, Dianna's favorite fanboys."

"I can tell you without having attended your 802 session yet, they're planning to paint you as a heretic bent on revenge regardless of the body count. The public has been screaming for blood after Apophis. Dianna's offering you as the sacrificial lamb."

"I'M A GODDAMN HERO!" Marcus fought back renewed tears of frustration.

"Do you seriously think you have to convince me of that? I knew you were right all along, and I know Dianna hates you for it. Calm down and tell me who I can call to testify on your behalf. We're going to fight the ice bitch with everything we've got."

The nickname provided a fleeting chuckle.

"Dianna's killed them all."

"And you can prove this?" Antony challenged.

"No."

"Then let's keep the conspiracy theories to ourselves. Who among the living knows you, owes you, or loves you? It's time to cash in every favor you can."

"Bill for sure. And Monica."

"What about people who aren't so close to you? People who had an arms-length work relationship and will be honest on the witness stand?"

"Bryan and Duygu are the only ones that come to mind, but both still work for the PDF."

"That doesn't matter. Dianna would have to kill them to silence them. Even assuming your theory is correct, the world is watching now so she won't risk contacting them, let alone touch them."

"What do you mean the world is watching?" Marcus put his hands on the back of his head and began to pace.

"Dianna held a press conference hours after your arrest. It's the biggest story in the world."

"How soon can you get me out of here?"

"Is the end of your trial soon enough?"

"I thought they could only hold me for seventy-two hours?"

"You've seen too many movies, brother. If they want to, they'll keep dropping the charges and recharging you every couple of days. When you've been confined like this," Antony pivoted in place, with arms spread, "they aren't letting you out till you're free. Or dead. Like I said, everything's stacked against you."

Their time alone ended as two unfamiliar men, dressed in the standard blood-red PDF uniforms, traversed the concrete space to join them jail side.

"Hello, gentlemen. I'm Luke Kelly, and this is Lucius Duston. We're Marcus's military-appointed counsel from Trial Defense Services."

"Why have one lawyer when you can get two for twice the price, and on the taxpayers' dime?" Antony said.

"This is a high-profile case. Given the possibility of capital punishment, TDS sent both of us. Are you Marcus's civilian defense counsel?"

"I am. Antony Adams. Nice to meet you both."

"Oh, you're related?" asked Lucius.

"At the genetic level no less," Antony responded. He turned back to face Marcus, whispering, "I'm going to take these two outside and make sure they're on the level. You need anything?"

"Water. Please."

"I'll do one better and get you out of this shit hole."

"What time is it?"

"A little past one in the morning."

"What day is it?"

"Wednesday, the 2nd of May … 2040," Antony was concerned about his brother's head again. "You were arrested fifteen hours ago."

"Where am I?"

"In the basement of a maintenance building on the University of Utah campus."

"What? Why?"

"The whole world will watch this trial. Dianna's counting on the public spectacle. To her credit, it's poetic she brought things back to where everything began. Your trial is happening in Kingsbury Hall on the same stage your doomsday algorithm was announced. It'll happen in front of a live audience and will be streamed to what's left of the world. Arraignment is later today. I'll be back soon, don't get lost on me," Antony smiled widely.

Marcus laid down again and surrendered to sleep, but rest escaped him since nightmares followed wherever he went. The dreams had plagued him for decades, coming in a dozen varieties. But each showed the same thing: the horrific destruction Apophis eventually brought down upon Earth.

Antony made good on his promise, and later that day, the MPs moved Marcus to a modern cell at the campus police station. He appreciated having running water, a toilet, and a cot for his battered back. When the time arrived for his arraignment, he was in such physical pain he couldn't stand and had to stay behind.

Antony soon returned with news. "I tried to have the case dismissed on the grounds you're a civilian, but that motion was denied. The good news is I got the Article 85 desertion charge tossed. The prosecution moved to exclude evidence connected to this, but the judge is letting us introduce it without facing the charge. It's a small win, but the communications I saw about your Article 32 investigation along with the JAG opine paint an unfavorable picture of Dianna for including that desertion charge."

"But the others will go forward?"

"Yes. I entered a not guilty plea for both and requested a special trial so we'd only have to convince a judge and not a jury. That was also denied because the prosecution is seeking capital punishment for your mutiny charge, which makes this a general court-martial with a jury."

"Death?"

"Yes. By decimation."

"What the hell is that?"

"Don't worry about it right now. Focus on what's immediately in front of us, and within that, only on the parts we can control. Everything else is a distraction. We have to build the case you're a hero who the world refused to listen to, and that Dianna is abusing her power to make you the scapegoat for the PDF's failures. Then we have to sell this to a hostile jury of your peers."

"I'm doomed."

"Don't abandon hope. Luke and Lucius seem like sharp guys willing to extend you the benefit of the doubt. And there are witnesses ready to speak on your behalf. Dianna has it out for you in all of her communications. That alone should ensure you avoid the death penalty—assuming you're even found guilty. It's small, but you've got a fighting chance."

Marcus was silently skeptical.

"But we need to talk about something," Antony said somberly. "Maybe your memory was jarred during the beating, but you said you didn't sign your charge sheet."

"I know I didn't."

Antony held up a copy with Marcus's signature.

Marcus stared back in disbelief, unable to reconcile his memory and the existence of this document, "I … I know I didn't sign anything. I was dragged from the room right after they read the charges. Monica can back me up."

"I already asked her about it, and that's exactly what she said. But how'd they get this signature then? If Dianna lifted it from any of your PDF personnel documents it would've been flagged as a duplicate. This has to be a unique signature."

"I have no answer. I'm stunned. Dianna's up to something."

"The prosecution says Sarah will testify she was present as the second officer at your arrest, and that she saw you sign this."

"Sarah wasn't there. It's her word against Monica's."

"We can't have Monica make that claim if you don't know where this signature came from. They'll paint her as the emotional wife and it'll destroy her credibility as a character witness. Our bench isn't that deep. We need her."

Marcus paused, then blurted, "My resignation letter!"

"What about it?"

"Dianna made me sign a resignation letter when I left the PDF. She never turned it in, that's why I wasn't officially discharged. That signature wouldn't be in the database to get flagged."

"It was a small-time move. She can't use it again, since it's in the system now. But at least we know she's playing dirty."

"What happens next?" Marcus asked.

"Jury selection. Twelve individuals will be picked, all from the PDF, and four have to be enlisted officers. Each of them will be put through a *voir dire* process, providing procedures that ideally give you as fair of a trial as possible. Meanwhile, Luke, Lucius, and I will build your case. Once that's done, a trial start date will be set. My guess is it'll be about three weeks. Dianna is doing everything she can to fast track things."

"How long can the whole trial last?"

"In a capital case like yours, months. We should have a verdict by fall, before the holidays."

"This is ludicrous. What about the rest of my life?"

"I don't control the whole world yet, Marcus. Make the most of your new-found free time. Have you thought about meditation?"

Marcus used the last of his energy to flip Antony the bird.

18

GENERAL KOS

J ury selection began immediately and turned into a circus just as quickly. Every time Antony agreed to a juror, the prosecution discovered dirt that ensured they were removed. The final list was a gaggle of wild card individuals, hand-picked by the prosecution: Che, Velia, Ashley, Charles, Su, Virgil, Bonnie, Jack, Nicole, Ameda, Lindsay, and Quinn who, as the highest-ranking member, was appointed the jury foreman.

Marcus's nerves where shot by the time trial arrived. He hadn't worn normal clothes in weeks, and the ruins of Kingsbury Hall were the first new space he'd seen since being arrested. The theater was missing its roof, another of the many victims from post-strike earthquakes along nearby fault lines.

"This is apocalyptic." Marcus looked at all the people packed into the dilapidated theater.

"That's because it is," Antony smirked.

The judge's bench occupied the highest position on the stage, flanked on either side by the jurors in a half-circle wrapping around the witness stand. The defense and prosecution had their counsel tables in the old orchestra pit between the stage and the front row. Spectators filled every surviving theater seat, balcony box, and walkway; it was remarkable to have public access to any military tribunal, especially Marcus's. Cameras were omnipresent, broadcasting proceedings to the rest of the world.

"Order. ORDER!" the Judge yelled over the rambunctious crowd. "Quiet down, people! I won't hesitate to clear this room of observers and cut off the cameras if it gets out of hand!"

The theater came to a silent standstill.

"This is the case of the government against Marcus Winthrop Adams. I'm Judge Jordan Kilravock, but you can all call me Judge Jordan for short. The defendant in this case, Mr. Adams, is charged with Article 107, making false official statements, and Article 94, mutiny. Everyone but the jury may be seated, bailiff please swear in the jurors then the prosecution has the floor."

With their promise of impartiality proclaimed, the jury sat. Benedict walked the small set of stairs from the orchestra pit to the stage, beginning the prosecution's opening argument. "Thank you, Your Honor. The story we will prove is about a man who would not accept change when it eroded his privileged position. It's the story of a man who only cared about his ego and fame, not the truth. Over the course of this trial, our evidence and witnesses will prove, beyond a shadow of a doubt, that Marcus Adams was an enemy of the people, who intentionally spread discord and disinformation at every turn, especially among the young and most impressionable. We will prove that Marcus Adams acted in a premeditated fashion for decades to ensure the outcome he wanted: a mutiny at the PDF which allowed Apophis and its asteroid moons to hit this planet. You all know the ending to this tragic story—the deaths of nearly two billion people.

"You may wonder why a once-beloved public figure would do something like this? The simple truth is because he resented his superior officer, in large part for being a woman. He was enraged she wouldn't blindly believe him, despite a long history of THAT MAN predicting things that never came true. You'll hear from those closest to him about how he let his emotions run rampant, how his toxic personality resorted to bullying whenever he couldn't get his way, and how he abandoned his post when faced with disciplinary action for an incident of workplace violence. You'll also hear how he retaliated by hacking and sabotaging the NostRa mission to crash the only probe that could've provided data to save us from the catastrophe we've lived through. However, billions of others weren't so lucky.

"Our evidence will also show how the defendant masqueraded as an employee of the PDF pushing fake data to confuse the public and fuel uncertainty, leaving us vulnerable to the unanticipated impact of Apophis. Other stories could be told from the evidence of this case, like how Apophis represents the darkest day in human history, and no one has more blood on their hands than Marcus Adams. But regardless of which version is told, the moral of this story must be written by you, a jury of his peers, and our evidence will provide everything you need to do right by the souls of the ascended."

The room was silent. Marcus could feel the weight of the entire world against him, and he hated it. Antony led the defense and deferred their opening argument until a future moment when the prosecution would rest its case.

"We call our first witness, Your Honor," Benedict said.

Dianna rose from the front row of floor seats and joined Benedict on stage, sitting in the witness stand below the judge and jury. Despite being far away, she stared straight through Marcus, sending his heart racing and blood boiling again.

"Don't let anyone see her make you emotional," Antony whispered to Marcus. "No matter what, stay calm and quiet."

"Would you please introduce yourself for those who don't know who you are?"

Benedict's question got its desired outcome, and the room resounded with laughter; Dianna was a well-loved science celebrity.

"General Kos, President of the Planetary Defense Force."

"That's an impressive title. Can you tell me how you earned your position and how it relates to your role with the defendant?"

"Let me answer your second question first since the first requires a longer explanation."

"Go ahead."

"I was the only faculty member studying asteroids in the Department of Physics and Astronomy in the College of Science at the University of Utah in 2004. The defendant was a master's student looking for a final project. I'd heard about the Kit Peak team's success detecting Apophis and told him to consider their data for his work—"

"Real fast," Benedict interjected, "can you explain how the asteroid got that name?"

"Tucker, Tholen, and Bernardi, the asteroid's discoverers, were *Stargate* fans and named Apophis after the show's antagonist."

"An alien committed to destroying humanity?"

"That's my understanding. I wasn't a fan." The room cackled at Dianna's curt retort.

"Did Marcus take your advice and use the Kit Peak data?"

"Yes, he did."

"Did he do it alone or under your guidance?"

"I helped Marcus obtain their data, since he was an intellectual nobody at the time, and advised him every step of the way on simulations to assess if Apophis was a real threat."

"You're referring to his nefarious doomsday algorithm?"

"Yes. It was mid-December. I remember because I was grading final papers for fall term when Marcus burst into my office in a panic."

"What was your reaction when he told you the model results?"

"Neither of us could believe it. We were stunned."

"What was it that stunned you?" asked Benedict.

"Apophis was going to strike Earth. Given the early estimates of its size, which was about three football fields, it would've hit with a force equal to every nuclear weapon in the world, all 15,000 of them, going off at the same time."

"What was his date for this terminal moment?"

"This gets to the answer for your first question, about how I got my position. I didn't know Marcus very well at that point, and I worried about his methodology. I reviewed everything multiple times. It looked okay. He had questionable assumptions built-in, but it seemed safer to assume worst-case scenarios at that time."

"I'm jumping ahead a bit," said Benedict, "but was the defendant's methodology something you'd continue to question during your career?"

"Yes. His doomsday algorithm turned out to be the first of many false findings."

"When did his doomsday algorithm predict the earliest strike?"

"In 2013," answered Dianna.

"We all know that didn't happen. Why not?"

"Marcus's model was way off. Apophis passed us at a safe distance of nine million miles that year."

"Why was his model, and by extension him, so wrong?"

"His early assumptions were incorrect. This became obvious as we collected better data on Apophis through more measurements."

"But after his failed prediction in 2013," Benedict added, "and even with more accurate data, Marcus wouldn't abandon his theory that Apophis was a threat?"

"Correct. He started saying 2029 was the new impact date."

"For the record, remind the court when Apophis actually collided with Earth."

"Impact was in 2036," Dianna replied.

"Did this match any of the defendant's models?"

"No, he was certain Apophis would've hit before that point."

"So he never got the date right. What about other predictions?"

"Later in his career," Dianna explained, "he said Apophis would strike multiple sites, either in South America or in the Pacific Ocean. The reality was far from his predictions though. Apophis broke into multiple fragments in the atmosphere, so those pieces, along with the asteroid moons it picked up, collectively destroyed eleven megacities. Two hundred million people were instantly annihilated. But most of the total deaths came from after-effects like wildfires, crop failures, earthquakes, famines, diseases, and social unrest. All that dystopian stuff."

"What about the echo strikes?" asked Benedict.

"No one saw those coming. With our budget and the legacy systems we inherited from absorbing older agencies, we could only hunt for the biggest asteroids. We didn't know a smaller secondary cluster was out there until it hit the moon earlier this year."

"Were you head of the PDF at that point?"

"No, Dr. Ed was," Dianna invoked her former superior and fellow science celebrity; the public lovingly called him the Chinese Mr. Rogers.

"So Marcus had a sordid history of being wrong by the time he was finally right?" asked Benedict.

"I don't know if it's fair to say he was ever right."

"And why is that?"

"I went back and reviewed every report he ever filed while working for the PDF, and 2036 never shows up. He only started pushing that date after he leaked the fake NostRa mission data in 2023 and again after his predictions for a 2029 impact proved false. It might be fair to say he was right for the wrong reasons. But as a scientist, that reeks of random chance to me."

"Your Honor, the prosecution introduces the forty-two reports Marcus Adams filed as a member of the PDF, along with the fake leaked mission data."

"Objection," Antony said from the defense counsel table, "the validity of that data can't be determined either way, and my client maintains it's real. Neutral language is appropriate."

"Sustained. Prosecution will refer to it as the 'disputed data' or 'leaked data' from this point forward," said Judge Jordan.

"Understood," Benedict replied, returning to his questioning. "General Kos, as the defendant's superior, what did you feel was his core motivation during your time together?"

"Objection, Your Honor." Antony shot up from his seat again. "This is speculation."

"This goes directly to motive," Benedict shot back.

"Overruled," said Judge Jordan. "Please answer, General."

"His ego. Can I back up a minute?"

"Sure," said Benedict.

"After his first doomsday algorithm, and some replication and validation by other scientists in early 2005, Apophis was moved to the highest threat level on the Torino and Palermo scales."

"Please explain those for us."

"They're different ways astronomers rank asteroid threats."

"So at least initially," Benedict probed, "Apophis was the biggest threat of all known asteroids?"

"Absolutely. No other asteroid has ever ranked with such a high threat level, not before and not since."

"That would've made Marcus a celebrity, wouldn't it?"

"Yes, it did. And he loved it. It was an important moment for his career. This kind of notoriety is common for academics, and occasionally for Ph.D. students, but it was unheard-of for someone with his credentials—"

"Is that why you were the one to break the news about Apophis at the infamous January 14th press conference, in this very hall, instead of him?"

"I had authority, he didn't. We discussed it beforehand and he was fine with it."

"Objection, hearsay!" Antony was vehement. "There's no evidence this conversation happened, and my client disputes it completely."

"Overruled," replied Judge Jordan.

"Please continue," Benedict encouraged Dianna.

"I went public with our findings. The first possible impact moment was only eight years away, and back then, it could take ten years or longer to plan and execute a space mission. The clock was ticking. In 2006, the Planetary Defense Force was formed by merging a large number of other organizations around the world, all under the former Planetary Defense Coordinate Office at NASA, answering to the UN with Dr. Ed as President. We had a mandate to succeed in our mission, by force if necessary. This included the power to conscript the world's most brilliant minds, called Superforecasters, if they hadn't already volunteered."

"Sounds like an exciting time," Benedict gushed.

"It was. We were a global team empowered to save the world. Our headquarters were established here in Utah under the Oquirrh Mountains near the old Dugway Proving Grounds west of Salt Lake City. We expanded to incorporate the former NSA data center at Camp Williams to the east, the historic site of Camp Floyd to the south, the Salt Flats to the west, and the Great Salt Lake all the way north to Hill Air Force Base. This part of the Great Basin has served as our base of operation ever since."

"Why this particular location?"

"The composition of the landscape, the local climate, and the relative isolation. There were a few homes within our boundaries, but mostly it was empty space that already had military assets on four sides of a resource-rich mountain range."

"What happened to the houses within the new boundaries?"

"They were incorporated under eminent domain to house PDF members. We became a community in the world but separate from it. I was offered the founding position over a program that went on to include Project Invictus Nostradamus Ra aimed at stopping Apophis, which we called NostRa. I immediately invited Marcus to be part of my crew."

"And he turned you down?" said Benedict.

"Yes."

"Why?"

"He said I'd stolen the spotlight from him at the press conference by taking credit for his doomsday algorithm, which wasn't true. It felt so petty to me at the time, considering he believed his own models more than anyone else on the planet. Here was an opportunity to help, but he was focused on his five-minutes of fame."

"Why didn't you just conscript him?"

"I already had plenty of capable volunteers. We were working on the most exciting project on Earth."

"But eventually, Marcus did join you?"

"Yes, once he cooled off. March 15th, 2006, was his first day."

"How long did you work together?"

"For the next fifteen years, approximately."

"A decade and a half is a long time to be on the same team. Did you become close with the defendant?" asked Benedict.

"I did, and not just with Marcus but also with his wife, Monica. We were close at a personal level. I considered her a great friend, and Marcus was an important colleague."

"But not equals? Without exception, you were always his superior?"

"Yes, and he openly resented it. I was promoted multiple times until I was the second in command of the PDF. He never congratulated me on any of the achievements, even though my success meant his success. He rose with me."

"Overall, how would you describe your professional relationship with the defendant?"

"Toxic," answered Dianna.

"Please elaborate."

"Nothing was ever easy. Marcus is one of those brilliant minds that's never satisfied. Most of the time, this is a great quality, but once a problem was solved, he'd keep picking it apart at the expense of other priorities. It's why NostRa was so delayed."

"So, in 2020, after crying wolf about the doomsday, what ended your professional relationship with the defendant?"

"At the PDF they call it the 'Great Christmas Chicken Incident.' "

Laughter scattered across the crowd. Judge Jordan intervened to restore order.

"Will you please explain," asked Benedict.

"You should talk to Hannah. She was the team's personnel support member and investigated the incident. She'll know the details."

"But Marcus left the PDF as a result of this incident, correct?"

"He went AWOL instead of facing a one-time sanction, and then spent his time slandering us and our mission in public while trying to corrupt our team," Dianna said sternly.

"I want to fast forward again to 2022, to the 'PR event of the Century' as it's known, when the NostRa mission ultimately failed, because you have irrefutable evidence it was the result of Marcus hacking your system and accelerating the mission probe directly into the asteroid?"

"Objection!" Antony protested. "Saying the evidence is irrefutable assumes facts not in evidence and is argumentative."

"Overruled," said Judge Jordan. "Please answer the question, General."

"Yes," replied Dianna.

"Your Honor," Benedict continued, "we'd like to enter the corresponding NostRa mission control access log data into the record to show the validity of General Kos's claims." Benedict retrieved a large binder of papers. "It shows remote access from Marcus's mountain home using General Kos's credentials, despite dozens of witnesses placing her at PDF headquarters during the same time."

"Noted. Continue with your witness," said Judge Jordan.

"What happened after the failed mission of 2022?" asked Benedict.

"NostRa was dead, so we were back to square one, with the next possible impact in 2029."

"What happened with Marcus after that?"

"He went into a conspiracy theory meltdown, and the public stopped paying attention to him," replied Dianna. "He accused the PDF of sabotaging NostRa ourselves, and he leaked supposed mission data claiming it was from the 2022 probe and proved a strike in 2029 was imminent. He also said I was personally killing colleagues, a particularly nasty accusation considering these were people I knew and worked with on a daily basis. When the asteroid didn't hit in 2029, his credibility was shot, and by 2030, Marcus had dropped off the radar. I didn't think much about him again until Apophis struck in 2036, and only briefly because we were busy helping humanity survive. When the echo strikes against the moon happened earlier this year, there was public demand to open an investigation against him, which I did immediately upon assuming control of the PDF."

"On behalf of everyone here, and around the world," Benedict praised, "thank you for the fine job you've done. No one has ever inherited a bigger crisis. No further questions, Your Honor."

The room burst into thunderous applause as Benedict left the stage, forcing Judge Jordan to get the crowd under control again.

"Your witness," Judge Jordan said to Antony.

"Thank you, Your Honor. And to General Kos, I appreciate you taking time to be with us today. I was surprised you were available, given your importance to our collective survival." Antony was a professional patronizer, laying it on just thick enough to still pass as a compliment if necessary.

"You're welcome," Dianna said through grit teeth.

"I only have two questions for you. Earlier you said you were personally involved with Marcus and his wife, Monica."

"I did say that."

"Did you have the same kinds of relationships with the rest of your team or just with Marcus?"

"It's a normal part of my role as a leader to be invested in the personal lives of my team members and their families. There was nothing unique about my relationship with Marcus."

"Great. Tell me how Marcus's coworkers died."

"Excuse me?" Dianna feigned offense.

"It's a simple question. For all of the people you cared so much about, can you list the details about how they kicked the bucket?"

"That is insulting and disrespectful."

"We're all going to die, Dianna. How did the people you worked with face the music? Just the facts, ma'am."

"It's General, or Dr. Kos."

"Got it. How'd they die, Doc?"

"Cancer, heart attacks, car accidents, everyday events …"

"Can you be more precise? Tell us, for each dead individual from the Apophis team still working on the mission after Marcus was pushed out of the PDF—"

"He went AWOL," Dianna interjected.

"—how did each of them die? There were only eight. You would've mourned with each of their families. Don't you remember the details?"

"I don't want to misspeak. I'll get back to you."

"No need," Antony held up a piece of paper. "I have the list right here. You probably remember Diksha, right?"

"Of course."

"She died from cancer."

"I just mentioned that as a cause," Dianna responded.

"Oops, my bad, I'm reading this list wrong. Diksha died from a car accident, just like Komson. Each was part of your innermost circle, and both were present in the Tactical Operations Center, or TOC, with you when NostRa crashed. Zain had a sudden heart attack at the ripe old age of forty-one, Garret was murdered in a still-unsolved carjacking, Sanchit appears to have been too fond of opioids, and Rick drowned in his tub despite being a former college swimming champion. Rick was also in the TOC with you the night NostRa failed, just like Corina, who committed suicide-by-cop while holding a machete and rambling about silencing voices in her head."

"Each death was tragic. What's your point?"

"They don't read like 'everyday events.' But there's one more name on my list, Dr. Ed. He wasn't just your superior at the PDF, he was also your personal mentor, right?"

"He was."

"How'd he die?"

"Suicide."

"What are the chances?" Antony sassed.

"Objection," said Benedict. "Correlation doesn't equal causation. Defense counsel is speculating if he's implying the witness or the PDF had anything to do with Dr. Ed's undisputed suicide. He was seventy-seven years old, and emotionally broken after Apophis and the echo strikes."

"Sustained. The defense better proceed carefully. I've had my fill of showmanship," warned Judge Jordan.

"Roger Roger. My point is that all of these deaths in isolation might appear to be random, but each person was also close to Marcus because of NostRa. Having half the people from such a small team die within less than twenty years of their failed mission is way beyond statistical probabilities. I'm a simple lawyer and hope General Kos, the beloved scientist, might explain what's happening … theoretically."

"You don't have to answer," Judge Jordan said to Dianna. "That's your final warning, Mr. Adams."

"It's fine, I want to," Dianna took a moment to compose her response. "Just because something is unlikely that doesn't mean it's impossible. Each death was a major loss for the PDF and our mission. But they were all independent random events. It might seem unlikely, but it is statistically possible."

"Thanks, General," Antony continued. "Next question, you said as of 2030 Marcus dropped off the map? Is that right?"

"Actually, I said he'd dropped off the radar. He wasn't in the public eye anymore, but I understand Marcus maintained a small following of deluded youths. He called them 'students' and used his past at the PDF to give the false impression he was still a sanctioned authority, not just a subject matter expert."

"If Marcus only proved to be wrong, like you've testified here today, how do you explain people's willingness to listen to him about Apophis?"

"You'd have to ask them."

"But as a scientist, it's got to irk you that people embrace ideas from someone spouting what you consider to be pseudoscience?"

"Unfortunately, everyone is entitled to their own opinions."

"Unfortunately?" Antony scoffed.

"We shouldn't pretend opinions are equal," Dianna grew aggressive. "Some are right because they're based on expertise, others are wrong because they're based on uninformed SWAG."

"I'm not familiar with your jargon. Can you explain the acronym for the court?"

"SWAG stands for a scientific wild-assed guess."

The room echoed with repressed laughter.

"It's our way of mocking unscientific ideas. In the case of Marcus, especially later in his career when he continued to fight against scientific consensus, his predictions proved to be SWAGs."

"So that's why you de-platformed him?"

Luke and Lucius arrived on stage, arms overflowing with stacks of binders. Turning to Judge Jordan, Antony said, "Your Honor, we'd like to enter the following PDF communication from General Kos to the media, to members of her team, and to other individuals of influence into evidence. In all cases, it shows how General Kos used her authority, and spent massive amounts of time, ensuring my client was ostracized from the public through systematic de-platforming from 2030 onward—"

"He was an enemy of truth, trying to confuse the public," Dianna barked. "I was ensuring people had the complete picture."

"There are tens of thousands of messages proving you spent valuable time convincing or intimidating others to ignore him. He only went silent because you personally silenced him."

"We disagree on our definition of how much of *my* time was spent combating his disinformation."

"Maybe, but we can both agree that in 2030, any time spent on these communications came at the expense of stopping Apophis."

"I'm fully capable of managing my time, Mr. Adams. That's why they made me a general and gave me an army to draw on."

"Fair enough. Earlier I said I had two questions, but I have a third before I let you go. Do you think it's a statistical coincidence the only people acting as witnesses for the prosecution come directly from what remains of your inner circle? Was no one else still alive to corroborate your description of Marcus and events leading to the strikes from Apophis"—Judge Jordan tried to intervene, but Antony persisted—"an impact you failed to stop since you ignored his advice, General?"

Dianna snapped, standing and yelling indiscernible things at Antony while a wave of outrage spread across the theater.

Judge Jordan ordered the bailiff to take Antony into custody. "We're ending here. I want the counsel in my chambers! Now!"

19

REBURNING BRIDGES

Marcus paced in his cell, awaiting the outcome of Antony's mandatory 802 session with the judge and prosecution. After a discouragingly short amount of time, his brother arrived. "Shout and cheer, Antony's here!"

"What happened?" Marcus asked.

"I got my ass handed to me. If I wasn't your brother, and if the rest of the world didn't already have it out for your blood, I would've been cut, and TDS would be taking over from here."

"But you can stay?"

"*Senza la famiglia non c'è vita!*" Antony invoked one of their family's dictums. "I knew I could take a bite at the apple once, so I used it against Dianna. I figured the worst they could do is kill us both."

"Thanks." Marcus was finally smiling.

"I'm glad you've found your sense of humor again. If you can't laugh through this, the stress will kill you before the general gets her chance. The jury saw a crack in Dianna's facade today. They can't unsee that even if the judge orders them to."

"Are we going back to court?"

"No. We'll start fresh tomorrow. The prosecution is calling Sarah and Hannah as witnesses next. Get some sleep."

Marcus's nightmares continued to haunt him. In the most common version, a smiling young girl holding a red balloon walked by in the street. His intuition said something was off about her, but he never tried to stop her. The dream ended with the realization she was a decoy before destruction engulfed him and mushroom clouds lit up the daytime sky. Then he'd wake up.

These visions only worsened after Apophis hit, and intensified following his arrest. The staying power of the visions forced him to sleep in short bursts, making the waking world feel surreal.

The next few weeks of the trial saw the prosecution guide Sarah's testimony in attacking every aspect of Marcus's work. Each mistake was convoluted to its extreme, so something as simple as botching one citation out of every hundred was evidence of an intent to plagiarize. The intellectual nitpicking was painfully meticulous, and Marcus was emotionally exhausted by his inability to refute her gross misrepresentations of his life's work. Sarah's narrative also perpetuated Dianna's picture of him as a difficult coworker and misogynistic subordinate who roamed the PDF looking for victims to sacrifice on the altar of his failing ego. When it came time for cross-examination, rather than rehash each detail she'd provided, Antony attacked Sarah's objectivity, given her loyalty to Dianna, then dismissed her.

But when Hannah took the stand, Marcus knew he was in for an even rougher ride.

"Please state your name," asked Benedict.

"Hannah Darrow."

"For full disclosure, are you my sister?"

"I am, but in no way does that obfuscate my ability to provide a factual recounting of my time at the PDF with the defendant."

"The defense has recognized this fact and waived their right to motion for your dismissal. Please explain for the court what you do as a personnel support member on General Kos's team?"

"It's a rebranding of 'human resources,' because we've progressed. We understand that a person doesn't exist in a vacuum. Since the PDF wants the best from its members, it gives the best support possible. My role was to bridge that divide."

"Can you give us a more concrete example of your day-to-day tasks?" asked Benedict.

"That's tough because it's whatever helps an individual in their personal lives. For some team members, this means having a person listen to them vent. For others, it's securing a special medical procedure for their sick child. My mandate was to be an advocate for all members and their families so the team could focus on our mission of saving the world."

"Thank you for that background. Given your role, can you please tell us about the 'Great Chicken Incident of 2020'?"

"It's the 'Great *Christmas* Chicken Incident,' to be precise—"

The audience suppressed their collective giggles and Judge Jordan let it slide.

"After fifteen years with the PDF," Hannah continued, "and so many failed predictions, Marcus developed a bad reputation among his colleagues. Frankly, he'd created an army of enemies. Behind his back, people were calling him Chicken Little because he constantly ran around saying the sky was falling despite scientific consensus to the contrary. People also joked about him wearing a tinfoil hat to bed because he believed someone, or something, was implanting nightmares to sabotage his work."

"Did Marcus know they were saying all of this?"

"He did, and over time it further strained his relationships with the entire NostRa team," said Hannah. "Marcus never helped his own case. People didn't want to be around him because of his behavior. They felt he was toxic. What happened in 2013 was an important turning point that made the incident in 2020 inevitable."

"Explain the connection between these events."

"The world was on edge because of the 2012 Mayan calendar hysteria. The end of the world was supposed to take place a few weeks before Apophis would reach Earth in early January 2013. Marcus repeatedly mentioned the Mayan prophecy when he spoke about the 2013 impact date in public."

"So he thought the Mayans predicted the end of the world?"

"He played it off as a joke, but privately when you talked to him, it was clear the humor was meant to deflect from his true feelings about the efficacy of ancient premonitions. It was a terrible thing to tease about when emotions were already high, so when the asteroid didn't come close to Earth in 2013, the public pounced. Everyone, even late-night talk show hosts, piled on Marcus. The world was exhausted from a decade of doomsday predictions, and he paid the price for alienating everyone. No one wanted to stand between him and the public rage."

"So what happened with the 2020 incident itself?"

"Someone put a rubber chicken wearing an ugly sweater and a tinfoil hat on Marcus's desk. I was standing in the Pit at the time, which is what we call the open office area with everyone's desks.

He had a complete meltdown when he saw it. I'd never seen a person act like he did at that moment. He was literally spitting as he shouted accusations and expletives at everyone. Then he smashed a bunch of stuff, including a mission-critical 3D printer. When the MP's arrived, they had to forcibly restrain him."

"We'd like to enter the following PDF personnel incident report to the record, Your Honor," said Benedict as Toby scurried like a spider onto the stage to hand him a paper copy. "Ms. Darrow, can you confirm this is your report about the incident?"

"Yes, that's it."

"Can you give us the 'too long; didn't read' version of what it recommended?"

"There was no doubt this was workplace violence, but Marcus hadn't actually touched anyone. The recommendation was he face sanction, which meant he'd have to make a public apology to the team, sign a contract placing him on probation until he completed an anger redirection program, take a demotion in rank, and forfeit 20 percent of his salary indefinitely."

"But you didn't advise he be discharged?"

"That's correct," answered Hannah.

"Who read your report?"

"General Kos, since she was his superior, along with Dr. Ed and other PDF leadership at the time."

"What about Marcus? Did he get a copy?"

"Yes."

"What was his reaction to it?" asked Benedict.

"I don't know. He went AWOL."

"Did you communicate with Marcus after that?"

"Not as much as I should have. I tried though. I got the feeling he resented me because of my report."

"Just for doing your job?"

"We never had a conversation about it, but that's how it felt. I contacted him to smooth things out, and he refused to respond. He became socially isolated," said Hannah. "I checked on his public commentary from time to time."

"Why?"

"I cared about him. He was brilliant. He just couldn't control his demons in the end. It was sad, and a loss for the PDF."

"Has his social isolation continued to today?" asked Benedict.

"Yes. But there are two distinct phases, with it getting worse over time. The first was 2020-2029, when Marcus was criticizing the PDF and raging against our work in public. The next phase was from 2030 until now, when Marcus has been mostly silent. Something changed after his 2029 prediction failed."

"But the punchline is after he left the PDF, he was a social pariah? People weren't whispering anymore—they were screaming at him to stay out of things."

"That's a fair assessment of the situation, yes."

"No further questions, Your Honor."

"Your witness," Judge Jordan said to the defense.

"Hi, Hannah," Antony began cross-examination.

Hannah responded with a siren's smile. "Hi."

"What did Dr. Ed think of Marcus?"

"He was probably his biggest fan. They had a special relationship among the PDF team."

"Your Honor, we'd like to enter this cache of internal PDF communication between leadership, including Dr. Ed and General Kos, about Hannah's incident report."

"It's admitted," responded Judge Jordan.

"Hannah, to borrow your brother's phrase, what's the 'too long; didn't read' version?"

"Dr. Ed thought the sanction was too harsh and it'd drive Marcus away. But he was part of General Kos's team, so Dr. Ed left the decision up to her."

"That turned out to be a true prediction, so why didn't the ever-wise Dianna listen to him?"

"Well, *General Kos* wanted to send a message."

"Which person do you agree with on the matter?"

"The general," Hannah said without hesitation.

"Why?"

"She had a front-row seat to Marcus's madness since before the PDF existed, plus I trust her judgment as a leader."

"I only have one more question: why'd you visit Marcus on April 29th—two days before his arrest?"

"I wanted to check on him. It'd been a long time and my other attempts had failed, so I thought I'd stop by his house."

"This is where you and Marcus agree. It'd been a very long time. In fact, it'd been since 2020. So why, two decades later, did you visit him on a Sunday, just days before his arrest?"

"It's a coincidence," said Hannah. "General Kos can confirm I had no connection to, or visibility into, his investigation since he wasn't a member of the team."

"Coincidence could be the catchphrase of this trial."

"Watch yourself, Mr. Adams," warned Judge Jordan.

"Where you disagree with Marcus," Antony probed, "is in the reason for your visit. He claims you said Dianna needed his help and would be reaching out. Then she did. Is that true?"

"I never said anything of the sort. He was extremely drunk when I got there and rambled on about how unfair everything turned out to be, how he'd ruined himself financially, his fallen status, and started listing other people from history who'd been exiled. He was stammering about difficulty sleeping because of nightmares when he passed out. Then I left. It was all very sad."

"Monica, his wife, also says you delivered the message about Dianna needing Marcus's help. How do you reconcile the fact two different people are contradicting your version of the conversation?"

"I'd probably lie too if I loved him and wanted to shield him from the consequences of his actions."

"So you believe he's guilty?" Antony moved toward Hannah.

"One of the things I learned from being put in charge of caring for team members' well-being is that my beliefs don't matter. The facts do. He did what he did. The evidence is clear, just like the rules were clear. This court will determine what to do about it. My motivation from day one with Marcus was to be helpful, but there was nothing I could do because he never wanted help."

"You can't save people from themselves?"

"Exactly," Hannah smiled.

Antony ended his interrogation and ceded the stage to the prosecution, who rested their case. When time was turned over to the defense the next morning, Antony delivered a short and simple opening argument extolling his brother as a hero. He emphasized that his evidence and eyewitnesses would point to one indisputable conclusion: Marcus had been right that Apophis was a real and growing threat to humanity, and no one in power listened.

The next three weeks were consumed by three witnesses for the defense: Monica, Bryan, and Duygu. Each of them talked at length about Marcus as a thoughtful person, researcher, and colleague. Their anecdotes helped humanize Marcus in the eyes of the audience, and a lighter presence could be felt in the courtroom. All three of the witnesses also agreed Marcus had been unfairly singled out for the wrath of the public, he'd consistently been a man of honor when treated fairly, and the world would've been wise to heed his warnings. The prosecution's cross-examination failed to rattle any of the witnesses. Things were looking bright when the defense called their next witness on the heels of the Fourth of July holiday, an obligatory tradition of a pre-PDF world.

"Welcome to the center of the known universe," Antony smiled. "Please state your name and title."

"William K. Martin, but call me Bill. I was the program manager for Project Invictus Nostradamus Ra at the Planetary Defense Force and worked with Marcus, General Kos, and Dr. Ed."

"We appreciate you being here."

"I wouldn't miss it for the world," Bill said, setting off murmurs of offense for his phrasing.

"Is it fair to say you knew NostRa better than anyone else?"

"No."

"Why not?" asked Antony, "You were the program manager."

"Marcus had a better picture of the mission than anyone, including me."

"But after him, you'd be next?"

"Yes," replied Bill.

"Great. Let's start with a softball question then, can you explain the meaning of the mission name?"

"Nostradamus was the name of the probe because an anagram of Apophis shows up in the work of the famous French seer as a 'strike from the sky.' Ra was the name for the lander it carried, named after the Egyptian sun god who constantly opposed Apophis, also known as Apep."

"What about Invictus? I'm rusty on my non-legal Latin?"

"It means undefeatable. That's how we felt about our fight against this strike from the sky."

"When Marcus was a part of your team, how'd you feel about him?"

"I loved him. So did Dr. Ed. Marcus was the man, at least in those early years. He could walk the PDF with his head held high knowing his algorithm was the reason we were all there," replied Bill.

"Curbing your enthusiasm for a moment, how'd the rest of the NostRa team feel about Marcus?"

"After 2013, it was all downhill. Hannah described it well."

"As a manager, could you tell if this conflict had any impact on the mission and its repeated delays?"

"Yes, the low morale was like pulling an anchor around," Bill explained. "At first people did the minimum or stayed silent when they saw ways to increase mission success. But eventually, most of them actively opposed, and occasionally subverted, the mission as a way to hurt Marcus."

"Can you explain how the mission was supposed to go down?"

Gasps of outrage rumbled through the crowd again, this time at Antony's insensitive word choice.

"Just give us a high-level picture," Antony asked.

"The mission was simple. Send the duo to intercept the asteroid, where the probe would take remote measurements and film as the lander made contact with the rock. Standard stuff."

"What was the main mission objective?"

"To remove uncertainty. With the mission data, we'd learn what we were facing and could plan an effective response. The data was everything."

"Was this all Marcus's design?" Antony asked.

"Yes. Every detail came from his mind."

"Would you describe your relationship with Marcus as toxic?"

"Absolutely not. It was the complete opposite."

"But that's the term others on your team used."

"Relationships are a two-way deal. He and I got along splendidly."

"During your time together, did you see Marcus act disrespect-fully toward superiors?" asked Antony.

"Only when he was right and they didn't listen."

"Can you give us an example of when Marcus was right, and leadership ignored him?"

"I can give you examples, as in plural. The q-type density coefficient for the asteroid's mass, the fact Apophis was a contact binary asteroid—"

"Explain what that is, please."

"Individual asteroids traveling so close they're touching, leading us to falsely believe they're a single celestial body."

"Was that all Marcus was right about?"

"No, he also predicted Earth's keyhole effect on Apophis's orbit."

"What's a keyhole, in astronomical terms?"

"A gravity sink around the planet six football fields wide. If an asteroid like Apophis goes through it, this changes the orbit and virtually guarantees a future impact with Earth."

"When?"

"That depends on all the relevant variables, like the asteroid's speed, density, and its Lagrangian points with other objects in space. This is the kind of data NostRa promised to get for us."

"But once Apophis passed through the keyhole, it was no longer a question if it would hit, but when?"

"Yes," said Bill, "when Marcus was still at the PDF, the keyhole effect was being debated, including the Lagrangian point effects with other celestial bodies."

"You're referring to the asteroid moons Apophis eventually towed to Earth in multiple waves?"

"Yes. Marcus was certain Apophis would collect asteroid moons as it traversed space, like when it passed by an asteroid called 2004vd17 in 2034, and sure enough, this one eventually hit the moon in the echo strikes of 2040. He was right because his model correctly assumed Apophis was a high-density q-type contact binary asteroid with more mass than early light measurements indicated. Technically, it turned out to be a contact trinity, but no one could've known that without NostRa's observational data."

"From what you observed as the mission project manager, why do you think no one listened to him?"

"He'd cried wolf," Bill said bluntly. "He'd been wrong about too many impact dates, so it was easy for leadership to ignore him."

"How's that possible when hindsight shows he had the right assumptions built into his models?"

"Predicting the future isn't the science we want to believe it is. Omitted variables, meaning things that aren't accounted for in the model, cause bias and there's an infinite number of omissions we didn't know about," Bill clarified.

"Can you give us a few examples?"

"The asteroid's mass, its physical shape, and direction of rotation. Even the surface composition of the asteroid was uncertain, so the impact of the sun's heating and cooling was unclear. All these things affect the orbit and a possible collision with our planet or our moon."

"Is this problem unique to Marcus's models?" asked Antony.

"No. After his first doomsday algorithm, the debate over the chances of an impact at various transit points, like 2013 and 2029, swung wildly. The consensus finally settled around 1 in 100,000 just months after Marcus joined the PDF, which was the first time Apophis was downgraded as a threat."

Antony said nothing, so Bill filled the void, "For context, that means a strike from Apophis was three times more likely than dying from fireworks, or eleven times more likely than dying in a plane crash. But there was one more thing Marcus was right about."

"What's that?"

Bill interlocked his fingers. "With sufficient time before the strike, we only had to nudge Apophis 1mm per second in a different direction to avoid the collision with Earth. Dr. Ed used to say 1mm is a fraction of the distance an ant moves in any moment. Prevention would've been a far easier option."

"The public, including PDF leaders like Dianna, have smeared Marcus as a heretic. Do you agree?"

"No."

"Why not?" asked Antony.

"Marcus was genuine about saving the world. All of these people saying his ego drove the narrative are dead wrong."

"Why are you so sure of this?"

"Just look at what he did with the leaked data."

"What do you mean?" asked Antony.

"It was an incredible amount of information. Marcus knew the moment of no return was approaching faster than Apophis was traversing the solar system, and he believed the data would be censored when he leaked it. He did something no one thought was technologically possible at the time. He compressed petabytes of information into gigabytes and distributed it across crypto blockchains, with all the code necessary to reassemble the original data."

"Why does this make you believe he was trying to save the world?" asked Antony.

"It was a stroke of genius for him to post the data like this because it became immutable. Leaving aside if the data was real or not, what he posted was clear for anyone to see and for no one to change. It cost him every penny he had from his family inheritance, all the money he'd made himself, and donations people had given him. It literally cost him a fortune."

"So it's strictly a monetary calculation for you?"

"He put his money where his mouth is," Bill replied. "Few people can say something similar. He believed in what he was doing, and I believe he was trying to save us all from Apophis."

"No further questions, thanks for stopping by."

The prosecution exercised their right to cross-examine Bill the following day but fumbled an attempted character assassination over his part-ownership in a Salt Lake City strip club long before volunteering for the PDF. As Bill was being dismissed from the stand, a car bomb outside rocked the ruins of the theater, sending people scattering in all directions.

"SECURE THE DEFENDANT … AND THE JURY!" screamed Judge Jordan. Marcus was grabbed by the bailiff and escorted into a nearby corridor. He could hear the muted sound of gunfire. Seconds later the jury appeared, flanked by a pair of MPs with rifles drawn. Marcus's mind wandered to his brother as a second explosion shook the concrete corridor.

"WE NEED TO MOVE!" one MP screamed to the people huddled in the hallway. Marcus was between Velia and Virgil as they traversed the underground labyrinth. The gunfire was getting louder; whoever was shooting was closing in on the group.

"CONTACT, REAR!" the bailiff screamed before his head exploded from a gunshot. The remaining pair of MPs engaged a gang of masked assailants at the far end of the corridor as the jury scurried in every direction. A flashbang grenade bounced beneath Marcus before bursting, searing the skin across most of his body, and incapacitating him with blinding light and deafening sound. Marcus was limp on the ground when unfamiliar hands grabbed both of his arms and dragged him away from the firefight. With his limited vision he thought it was Velia and Virgil.

The echo of automatic gunfire pulsed through the passageway. Marcus was experiencing everything in tiny bursts of confused consciousness. His back was on fire, and his legs felt like they were submerged in a warm bath. He wasn't sure what was real anymore. Marcus had visions of a spaceship cockpit, with endless panels of flashing lights, buttons, switches, and dials, all labeled in an unfamiliar script resembling hieroglyphics. As his eyes closed for the final time, fragments of sound, from two voices—one male and one female—continued:

"Alive? ... barely... chances of surviving ... fuck! ... not supposed—"

Gunshots.

"Where the hell ... they? ... they... rally point ... hallway ... sloppy? ... shot!"

Explosions.

"Face ... gunshots don't kill ... infection ... still breathing? ... breathing?"

Gunshots.

"Capture ... no? ... containment? ... no! ... fine, kill ... fine!"

Door opening.

20

PREMONITIONS

Marcus struggled to open his sedated eyes. His ears were ringing, and for a moment, he could only see his brother's mouth moving.

"What?" Marcus murmured.

"I said, you're one tough mother," Antony smiled.

"Where am I?"

"The University hospital. You've been in an induced coma, but you're healing, that's all that matters."

"What?" Marcus couldn't make sense of Antony's explanation.

"What do you remember?"

"An explosion. On a spaceship. And voices. Arguing."

Antony roared with laughter. "They found you in a utility closet in the basement of Kingsbury Hall. You probably thought it was a spaceship because of all the power breakers."

"What?" Marcus asked again.

"You were shot in the back multiple times. You're lucky to be alive. It broke a bunch of vertebrae and most of your ribs, but it didn't puncture any organs. They're pretty sure you'll be able to walk again."

Marcus's face itched something fierce, but his hands were wrapped tighter than a mummy. "Why are my hands covered?"

"Most of your body was burned during the attack, so you can't scratch anything yet. There's fish skin under all those bandages!"

"Why don't I remember any of this?"

"You suffered severe trauma. The court was attacked. They were after you. Two of the jurors managed to drag you to safety."

"Who?"

"Velia and Virgil," Antony answered.

"No, I mean, who attacked the court?"

"The PDF is investigating, but none of the attackers could be identified by their bodies. They were well trained though— special forces mercenary types. My money is on you-know-who."

"Dianna?"

"She has motive, now if we could prove intent."

Marcus was speechless.

"You need to rest," Antony leaned in to kiss Marcus's bandaged forehead. "I'm thankful you're alive, and you're reacting so well to the nanobots and oxygen chamber therapy. You've got a long recovery ahead, but I'm here, every step of the way."

The intravenous narcotics distorted Marcus's dreams. In place of the normal Apophis horrors were flashbacks of his attack. Fragments of his memory intermixed with possible imagination until a continuous stream of dialogue repeated like an incantation:

Virgil: "Is he alive?"

Velia: "He's barely breathing. His chances of surviving are low. He's been shot three times."

Virgil: "Fuck! He's not supposed to die."

Gunshots.

Velia: "Where the hell are they? They know this is the rally point, right?"

Virgil: "Yes. They'll be here once they've cleared the hallway."

Velia: "How could they be this sloppy? He wasn't supposed to get shot! And how'd they manage to burn him up!"

Explosions.

Virgil: "His face is fucked. If those gunshots don't kill him, the infection from the burns will. Is he still breathing?"

Velia: "What!"

Virgil: "Calm down. Okay? Is he breathing?"

Gunshots.

Velia: "Yes. But capture isn't an option anymore."

Virgil: "No?"

Velia: "No!"

Virgil: "What about containment?"

Velia: "No! He's going to die!"

Virgil: "Fine, kill him then."

Velia: "You sure?"

Virgil: "Yes. Just suffocate him."

Velia: "Fine!"

The dream ended the same way, with the door bursting open, but Marcus couldn't see who it was. According to Antony, the hero of the moment was an MP named Tony, who killed all the masked assailants before following the blood smear from Marcus's gushing back wounds to the utility closet. EMTs barely revived him, and he'd suffered multiple heart attacks before they induced a coma to give him a fighting chance.

Recovery came slowly. *It was ironic*, Marcus thought while lying in bed, *all this effort to keep him alive just so he could return to the trial and the possibility of the death penalty.* Velia and Virgil were hailed as heroes, but Marcus couldn't shake his vision of them conspiring to kill him. After three months of intensive physical therapy, Marcus could walk again, but only in a hunched posture. It wasn't until the eve of his trial's resumption that he dared look in a mirror. His fears proved valid. His disfigured face and half-hidden left eye made him unrecognizable.

Armed with callous signs, protesters swarmed Kingsbury Hall. One said it was unfortunate the attack, which killed dozens of people, hadn't saved society the trouble of a trial. Many others mocked Marcus as the 'Hunchback of Nostradamus Ra.' The entire campus was in FPCON Delta, and PDF soldiers were out in force; only the system itself would be allowed to kill Marcus.

"No matter what happens today, no matter what I say or what Benedict does, DO NOT lose your cool," Antony emphasized as they walked into the ruined shadow of Kingsbury Hall. Everyone gawked at Marcus's ghastly appearance.

"Do you hear me?" Antony grabbed Marcus by the wrist.

"Yes," Marcus sat at the defense counsel's table.

"Welcome back, everyone," Judge Jordan addressed the room. "It's been a long road to get here, but we'll pick up exactly where we left off. Before we begin, however, I'd like to address the continued presence of two jurors who were instrumental in saving the defendant from vigilante justice. Exigency, in addition to the consent of both counsels, means they'll stay on for the remainder of our trial. That said, I'll remind all jurors that despite any feelings created by the failed attack on the defendant, you're still bound by your oath to be objective in this case. Now, with pleasantries out of the way, the defense has the floor."

"We call Marcus Adams, Your Honor," Antony announced.

Sitting on the stage, instead of at the defense table, was a totally different experience. It seemed the cameras were jeering at him harder than people in the audience. He hated having his back to the judge and jury; it triggered memories of Dianna's hovering, unseen, at his polygraph months earlier.

"State your name for the court," asked Antony.

"Marcus Adams."

"The luckiest man in the world."

"Something like that."

"One fact that's already emerged in this trial, and its ancillary moments, is you're not a universally-loved individual. It must be a heavy burden to carry. Other people throughout history, facing far less, have simply killed themselves."

"I didn't come this far to only get this far," Marcus replied.

"Good to hear. I don't think it's an exaggeration to say the entire world is on the edge of their seats, so let's jump right in. Were you right or were you wrong that Apophis posed the biggest existential threat humanity has ever faced?"

Marcus's heart was pounding, making him weak for breath. He'd believed the answer to this question so fervently for so long, but now he had to say it aloud to the entire world. "I was right."

The room muttered, and Judge Jordan did the usual settling to restore order so Antony could continue, "I'd like to pick up where Bill's earlier testimony ended, on the idea of prevention. That was your ultimate recommendation, right?"

"Yes," Marcus answered.

"Months ago, Benedict said the story of your trial was waiting to have the moral written by this jury, but that isn't true, is it? The moral of the story was written when leadership refused to listen to you. When they refused to follow your plan of prevention. Because if they had, we wouldn't be here today, and you'd be free to do something else to help the world instead of taking the stand."

"Objection," said Benedict, "he might as well be laying bread-crumbs along the floor of this courtroom with how hard he's leading this witness."

"Sust—" Judge Jordan started to say.

"Yes. That's all true." Marcus replied.

"Sustained, Mr. Adams. I'm going to let that slight slide on account of the hearing damage your client suffered during the attack. But both of you have no wiggle room left, do you understand?"

"Yes, Your Honor," Antony returned to Marcus. "Tell us your version of the story this court heard during previous testimony."

"We have to go back to where this started, the academic year of 2004. It was my final year as a grad student. I'd completed my classwork and had to prove myself with a project. I bounced around until I was sent to Dianna. I didn't seek her out."

"Do you feel she was the stellar mentor she described to this court?"

"Not at all. Yes, she used her credentials to get the data, but it was all me. Dianna had no idea how to handle that much information or how to efficiently model it. Her suggestions were shallow and often wrong. It was my code. My algorithm."

"So she stole your thunder."

"Yes. It's sad because before I started graduate school, our father told me to watch my back since some academics were fine stealing other people's work to advance their own careers. I was more than naive, Dianna knew it. She played me."

"Then why did you eventually join her at the PDF?"

"I had a gut feeling it was the right thing to do. I hated the idea of working for her. But it was my best shot to stop Apophis."

"Briefly tell us what it was like at the PDF."

"It was the greatest time of my life—"

"Why?" Antony interrupted.

"For the same reason Dianna said: we were saving the world. People don't appreciate how close we thought the 2013 strike was going to be. Apophis was literally upon us."

"But it didn't hit?"

"Right. Whenever you're dealing with data, it's a sample, a small piece you can use to predict the future. There's no guarantee you'll be right, so you weigh the consequence of outcomes against their probability, which were high for 2013 and 2029."

"But it hit in 2036," said Antony.

"Yes, because Apophis came so close in 2029 that it passed through our keyhole, which is something I said could happen."

"Why didn't the PDF alert the world about 2036 then?"

"Their newer models assumed Apophis didn't pass through Earth's keyhole."

"As time went on, and your predictions didn't materialize, you found yourself surrounded by people who didn't just ignore you. They openly ridiculed you, making it impossible to do your job."

"There were exceptions, like Bill and Dr. Ed."

"I'm glad you mentioned the late doctor because I have this hand-written letter I'd like to enter into evidence, Your Honor."

"Has this been authenticated?" Judge Jordan inquired.

"Yes," both counsels said simultaneously.

"Alright, you may continue, Mr. Adams."

"This letter is from Dr. Ed to you, Marcus. In it, he praises your character, your commitment, and your intellect."

"I had a great relationship with Dr. Ed. He was a father figure. We had a lot in common. We'd both wrestled in high school, and he loved card tricks like me. He was an honest intellectual. Dianna resented our relationship for being an old boys' club."

"When is this letter dated?" Antony asked.

"Sometime in 2034."

"January 2034, to be precise," Antony answered, "a few short years before all hell broke loose. At the depths of your social ostracism and public exile."

"Yes."

"While we're on the topic of Dr. Ed, explain how NostRa competed with his Sentinel mission."

"When Apophis didn't hit in 2013, its threat level was downgraded again. Sentinel was next on deck. I knew he was doing important work because we discovered Apophis on a fluke. It just suddenly showed up in the sky. Dr. Ed's project would scan the heavens for all the other asteroids we hadn't seen yet, like the secondary cluster Apophis was towing."

"By 2014, his project was the PDF's top priority?"

"Yes. Everyone knew the 2019 flyby of Apophis wasn't going to hit, so our next big milestone was intercepting the asteroid with NostRa in 2022 to confirm if the 2029 flyby was a serious threat like I predicted. We had time for Sentinel to take priority."

"So you supported Dr. Ed's vision for Sentinel, even though it meant de-prioritization of yours?"

"Yes."

"That doesn't sound very egotistical to me," Antony was patronizing again. "What happened between 2013 and 2020 when the chicken incident Hannah described took place?"

"Everyone turned against me. The abuse at work hit critical levels, but Dianna never intervened."

"So she never sent Hannah, the team's personnel support member, to step up on your behalf?"

"Never. Dianna knew how I felt about her because I'd seen the real person underneath that fake smile. She had it out for me, and let everyone else do her dirty work of tearing me down."

"Why do you believe she targeted you?"

"Because I'd call her on her bullshit, and I wouldn't back down when I was right. Almost everything I assumed proved to be true. I knew it in my bones. I wasn't going to let her silence me."

The room resounded with snickering.

"She's calculated," Marcus continued. "Dianna used the team to push my buttons, then forced me out when I finally snapped."

"But the esteemed general said you went AWOL. Is that your understanding of what happened?"

"She used Hannah's report to make me resign."

"Did you ever read Hannah's report?"

"Not until this trial, no. At the time, Dianna used it as a prop. She said it contained enough evidence to dishonorably discharge me. But instead, she'd prepared a letter in my name saying I was resigning from the PDF. I read it and signed it. Then I left."

"She knew you were leaving?"

"Without a doubt. It was her idea."

"Your Honor, we want to enter the plethora of communication evidence showing General Kos pushing the narrative that Marcus went AWOL even though for two decades, the PDF didn't arrest him for desertion. The communication also shows how she pushed for an Article 85 charge in this trial, which was eventually tossed."

"Noted," said Judge Jordan.

"But that wasn't the end of your saga, was it?"

"No. A few days later, she was on the news saying I deserted. She's said the same thing hundreds of times since 2020 and claimed the PDF had an ongoing investigation. Nothing ever came of it. I learned to live with possible prosecution hanging over me."

"Tell us about your alleged 2022 hack of NostRa."

"I knew the mission control VPN access points, and guessed Dianna's credentials to gain entry."

"How'd you guess them?" Antony asked.

"It was a simple sequence of numbers."

"Is Dianna always that sloppy with security?"

"No," Marcus said. "It was a trap. She knew I couldn't resist."

"What did you see when you logged in?"

"The video feed from the probe as it approached the asteroid, along with all the relevant mission control metrics. It was all shown in a master dashboard built for Dianna."

"What did that moment feel like?" Antony pushed the palms of his hands together, reverentially resting them against his lips, like he was offering a prayer.

"It was a spiritual experience. I was staring face to face with this amazing chunk of rock zipping through the cosmos at 65,000 mph. It was like the asteroid was calling out to me through space."

"Did anyone else, other than you and those in the TOC with General Kos, have visibility of the mission dashboard?"

"No."

"How can you be certain?" Antony challenged.

"Because I designed the dashboard. What it showed, how the public feed worked, and who had access to which parts."

"What was the last thing you saw before the feed went dark?"

"The probe had successfully moved into orbit around the asteroid, which was key for launching the probe and taking data measurements. I saw Apophis wasn't a contact binary like I'd theorized … it was a contact trinity. Three gigantic rocks traveling in perfect parallel. I also saw a reflection of light off of an asteroid moon being dragged behind it. Then the feed cut out."

"You've seen the public feed. It doesn't show any of this."

"The public saw things hours after they'd actually happened."

"What caused the mission to fail?"

"Well, the official story is the probe crashed into the asteroid before getting into orbit."

"But you don't believe that?"

"No. I saw it in orbit. I saw the system data, and it was all fine."

"Then what do you think happened? Because you aren't claiming the probe is still alive, are you?"

"No, the probe is dead—Dianna crashed it into Apophis."

Gasps spread through Kingsbury Hall.

Judge Jordan intervened, "ORDER! Quiet down, people."

"How do you know this?" asked Antony.

"Because Komson told me," Marcus replied.

"Who is he?"

"Komson was a member of Dianna's inner circle and was present in the TOC the night NostRa crashed. He's also the one who eventually leaked the mission data to me. He said that when Dianna learned I was remotely viewing the mission, she cut all feeds, took over the controls, and manually drove the probe into the asteroid."

"Intentionally?"

"Yes."

"Why hasn't anyone else confirmed your story?"

"They're afraid," said Marcus. "Komson died. So did Rick, who was also in the TOC. She swore everyone to secrecy on the punishment of death, and they all knew how ruthless she is … ultimately, she made good on her threats, so the survivors have stayed silent."

"So four years after the failed mission, and just prior to his own death, Komson gave you the leaked data which you released despite the technical limitations of sharing such large files, under the penalty of death?"

"Yes, I did. I ran more algorithms, and it was clear the 2029 transit would be too close for comfort."

"How close was too close?" asked Antony.

"Apophis would pass between us and our artificial satellites. The public needed to know, but Dianna hadn't said anything yet. Time was running out to avoid the consequences of her inaction."

"Why would the general crash the probe and hide the data?"

"Because she saw, with her own eyes, that I was right about all my assumptions. Without me, she had no solution for Apophis, and she didn't want to lose her power, so she buried the truth."

"What happened after you published the data?" Antony asked.

"I was crucified. Dianna accused me of being a doomsday charlatan, and people attacked my ideas, then me personally."

"But in 2029, for the second time, Apophis didn't hit?"

"True," Marcus leaned forward like he was itching to fight, "but it was by a razor-thin margin. It was another fatalistic day, Friday the 13th. Apophis was so close we could see it with the naked eye for the first time in recorded history. I was outside watching it and thinking how far we'd come from a small white dot on a dark screen in 2004."

"What was the public reaction when Apophis didn't strike?"

"I was completely de-platformed. I couldn't go into public without being physically abused. Beyond face-to-face conversations and small unlisted online gatherings, I was silenced."

"Then, seven years later, on April 9th, 2036, Apophis finally struck Earth," Antony said before taking a long, dramatic pause. "Tell me what you were doing on impact day?"

"I was asleep, and my wife, Monica, started shaking me and yelling about the news. The main asteroid and a few asteroid moons had already taken out multiple cities across Europe, Africa, and Asia. No one knew how many more were coming over the next few hours. I can still feel the teeth-rattling roar as one large asteroid passed over us. Monica and I ran out to our porch and watched it blaze a trail eastward across the atmosphere."

"That one hit New York City, killing everyone in the metropolitan area instantly, didn't it?"

"Vaporized them. Like everyone else in the other ten megacities Apophis destroyed. This collision was determined four and a half billion years ago when our solar system formed. It was a feeling of utter disbelief that I was alive to witness this. It took days for the strikes to play out, but then we plunged into the real hardship of rebuilding."

"What cities were hit? Can you list them all?"

"Paris, Kinshasa, Cairo, Moscow, Istanbul, Delhi, Shanghai, Tokyo, Mexico City, New York, and Sao Paulo. Dianna was off by 17 percent when she said two hundred million died in the megacities. It was two hundred and thirty-four point two million."

"What'd you feel when this was happening? You'd warned everyone—now it was real."

"Sadness. Anger. Fear. Empathy. The emotions came in alternating waves. But I recall feeling frustrated it could've been avoided. With gradual intervention, we could've ensured Apophis wasn't a threat. I'd been right," Marcus had an ocean of tears in his eyes, "but I still failed to stop it."

"No more questions, Your Honor."

The court was silent.

Benedict lost no time in launching an attack against Marcus during cross-examination, "Mr. Adams. Your story is tragic, but how much of it is your fault?"

"I don't understand what you mean."

"It's clear from everyone's testimony, that you were hostile toward superiors. Do you deny this?"

"No, because I was right."

"Yet, you failed. You said so. Because every step of the way, you turned allies into enemies. If you believed your conclusions, then wasn't a more political path prudent?"

"Possibly."

"You claim to be an optimistic man—"

"Absolutely. I may not be as enthusiastic as I once was," Marcus interjected, "but I still believe in our collective power to improve the world. Tomorrow will be a better day."

"Do you give people the benefit of the doubt?"

"Yes."

"Then why is there no example of this behavior between you and General Kos? From what I can tell, it was a purely antagonistic relationship where you repeatedly screamed about the sky falling while berating her for not believing you, despite your many false prophecies. That doesn't seem to match your own description as optimistic and accepting."

"That's because I saw her for what she really—"

"Mr. Adams, she is a decorated—"

"Accolades and commendations don't mean shit. Promotions are all she cared about, so of course she got them. I already said she was calculated. She used to joke that she joined the PDF because soldiers would be the last ones to starve if Apophis hit."

"And you have evidence of this conversation?"

Marcus was silent.

"I didn't think so. Just like you have no evidence that General Kos had you sign a resignation letter, or that she killed your old colleagues, or that you can recall what Hannah said when she visited because you were drunk. The thing about you, Mr. Adams, is you're a magnetic personality. You tell a great story. But General Kos saw through that, and the fact you couldn't control her drove you to insane lengths. You resented being secondary to her over the years. All we need to do is look at your social media posts to see how you default to hyperbolic and incendiary comments to hurt General Kos. Your behavior shows you wanted to muddy the waters to create a mutiny. Disrespecting superiors was standard operating procedure. You're a toxic bully, Mr. Adams, who destroyed your own office. Can't you admit it?"

"Object—" Antony started to shout, but it was too late to stop his brother.

"I was right and they were wrong." Marcus was seething on the stand.

"Are you even listening to yourself? You're proving my point," Benedict baited. "You doomed us to suffer the worst genocide in human history."

"HOW DARE YOU PUT THIS ON ME YOU PIECE OF SHIT!"

"Your Honor, the prosecution would like to introduce nearly identical comments from the defendant aimed against General Kos during his arrest and then again during his interrogation. In it, you'll see Mr. Adams resorted to the same tirades and threats after the polygraph deemed him to be deceptive."

"She forced me to take that," Marcus fidgeted.

"Can you repeat that?" asked Benedict.

"Recess request to speak with my client, Your Honor," Antony said from the orchestra pit.

"Overruled. You'll answer the question, Mr. Adams," Judge Jordan commanded.

"At every step along the way Dianna has been doing things outside the law to ensure I'm convicted, that way she'll have a scapegoat to pin the public outrage on. She did this with my resignation letter, she did it again when I was arrested without signing my charge sheet, and she never got my consent for the polygraph. She's playing me, you, all of us."

Antony didn't have to hang his head for Marcus to know he was disappointed. But before he could feel any regret, Benedict hit again, "Your Honor, we'd like to enter the signed charge sheet from Mr. Adams's arrest along with his video consent to be polygraphed into evidence."

"I never filmed a consent video," replied Marcus.

Benedict played a short clip on screens throughout the theater showing Marcus in the interrogation room telling the camera he was willing to take a polygraph to clear his name. His ears were ringing, and the hair on his body was standing on end. She'd already faked whatever evidence was necessary to prove the case against him.

"What do you make of that, Mr. Adams?"

There was a long pause.

"MR. ADAMS," Benedict shouted, "the video is irrefutable proof that what you just said was a lie."

"It's a deep fake," Marcus slouched. "Generated with AI using footage from my polygraph. Give me a computer and a few hours, and I can make a video of Dianna proclaiming my innocence."

"So your answer to official PDF evidence, which resulted from a transparent chain of custody involving dozens of individuals, is that a grand conspiracy is being played out against you? Everything you've claimed has been proven categorically false time and time again. The only people vouching for your character at this point have questionably close relationships with you, and none has the spotless credibility of General Kos. You're the trickster in this, Mr. Adams, not everyone else. You said you love card tricks. What are they if not an act of deception, a skill for which you are an undisputed master? You're also a heretic, Marcus, talking about Mayan calendars, Friday the 13th, and Nostradamus doomsdays despite a scientific consensus to the contrary. How can you sit before this court and public, playing the victim? Billions died because of you!"

"I KNEW I WAS RIGHT AND THEY DIDN'T LISTEN!"

"You're blindly overconfident," Benedict said.

"You have no idea the burden I've carried. I spent every moment, literally every single minute I was awake, trying to prevent

Apophis. I bankrupted myself warning the world because I knew the voice in my mind and my gut feelings were correct. Apophis was a clear and present danger."

"A voice? Like a demon?"

"No. A daemon, not a demon. Like the voice Socrates said inspired his greatest ideas and actions. That voice has been my companion every moment of every day. And at night, I was haunted by lucid visions of the carnage to come. I thought they'd go away after Apophis hit, but they never stopped. You don't get to pretend as if you know what that's like, or the emotional drain these dreams—"

Benedict cut him off, "Your Honor, we move for another Article 32 investigation to obtain the defendant's dream data from any of his various biometric devices. It's our belief this data goes directly to the defendant's motive under the prosecuting articles of this case."

"Objection," Antony was dismayed. "Separate charges mean a separate trial."

"The prosecution is willing to dismiss the current charges and bring them again after his dream data is analyzed," replied Benedict. "The trial can start over if the defense wishes."

"Isn't that double jeopardy?" Marcus asked.

"This is a military court. You don't have that protection," Judge Jordan explained before turning to the defense counsel. "Mr. Adams, what would you like to do?"

Antony recognized their defeat. "We consent to the Article 32."

"We'll pause here," said Judge Jordan. "We'll set a date to resume as the investigation unfolds. Bailiff, escort the defendant back to his cell."

21

MEMBERS ONLY

"What does this mean?" Marcus asked through the bars of his cell.

"We wait. That's all we can do," replied Antony.

The weeks dragged on. Marcus endlessly paced the small path of his personal prison. Feelings of dread and uncertainty where constant companions. He knew everything was going against him right now, but he was committed to staying calm and tried to remain centered. Then Antony arrived.

"I have something serious to talk to you about."

"Okay?" Marcus replied.

"I got this note claiming to be from Lindsay."

"I never worked with a Lindsay at the PDF."

"She's one of the jurors. If this document is real, it'll blow our case apart. She can't be contacting you, and that says nothing about Lindsay's claims in the letter."

"Let me see it," Marcus scanned the note.

"She says Dianna put her on the jury and gave her explicit directions to vote guilty," Antony explained. "She suspects that the rest of the jury has been similarly instructed."

"How could a juror get something like this out?" Marcus asked.

"They can't. They're on total lockdown."

"This is Dianna. She's gloating. Like how serial killers taunt the police."

"Why would she send a letter exposing herself?"

"So she can know that I know the extent of what she's done to me."

Antony's face turned white. "God. Damn. It."

"We can't prove this letter is real, right?"

"Not unless Lindsay admits to writing it and can explain how she got it to us," said Antony.

"Packing the jury is a very Dianna move. She wants me to know my fate is sealed."

"Stop."

"NO!" Marcus shouted, "YOU STOP, ANTONY! Dianna played this masterfully, down to the most minute details. Like you said when this started, I'm in checkmate. I felt it then and hoped it wasn't true. But it is. I can accept it now. You need to too."

A long silence dragged on before Marcus spoke, "Dianna knew about the dream data long ago. I told Hannah in detail about the nightmares when she visited me."

"Why would you do that?" Antony asked.

"I was drunk. She made me feel safe. Dianna knew she could use this against me. It's her October surprise."

"We have to try and—"

"You're not listening," Marcus snapped. "I'm done playing her game. It's taken me thirty-five years to realize I was playing. I'm done fighting, and I order you as my lawyer, and beg you as my brother, to please stop fighting."

"I love you so listen—"

"No! I won't, Antony. It's over. She's going to ensure I die. I'm fine with it. Focus only on what's in front of us, right? That's what you said. Death is what's in front of me now. All I can do is face it with my head held high. The ice bitch won."

News coverage of the investigation had hit a fever pitch by the time trial resumed on Halloween, a holiday that—unlike the Fourth of July—had been a casualty of Apophis. Benedict called Dianna to the stand again, introducing Marcus's biometric data into evidence. The video he played of Marcus's dreams was a near-perfect match of the publicly available video of Apophis's annihilation of the eleven megacities. Timestamps of his dreams showed they'd preceded the real footage by decades.

Marcus knew this data was genuine; he'd lived it nightly. And now that he'd resigned himself to fate, the trial felt like it was in fast forward, only being interrupted by key moments like Benedict's final questions for Dianna.

"Dr. Kos," Benedict emphasized her persona as a science celebrity now rather than a military general, "how do you explain the near-perfect match between visions captured in Marcus's dreams and the actual destruction caused by Apophis? Is this random chance? Another unlikely, but possible, outcome?"

"No."

Chatter spread around the theater, which Judge Jordan was unable to stop for several minutes.

"Please repeat your answer," said Benedict.

"No. As a scientist, there's no way I can believe this is random chance. The joint probability is so low it defies credulity. Yes, it is randomly possible, but it's incredibly improbable."

"What are you saying, General?"

"Marcus claimed our megacities were destroyed by a sequence of events that began billions of years ago. Maybe. Another explanation is someone, or something, used a master algorithm against us."

"Please explain what that is," Benedict asked.

"If the universe follows deterministic rules, then there must be an algorithm that can be used to understand, predict, and manipulate everything within those rules. It seems clear to me this wasn't a random event at all. Someone sent those rocks raining down on our homes. It's clear from his dreams, and the demon voices he admitted to hearing, that Marcus was an agent, unwittingly or not, for this unknown enemy. It's also clear this force has military superiority and they've fired the first shot at humanity. Finally, it's clear to me that the world needs the PDF more than ever. War is upon us, and we're just realizing we're in the fight."

"Your witness," Benedict said as he left the stage.

"We meet again, Dr. General," said Antony.

"Charmed."

"Why did you wait all these years to come after Marcus? It'd been eighteen years since the NostRa mission failed."

"I was busy saving the world, remember?"

"Well, that was a colossal waste of time, because you failed, General. The asteroid hit. Look around," Antony spun in place with his arms out, "is this your idea of victorious salvation?"

"We faced the biggest crisis in human history, and despite the disinformation and interference from your traitorous brother, we're still standing. Tomorrow will be a better day."

"It's funny you say that, because that's something Marcus says all the time, and you've never listened to him. Not about this. Not about Apophis. You had it out for him from the beginning because you resented his premonitions. Now you're trying to appropriate his narrative, just like you did with his work during your career together. When he pushed back, you drove him out of the PDF in a way you knew you could leverage. When he wouldn't back down, you de-platformed him. You insisted on the desertion charge against him because you hoped it would get him killed before trial. Let's not even mention the mysterious attack on this court, or how you've repeatedly forged evidence and packed this jury with people loyal to—"

"Objection, intimidating the witness," Benedict said.

"How can I intimidate one of the most powerful individuals in the world?" Antony mocked. "She's a general for God's sake."

"Overruled. Mr. Adams, we're in the final stretch, so reflect on the outcome you hope to accomplish for your client, and modify your behavior accordingly," said Judge Jordan.

"General, I'd like you to look at something." Antony received a single piece of paper from Lucius covered in mathematical proofs.

Dianna disinterestedly reviewed it.

"Can you tell me what that is?" Antony asked.

"Math," Dianna replied.

The audience shared a moment of nervous laughter.

"What does it say? You're a scientist, translate it."

"I'm not going to do that."

"Why not?" Antony asked.

"Because I'm done playing games with you."

"You can leave when you answer my question. Hand to science," Antony said as he placed his left hand over his heart and held his right hand to the sky.

There was a silent standoff between them.

"You can't do it, can you, Dianna?"

"GENERAL KOS! I'm a leader! Calculus is below my pay grade."

"Right. What about probability? That's below you too? Is that why you gave contradictory answers about the chance of your inner circle dropping like flies and my brother seeing a reality that ultimately came true? Which you claim was the work of an unseen force? And you have the audacity to call him crazy? For the record, General, the paper you're holding is the Lagrangian point calculations Marcus made for Apophis, showing it'd capture asteroid 2004 VD17 in its 2034 flyby. The very same asteroid that just hit our moon. You're a scientist who can't science. And while I suspect you're a brilliant strategist, you've been so blind in your desire to get Marcus you've never looked beyond his death. What will you do if he's executed? How will you succeed in a fight against this unseen force once Marcus is gone, given you've siphoned all your ideas off him? He's not another disposable colleague you can kill."

"MR. ADAMS!" yelled Judge Jordan, "I AM FINDING YOU IN CONTEMPT OF COURT. YOU WILL SERVE A MONTH IN THE BRIG AFTER THIS TRIAL FOR THAT LAST COMMENT!"

"A month? That's a steal of a deal. Hey, Dianna," Antony said in his best game show voice, "gooooooo fuck yourself."

The room exploded with shouts of disapproval, and people threw whatever they could find at Antony and Marcus; their lack of precision rained down havoc on everyone in the lower theater seats.

"YOU'RE AN IMPOSTER AND YOU KNOW IT!" Antony shouted over the crowd. Dianna sat confidently amidst the chaos.

"THE DEFENSE IS DONE! YOU'VE EARNED YOURSELF SIX MONTHS, MR. ADAMS!" Judge Jordan regained composure. "General Kos, you can step down. If there are any more issues with the defense or his counsel, they'll be mediated by force. Do we understand one another?"

"I did the crime, I'll do the time, Judge. Best behavior from here on out," Antony replied.

"We're moving to closing arguments," Judge Jordan barked. "Prosecution has the floor."

Benedict was eloquent and articulate, creating an emotionally charged moment as he repeated his indictment of Marcus's character, again blaming him for the fate of the world. Antony took the opposite approach, briefly reminding everyone in simple terms that Marcus had been right and was railroaded by the PDF for their own failures.

"Does the prosecution have a rebuttal?" asked Judge Jordan.

"I don't believe one's needed, Your Honor. The Adams brothers showed their character throughout the trial. We're ready to move to the verdict."

Judge Jordan instructed the jury on what their obligation was and sent them off to vote. Before anyone could clear the run-down theater, the jury returned. Foreman Quinn read their verdict. "On both the article 107 charge of making false official statements and the article 95 charge of mutiny, we find the defendant Marcus Winthrop Adams to be guilty."

The whole world seemed to erupt in cries of jubilation. Judge Jordan didn't try to control them, opting instead to update the charge sheet against Marcus while waiting the room out. After a few disorderly minutes, the court was quiet again.

Judge Jordan continued, "The prosecution and defense waived their rights to aggression and mitigation over the convict's redeemable qualities—"

Marcus felt a tinge of pain hearing himself called the convict and not the defendant.

"—the prosecution is recommending death. We'll hear directly from Marcus Adams, who may offer an apology and propose a different punishment before the jury's sentencing vote."

Marcus knew he'd do nothing of the sort as he limped onto the stage, standing silently before speaking. "During the months of my confinement, I've thought about this moment a lot. I dreaded it, but now that it's here, I don't understand why I was ever so afraid. During the uncertainty, I prepared dozens of speeches, but instead, I want to say two things: you're all so important, it'll be you who builds the better tomorrow, not Dianna and other leaders. Beware of wolves in shepherds' clothing. Second, I have no doubt you'll regret this moment, to see it for what it is, a mark of historical shame. Please remember I've already forgiven you."

The room was ice cold.

"Your alternative sentence?" asked Judge Jordan.

"I don't have one."

"Well, you need to offer something, Mr. Adams."

"The PDF could give me Dianna's job and support my family until I die of natural causes."

The court snickered again at Marcus. Judge Jordan instructed the jury on how to proceed, and just as before, they returned quickly, this time voting unanimously for death. The room renewed their euphoria as Marcus was escorted out by guards to ensure the mob didn't attempt vigilante justice.

Marcus was sitting silently in his cell when Antony arrived with Monica. Everyone was crying, but they knew they had to say goodbye, which helped them focus on the happy memories they'd made together. After Monica left, Antony explained decimation, "This is something I hoped we'd never discuss."

"Out with it," Marcus gripped the cell bars with steady hands.

"Tomorrow, you'll be moved to a pre-confinement chamber. It's a windowless pod they'll haul out to the Salt Flats. On the way, you can eat your final meal—"

"Pass. Food is scarce, and I won't get any mileage out of the calories."

"A kind gesture for an undeserving world."

"It will help," Marcus insisted.

"I hope you still feel that way when you reach the Salt Flats and witness the true nature of this thankless mob."

"Will it be broadcast?"

"Yes. Dianna wouldn't waste the chance to prove her power."

"One final moment to be the center of attention," Marcus got a small laugh from Antony, who wiped a stray tear from his eye.

"When they open your pod," Antony continued, "you'll be facing a pathway a hundred feet long running eastward with nine of your coworkers from the PDF lined up along the way. You'll face each, one at a time, as you approach your funeral pyre at the far end of the path. That's where you'll be killed and cremated."

"I'd be shocked if Dianna can find nine people from our team who are still alive."

"She only has to find eight."

"Why? It's decimation, me plus eight doesn't equal ten."

"She'll be the final person you'll face. Everyone gets a moment to say something to you. I can only imagine what she's prepared."

"It doesn't matter. How do I die?" Marcus stared at Antony.

"Two MPs will escort you to the pyre. You'll have a black hood placed on your head and a golden plasma pulse collar secured around your neck. You'll lay down, and the collar will send a focused beam of energy through your neck. It's a guillotine for the digital age."

The next morning came quickly despite a sleepless night that'd been sacrificed for final reflections. Marcus found his pre-confinement pod to be a unique and interesting space, another new place beyond his cell, the hospital, and the roofless theater. When the door was finally opened, the pure white of the Salt Flats scorched his eyes, making it impossible to see anything as he was pulled from the pod. When his vision returned, he didn't recognize any of the PDF members tapped for the macabre task. Their uniforms popped against the canvas of salt they stood upon.

The public surrounded him, ready to receive his blood offering. They'd donned the PDF's colors, creating an expansive sea of crimson.

Marcus was pushed forward. He didn't internalize a word anyone said to him; he was focused on his pyre until he reached

Dianna. Smiling, she leaned into his right ear and giddily whispered two words: "I won."

She stepped back, resting her hands on his shoulders. Marcus was pushed again to the end of his path and the base of his funeral pyre. The large pile of pinewood, fueled with a potassium chloride accelerant, would engulf his body in a beautiful blue hue.

Marcus shook off the MPs, who turned to face Dianna for approval. She nodded, and Marcus walked himself up the pyre, placed the hood on his head, and secured the golden collar around his neck before laying down, skyward, to face his fate. The noise of plasma charging in the collar drowned out the roar of the mob; it was a soothing sound.

[Sequence ID# 417] [Data Ends]

Marcus woke, memory clean, and sicker than ever. Brad was waiting in the locker room with a mammoth smile. "Congratulations, Marcus. I'm happy—no, I'm OUT OF MY MIND to say you've passed Selection!"

"What?"

"You're done."

Marcus thought this moment was far in his future.

Brad motioned toward a locker.

19. MARCUS

"You said this would take months."

"Could, not would. I gave you an average. Under normal conditions, half the proxies do it faster, and half do it slower. No one's been this fast! I know outliers like you exist, they're why I get up every morning, I just haven't met one yet!"

Marcus wasn't convinced.

"You're one in a billion!" Brad's words were flying faster than Marcus could catch. "At most, there are six others like you on Earth. You can accelerate Project Noble to the first milestone, M1, and integration beyond that, by accepting your rightful position in the Cohort."

Marcus was frozen.

"If you say no, there'll be no hard feelings. But you won't be able to come back. If you say yes, you'll never be turned away. Ever. Those are your paths. Choose one and start walking."

"I'm in."

PART VII

AMOROUS VOX

FRIDAY, MARCH 18, +1 NE

22

PROPITIATION

Marcus was almost home when it finally sunk in: he was a member of the Cohort now. He wanted to scream what he'd accomplished to the world, but no one was listening. Dianna wasn't speaking to him, Antony was recovering, and he didn't know the woman from Nerio's name or number. *It was lonely at the top*, he thought as he headed home. *Jordan was his only hope.*

Marcus found Jordan alone at their ornate dining room table, laughing hysterically at something on his tablet. The slow sway of his upper body indicated his state of intoxication as he shoveled forkfuls of Costco chocolate cake into his mouth.

"Are you going to eat the whole thing?"

"Welcome home, bro." Jordan didn't look up. "Probably."

"That has more sugar than a colonial American ate in a year …"

"USA! USA! USA!" Jordan chanted. "Ameda and Bonnie were helping me with it earlier. Fucking quitters."

"Where are they now?"

"Basement. We've been working on a track together." Jordan spun his tablet around to face Marcus. "You gotta see this."

"What am I looking at?"

"This group recruits ugly people for a blind date with one of their friends. Then they program a Tek complement to transform the beast into a beauty. Everything's recorded POV-style through the Tek. If their friend bangs the beastie, then a bet is on."

"If they're having sex, what's the bet about?"

"Whether their friend will turn off the Tek and reveal the real person they're with. It's called 'whiting out' because if their friend is brave, they'll remember everything, even if they don't want to."

"I thought Tek was the devil ..."

"Finding this hilarious and knowing Tek is the end of society aren't mutually exclusive. You're home late for a school night."

Marcus was so high from success that he'd lost track of time.

Jordan noticed the hesitation. "What time do you think it is?"

Marcus used the fact it was dark outside to guess, "Eight?"

"WRONG!" Jordan screamed. "It's half past midnight."

"What?" Marcus paced the house looking at all the clocks; each confirmed Jordan's truth.

Jordan continued his friendly fire, "Jesus, dude. The Federation is scrambling your brain in that Lab."

Jordan was decked out in late-1980s neon green, so Marcus pushed the focus back onto his friend. "What's with the outfit?"

"Bonnie, Ameda, and I snuck into a Paddy's Day pub crawl. We got busted, but not before we consumed enough green beer to kill a baby rhino. Word on the street, though, is the best party happens at Nerio …," Jordan tested Marcus, "… where were you last night? I let Bonnie in around 2:00 a.m., and you were AWOL."

"I was with Antony at the Black Market. But you knew that already, or you wouldn't be on this fishing expedition."

"Just checking," Jordan said, stuffing his mouth. "I'm just trying to gauge when the Federation's mind control kicks in."

"I passed Selection tonight. I'm officially part of the Cohort."

Jordan was sobered by the unexpected news, and focus returned to his eyes. "Fuck … I mean congrats—wait, what does this mean?"

"I'm not sure yet. I know it won't change anything about my normal life. But I'll get to work with the rest of the Cohort now."

"Normal life? It's laughable you can use that word to describe this situation. NOTHING ABOUT THIS IS NORMAL, MAR—!"

"Please don't do this," Marcus cut him off, "not tonight."

"You said you'd respect my ability to rant, AND THIS IS WHAT THAT LOOKS LIKE, BRO!"

Ameda and Bonnie appeared, summoned by Jordan's shouting.

"Is everything okay?" Ameda asked.

"Yes," Marcus abated.

Bonnie stood next to Jordan.

"Do you guys mind? We were in the middle of a private conversation."

"What happened to Mr. Aboveboard?" Jordan taunted.

Brad's advice about discretion kept looping in Marcus's mind.

"I told you how the Lyceum conspirators were scanning Tek," Jordan leaned his chair onto its back legs, "they switched tactics since it made them sick, and scanned users' brains instead. Good thing too, because we've figured out how Tek functions, which by extension, is probably also how your Sequences work."

Marcus accepted his loss of informational control. "And?"

"They're hallucinations. Whenever a person started using Tek, their pineal gland came alive with activity. It was subtle until we knew what to look for, then we realized it was going crazy."

"What's the pineal gland?" Bonnie asked.

"A pinecone-shaped lobe the size of a grain of rice dead center in the brain," Jordan explained. "Ancient cultures called it the third eye, which is amazing since it evolved to help with vision."

"Bill talked about this in class," Ameda asserted.

Bonnie scrunched her brow. "Why don't I remember this?"

"Don't feel bad," Marcus answered. "Neither do I."

Jordan smirked. "Bill told us the philosopher Descartes thought the pineal was the seat of the human soul because it isn't divided into two lobes like the rest of the brain. Technically it's not even part of the brain because it sits outside the blood-brain barrier."

"You've lost me, dude," Marcus folded his arms.

"The pineal gland is a bridge between the brain and the body. It controls the release of melatonin, which regulates our biological clock and tells you when to go to sleep or when to wake up."

"Seriously, bring it home," Marcus challenged. "What does this have to do with Tek ... or Subsumption?"

"You experienced time dilation tonight because Brad's been fucking with your pineal," Jordan was spitting chocolate with his words. "Remember the documentary I asked you to watch?"

"You'll have to be more specific," Marcus grumbled. "There've been hundreds of those over the years."

"The one with Joe Rogan about DMT," Jordan clarified.

"The Spirit Molecule?" Bonnie asked.

"Yes," Jordan affirmed. "Dimethyltryptamine is made by the pineal gland. It's involved with hallucinations, near-death experiences, and God knows what else. Federation technology is just controlled hallucinations using the pineal. The user's eyes even dance around like they're in REM sleep when using SIMs."

Marcus rolled his eyes. "It's an interesting theory."

"It's irrefutable if you're brave enough to connect the dots."

"Great chat, everyone. Good luck with the music-making." Marcus accomplished a ceasefire by moving to his room. *Jordan had violated his trust tonight by forcing the issue in front of other people*, Marcus thought while lying in bed. *This was a disturbing new pattern between them whenever the Federation was involved.* Angry and unable to sleep, he was deep into studying when his phone rang; Dianna was calling. *Had Jordan already told her about passing Selection?*

Marcus took a deep breath. "Hello."

"Hi," was all Dianna replied.

A silent standoff ensued.

Marcus blinked first, "How are you?"

"Not good, Marcus. Not good at all. I've been experiencing waves of anxiety since our fight. Then last night, it was like someone flipped a switch, and I couldn't feel our connection anymore. It was impossible to sleep. I went to the clinic and buried myself in work, but all day it kept building—it feels like a giant rift has opened between us. I hate it. A few hours ago, it spiked again. Something has to change. I can't live like this."

Marcus suspected she knew about the Cohort, and this was a roundabout way of testing him. "Have you talked to Jordan."

"Yes," Dianna confirmed.

His stomach churned, "When?"

"He called after your class yesterday and apologized for the text message. He said you planned to tell me about Selection, but he beat you to it. I explained how you'd lied and how mad I was, then he helped me focus on how special you are and the connection we share. He said your chances of passing Selection are basically zero, so I'm worrying for nothing."

Marcus had emotional Déjà vu, but omission wasn't the same as lying, so he said nothing about already passing Selection.

"We need time alone, Marcus. To reconnect and talk like we used to before the world drove a wedge between us. I want us to understand each other more and figure out what future we can still make together. I don't want things to end like this."

Marcus desired Dianna more than he wanted to admit. "What if I take you to my family's house in the mountains tomorrow after class? I can cook for us. We can build a fire and talk through things. We'll have the entire weekend if we want it."

"Sounds lovely!" Dianna did an emotional one-eighty. "Thank you, sweetheart. I can't tell you how much better I already feel."

"Me too."

"I hate to go, but someone just walked into the clinic."

"It's okay. See you soon," Marcus replied.

Dianna kissed the air.

23

QUAKING POPULARES

Marcus woke up with his face pressed into a textbook. A pool of drool warped its words into an inkblot resembling one of Dianna's Rorschach tests. The sun wasn't up yet, but he felt rested for the first time that week. Marcus usually spent Fridays with Jordan, but the Lab was calling his name, so he completed his daily affirmation, wrote a note promising to catch up with Jordan at class, and walked to Carlson Hall.

"Like the rising sun in all its splendor, behold Marcus!" Brad's eyes were alight. "Since you're part of the inner circle now, I'll introduce you to another Cohort member. She's in a Sequence at the moment. Sit down and let's catch up first. Want a coffee?"

"That'd be great."

"Give me a sec."

Marcus hoped a Black-Market-like orb would deliver his drink, but Brad fetched it himself. The woman from Nerio was right; normal life felt inconvenient. Her memory had imprinted on him so powerfully that for a moment, he could smell her perfume again.

"How's it going?" Brad handed Marcus the drink. "Have you decided how much Tek you want for your quota?"

"I thought I just took whatever you gave me."

"What is this, the Soviet Union? That'd be a ration, Comrade!" Brad said in his best Russian accent before seamlessly switching back to his usual self. "A quota is different. It's your reservation price, what you need in exchange for your time. You're the only person who knows your worth, so you tell me."

"I'm not doing this for the money—"

"Altruism is admirable, but everyone's got to eat."

"I don't want the headache of selling it."

"It's a frictionless process," Brad encouraged. "You tell us what portion of your quota you want sold and we deliver it to Tek-Mart, then you get paid to a crypto account only you control. Everything happens in the background, so you don't have to do anything."

After Antony's warning about the Darrows, Marcus had zero desire to do business with Tek-Mart.

"There's no rush. Take all the time you need to decide, and we'll settle up later. I'm good for it."

"Plus, I know where you live," Marcus said, eliciting a hearty laugh from Brad. "I have a couple questions for you, not about the quota, if that's okay?"

Brad grinned. "And I have at least three answers."

"What can you tell me about the Confederation?"

Brad removed his glasses, rubbed the bridge of his nose, and placed them back on his face. "What I'm going to share with you is need-to-know information. Your governments requested we wait until M1 is reached before sharing these details with the general public, so discretion is advisable."

"I'll keep my mouth shut," Marcus promised.

"Seriously though," Brad continued. "You saw how quickly your form lost its collective mind from a submicroscopic pathogen with a 99% survival rate. The existence of hostile humanoid giants could send them into another toilet-paper buying tizzy."

"Giants?"

"The Confederation's Form comes in two sizes. It's a result of their segregated society, which occupies two planets in their home system of Vega. The majority of their Form are indistinguishable from your own—same size, appearance, and biological functionality. These individuals occupy Vega Major, a planet with similar mass and atmospheric density to Earth. But the elite class live on Vega Minor, which has less mass and a thicker oxygenated atmosphere. They still look identical to your Form but are 40 percent larger. The typical citizen of Vega Minor is over eight feet tall."

"Holy shit!" Marcus leaned forward.

"Their size isn't as advantageous as you might think. Their response time is fractionally slower since electrical signals in their body have to travel further. It's harder for them to maneuver on a planet like Earth because their bodies are conditioned to lower gravity."

"Do they ever leave Vega Minor?"

"Rarely. They have something like your EXO if they venture beyond their planet, but Confederation elites are religious zealots hiding behind ancient doctrine so they can shelter-in-place."

"How are they planning to invade Earth then?" Marcus asked.

"The citizens of Vega Major are their strike force. These troops, assisted by artificial entities similar to Hi!-D, have conquered the rest of the known universe, turning everything they touch into a Confederation colony. *Imperium sine fine.*"

"An empire without end," Marcus translated.

"Bravo! Do you know about the Fermi Paradox?"

"It sounds familiar."

"Your mother would be rolling in her grave! It was a theory put forward by Italian-American physicist Enrico Fermi to explain the absence of evidence for extraterrestrials."

"You guys blew that one out of the water," Marcus mused.

"Indeed," Brad smiled. "The Paradox's answer is rather elegant. The Confederation controls everything other than Earth, and they're silently stalking you from afar in anticipation of an invasion. Like a pack of wolves, they've surrounded you, relying on the element of surprise. It's one of the reasons we warned you. We don't want to see you ambushed … if you're going to fight, you should at least see it coming."

"How have you survived their conquest?"

"In every sci-fi story, the galactic empire faces a rebellion. We're mobile and outside their domain of control. Earth is their final prize. It's why you're so important, and why we're helping. Not to sound unnecessarily dramatic, but the fate of your world will literally determine the universal balance."

"What do they want?"

"Borrowing from your astronomical lexicon, you should think of the Confederation's goal as a Redshift, focused on creating divisions within a Form and drawing them ever further apart so they can be controlled. The Federation's goal is the opposite, a Blueshift, focused on creating unity within a Form to help them reach higher stages of enlightenment and progress."

Marcus paused to mentally catalog the details of their conversation, finding a final unknown. "How similar are their artificial entities to Hi!-D?"

"Hi!-D is one of a kind because she was built using your Form as the foundation of her social cortex. She has no equal."

"What's a social cortex?" Marcus asked.

"There are many ways to create artificial intelligence. In Hi!-D's case, she's based on a Subsumption architecture—"

"Is that where the Cohort got the name for the Sequences?"

"Yes," Brad admitted. "I biased things when I explained Hi!-D to the first member of the Cohort. The name stuck. Instead of navigating the world through mental representations of every possible detail, Hi!-D couples her sensory information with stream-of-action information in a 'bottom-up' layered approach. She's far more complex than her Confederation counterparts built with a 'top-down' approach."

"Where does all the action information for her social cortex come from, if it's not the result of her own sensory experience?"

"From you!" Brad beamed. "Largely from the Sequence data."

Marcus was lost in thought when Brad probed him, "What was your second question?"

"I don't remember anymore."

"It'll come back to you. Speaking of Sequences, we didn't follow up on your sickness. Did it happen again?"

"Yes. I felt terrible, but it faded fast because of my excitement over passing Selection."

"That was exciting, and this is very interesting. Yesterday was far and away the longest Sequence we've done together. I thought it'd make your sickness worse. Your issue must be logarithmic."

"Meaning?" Marcus inquired.

"It climbs quickly to an upper plateau, then stays there. Length has nothing to do with it. In some ways, that's good news for you."

"Great … so I'll get equally sick from any length Sequence?"

Brad glanced at his notes before replying, "Yes. Though it wasn't my intention to go so long yesterday. I just determine the set and setting. It's your job to navigate the space. You committed to continuing, and that stamina pushed you across the Selection finish line." Brad raised his drink to salute Marcus. "How's the rest of your life? You balancing everything?"

"Things are improving. Dianna wants to reconcile."

"What did she say about passing Selection?"

"That's to be determined. I'm taking her to my family's house at Sundance after class. I'll tell her when the moment is right. She requires a lot of personality management."

"That's on Mount Timpanogos?"

"You know it?" Marcus challenged.

"I've never been, but I've studied the quaking aspen trees all around those mountains. Your Form gave them a perfect name."

"Populus?"

"It's such an old word that we don't know where it comes from."

"It means 'the people,' right? That's what my dad said."

"Your dad would've cleaned up on *Jeopardy*. It's a fitting name since each tree gives an illusion of being an isolated individual."

"How's it an illusion?"

"An entire colony of fifty-thousand trees spread out over tens of thousands of feet is a single life form with one genetic code and a common root system. This invisible connection shows up when the trees of each colony change color in unison. I haven't seen it for myself. Yet."

"It's true. Every fall night, my mother took us hiking through the forest to see the patchwork of colors on the mountainside."

"What great memories."

"It's why my family moved there. My mom loved the aspens. She thought they were immortal. She was very superstitious."

"She might be correct. An aspen can live thousands of years, and no one knows how long their roots survive. Have you visited Pando here in Utah?"

"Not that I know of."

"It's one of the oldest life forms on your planet. It's at least 80,000 years young. Some of your Form think it's capable of living millions of years. Aspens are survivors, adapting to every climate across the planet. Plus, they can legit clone themselves."

"Is that how they live so long?" Marcus finished his drink.

"No, cloning creates monoculture, and an identical genetic version of a Form makes it vulnerable to freak mutations, predators, and competitors. Cloning has pitfalls, like in that movie *Multiplicity*."

"Never seen it," Marcus replied.

"What?" Brad bounced with excitement. "It's Batman at his best! Michael Keaton's character clones himself, and when one of his clones copies itself, it's like the worst of royal inbreeding. A copy of a copy is never as good. How tall are the Aspens by your house?"

"Maybe fifty feet? I know they're taller than usual."

"Aspens don't do well in the shade, so that colony expresses an advantageous difference. But what if it went the other direction and the colony only grew two feet high? If it kept cloning itself as taller pine trees showed up, the whole colony would collapse."

"I've seen that, where the pines snuffed out all the Aspens."

"They can't compete with the taller conifers. But below ground, their root waits for a fire to clear the forest, then it sends out thousands of new Aspens unobstructed. It's a poetic image of life rising from the ashes. Like I said, they're survivors. I love them."

"You should come to Sundance in the fall and see the colors for yourself."

"Deal! I'll bring the good looks, humor, and charm. You bring me."

Marcus could feel their bond deepening.

"So you're here to work, yes?" Brad asked.

"Yup. But I have to be gone before noon for class."

"You're the boss now. Let's go meet Monica."

Monica was sitting at the far end of the locker room, back towards the newly arrived pair, watching a holographic projection of Antony's fight. The sight of his brother in the final moments of victory over Zedd stole Marcus's attention, so Brad jabbed an elbow into his abdomen to ensure a proper first impression. "Marcus, this is Monica Eames. Monica, this is Marcus Adams."

Marcus's heart fired like an errant rocket.

"It's nice to meet you, Marcus."

"Again."

"Yes," she clarified. "Nice to meet you *again*."

"You know each other?" Brad winked.

"We met at the Black Market. She's the woman I danced with."

Monica wasn't dolled up. Marcus's mother used to say "powder and paint make a girl what she ain't," but Monica was naturally beautiful.

"Welcome to the Cohort!"

"I know you just finished, but do you want to go again?" Brad asked.

"I'm always down for more." Monica winked.

"Suit up. Separately, for the sake of time and lawsuits."

"See you in a sec." Monica moved toward her locker, turning for a moment to gaze back at him before disappearing from view.

Marcus was disappointed to find his locker indistinguishable from the one he'd used as a proxy. As he entered the Liberty Bell, he noticed a subtle change in his EXO; the honeycombs over his heart were gold, forming the Roman numerals XIX.

"You'll have to be gentle," Brad announced over his invisible PA system. "This is Marcus's first tandem Sequence."

"What's that?" Marcus asked as the pair floated.

"A Sequence involving multiple Cohort members," Brad explained. "Same rules apply, but you'll share the set and setting."

"You're in for a treat," Monica replied. The golden numeral on her EXO expressed authority; she was the Cohort's first member.

Though he couldn't see her face through the suit, Marcus felt their connection coursing through his veins like it had at Nerio.

"This feels like a bad rom-com," Brad said over their silence.

[Sequence ID# 538] [Data Begins]

The last thing he remembered was saying he loved her, though not directly, so he clarified, "What I mean is if years from now you asked for the moment I knew I loved you, this would be it."

They'd stopped at the center of three converging alpine valleys. A towering ridgeline on three sides formed the outline of a bird of war; wings to the side, head held high in profile. They were standing on the heart of this imaginary bird, surrounded by red lupines and stargazers, Monica's favorite flowers. Their sweet scent of grapes saturated the nighttime, carrying off the pair's problems with the crisp mountain air. Moonlight bounced off a glacier descending one of the ridges, coming to rest in a nearby emerald-colored lake. Behind them, from where they'd come, rolling mountains faded from view. The silver underbellies of the lupines magnified the moonlight, illuminating everything.

Thousands of feet above them was the summit, capped by a small white shack on the edge of the sheer cliff face. Monica took his hand, and they continued their journey. It was silent here, allowing Marcus to hear the flowers sway in the soft wind. She guided him up a steep section of rock to the saddle, a low point in the ridgeline where they could look down both sides of the mountain. He scanned the western valley, but it was empty. There were no city lights, just a large body of water surrounded by wilderness. In the other direction was the aspen forest they'd traversed. The Milky Way was brushed boldly across the sky, each star feeling like it pierced through his skin, especially Orion's constellation.

"We need to sit," Monica said. "We'll be shown something soon."

They found a spot overlooking the blood-red meadows. The colors of this world pulsed in unison with the twinkle of the stars. It was so subtle Marcus questioned if it was happening.

"Do you see that?" he asked.

Without breaking her upward gaze, she whispered, "Shhh ... it's starting." Waves of auroras washed across the sky. Intense fields of purple, blue, and green slithered like silk scarves in the stellar wind. Marcus stood, inspired to try and get closer to the power of what he was seeing. Monica reached out and took his hand again. Together they stood immersed in the infinite, never looking at one another. Even the aspens were given eyes to bear witness to this moment.

[Sequence ID# 538] [Change Point, Data Restarts]

The last thing he remembered was standing in the middle of the lupine fields. The meadow changed colors with the light of Auroras racing overhead. Marcus had a strong feeling of Déjà vu. Monica was a hundred feet ahead, back facing him, as the valley turned a blue hue. She pointed westward; Hecate was rising. The intensifying light washed their eyes with pain as the planet peaked the ridgeline. It felt larger and closer than it should be. Without warning, the volume of the world amplified. Each sound had momentum, like a locomotive bearing down on them. Marcus grabbed his ears and squinted his eyes, he didn't want to lose Monica, but he was overwhelmed and fell to his knees in anguish.

Vibrations ricocheted across the meadow, knocking the breath from his lungs. He gasped for air, but none came, making it impossible to scream for help. Then, all was silent; the sound subsided, and the light faded. Monica was still standing with her back to him. He stood, stepping toward her when everything shook violently again. The ground tore open, creating an impassable rift filled with waves of liquid fire. The deafening roar returned ten times louder now, and the ridgeline that once stood powerfully over them crumbled into dust. The world was falling apart. Marcus forced his eyes open, suffering the blinding light again, only to find Monica had disappeared.

[Sequence ID# 538] [Data Ends]

Marcus woke up feeling as expected, sick, and with no memory of the cause. But he was happy to be beside Monica. As they lowered to the floor, his body begged for mercy, and he doubled over.

"Are you okay?" When Marcus didn't respond, she panicked. "Brad. BRAD!"

"I'm fine, Brad already knows about this. There's nothing he can do." Marcus tried to calm her concerns. "I get like this after the Sequences. It fades quickly. Really, I'm fine."

"I was going to ask if the Sequence was as good for you as it was for me, but that doesn't seem funny anymore," Monica huffed, getting a laugh from Marcus as he walked toward his locker.

His human clothes felt strange after a Sequence because, unlike the EXO, human fabrics rested against the skin. He checked his phone; four hours had passed.

Monica was waiting in the locker room in a chair that'd melted to conform to her curves. "It's great we'll be working together," she said. "Sit."

The chair moved as if it were alive, releasing its hug on Monica to make a second seat beside her for Marcus, but he didn't budge. The rest of the room was dark. No patterns or colors were scrolling across the walls; their thoughts were fixated on one another.

"I wish I could stay. I have class," Marcus lamented.

"Well, if we're going to work together," Monica stood and walked to him, "we should exchange info. Can I see your phone?"

He handed it to her, knowing what would happen.

"It was nice to see you again, Marcus. And to learn your name this time. Call me."

Marcus would have to run to class for the second time this week, but thankfully it was a warm day without a cloud in the sky. He caught up to Jordan at the Legacy Bridge, the three hundred-foot suspension walkway joining the old military fort to the main campus. The view from the platform was amazing. Mount Olympus was in the distance, its imposing peak visible from anywhere in the valley; Marcus climbed it every summer with Antony. Before he greeted Jordan, Hi!-D delivered a Public Service Announcement:

> "Good afternoon, citizens, and welcome to another wonderful day! You've heard it said that everybody needs somebody to love. Or that love is louder, brighter, and fuller of life than any other emotion. Yet most of the time, we wait around, hoping other people will make the first move. Today, tell a stranger you love them. They're probably eager to say it back. Because together, we're unbreakable."

It was noon.

"I. Love. You. Marcus," Jordan said in a robotic voice.

"And don't I know it."

"Can you imagine if you actually listened to their Manchurian programming and walked up to a random person and said you loved them? They'd think you were a mental case."

"Sad but true," Marcus moaned.

"Do the PSA's remind you of a softcore version of Orwell's two minutes of hate?" Jordan crossed his wrists and held his hands toward the sky. "GRASP AT VICTORY AND SHOUT HIS NAME, MARCUS! WAR IS PEACE! FREEDOM IS SLAVERY! IGNORANCE IS STRENGTH!"

24

AIDING THE ENEMY

J ordan and Marcus hustled to class at the Honors Center, a former military barrack built in -146 NE. Fort Douglas's position on the hill gave military supremacy over Mormons and indigenous tribes during the Civil War. But economic integration between the church and the military had eased tensions. Today, the fort was the most beautiful part of campus, graced with tall trees, ample green space, single-story colonial structures, and a sports field that once housed the parade grounds.

Marcus overheard Che, Bonnie, and Velia gossiping about Bill as he took a seat; sound bounced easily off the hardwood coffered ceilings and intricate wall moldings of their classroom.

"What about Bill and a strip club?" Marcus asked.

"Nothing. It's stupid," Velia dismissed.

Jordan crooned at Bonnie and she cracked, "Velia told us Bill was a partial owner in a topless bar before the Federation arrived."

"I've heard that one, I've also heard Bill is way older than sixty-one like he claims," Charles added. He was an outdoorsman who regularly swapped hiking tips with Marcus, but his main claim to fame was descending from Benjamin Franklin. There was zero physical resemblance; Charles had thick short brown hair, bright blue eyes, and a stubble-covered jawline.

Jordan had no love for moralistic rumors and turned to focus on Marcus. "Will you be at Sundance the entire weekend?"

"How'd you know?" Marcus raised an eyebrow.

"Dianna told me this morning."

"Do you two have a hotline set up?"

"Just answer the question," Jordan challenged.

"Depends on tonight. Things can go sideways with her, fast."

"She's a great girl. She loves you."

Marcus cut to the point, "Did you tell her about the Cohort?"

"Nope. But what's your plan to break the news?"

"Like I said, it depends on how tonight goes. If we're staying together, then I'll tell her. Otherwise, I don't see the point."

"She's worth fighting for, dude," Jordan encouraged. "She's got an incredible work ethic, she's brilliant, and she's generous with her time. You couldn't hope for more in an eventual baby momma."

If only things were that simple, Marcus thought before leaning in to whisper, "Want to hear a crazy story about the Cohort?"

"Deflection doesn't work on me," Jordan chastised.

"I met a woman at the Black Market. Right after Antony's fight. Well, technically, I saw her earlier that night when we locked eyes across the club. After the fight, she approached me, and we had a few drinks, danced, and talked until Antony recovered—"

"So far, this hasn't been a very crazy story."

"She never told me her name. This morning, Brad introduced me to Monica from the Cohort. Monica is the woman from Nerio."

"When you were cozying up to Monica, did you mention your girlfriend, Dianna? Because *that* would be a CRAZY story."

"Settle down," Marcus omitted any details about their kiss, given Jordan's splintered loyalties of late. "It's crazy because nothing like this has ever happened to me. It was synchronicity. What are the odds?"

"Let's ask." Jordan turned to their classmate. "Hey Jack, Marcus has a story and wants to know the odds of it happening."

"Afternoon, everybody." Bill entered the classroom like a late-night host, waving and acknowledging each student individually.

"It's a beautiful day to be aiding the enemy," Jordan replied.

"Indeed," Bill smiled. "Today is our synthesis discussion about choice and free will. Then, if time allows, I'd like to end with some Federation art. But before we begin, how are you all doing?"

"I'm worried about the weather," Jordan blurted.

"Let's talk about the weather then," Bill replied.

"Since the Federation arrived, we've seen two winters with almost no snow, a super wet spring that we're likely to repeat this year," Jordan's words were coming quickly, "and last summer was so lush our desert valley could've been confused for the pacific northwest. Is Hecate messing with our weather?"

"Interesting idea," Bill nodded at Jordan, "the Federation agrees weather around the planet is erratic relative to the available historical data. That's point number one. The Federation has also stated, publicly and repeatedly, that Hecate is Hicks-Neutral. Meaning, it has zero effect on the Earth as a biosphere. So, if we believe them, the weather patterns you described are coincidental."

"THEY'RE LYING!" Jordan shouted, "I don't know why that's hard for everyone to accept. If roles were reversed, we'd lie too."

"Why?" asked Marcus.

"Because it'd give us control. Why's the Federation different?"

"Bold claims should be supported by evidence," Bill replied.

"The evidence is obvious. One minute it's a gorgeous sunny day, the next, it's raining so hard no one can go outside. We've had titanic swings in temperature and humidity. We can't predict what the weather will be like a few hours into the future. These problems didn't exist before the Federation arrived."

"This is a classic example of correlation and causation," Bill began, "you tied two patterns together: the Federation arrived, and the weather has been erratic. But you haven't explained how they're connected. You haven't shown us clear causation."

"Their ginormous fucking planet is the causation," Jordan rasped.

Quinn jumped in, "If they can move a planet across the universe, they probably know how to keep it from affecting Earth."

Marcus led a chorus of nodding heads.

"That's an appeal to authority fallacy," Jordan replied. "You're assuming they don't want to affect Earth."

"What about HAARP?" asked Sukanksha.

"What about it?" Jordan turned to face her.

"Don't conspiracy theorists believe weather modification is the primary reason it was built?"

"That's a red herring," Jordan dismissed.

"A what?" Su asked.

"It's a deflection from HAARP's real use in mind control."

Bill opened the discussion to the rest of the class, but Jordan was outnumbered. Everyone except Bonnie, Ameda, and Velia felt the Federation was trustworthy, and the inexplicable weather was a coincidence.

Jordan remained unconvinced, "Okay, let's ASSUME the Jupiter-sized planet orbiting us ISN'T causing the sudden swings in weather ... you know, because the virtuous Federation says so. What about the psychological impact? That could be impacting the weather."

The class broke into riotous laughter.

"Why is that funny?" Jordan snapped.

"It's an interesting idea," Bill said.

"It's more than an idea," Jordan retorted. "A researcher at Princeton used decades of data and found a statistical pattern between large public gatherings and improved weather: if enough people wished for good weather, it actually happened. If that's the case, why couldn't it go the other direction? As people worry more, the world's environment gets more chaotic."

"You might be onto something," Bill paced the room like a general again, hands behind his back fingers interlaced. "This is a perfect bridge into our synthesis discussion about choice. If we can wish for good weather and make it happen, like Jordan is proposing, that implies a choice. If that's true, it means the opposite must also be true—we're *choosing* the chaotic weather."

"Is it really a choice to be terrified?" asked Nicole. Marcus thought she was the prettiest girl in the class. She had curly chin-length black hair, rich brown eyes, and a graceful French face. They'd been in a History of Rock and Roll class before the Federation arrived, and Marcus asked her out, but she shot him down. He started dating Dianna a week later.

"So we can only choose the good things?" Bill challenged.

"Last class, you said fear clouds our minds," Nicole replied.

"And that's true," Bill emphasized. "Fear fires up your reptilian brain. But can we control our fear response?"

The class was evenly split on the idea.

"There's a quote I want to read," Bill retrieved a small journal from his desk at the front of the classroom. " 'Between stimulus and response, there is a space. In that space is our power to choose our response. In our response lies our growth and our freedom.' "

"Viktor Frankl?" Nicole asked.

"Very good," Bill smiled. "What does it mean?"

"We have choice in all things," Nicole conceded.

"What about path dependencies?" asked Che. "You mentioned that last time too. Frankl survived the Holocaust, but that was way beyond his control. How is that free will?"

"SIC VOLVERE PARCAS!"

"Say what?" Che stammered.

"Thus fate has decreed!" Bill answered. "It's a line from Virgil's *Aeneid,* a Roman reboot of the earlier Greek epics the *Iliad* and the

Odyssey. And there's some truth in that. Whether it's dinosaur-killing asteroids clearing the way for mammals to evolve, volcanos and comets breaking the grip of an ice age thousands of years ago, or the rise and fall of empires—"

"Rome?" asked Jack.

"Rome had the most direct impact on our present situation. There are others we know nothing about since material evidence decays rapidly the further back in time you go. But the existence of genetic bottlenecks tells us that human populations fell to a few thousand people globally, more than once. Yet here you are, like Frankl, a survivor with the ability to choose what to do next."

"Stoicism shares the same idea," said Marcus. "Regardless of what has happened, we have a choice about how to respond."

"Hinduism is the same way too," Su added. "The Bhagavad-Gita talks about *Svadharma*, one's duty to choose an action that aligns with your true nature within the bigger context of the universe."

"Isn't this also similar to Transcendentalism?" asked Ashley from the back row, surprising everyone. She had bright pink hair, amplifying her Asian persona. The entire class assumed her shyness was because of a language barrier, but she was a California native who spoke perfect English.

"Yes! Excellent connection!" Bill's pacing intensified. "The Transcendentalists are the perfect example, because like the Stoics, they focused on the existence of choice and its importance in this material existence, but added the Hindu beliefs about choice and its impact on an immaterial consciousness subject to reincarnation. This is what Emerson famously called the 'Over-soul.' The choices we make individually impact humanity collectively in this life and beyond. Despite everything being determined before this moment, you still have a set of choices you can make right now. That's an amazing power, even if your choices are infinitesimal in terms of the Cosmic Year. Some choices will be right, and other choices will be wrong. Some are good, some are evil. It's in line with Frankl's ideas too. They all believe choice exists."

"To what end?" asked Bonnie. "Why does any of this matter?"

"That's a fair, if Nihilistic, question," Bill replied. "If we use Ameda's definition of free will as our ability to push back on the universe, then making the right choices allows society to progress and individuals to flourish in this life and beyond. If we get it wrong, societies collapse, and people die horrible deaths en masse to be reincarnated and start over. The choice is ours to make."

"Wednesday," Bonnie challenged, "you pointed out how much uncertainty we face and how limited human knowledge is. How can we possibly make the right choices in that situation?"

Nicole, Che, and Ameda nodded in agreement with this idea.

"Transcendentalists like Emerson believed human intuition was the key since it taps into the Oversoul," Bill replied. "We can also use logic, and can rely on experts in this material existence."

"Most experts aren't much better than chimpanzees," said Jack.

"I've never heard this," Bill belly laughed. "Can you explain?"

"The Good Judgment Project hired an academic to test if people could predict the future. He needed a control group, so he trained chimpanzees to throw darts at a wall to randomly pick outcomes. The experts barely outperformed the chimps."

"How can we make the right choices then, if we can't predict the future?" Bonnie echoed her concerns.

"Some people could predict the future pretty well, they're called Superforecasters," Jack countered. "They just aren't what you'd normally expect an expert to be. They were able to process new information and update their prior beliefs quickly. Their intellectual flexibility was key."

Bill continued laughing to himself when Lindsay waded into the discussion, "What's so funny?"

"Predicting the future only matters if you believe you can make it better through correct choices," Bill answered. "And even then it requires cooperation between lots of individuals to pull off. How do all of these different people in the world know what the right choices are?"

"It's the 100th monkey effect," said Jordan. No one responded, so he elaborated, "Ideas spread rapidly through a population once a critical mass knows about them. It's an emergent phenomenon. It lends a lot of credibility to Emerson's insistence on the importance of intuition."

The synthesis of ideas continued among the class for the next hour, focusing on the interplay between choice and progress. When dissent seemed to be exhausted, Bill proposed a vote, "We've arrived at the terminus of our topic for this week. By a show of hands, who believes humans have free will and the power to choose?"

Everyone, even Bonnie, had become a believer.

"Lindsay will have to check the class records," Bill said, "but I think this is the first time we've been unanimous in our opinions."

"It is." Lindsay was confident in her memory.

"I want to add a small post-script to this discussion then, for consideration as you cerebrate over the weekend: what would you choose if given the promise of a life without death, even if it meant you had to surrender your ability to choose for the rest of your existence?"

"Are you talking about the Federation?" asked Nicole.

"No, actually, I was talking about the Confederation. According to the Federation, that's how they will enslave humanity: a final choice between life largely free of death under their rule, or a life in opposition to them which guarantees an eventual demise."

Marcus looked at Jordan. He was foaming for a chance at rebuttal, but Bill commandeered the class's trajectory, "NOW, TIME FOR ART!"

In perfect choreography, Lindsay pulled down the projector screen at the front of the classroom and turned off the lights while Bill shut the blinds, moving into position at the back of the room. In contrast to Luke's media-rich symposiums, Bill was old school, preferring an overhead projector with single-sheet transparencies.

Marcus couldn't relate to the Federation art; it was a mess of colors and shapes. He retrieved his phone and navigated to the call log, highlighting Monica's number. He thought about texting her.

"The brainwashing only works if you're looking at the screen," Jordan startled him with a whisper.

"I don't get any of it," Marcus whispered back, heart racing.

"There's nothing to get. It's another way to probe our minds. I know a Rorschach test when I see one. Plus, it looks like a bad *Unarius* rip-off." Jordan was referring to the San Diego cult's public access TV dramas they'd watched as kids thanks to Antony's bootlegged VHS tapes.

Bill's exhibition only lasted a few minutes, then light returned to the room. "I hope you enjoyed that in your own way. For me, that's the thrill of art. We collectively experience it as individuals.

Enjoy your weekend, and good luck cerebrating on our final question. See you all Tuesday."

The world had transformed while they were in class. Heavy clouds stretched across the sky, and static electricity filled the air. The PSA screen flashed an emergency weather alert instructing everyone to seek shelter.

"See," Jordan taunted.

"Wish harder." Marcus smiled. "Race you home?"

"I don't know, dude. After that lecture and the art, I'm feeling pretty—" Jordan feigned before scampering away. Marcus gave him a head start; Jordan would need it. The two dashed over the Legacy Bridge and into the heart of campus. The entire sprint was downhill, and the sensation of resisting his own momentum gave Marcus flashbacks to running in the mountains when they were kids. He held back to keep the pressure on Jordan until they'd reached their street, then he blew by him. Jordan slowed to a walk.

"Time to hit the cardio," Marcus boasted from their porch.

Jordan caught up, arms above his head, struggling to breathe. "You're lucky … to be born with … an athletic body … I'm going downstairs … to die."

25

DANGEROUS THINGS

Marcus prepared for his weekend with Dianna. He could pack lightly; most of what he needed was already at his family's house. With bag in hand, he braved the bad weather to reach a freestanding single car garage at the back of their property. He carefully lifted the splintered old door to reveal his family's most prized possession: a Blue Tahiti 25th Anniversary Lamborghini Countach. The car was so ahead of its time that forty years after being built, its exterior still looked futuristic. The Lamborghini wasn't like new—it was new. His mother had loved the car so intensely that she'd put less than a thousand miles on it during her lifetime.

As Marcus shut the vehicle's iconic scissor door, the volume of his world fell away. No rain. No street noise. He closed his eyes and inhaled slowly through his nose. Pop culture said that by depriving one sense, humans could increase another; focusing on the smell of the car's interior helped Marcus conjure up memories of his mother.

The roar of four hundred and fifty horses broke the silence as the Countach came to life. It was dangerous to reverse the car without hanging halfway out the open driver's side door; the vehicle had been designed with moving forward in mind. Marcus's tiny garage made that maneuver impossible, so he had to rely on muscle memory.

Dianna arrived on foot in time to witness his act of blind faith from beneath the safety of her umbrella. Marcus parked, then ran to hug her. "Let me take that for you," he said, grabbing her small bag. "It's good you're traveling lightly. I don't have much of a trunk."

"Is that your car?" Dianna's eyes widened. She'd never seen the Countach since their romance had been confined to campus or places accessible by public transit.

"Come get in." The engine's purr was drowned out by the unrelenting rain. They were finally alone.

"This is incredible. It feels so snug." Dianna glanced around. "This car is probably worth more than the duplex I grew up in."

"It was my mom's. She left it to me when she died."

"Forgive me, sweetheart," Dianna's voice lowered.

Marcus hadn't shared the details of his parents' death with her, and as a psychologist, she understood not to pry at such a sensitive topic until he was ready.

"I'm excited to see where you grew up. I think it'll give me a better sense of who you are, and what makes you tick, you know?"

Despite her code of ethics when it came to prying, Dianna never missed an opportunity to analyze something once he'd opened up about it. But she was right; growing up in the mountains had defined him.

The car's monstrous windshield wiper furiously flung the rain aside. The large performance tires and extra-wide frame made the Lamborghini feel invincible as they raced against the weather's onslaught. The interstate was empty, allowing Marcus to speed through the surrounding environment. *The acceleration was different from floating during Subsumption,* he thought, smiling at Dianna. She was glowing as she smiled back; he hadn't seen this side of her in a long time. Dianna was intuitive, which made Marcus nervous. *He couldn't wait forever to tell her about the Cohort. Even if this weekend succeeded in resetting their relationship, he questioned if their bond could survive his full disclosure about the Federation.*

"When did your mom buy this car?" Dianna asked. "The more I look around, the more dated it feels."

"Sometime in the '80s. It was a gift from my grandfather since she was the first person in her family to graduate from college."

"So she was already rich?" Dianna asked.

"Yeah, my grandfather made his fortune selling Italian cookies in grocery stores. He paid for her to go to college, and she did the intellectual heavy lifting. Technically, he paid for my college too."

"What were your grandparents like?"

"I only know from stories I've heard. My parents were old when they had me. Antony basically grew up as an only child. I arrived in his senior year of high school. My father's parents and my mom's dad were all dead by that point. I was five when my mom's mom died. I have spotty memories of her."

"I didn't have grandparents."

"They've all passed on?" Marcus asked.

"Not sure, but probably not. My mother hopped trains to LA when she was fifteen to escape her Greek Orthodox parents. She turned seventeen the day I was born, so I assume they're still alive and operating their diner somewhere in the Midwest."

"What about your father's parents?"

"Never knew him, so I have no idea. I wanted a grandmother so badly when I was a kid. Now, as an academic, I appreciate the important role they provide for our personal development. I never forgave my mother for denying me one."

Marcus and Dianna raced out of the city, beyond the grasp of suburbia, and into the mouth of a colossal canyon. The river running alongside the narrow mountain road was swollen from rain, and heavy clouds cast a perpetual darkness.

"This road is really narrow, especially for how fast you're driving." Dianna furiously twirled a lock of hair.

"Don't worry. It fits two normal-sized cars."

"Where are we?"

"The Uinta National Forest. This road is by Federal design, but it cuts twenty minutes off our drive. Plus, it's prettier than the other routes ... when you can see things."

Dianna's tension was rising faster than the river.

"I've driven this a thousand times," Marcus assured. "I doubt we'll see anyone. You can relax. We're safe."

Dianna shot forward as they passed a sign for Timpanogos Cave. "This is American Fork canyon."

"Yes," Marcus replied. "Why?"

"Ted Bundy dumped Laura Ann Aime here."

"Am I supposed to know who that is?"

"She was a runaway he grabbed on Halloween in 1974. They didn't find her body until Thanksgiving, somewhere right around here …"

Marcus was the uncomfortable one now. Dianna sensed it and explained, "Before we met, I completed a Master's thesis about the celebrity status of mass murderers: genocidal governments, public shooters, organized criminals, serial killers, those types."

"Okay?"

"During my research, another student told me about Bundy and this canyon. He said there's a small cave nearby people go to because they think he kept Laura captive there, which isn't true."

"Mormon kids in my high school thought paranormal stuff happened in this canyon," Marcus mused. "They blamed most of it on devil worshipping. The stories usually involved some tragic female figure, so I'm sure the Bundy connection fueled their fire."

Marcus's car climbed the winding road. The clouds faded as their elevation increased, revealing the domineering mountaintops covered in densely packed pines. One millimeter of vertical movement per year produced these dramatic peaks, but this was a misleading statistic because the landscape instantly jumped twelve feet when the fault line slipped.

"Despite any imaginary evil," Dianna sighed, "this is a beautiful place."

Marcus's car seemed to perform better as they passed the summit and descended into Sundance Canyon, like it knew they were home. Normally, the Alpine Loop they were driving wouldn't open until Memorial Day, but the lack of snow and rapid onset of spring made it navigable months ahead of schedule.

Dianna ran fingers through Marcus's hair, sending chills across his body. "The scenery really changed."

She was right, Marcus thought. This side of the mountain was dominated by aspens and a thick bed of forest ferns instead of tall pines.

"The micro-climate on this side of the mountain is special. It's why Sundance has always been a resort, even for the Ute Indians before Mormon settlers or Robert Redford."

"The film festival guy?"

"He was an actor too," Marcus clarified.

"I know, my mom was obsessed with his movies."

"He bought this entire canyon to control its development. It's sad … they had to close the resort months ago because there's no snow."

"Why is it called Sundance? After the Indian ritual?"

"Indirectly," Marcus replied. "It's the name of a character Redford played who was part of the Wild Bunch gang."

"Speaking of mass murderers—"

"The Sundance Kid never killed anyone during their bank robberies," Marcus explained. "He got his name from Sundance, Wyoming, which is named for the Indian ritual."

"Have you ever seen the dance in person?"

"No. They don't do rituals here, at least not the Indian ones."

"What does that mean?"

"Every year around Pioneer Day, thousands of people used to climb the mountain at once. My dad did it as a young transplant to Utah. They shut it down a long time ago because it destroyed the environment, especially the waterfalls."

"There's a waterfall?" Dianna shot forward again.

"A few. Stewart Falls is the closest to my family's house. If the rain stops, we can go. It's a fun hike."

Dianna was wide-eyed as they drove through Marcus's neighborhood. "I've never seen anything like this. I had no idea people lived this way."

"In the mountains?" Marcus asked.

"With this much personal space. The houses are so spread out, set back from the road, and hidden by trees. What are they?"

"The trees?"

"Yes. They're beautiful. They have eyes."

"Quaking aspens."

"Are there wild animals here?" Dianna scanned the horizon.

"A bunch! Moose, bears, rams, cougars, bobcats, and turkeys."

"I thought turkeys were from Massachusetts?"

"There are huge flocks here. They shit on everything."

"It was a bad joke," Dianna backpedaled.

"Benjamin Franklin wanted them to be our national bird."

"Turkeys?"

"Yeah. He thought eagles had bad moral character."

"Why?"

"Because they use their size to take whatever they want."

"Might makes right," Dianna replied. "How do you know all these little facts, sweetheart?"

"My parents taught me," Marcus said as he pulled into the driveway. "We're here."

Dianna's eye was drawn to indecipherable inscriptions over the door. "What do those say?"

"The first says *know yourself* and the second says *nothing in excess*, they're Greek maxims from the Oracle at Delphi. The third is Italian. It says *abandon all hope you who enter*."

"What does that mean?" Dianna squinted.

"It's my father's dark sense of humor."

"I don't get it."

"It's from Dante's *Inferno*. It's inscribed over the gate to Hell."

Marcus turned off the car; all was quiet again. Dianna leaned over the center console and kissed him. "Thank you for bringing me here. I realize what this means for you. For us."

Marcus stared into her eyes. "This feels like a first date."

Dianna smiled and kissed him again.

"Let me give you the tour," Marcus offered.

Dianna was speechless as they entered the house through its media room. "You could fit my entire childhood living space into this area. The hardwood floors are gorgeous ... what are they?"

"I'm not sure," Marcus said as he led her to the main landing. "Through that door is Antony's part of the house. Don't go in there."

"Will he be here this weekend?" Dianna flexed her jaw muscles.

"Not this weekend," Marcus clarified.

A winding set of stairs led them to the second-floor dining area.

"This house is incredible!" Dianna paced around the wooden dinner table. "I love all of your parents' art! It's so eclectic!"

"My family traveled a lot. It's from our trips."

"It looks like you had some incredible adventures."

"We should go somewhere together."

"We'll see," Dianna dismissed. "I'd have to budget for it."

Marcus showed her the rest of the house, pausing at the family's third-floor library. "My mother wanted this in the house because her parents, as intelligent as they were, never owned books."

"This. Is. Amazing!" Dianna stood on a small rolling ladder, and Marcus gave her a push, sending her across a short wall and around a soft curve to another. "It's peaceful here."

Marcus led her to the master suite, situated at the highest point in the house. "When it's clear, you can see the entire valley."

"This is your parents' room?" Dianna whispered.

"It is." Marcus peered through the room's large window.

"Do you sleep here when you visit?"

"Sometimes. But we'll stay in my room off the kitchen."

There was a pause as Dianna inspected the space.

"Are you hungry?" Marcus asked.

"I'm starving!"

"Follow me. I have something special for you."

26

MEMENTO MORI

After gathering ingredients, Marcus paused to pour them both Moscato white wine from his family's collection.

"It's rare to find a guy who knows his way around a kitchen, especially at your age."

"My parents were great cooks. I grew up in here every night."

"I'm a lucky lady," Dianna replied. "What are we eating?"

"Angel hair pasta in a pesto sauce."

"I love pesto! Is that weird, since I don't know what's in it?"

"It's olive oil, basil, parmesan cheese, garlic. Most people use pine nuts, but my family recipe calls for walnuts. The Roman's had something similar made of olive oil, cheeses, and herbs. Pesto means 'pounded' since you grind it all in a pestle and mortar."

"You were lucky. Italian food in my house was microwavable mac and cheese. It's nice to see that you appreciate your privilege."

"One time, when I was really young, we visited my grandma, and I had a meltdown over what we were eating. My mother smacked the back of my head, smushed my cheeks together, and said I was a fortunate soul to have so much because somewhere in the world, a child was begging his mother for food, and she was crying to God since she didn't have any. Every time I eat, I still think about that."

"Every kid is like that. She shouldn't have hit you," Dianna's jaw muscles were flexing again. "What were you upset about eating?"

"Pesto, actually." Marcus extended his hand, "*Dame la mano.*"

"What does that mean?"

"Give me your hand." Marcus led her to a sheepskin rug in the living room. "I'll build a fire for us, then finish cooking."

"This feels amazing," Dianna said as she ran her fingers through the rug. "I'm against fur, but this is the first time I've felt it."

"It's a necessity here. When the heat goes out, you learn to appreciate the warmth of fur real fast."

"I bet there are other uses for it. ..." Dianna bit her lip.

Marcus kissed her. "Dinner first. Enjoy the anticipation, right?"

After a short time working in the kitchen, Marcus returned with two bowls of pasta to find Dianna asleep under a cashmere blanket before the roaring fire. He set the food on the hearth and kissed his sleeping beauty.

"I'm sorry," Dianna rubbed her eyes, "it was so serene."

"Food's ready. We can eat right here if you want."

Dianna sat up and tightened the blanket around her body. The smell of basil and fire danced around them. Her taste buds delighted in Marcus's creation; she closed her eyes and tipped her head back, savoring the edible experience.

"This is unbelievable!" After a few more bites, she reignited their discussion, "How did your parents meet?"

"My dad was my mother's Roman history professor. She said it was love at first lecture."

"Did they get married right away?"

"No. My mother's parents were skeptical. They worried my father was in it for the money since he was fifteen years older, but he had no idea they were wealthy. They got my grandfather's blessing when she graduated and married the next year on the Fourth of July. Six months later, Antony was born, a sin my father never absolved even after converting to Catholicism."

"How long were they married?"

"They would've celebrated their twenty-ninth anniversary the year they died. They never spent a single day apart ..." Marcus dropped his head into his hands, rubbing his face before sitting up straight to look directly at Dianna. "Then, they died together."

The floodgates opened on Marcus's confession; this was his chance to move their relationship forward, through vulnerability. "Every year, we'd travel as a family. I loved those trips, especially when Antony was still coming. We went to ancient ruins, we saw the space shuttle launch, we explored Redwood Forests, we went on Safari, and we did service work in places like Soweto. I felt like I lived a lifetime with each adventure. Like I was a wiser person for having seen it all myself. Then Antony got busy with school and work and stopped coming. I was nine the year they died.

"We were supposed to visit Greece without Antony during spring break. I wanted to stay home to be close to Jordan. We'd lost so many classmates to a cancer cluster that year, and other kids had died from accidents and suicide. There was even one girl who was murdered by her mother. Experts came to our school and did interviews, but no one had answers, so all it did was make me more fearful of losing people in my life. I felt safer with Antony and Jordan at home. This erupted into a huge fight with my parents. My mom was crying, and my father was threatening to beat me senseless. I stormed out and went to Jordan's. The next day, they left without me. We made up by phone, but I could already feel that nothing would be the same. A few days later, they got on a plane for Delos and disappeared over the Aegean Sea. I was at Jordan's when Antony called. He told me to get home immediately. I knew something was wrong. I could feel it … they were gone."

Marcus paused to take a deep breath. Still choking on his words, he continued, "Hearing Antony deliver the news made it real. I was unable to stand. I was crying. Screaming. I kept making this horrible guttural wail I had no control over. All I could think about was our last time together. Spent fighting. The image of my mother sobbing … my father in a rage—when I'd sleep, that's all I'd see. I convinced myself that if I'd been with them, it would've ended differently. We would've slept in and missed a taxi, or I would've needed to find a bathroom and delayed us. Any small change would've put us on a different path to a different plane … that if I'd wanted to be with them more, they'd still be alive."

Marcus looked up at Dianna. Her eyes were flowing. As she moved closer, he couldn't hold back his own tears. "No one knew where the plane crashed. For months we waited. Hoping they'd be found alive with a miracle story. We never got to say goodbye. There was so much hysteria that year because of the Mayan calendar. When doomsday didn't happen, everyone was relieved. I wasn't. I'd been hoping for it. An apocalyptic prophecy for nothing. It was like the universe made that moment to mock me.

Only my world ended that year. My entire life, people had told me how lucky I was, but at that point, I couldn't see it anymore. I felt defeated."

Marcus stood, drying his eyes, and led Dianna onto the covered second-story porch to cuddle in a hammock overlooking the valley. Despite the rain's ferocity, the wind chimes continued singing their soft song. The sky was prematurely darkened, the result of an eclipse taking place beyond their view on the other side of Mount Timpanogos, as Marcus continued spilling his soul. "My anxiety hit critical levels after their deaths. I burned through therapists. I was fearful and hateful all the time. Antony tried his best, but nothing changed until I met Garret."

"He must be an important person," Dianna whispered.

"After Antony and Jordan, he's the most important man I know. Maybe it's because he'd been a colleague of my father's, or because I'd grown up seeing him at Christmas Mass and Easter Vigil, but he was able to break through like no one else could."

"How so?"

"He taught me about Stoicism and gave me a daily affirmation ritual. It helped turn things around for me."

"Do you still do the daily affirmation?"

"Religiously. It makes or breaks my entire day."

Marcus retrieved his Memento Mori coin. Dianna inspected it closely but couldn't decipher its meaning. "Why is there a skull, and what are these other things to the sides of it?"

"They represent the three essentials of existence: life, death, and time. Those other symbols are an hourglass and a tulip. The coin is a physical reminder of my mortality, so I can face life with clarity of purpose and not from a place of fear. Garret said my dad gave him this coin decades ago when they first met, and he'd carried it for years without knowing it was meant for me. Now I carry it every day, everywhere I go."

"What's your favorite memory of your parents?"

"For my dad, it's paintballing here in the woods," Marcus said with nostalgic elation. "There are old sheds down by the river from the Mormon settler days. He got paintball kits for everyone, including Jordan, and showed us how to work as a squad by maneuvering between cover so we'd be unstoppable in a firefight."

"Was he in the military?"

"No. He just came from a long family tradition of being the first line of defense. He was an Adams, after all."

"Is that supposed to mean something?"

"You said it earlier: might makes right. History taught him the strong prey on the weak. He thought it was important to keep yourself from being easy prey. It's why we had guns growing up. He was a modern Minute Man, forever at the ready."

"I hate guns."

"Have you ever shot one?" Marcus asked.

"No. I've never touched one and don't want to. What about your mother? What's your favorite memory of her?"

"That's easy," Marcus said with a smile. "When we were in public and saw a column on a building, she'd quiz everyone about its type: Doric, Ionic, or Corinthian. She said it was her way of civilizing the barbarians. Antony and I teased her mercilessly for it."

"Were you and Antony always so close?"

"Always. After my parents died, everything changed. He had to raise me. He did a great job too. He made sure I had someone there every day after school, so life felt normal, as much as that was possible."

Dianna turned to face Marcus. "There's something I want to tell you. The reason I don't get along with your brother is last year he intercepted me on campus—"

"What?" Marcus sat up in the hammock. "When?"

"It was a few weeks after the Federation arrived. He took me out for coffee to talk about you and school, but then he probed me about my family. He was insistent about that. When I wouldn't give him details, he offered me two million dollars in cash to leave you alone. He had it in his gym bag. He said if I was after easy money, this was my chance. It was so sexist! If he were anyone else, I would've thrown my coffee in his damn face. We haven't said a word to each other since."

"I'm so sorry. He thinks he's protecting me. I hope you know I didn't ask him to do that."

"I know," Dianna pressed on Marcus's chest, getting him to relax back into the hammock.

"Is this why you've made a big deal about paying for everything?"

"I don't need anyone's money. I was like this before your brother's bullshit. I pay because I'm capable of taking care of myself. Like your dad, I want to be my own first line of defense."

"It isn't necessary. I want to help make your life easier."

"I love that you want to help. I do. But I'm worried I'd lose my identity. My mother worked multiple jobs just to keep us stuck in poverty. I'm not in that place anymore, and I'll never go back. No one will control me through money."

Marcus kissed her forehead.

Dianna spoke softly, "Do you think about your parents often?"

He wasn't ready to tell her about the voicemails but didn't see the harm in being general, "Every day."

"I think that's healthy. Lots of cultures have ancestor worship as part of their daily rituals. They believe if you say a person's name, it makes them immortal. Their memory lives on forever."

"I hope that's true," Marcus whimpered.

"Whatever happens between us," Dianna looked into Marcus's eyes, "promise me I won't be a memory that fades away."

27

WANDERING INTO A CARTHAGINIAN'S CAVE

A clap of thunder woke the pair from their slumber; they'd fallen asleep in each other's arms under the comfort of a heavy blanket. The source of the sound was a mystery since the sky was clear. The moon and Hecate both soaked the world in their reflective light.

"Still want to go to the waterfall?" asked Marcus.

"In the dark?" Dianna muttered.

"We'll be fine. There are jackets in the closet by the front door. I'll pack some supplies and meet you downstairs."

Marcus was raised on the Boy Scout's motto to always be prepared. He gathered a backpack, water, blankets, fire starter, a headlamp, and rain protection; the weather changed faster in the mountains than it did in the valley, and he wanted to be comfortable if they got pinned down somewhere. He found Dianna lightly bundled, phone in hand, ready to go.

"Lead the way," she said with a nervous smile.

Marcus led them through the tranquil neighborhood to a dead-end spur. The mountainside took off at a sharp angle, making their ascent through the thick cover of wet ferns difficult. The ground was uneven, requiring constant balancing. Fallen trees occasionally obstructed their path, a narrow trail used for cross-country skiing in the winter and horse riding in the summer; this time of year, it was empty.

Tall trees encircled them, cutting Hecate's blue light into zigzag patterns of shadows. Still, it was hard to see more than fifty feet ahead, though the occasional glow of a highly reflective flower pierced the darkness like a lighthouse. The random snap of branches in the surrounding woods triggered fleeting fright in Marcus, but the soothing rustle of new spring leaves in the wind quickly calmed him. They could barely hear the distant rumble of the falls over the chorus of crickets.

"If you count how many times the crickets chirp in fifteen seconds and add thirty-seven, it's an accurate way to get the temperature," said Marcus.

"Seriously?"

"As a heart attack."

Dianna listened intently, then did some quick math. "Fifty-four degrees?"

"I don't have a thermometer, so I'll take your word for it."

Dianna laughed, and they continued along the midnight mountain path. Dead grass from the year before was interspersed with new life, and spiky plants flicked across the exposed skin of their hands. The air was a heavy mix of oxygen from the trees and lingering ozone from the storm.

They emerged into a massive meadow. The glow of civilization haloed the northern and western mountain ridges. Dianna held

Marcus's hand as they both stared, transfixed, at the canopy of twinkling stars.

"This is a new world for me."

"Hiking?"

"I never had access to wilderness growing up, despite my mother being a New Age zealot. She didn't take me into nature. As an adult, I rarely leave campus. I never would've seen this without you. Thank you, sweetheart."

"I'm glad I can share it with you."

Their peace was interrupted by a scream echoing across the meadow.

Marcus was on full alert. "You heard that too, right?"

"Yes. What was it?" Dianna looked around anxiously.

"I have no idea."

The sound continued.

"I think we should follow it," Dianna suggested.

"You're really getting into the spirit of adventure! But it could be an animal killing something. You sure?"

"Yes."

Dianna led the way. The noise was coming from the middle of the meadow. Once they were within thirty feet, they saw what'd happened: a buck was lodged by the antlers between two inopportunely spaced trees. He was thrashing in a failed attempt to free himself. The screams were from his female companion frantically circling her stuck mate.

"We need to help them," said Dianna.

"How?" Marcus cautioned, "If you get too close, that buck will impale or kick you. He's already pissed."

"I'm going to help. If you want to join me, feel free."

Dianna inched toward the animal, who continued to struggle against the trees' grip. The doe now stood frozen. Dianna crept closer to the buck until she was gazing directly into its eyes. After a few moments of close proximity, Dianna tried to touch his forehead, causing him to thrash again. Following half a dozen similar attempts, Marcus couldn't believe what he was seeing: Dianna had gained the buck's trust and was stroking the placid animal's forehead.

"If we push on his horns, we can get him loose," said Dianna.

"Not to split hairs, but they're antlers. And they're dangerous if he decides to swing them around."

"He won't hurt us. He understands we're here to help. She understands too." Dianna nodded at the doe.

Marcus decided to trust Dianna. After a single push, they'd freed the animal. It stumbled backward, shaking its head while letting out a series of snorts. Marcus moved between Dianna and the deer, but she stepped around him. The reunited mates looked at her with discernible gratitude, then bounced off into the forest.

Dianna was smiling ear to ear. "That was a rush!" She leaned in and kissed Marcus again. *This was the most intense embrace of the evening, an echo of their physical fireworks before the Federation arrived*, Marcus thought.

"How much farther is it to the falls?" Dianna asked.

"A mile, we can get there in twenty minutes."

A few steps into their journey, Dianna stopped and took a deep breath. "I have something I want to share with you, but I'm terrified."

"Okay?"

"You were vulnerable with me earlier, which says a lot. But I have to know I can trust you."

"You can," Marcus assured.

"I've never told this to anyone."

"If you aren't ready, don't do it."

"I feel like I have to," Dianna replied. After some hesitation, she began her own confessional, "You truly are lucky. I hope you know that. I'm not trying to diminish your pain, so please don't interpret it that way. But this is heaven on Earth, Marcus. To grow up here ... surrounded by such beauty and so much love. My life has been a living hell. I've only known real peace since I left home. Every horrible thing that could happen to one family happened to mine. My mother had delusions of Hollywood grandeur when she ran away and it ruined us. She had no education, no family, and two babies. She ended up waiting tables and living paycheck to paycheck. When that wasn't enough, she prostituted herself to wealthy old men she met through her New Age groups. They liked the power they had over her. A few even propositioned me when I was a teenager. Drugs were a constant presence in my house, providing irrational 'hope-timism' for my mother. Despite all the horrible shit that'd happened in her life, she continued on like everything was fine. The low point came just before my sixth birthday."

Dianna took another long breath, struggling to hold back tears. "This is the same week my brother, Apollo, was abducted by one of my mother's men. For weeks, we bounced between search parties and my mom's crystal-healing circles. No one had any idea where he was or what had happened. Looking back, that period was worse than finding out he was dead or hearing the details of how he suffered. I felt so powerless. They found his body days before our birthday. For more than a month after Apollo's murder, my mother was certifiably crazy, telling me she could see his spirit and that he was happy because he'd rejoin us soon."

Dianna's story was interrupted by an uncontrollable bout of crying. Marcus stood frozen, unsure if he should comfort her. Before he could act, she'd regained control of herself, eyes full of fire. "I was so naive. One night, when it was just the two of us in our filthy kitchen, I asked my mother if Apollo was present. She said yes, so I asked if I could see him too. Without hesitating, she said that my spirit must not be good enough because otherwise, I'd already be able to. I've never felt pain like that in my life. Never. It's taken two decades for me to recover. If that's possible. It was at that moment I realized how alone I was in this world. I started planning my escape. I worked odd jobs under the table and turned my cash into gift cards, which I kept in a shoebox I carried everywhere in my backpack. By the time I was eighteen, I'd saved more than twenty-thousand dollars, which with my scholarships to the University, allowed me to leave home. I know the darkness you talked about earlier. I feel it whenever I think about what my mother denied me in life: a grandmother, a family, nature, sanity, and … love."

Overwhelmed by the magnitude of her sorrow, Marcus was unable to muster any words. He reached out and offered his embrace, which she eagerly accepted. Marcus held her tight, wishing he could protect her from the past trauma. *He'd learned more about her in the last few minutes than in the entire time they'd dated.* Without another word, Dianna let go and continued down the trail.

The roar of the waterfall was at full volume as they emerged from the forest. Hecate combined with the moon to pour dramatic lighting on the two towering tiers of the waterfall, and the Milky Way arched across the southeastern sky. Heavy storm clouds were beginning to accumulate along the mountain's ridgeline to their west.

"Why do they call it Stewart Falls?" Dianna asked.

"It's named for the Mormon polygamists that settled this canyon."

"Could you ever do that?"

"What? Polygamy?"

"Yeah."

"No," Marcus laughed.

"I like that about you." Dianna took a break from staring at the stars to stare at him instead.

Marcus found a heart-shaped rock near the edge of the water. It fit perfectly in his palm. He handed it to Dianna. "Do you know the myth about this mountain?"

"No." She inspected the stone.

"Timpanogos has many indigenous myths about it, all of which have a pair of heartbroken lovers. Tragedy is the only constant. In most versions, she dies of a broken heart after losing the love of her life. That's why people say the mountain's outline resembles a woman lying in state."

Unexpected hail sent them scrambling. Marcus grabbed Dianna's hand, leading her to a cave beyond the trees near the midpoint of the falls. The space was barely tall enough for them to stand. Marcus deployed one of his blankets before braving the hail to gather wood to build another fire. When the flames were blazing,

Marcus faced Dianna; energy streamed through the air between them. Then she pounced.

Their tongues danced across each other's hungry lips. They peeled off their clothing, piece by piece, a collapse of the barriers left between them. The mix of cold mountain air and heat from the fire delighted their bare skin.

Marcus pulled away from their embrace. He took big breaths of air, his chest rising and falling to control his racing heart as the glossiness of Dianna's eyes exposed her true desires. He smiled to reassure her of their mutual vulnerability. They took turns exploring with their lips and hands. Marcus nibbled his way from Dianna's neck to her inner thighs, eliciting deep groans. He drove his face forward, and she lifted her hips to get closer to the source of pleasure from Marcus's mouth. After being lost in her own gratification, Dianna matched his expert use of both tongue and lips. The smell of fire and flesh filled their cave as the storm continued to rage outside. Dianna stopped, laying back onto the blanket to speak the first words of their carnal encounter, "I'm on the Pill and want to feel you skin-to-skin."

Marcus was beyond rationalization and quickly consented; they both gasped as their bodies became one. Dianna locked onto his eyes throughout their rhythmic movement. The outside world melted away; all that remained was their connection.

Dianna's eyes rolled back in her head as she surrendered to Marcus's thrusting. A primal energy had taken over, accelerating them toward reciprocal bliss. Her excitement climbed until she was shouting for his fingers and mouth again. Marcus seized the moment, pushing Dianna to orgasm. She pulled the back of his hair, legs quivering, and voice trembling as elation gave way to tears of release.

Marcus was concerned by Dianna's cries, but she reasserted the nature of their experience, pressing him onto his back and climbing on top. It was Marcus's turn to be lost in the moment as she guided him back inside. Dianna rode him relentlessly until he couldn't hold back any longer. As he finished inside her, his roars reverberated into the night sky. Light from the fire's flames danced across the cave walls, while thunder rolled down the distant canyon. Dianna laid atop Marcus like a victorious warrior queen, chest to chest, gasping for air, and exhausted. Marcus gave her one last kiss. Neither knew this was fated to be the only time they'd ever be one.

PART VIII

THE TIPPING POINT

SATURDAY, MARCH 19, +1 NE

28

THE SUNDANCE KID

The faint giggles of children woke Marcus from a deep sleep. He listened for additional echoes of innocent joy, but none came. Dianna was still sleeping. She shimmered with atypical fragility, like a snowflake at thirty-two degrees reflecting its last light, as their fire smoldered. A hint of morning chill pierced the wool blanket covering their naked bodies; they were safe, oblivious to the demands of the waiting world.

The roar of the waterfall continued unabated, but the rain was gone. It was astronomical dawn, the stage just after night but before both nautical and civil dawn. From lived experience, Marcus knew there was a final phase at Sundance: when the sun breaks above the eastern mountains about forty minutes after official sunrise.

He held Dianna until blue sky emerged. Birds vocalized their jubilation for another day of life. *This moment was perfect*, Marcus thought, feeling the familiar cosmic lightning run up his spine. *He risked losing everything by telling her about the Cohort, but he had no choice.*

"Hi!" Dianna beamed brighter than the rising sun.

"Are you cold? Want me to get the fire going again?"

Dianna snuggled closer. "No. I'm content."

"What would you like to do today?"

"Read in your library. That'd be divine. And have you cook!"

"I'm hungry now."

"I bet you are," Dianna softly pressed into him.

Their opportunity was ruined by a dog darting into their quiet cave. *It probably belonged to the children that woke him.* "Stewart Falls is like Grand Central Station on Saturdays. We should go," Marcus said.

They quickly clothed. Marcus buried the embers of their fire, packed his bag, and set off with Dianna in the lead. They hiked for a long time without saying a word, taking in the sounds of life that had silently surrounded them the night before. The trail was steep and narrow to start, with trees encroaching on the path. Dianna's superior physical conditioning opened a large gap between them. Marcus pushed himself, but the distance continued to widen until Dianna stopped to stare at a single tree.

"What is it?" Marcus asked between breaths.

Dianna pointed to an aspen, branded by a former passerby:

M&M '74

The message was ringed by a heart-shaped scar.

Dianna was indignant, replying, "That's so selfish!"

"People didn't understand what they were doing back then."

"Or they didn't care."

"Maybe they didn't know they should care?" asked Marcus.

"How do you not realize that carving something into the skin of an innocent life, causing pain and agony in the process, is wrong?"

"They probably thought it was a romantic way to achieve immortality. These trees will outlive all of us by a long shot."

"Death drives like this make me sick."

"Death drives?" Marcus muttered.

"It's Freudian theory. Beyond pleasure, we're motivated by drivers that push us toward destruction and death. He stole the idea from Sabina Spielrein, but only after shitting on her first."

Marcus had nothing to contribute, so Dianna continued, "Death drives are exciting, so we keep going back to them. They push us to destroy the world around us, like this idiot did to the tree, or else we risk destroying ourselves. Your brother is the perfect example of this."

"People don't do this to pine trees. Just the aspens. I wonder if it's because their white bark looks like a blank canvas?"

"This is why I hate Stoicism," Dianna snapped. "It teaches people to blame the victims."

"Come on," Marcus scoffed as he rolled his eyes.

"You blamed the tree for being an inviting victim. Freudian theory might be ancient, but Stoicism is archaic. I'm glad it's helped you, really, but it's a regressive way to view the world."

"The aspen can't change what happened to it, but it gets to choose how to react. To keep living. To continue striving for sunlight. That's the point of Stoicism. And if we're being honest, it doesn't look like that scar has slowed the tree down."

"Stoicism turns people into robots by denying their emotions. Rage and anger have a function. A purpose. To push back on injustice. A constant state of positivity is incompatible with real-life because the world includes suffering. I cringe every time I read *Meditations*, but the esteemed Dr. Borland insists—"

"Dr. Borland?"

"Yes. He's the member of my committee holding things up."

"That's Garret."

"What?" Dianna rasped.

"Dr. Garret Borland. He was my therapist."

"I can't believe I didn't put the pieces together," Dianna huffed. "It's still a stupid way of thinking. Sorry, sweetheart."

Marcus wasn't prepared to die on this ideological hill and suggested they keep moving. Soon they'd reached the meadow. The new spring leaves were neon green, as if the trees had been uprooted and dipped like a paintbrush into Gatorade.

"Is this where we freed the deer?" asked Dianna.

"Yes."

"Do you know where the exact spot is?"

Marcus led the way back to their sacred spot. In the daylight, they could see one tree was an aspen and the other a pine. Normally eternal enemies, they'd curved their ascent around one another to thrive in the shared space.

"That was a magical experience," Dianna effused. "I've never felt that thrill of danger mixing with altruism. Pushing through the fear was exhilarating."

"You sound a lot like Antony."

"Don't joke like that!" Dianna thundered. "There's a big differ-ence in what we risk ourselves for. I helped an innocent life, he just does it to jeopardize his own. They're not equivalent."

"Antony doesn't want to live like he's waiting to die."

A large shadow passed over them. Marcus looked up, and Dianna followed his focus. An eagle gripped a snake in its talons, which frantically contorted its body in an attempt to get free. Beyond the predator and its prey, Hecate hovered in the western sky. *Thirteen hours had gone by in the blink of an eye*, Marcus thought.

"That's so sad. I love snakes."

"Why?"

"They're self-sufficient from the moment they're born."

"Well, that snake doesn't stand a chance," Marcus observed.

"It shouldn't fight back?"

"What's its end game? To be dropped from the sky?"

"Why are you rooting for the aggressor?"

"The eagle has as much of a right to life as the snake." Marcus recognized they weren't talking about the struggles of the animal kingdom anymore. He couldn't stop thinking about Hecate and the Federation. Now was the time to come clean about Selection, "There's something I need to tell you. It's important to me, and I'm excited about it, but I'm also worried about your reaction. If you want to wait until Monday so we can enjoy the rest of the weekend, that's fine. I just needed you to know it's eating at me."

"How could I possibly wait after that comment? Just say it."

Marcus could see the heartbreak building behind Dianna's eyes. Then she came apart, "SAY IT! YOU THINK I DON'T ALREADY KNOW? YOU REALLY THINK I'M THAT DENSE?"

"How do you know?"

"Because I could feel it, Marcus! I feel everything. SAY IT!"

"If you already know, why do I have to say anything?"

"So you can hear the words coming from your own mouth that end our relationship. Forever. SAY IT, MARCUS!"

"I passed Selection. I accepted a job in the Cohort."

"JOB!" Dianna scoffed. "You said this wasn't about money, REMEMBER! You also promised this shit was behind us."

"No, I promised not to drop off the radar again, and I haven't. You're the one who went radio silent on me the past couple of days."

Dianna clenched her jaw and drove her fingernails into her palms; he'd stirred the emotional nitroglycerin, and she exploded. "I was busy doing things a lot more valuable for society than helping those occupiers!" Dianna's words came in a frenzy, "You can call that project 'noble' all you want, but they're using the fear of annihilation to strip us of our rights. Just so they can peddle Tek! AND YOU'RE VOLUNTEERING TO HELP THESE MONSTERS! When people eventually revolt, you'll be branded as a collaborator. Do you understand that? You won't be forgiven."

"What annihilation are you talking about?" Marcus challenged. "Point to the spot of blood on the ground, Dianna."

"North Korea."

"I don't mean to victim blame here, but didn't they bring that on themselves when they attacked the Federation?"

"They were human beings. Like us. With people they loved and lives they hoped to lead. All cut short by the Federation. It was genocide, Marcus. You really are lost. I feel sorry for you."

"Then light a candle and say a prayer," Marcus mocked.

"DON'T PUT THAT FALSE POSITIVITY ON ME, YOU PIECE OF SHIT! OWN YOUR CHOICES! I DESERVE THAT!"

Marcus felt his anger building but chose to stay silent.

"I can't believe you kept this from me! I felt it and didn't listen to myself—why didn't you tell me before we—oh, GOD!"

"I wanted to tell you but—"

"YOU LIED! AGAIN! You could've told me when I called … before you lured me here to your fantasy land. You have no idea what you've done—I'll ruin you for this. RUIN YOU!"

"Calm down. Let's talk through this." Marcus stepped forward.

Dianna recoiled, falling to the ground, further accelerating her rage. "DON'T TELL ME TO CALM DOWN, AND DON'T YOU DARE TOUCH ME! YOU'LL NEVER GET TO TOUCH ME AGAIN!"

Marcus accepted the reality that she was beyond rationalizing.

Dianna dusted herself off. "I'm leaving. Don't follow me. Don't contact me. If you see me on campus, look down and run away."

"How will you get home?"

"I'll spend a thousand dollars for a ride if necessary."

"Do you even know how to get back to my house?"

"I logged it in my running app. I knew I couldn't trust you."

"I would've shown you the way. I'm not a monster."

"That's laughable, Marcus. Show me your friends, and I'll tell you what kind of person you are."

Dianna perfectly picked her Parthian shot; it was something Marcus's mother used to say, a fact he'd shared with Dianna early in their relationship. His mind replayed the fight, comparing it to the conflict outside the museum, but knew that Dianna would never forgive him. *She was really gone.* After standing stag in the meadow, he headed home, dawdling along the trail to avoid an encounter with her. He texted Antony on the way:

> *Dianna dumped me. I need your ear. What's your day like?*

He felt guilty for not telling her about Selection on their midnight call; it could've avoided this. *He wasn't perfect, even if that was Dianna's unrealistic expectation,* he thought. *It was her baseless, blind hatred of the Federation that was the real problem, not his choices.*

The house was empty, and Dianna's things were gone. Antony hadn't replied, so he texted Jordan, who answered immediately. He was at his parent's house and promised to come right over.

Jordan found Marcus swinging on the hammock. "Sorry, bro."

"… But …," Marcus moaned.

"But nothing. I'm sorry that you're heartbroken. I'm sorry you lost Dianna. I'm just sorry for you, dude."

"You're not going to use your 'told you so' card?"

"Not today. Not for this. No."

"Thanks," Marcus replied.

"What do you want to do now? Self-medicate? Nap? Party?"

Marcus was weighing the options when Antony texted back:

At Krav. Come get me. We'll pew pew and talk.

"Antony wants to meet at his Krav gym so we can go shooting."

"Perfect!" Jordan exclaimed. "I've got a delivery for him. I came to casa Kilravock this morning to do the harvesting."

"You didn't come to do a wellness check on me?"

"Can't it be both?" Jordan said, crossing his arms.

More heartbreak awaited Marcus in the garage. Dianna had thrown the heart-shaped rock through the windshield and carved "collaborator pig" onto the blue doors and hood of his Countach.

"Fuuuuck," was the extent of Jordan's empathy.

Fighting back the tears, Marcus could only state the obvious, "We'll have to take your car."

29

PLEASURES OF VIOLENCE

J ordan drove a nondescript Jetta from the late-1980s; the car had been his father's prior to his explosive career success. Jordan loved the vehicle, and the only modification he'd made was adding a vanity plate: FFYFF. Marcus slept the entire ride down the canyon. Visions of Dianna destroying his mother's bequest consumed him. He woke, heart aching, when the therapeutic hum of the Jetta's engine ended.

"We're here," Jordan announced.

Antony's Krav Maga gym was famous throughout the United States because of its instructor, Joseph. This man's singular focus on real-world skills, which included training against attackers with actual knives and loaded guns, had prepared Antony for his victory over Zedd.

"Do you remember what 'gymnasium' means in Greek?" Jordan asked, surveying the training space.

"I don't," Marcus conceded.

"The naked place."

"That'd really change the vibe in here."

They could see Antony's battered face from across the room. He was talking more than he was training, but as they approached, the extent of Antony's physical damage became clearer; torn skin dotted the local maxima of his face, which had puffed up like a baboon's butt. Dark pockets of blood pooled around his nose, and his eyes were partially obstructed by engorged eyebrows.

"It smells like bleached assholes," Jordan proclaimed.

If description was an art, Jordan was an aesthete.

Marcus cleared his throat, announcing their arrival.

"Guys, this is Sarah," Antony made introductions. "Sarah, this is my blood brother, Marcus, and this is Jordan, who's my brother from another mother … and father."

Sarah was slightly shorter than Antony, with piercing blue eyes and wavy blonde hair pulled into high anime-style double buns. For a fighter, she had a straight smile of perfect white teeth, matching the fair skin tone of her Anglo-Saxon ancestors. Her posture signaled unfailing confidence, and Marcus had zero doubt she could best him in a fight.

"Nice to meet you," Marcus said, shaking her hand.

"What are you boys up to today?" asked Sarah.

"That pew pew life." Jordan's attempt at humor didn't land.

"We're going shooting," Antony clarified.

"Why haven't we gone?" Sarah hit Antony in the arm, striking the spot he'd used to stop Zedd's many assaults.

She mocked his wincing, "I'm sorry, did I bruise your vagina?"

"Vagina means sword sheath in Latin!" Jordan declared.

The random factoid created an awkward, muted moment.

"Brick. Head. Home." Antony forced a smile past the silence.

"Exactly," Sarah struck the same spot again." You boys have fun playing soldiers in the desert. See you Monday, Antony."

Jordan couldn't constrain his curiosity as they walked away, "What does 'brick, head, home mean?' "

"It's something Joseph says all the time. It means you do whatever's necessary during a fight to ensure you get home safely. Speaking of which, we have to stop by my place to get the guns."

"Where'd you park?" asked Marcus.

"Sarah drove. I'll have to bum a ride off you guys."

As they turned to leave, Marcus noticed another familiar face in the crowded gym. "Is that Velia?"

Jordan squinted. "Looks like it."

"She joined after my fight," Antony explained.

Marcus rubbed his chin. "What the hell?"

"She's a harmless fangirl," Antony assured. "I'd love me too if I was her. She's also a natural fighter. We're glad to have her."

The cloud of chemicals dissipated as they reached fresh air. Marcus took a long breath in through his nose, exhaling out his mouth. The sight of Jordan's car, instead of his Lamborghini, was giving him PTSD.

Antony spoke in his best mafioso voice as they reached Jordan's Jetta, "It's Saturday. Yous got a package fors me or what?"

Jordan pulled a pound of cannabis from his trunk, tossing it to Antony, who sniffed it obsessively. "The mountain madness?"

"Indoor grown," said Jordan. "From Sundance with love."

Marcus took his usual seat as shotgun and Antony climbed into the back, hugging the bag of drugs, as the trio set out on their adventure. *This was a preview of the coming summer,* Marcus thought. *A dress rehearsal for their Grand Tour, which Jordan had just paid for in full.*

"So what happened with the ice bitch?" Antony invoked another of his endless nicknames for Dianna.

"Marcus bears some of the blame for this," Jordan insisted, "he knew she'd flip out over Selection and intentionally withheld—"

"Shhhhh," Antony interjected. "Let the involved party explain."

"Thursday night I passed Selection and—"

"What! Why didn't you lead with that? Congratulations, brother! I've got a graduation gift for you at my place—man, did I call this or what? I'm so proud of you, Marcus. *Sempre avanti!*"

"I'm glad someone's excited." Marcus looked at Jordan.

"What happened with Dianna?" Antony asked.

"She wanted to reconcile."

"Is that a euphemism for fornicating?" Antony simpered.

"No ... I mean, yes. Last night, we finally did. But it was a lot more meaningful than that. For a moment, I had the old Dianna back."

"You mean she wasn't always this batshit crazy?"

"How is it that the two of us," Jordan gestured in Marcus's direction, "have seen something good in Dianna that you can't?"

"Marcus is young, dumb, and full of cum. At least he has an excuse. I've never understood your platonic thing with her."

"It was going great, then I told her about joining the Cohort, and she went nuclear." Marcus withheld details about their mother's car, a necessary omission to salvage the rest of the day, especially for Antony.

"She's nothing if not predictable," Antony offered as Jordan glared at Antony through his rearview mirror. "So she's gone? For good?"

"Yes," Marcus and Jordan replied in unison.

"You dodged a serious bullet. I hope you appreciate how lucky you are." Antony whistled a bar of Miss Gulch's song from the *Wizard of Oz*. Jordan responded by blasting music through the car's stereo.

"I TOLD YOU, MARCUS," Antony raised his hands dramatically, "DON'T PUT YOUR DICK IN CRAZY. SHE'S NOT THE TYPE TO GO GENTLY INTO THE NIGHT. WATCH YOUR SIX, LITTLE BRO."

Jordan stopped beside a line of new Lamborghinis, four cars deep, each a different dazzlingly brash color, waiting at the traffic light.

"Fuck," Antony's voice was barely audible.

Marcus cut the music. "What's wrong?"

"Pull forward a few feet," Antony implored.

"Into the intersection?" Jordan's voice climbed three octaves.

"Just roll into the crosswalk so we're not next to this car. It's Benedict Darrow. I want to avoid another stop and chat. MOVE!"

Jordan's manual transmission slipped, lurching them a full-car length into the intersection. The blaring horn of an approaching semi forced them to retreat to their parallel position beside the leading Lamborghini.

"Maybe he won't see us," Marcus said.

"Anthony? ANTHONY ADAMS!"

"So much for that theory." Antony slowly turned the manual window crank. "Hey, BeneDICK. I'm surprised to see you outside of your gated community. Coming to see how the other half lives?"

"I was heading to the motorsport park with the boys, but the office called and there are fires to put out. You know how it goes, stuff seems to hit the fan whenever I try to take the day off."

"I can't relate. My team is great at preventing fires."

"I wish I had your tolerance for imperfection," Benedict didn't mask his disdain. "But some things can't be delegated down the food chain. Will I see you tomorrow?"

"On a Sunday? Not unless you're joining my Druid LARPing troupe to celebrate the spring equinox. Pisces is rising!"

"Interesting. There's a stakeholder meeting for One Identity ... I guess you weren't invited. I'll have my girl send the meeting notes on Monday." Benedict sneered. "Great car, by the way. It's very fitting. What does the vanity plate mean? FFYFF? I read it while you were obstructing the intersection."

Jordan leaned over Marcus to flash his Cheshire grin through the passenger window, shouting, "FACE FUCK YOUR FUCKING FACE!"

Benedict rolled up his window and sped off, retinue in step.

"That guy is the worst," Marcus grumbled.

"I sleep a little better every night knowing I banged his sister."

"What?" Jordan and Marcus said in sync for the second time.

Antony laughed. "At a gala years ago in the back of Benedict's limo. I think she got off harder than I did at the deviancy of it."

"Does he know?" asked Marcus.

"I hope so," Antony said, glowing. "I really hope so."

"What's One Identity?" Jordan inquired.

"A government contract for Know Your Customer and Anti-Money Laundering regulations. Basically, it's blockchain-based identity management tied to every individual on Earth. Banks have to migrate everything to Benedict's data systems. I've been tapped to build their master algorithm. Looks like he's trying to steer the project in a direction that minimizes me. He's datatarded though, and the government boys know it. I'm not worried."

"That was one hell of a car," Marcus admitted.

"Benedict doesn't own that car because he gets pleasure from the perfection of automotive technology. He bought it for one reason: to make you feel beneath him for not having one."

"It's a positional good," Jordan confirmed.

"Exactly. It's a way to elevate himself above everyone else, so long as they all buy into the same noble lie."

"Which is?" Marcus asked.

"That a car reflects the value of the person driving it."

The boys spent the rest of the trip lost in music and introspection. Antony's house was an old single-story structure surrounded by ten acres of fallow farmland in the shadow of the NSA's data center. A swarm of air- and land-based drones surrounded his property, custom-designed to alert Antony of any invaders in real-time. The eight hundred square foot home was meticulously clean but bereft of furniture, even lacking a bed since Antony slept on the floor. Small shoddy windows and century-old light fixtures gave the house a dark feel, and knee-high piles of well-worn books lined the cracked alabaster walls.

As they reached Antony's front door, Hecate began a transit of the sun, casting the world into shadows. The eclipses came in clusters over a couple of days, but then they'd occur out of sight on the other side of the horizon. Despite his fascination, Marcus had more important things to do than watch another eclipse right now.

"Kitty!" Marcus dropped to the floor and rolled across the foyer with Antony's middle-aged chocolate lab. It was a dangerous maneuver since her tail swung like a forged steel wrecking ball whenever she was excited.

"At least *that* bitch still loves you," Antony quipped.

Marcus stood and composed himself before following an unlit hallway to a bedroom-turned-walk-in-armory. *Violence is the last refuge of the incompetent* was inscribed into a fortified door that opened using a set of biometric sensors to remotely identify Antony by both his DNA and his electromagnetic signature.

"Pick your poison," Antony encouraged. Hundreds of pistols and rifles, along with suppressors, optics, tactical vests, and holster systems, were mounted on the walls. Ammo cans and bins of various magazine calibers lined the floor. Antony had survived a mass shooting at the Trolley Square Mall in Salt Lake City in -14 NE thanks to an off-duty officer carrying a concealed weapon. The experience shaped Antony, and he committed to never being a helpless victim again.

Marcus had flashbacks to his first Sequence with Brad as he pulled an AR-15 and a pistol from the wall. He added suppressors, loaded magazines, and selected a vest system. After a long delay, he found Antony waiting in the back yard, leaning against Bucephalus. The vehicle was designed by Volvo's Arquus division; although the armored vehicle's official name was Scarabée, Antony lovingly renamed it after Alexander the Great's warhorse. This modern incarnation was lighter, faster, stronger, and far more futuristic-looking than a Humvee, reminding Marcus of the Warthog from the *Halo* videogames, minus the infinite ammo turret.

Jordan was in lock-step behind Marcus. As they approached, Antony used his remote to open Bucephalus's sliding doors; this was the only way into the urban assault vehicle since it had no outward-facing handles. They were loading gear through the passenger side when Antony approached, sporting a devious smile. "It's dangerous to go alone! Take this."

Marcus was confused by the reference until Antony revealed a large sword, sheathed in elegant black leather with decorative silver inlays. He extended it to Marcus, showering him with more praise. "I realize I say this a lot, but I'm so proud of you and I love you."

"Thank you!" Marcus embraced his brother. "I love you too."

"I'm also glad I don't procrastinate!" Antony rubbed his head. "I picked that up yesterday. I was going to laser etch something into the blade, but you're too fast—for the Federation and for me!"

"It's beautiful. What is it?"

"A Gladius. Like the Roman soldiers used. Except this one has some seriously modern modifications. Does that feel like real leather?"

Marcus moved his hand across the scabbard's surface. "No."

"The outer layer is made of mini LEDs that project a pattern. They can also cloak the whole thing using tiny cameras. Push that little button on the side of the sheath," Antony instructed.

The Gladius dissolved into the background of Antony's yard. It was a strange sensation to swing it around since the sword's weight remained unchanged.

"The scabbard has a retractable three-point sling to keep it tight to your body at all times," Antony continued. "The inner layer of the sheath, below the LEDs, is a carbon nanotube core, which means it's nearly indestructible. But the coolest feature is the handle."

"Why's that?" Marcus asked.

"It doubles as a biometric lock. The blade can only be pulled from the scabbard by the hands of someone with Adams' DNA."

"No way!" Marcus bounced in place and freed the blade. "Maybe I should call it Excalibur?"

"You're mixing mythologies, but I'm progressive like that."

"No. Invictus. That's what I'll call it."

"Perfect," Antony encouraged.

"Is this metal?" Marcus inspected the black blade.

"It's cold steel, the high-carbon type, so it's strong and sharp as hell. But it will eventually fail on you. It's also the only part of the Gladius that can't be cloaked."

"Why not make the blade from the nanotubes?"

"For the same reason it isn't made of LEDs: they don't provide a good edge. See how the blade comes to a long, fine point? That's for piercing all types of body-armor. The blade itself is thick, but both sides are razor-sharp and tapered at the center, like an hourglass. That means Invictus is equally awesome for hacking and slashing in a pinch," Antony winked.

Marcus slid the blade back into the scabbard.

"Saddle up," Antony sang. "We're moving out."

"Where are we going?" Jordan asked.

"Global One," Antony answered. "In the western desert."

"Isn't that where the Federation Forces train?" Jordan protested.

"Soldiers and citizens alike are welcome there to perfect the ways of war. It has a shoot house and dozens of outdoor bays designed to simulate real-life run-and-gun scenarios. If you want to get crazy, there's even a track for defensive driving, and an airfield to master the art of jumping out of airplanes."

"It's awesome. You'll love it!" Marcus's enthusiasm eclipsed Jordan's hesitancy.

Despite weighing six tons, Bucephalus easily reached speeds of seventy-five miles per hour. Its three hundred horsepower engine ran on a blend of diesel fuel and electric energy. It could also crab-walk because its wheels turned sideways. Combined with independent tire controls, this allowed the warhorse to spin in place like a top.

As they drove a dirt road leading to Global One, Marcus noticed a historical sign. "The Pony Express came through here?"

"Child labor," Jordan said from the backseat.

"What is?" Antony inquired.

"The Pony Express. They hired twelve-year-old orphans because they were too stupid to know the danger, and were disposable if things went badly on the route."

"I've never heard this." Marcus turned to converse.

"Maybe that's why the Federation picked you?" asked Jordan.

Marcus smirked.

"Word to the wise," Jordan coached, "I'd survey your Cohort for other orphans if I were you, bro."

The second they parked, everyone at Global One descended on Bucephalus. Even for those in the military, this vehicle was a novelty. Following some small talk, smiles, and lots of selfies, the trio checked in and moved to the first shooting bay. The sounds and smells of gunfire lingered in the air. Earthen walls enveloped an expansive area filled with blue fifty-five-gallon drums, and a plethora of plywood panels provided mock cover.

"The idea is to navigate these obstacles while engaging the steel and cardboard targets," Antony advised. "Only one of us will shoot at a time, while another person holds the timer. We'll take turns as the safety officer, so let's remind ourselves about A-C-T-T." Antony looked at Marcus first, "What does the "A" stand for?"

"Always treat every firearm as if it's loaded," replied Marcus.

"What about the "C"?" Antony asked Jordan.

"Control your muzzle—"

"Explain what that means," Antony interrogated.

"Don't point the gun at anything we don't intend to destroy."

"Good, and the first "T"?" Antony echoed to Jordan.

"Be sure of your target's foreground and background."

"Excellent. Take us home, Marcus. What's the second "T" for?"

"Trigger control."

"And how do we accomplish that?" asked Antony.

"By keeping our fingers outside of the trigger guard until we're ready to destroy something." It was during moments like this, surrounded by men, that Marcus especially missed his father.

Antony had done an incredible job as a model of male behavior, Marcus thought, *but it wasn't the same thing as having their father around.*

"Suit up," said Antony.

Marcus and Antony looked the part in their battle gear, but Jordan's ill-fitting vest betrayed his unsoldierly body. Realizing this, Jordan offered homage to one of their favorite childhood movies, pointing his rifle skyward and shouting, "WOLVERINES!"

They followed Antony's lead, running each scenario and comparing their timed performances. The sweetness of expressed gunpowder clung to Marcus's lips. The kick of his rifle and snap of his pistol proved therapeutic, but his shooting was terrible. He was off by a wide-enough margin to make him more of a liability than an asset in any real-world parallel. His frustration built bay-by-bay, until somewhere around the eighth scenario of the afternoon, Antony spoke up, "Looking at your targets, I'd think Ray Charles was out here putting rounds downrange. Still letting Dianna get to you?"

"No … maybe. I can't get into the flow right now."

As they moved to the next bay, a realization hit Marcus harder than a 5.56x45mm NATO round: he'd skipped his daily affirmation. The remainder of the afternoon went much the same, with Marcus consistently taking up the rear ranking. It was unheard of for Jordan to outshoot him like this. When the crew had exhausted themselves and their supply of ammunition, they mounted a controlled tactical retreat to Bucephalus.

"Hold up," Antony paused at the shoot house. An eight-person squad expertly maneuvered through fortified positions, blasting at holographic targets, literally, with their arms.

"What are they using?" Jordan asked, stroking his beard. "It's like a Mega Blaster."

Antony laughed at the analogy. "You're pretty close. They're called Power Gloves. It's a Federation weapon that covers both arms up to the shoulder and offers a mix of offensive and defensive capabilities. I assume it works like Tek, using some kind of wireless connection to the Operator's brain. If they're facing fire, the Power Gloves can respond with ice. If they're facing armor, it can offer penetrating rounds. I've seen it a few times now. It's so badass."

"One Power Glove is shooting all those munitions?" Jordan squealed.

"One set. Yes," Antony answered.

The Gloves resembled the sleeves of the EXO, Marcus thought. "Where does the ammunition come from?"

"From what I understand," Antony speculated, "the Gloves use the surrounding environment to materialize the munitions."

They watched with awe as the squad trained in their simulated battlefield. Emblazoned on the shoulders of each Operator's Power Gloves was the Federation Forces logo: back-to-back F's within a circle of laurels, topped by a trio of five-point stars forming a triangle.

"Why didn't we do that?" Marcus asked.

"You have to be part of the Federation Forces."

"I know that guy," Jordan pointed to an Operator in the shoot house. "He's a YouTuber. I met him once at a local creator's event."

"Nutnfancy," Marcus recognized him too.

"Want to say hello?" Antony asked Jordan.

"I doubt he'll remember me," Jordan replied. "Are all the Federation Forces former military like he is?"

"Anyone can volunteer." Antony lit up, "Speaking of familiar faces—"

Marcus scanned the squad; it was hard to focus on individuals given the rapidity of their movement. Still, he recognized Antony's old head of security, calmly situated amid the chaos. "Tony?"

"I didn't know he'd joined," Antony uttered under his breath.

"Why's he sitting in the squad's line of fire?" asked Jordan.

"It teaches each Operator the importance of precision, and it proves they can trust one another in a crisis," Antony explained.

After gawking a little longer, they climbed into Bucephalus. Marcus was overcome by a flashback of the car accident in Provo canyon from his first Sequences; the set and setting had been built from one of Nutnfancy's videos. He felt dizzy for a moment, trying to parse out his real memories from the artificially-lived experience.

Antony noticed Marcus's wincing face. "Need some water?"

"Just give me a second," Marcus grimaced.

"I've seen that face a few times now," Jordan jumped into the conversation. "My working title for it is *Federation Fry Brain*."

"Sounds delectable," Antony replied. "I doubt that's how their Lab works, or they'd burn through guys like Marcus faster than they could replace them. We both know he's irreplaceable."

The drive back to Antony's was quiet, each of them riding the downhill slope of adrenaline. Everything changed when they reached cellphone service, where all of their devices surged with alerts.

"Shit!" Jordan was the first to process what was happening.

"What is it?" Marcus asked.

Jordan's arm was shaking as he held the phone between the front seats, revealing a *TMZ* headline with a yearbook photo of Marcus from high school:

Is This the Face of the Federation's Cohort: Marcus Winthrop Adams?

There was defeated silence among the weekend warriors.

"Improvise, adapt, overcome," Antony offered. "I've been the target of cancel culture, death threats, you name it. I'll show you how to stay safe. Don't let fear get into your head. You're safe right now. No one knows you're here. We can get you a security detail. And come Monday, you'll start training at Krav with me. We'll get through this. Together."

"I can't believe she'd hurt me like this," Marcus lamented.

Silence was the fourth passenger for the remainder of their drive.

Kitty, blissfully naive, greeted them a second time as they gathered around Antony's backyard fire pit for a night of revelry.

"Ready to sample my wares?" Jordan bounced anxiously.

"Everything is on the kitchen counter."

Jordan returned with enough weed for a Snoop Dogg concert, grinding and loading a bong before passing it around. Marcus declined, so Jordan hit it again, coughing on smoke. "Is my mountain grow suddenly too lowbrow for you?"

"I don't feel like it right now."

"He's stressed and heartbroken," Antony said. "Let the guy wallow for a minute. The only way forward is through the pain."

"I can't believe she'd expose me like this," Marcus huffed.

"I'm surprised by it too," Jordan affirmed.

"I'm not," Antony snapped. "You've both deluded yourself about that woman's true nature. For the love of God, if you learn nothing else from this, realize the simple truth: she's very, very dangerous."

Though for differing reasons, neither replied.

Flames crackled as the sun migrated beyond the western sky. Antony went inside, returning with three Cuban cigars and a bottle of scotch.

"Now that," Marcus's spirits climbed, "I will have."

"Where'd you get those?" Jordan was suspicious of the competing contraband.

"Irma."

"Your secretary? She's a million years old," Jordan hissed.

"She's sixty-seven. And she's an executive assistant, you dick."

"She doesn't look a day under one hundred," Jordan retorted.

"That's what a hard life does to a person."

Jordan didn't take the bait.

"She was a Peter Pan kid," Antony expounded.

"I loved that movie," Jordan hit the bong again.

"Christ, you guys really are the product of modern public education, aren't you? The Peter Pan kids fled Cuba without their parents after the country fell to the Communists. Irma was six when they started conscripting kids into military training. Her parents sent her to the US."

"How did you meet her?" asked Marcus.

"She was working in the campus bookstore when I was a grad student. I don't remember what textbook I was picking up, probably an economics one because we talked about communism and her story. When I needed an assistant, I thought of her. She's like a grandmother."

"A granny who bootlegs Cuban cigars?" Jordan mocked.

"A madam of mystery. Do you want one or not?"

Jordan acquiesced. As the three sat around the fire, Marcus's phone vibrated. It was Monica:

What R U doin? Wanna take a midnight ride?

"Who is it?" Antony suspected it might be Dianna.

"Monica. The girl I was talking with at Nerio the other night. Turns out, she's also a part of my Subsumption Cohort."

"That's crazy." Antony laughed incredulously.

Marcus looked mockingly in Jordan's direction.

"What do you think I should do?" Marcus asked his brother.

"Go enjoy the benefits bestowed by a benevolent universe."

"I don't follow," Marcus replied.

"It's a booty call, right when you need a rebound. Nothing helps you get over the last like the next. Plus, you'll be safe with her. Fate has teed this one up. All you have to do is take a swing."

"Or," Jordan hesitated, "you could stay here, smoke some of my weed, and listen to *Coast to Coast* all night."

Marcus texted back. She insisted on driving, so he pin-dropped his location. She was twenty minutes away; he had time to finish his cigar.

"Want to drop acid before your date?" Jordan dared.

"No thanks," Marcus shook his head.

"I'll partake," Antony said. "How much you got?"

"Fourteen tabs," Jordan answered.

"Perfect. We can each drop seven," Antony contorted his face to appear crazy as he placed the small papers in his mouth.

"The smell of sweat, dust, and cigars reminds me of a dream I had once," Jordan ranted. "I was being groomed by Hemingway ... he was an Incubus though, not a living person."

Marcus stared at the bouncing flames and tried to reground the conversation in the material. "Fire might be unique to Earth."

Jordan and Antony broke into riotous laughter. Antony accidentally inhaled a mix of smoke and scotch vapors, and through violent coughing, asked, "WHAT?"

"Jordan was talking about smoke. But fire is probably unique to Earth ... you guys love talking about random shit when you're high, so here's a kernel for you. Fire requires the perfect amount of oxygen to burn, and Earth is special in that way."

"What if the Federation is here for our fire?" Jordan could barely see through squinted eyes, "Maybe that's what your research Shadow is after."

Antony had a moment of clarity, "During my Disclosure Moment, Hi!-D said Marcus was special ... and that Dianna would get in his way."

"What?" Marcus turned to face Antony.

"Yeah. Hi!-D said my brother, that'd be you," Antony pointed with his cigar, "was very important to the Federation and that I should continue supporting him however I could because a woman would get in his way. It's the only thing I remember from that night. I was blotto."

"Always do sober what you said you'd do drunk. That will teach you to keep your mouth shut." Jordan smiled. "Hemingway said that ... not to me in the dream ... in real life."

"What do you guys remember from that night?" Antony asked.

"About the party or Disclosure?" Marcus clarified.

"Disclosure. When everything you knew about the world changed. I was an adult, but you were so young. You still are."

"I felt terror," it was Jordan's turn to be serious now, "and it's never gone away. I've carried that dread every day since. I got evil vibes from Hi!-D. She made the hair on my back stand up. She still does."

"I didn't feel fear at all," Marcus recounted, "just drunken excitement. The Federation has never made me feel like I was in any kind of danger."

Jordan and Antony continued to pass the bong back and forth between puffs on their cigars and sips of scotch. Eventually, they hijacked the conversation, debating the origins of EDM music. Marcus slipped off to complete his daily affirmation in the house's bathroom mirror. *Better late than never,* he thought, gripping his Memento Mori. Monica texted that she was out front, and he walked Antony's long driveway to a waiting FJ Cruiser. *The car perfectly fits her personality,* Marcus thought as he climbed in.

"Hi!" Monica beamed with a bewitching smile.

"Hi."

"Do I smell cannabis?"

Impressed, Marcus replied, "Yes."

"Really! Do you have any more?"

"It's not mine."

"Could you get us some?" Monica asked doe-eyed.

"Right now?"

"If it's not too much trouble?"

"Let me see what I can do." Marcus jumped from the car and ran the long driveway to the back of the house, where Antony and Jordan were more heated than the fire.

"BULLSHIT!" Antony shouted. "Without Trent Reznor, heavy electronic music never would've succeeded in the US—"

"The Prodigy was already laying the groundwork around the rest of the planet, bro. It was inevitable," Jordan bellowed back.

"I hate to interrupt this scholarly squabble," said Marcus, "but can I get some of that weed?"

"Sure—" Antony started to say through an inebriated smile.

"Hold up," Jordan protested. "You aren't in the mood."

"It's for Monica."

Jordan stared him up and down.

"Is that a yes or a no?" Marcus persisted.

"Just give it to him," Antony instructed.

Jordan handed Marcus three fat pre-rolled joints.

"Grazie." Marcus rubbed Kitty one more time, then headed for the driveway as his brothers dove back into their forge of intellectualism.

30

MIDNIGHT RIDE

Marcus arrived back at Monica's car, the hero of the moment.

She smelled each joint. "How much do I owe you?"

"Nothing," Marcus explained. "Free for me, free for thee."

"I see what you're doing," Monica radiated. "I'm into it."

Monica was a forward female, thought Marcus. *It was a big change from Dianna, and he liked it.*

"You have a serious commute to campus every day," Monica said as her FJ Cruiser roared to life, headlights cutting the darkness as they began their midnight ride. The air vents puffed out a pungent mix of melon body lotion and perfume.

"That's Antony's house. I live within walking distance of the Lab."

"Really?" Monica looked briefly over her shoulder as the property faded from view. "Do you live alone?"

"No, I share a house with my best friend, Jordan."

"If I keep you for the night, how will he get home?"

"He drove," Marcus answered. "So where are we going?"

"I have a house an hour from here in the western desert. I thought we'd go there. It's got a bar, a hot tub, and a movie theater."

"Sounds like a plan," Marcus affirmed.

Monica lit the joint as they reached the edge of civilization, taking a long hit before handing it to Marcus.

"This is the second time I've been out here today."

"Were you off-roading?"

"No." Marcus exhaled a thick cloud before passing the joint back. "We were at Global One. Shooting."

"I love guns!" Monica exclaimed.

"You do?"

"I sleep next to a pair of pink Glock 18's."

"The full auto ones?"

"*Face Off* specials. With suppressors to boot."

"Getting all those tax stamps must've been fun ..."

"It was painless. My lawyer did everything. Best seven hundred dollars an hour a girl can spend."

The darkness was fading along the edges of her headlights. He'd been conditioned by Dianna to expect confrontation in everyday banter, but conversations were natural and easy with Monica.

"How are you enjoying overnight fame? *TMZ's* a big deal. No one from the Cohort has ever been outted. You just made history."

The blood in Marcus's body surged to his stomach. "You saw?"

"About five minutes before I texted you."

Marcus was plotting his next comment, but Monica pressed on, "It'd been more than twenty-four hours since I gave you my number, and you hadn't made the first move, so I was looking for an excuse anyway."

"It's been a rough day."

"What happened?"

"I don't want to be a Debbie Downer," Marcus replied.

"First off, I love *Saturday Night Live*," Monica laughed, "second, I wouldn't ask if I didn't want to know. I don't do the typical female thing and dance around what I mean. You can tell me if you want to."

"I've noticed that about you. I broke up with my girlfriend this morning … then she leaked my info."

"I didn't realize you had one," Monica passed the joint again. "I'm guessing you broke her heart, so she put a target on your back?"

"Other way around actually. She dumped me."

"So that's why you're acting like Eeyore right now?"

"Ouch," Marcus suppressed painful laughter.

"She did it because you joined the Cohort?" Monica theorized.

"How'd you guess?"

"Didn't Brad warn you about 'mating partners'?"

"Yes," Marcus conceded.

"He really undersold the shit, right?"

"No joke."

"If she's too stupid to see what a great guy you are, regardless of her feelings about the Federation, then you don't want to be with her."

Monica sounded like his mother, Marcus thought. "I knew she'd be mad, but I didn't expect her to do something like this."

"If you're looking for sympathy, you won't get it from me. I gave up everything for the Cohort. And it was totally worth it."

Monica was driving into the depths of the Great Basin, a landscape largely devoid of life due to the lack of water. A scintillating cluster of lights sat on the horizon. *Nothing else was out here, so that had to be their destination.* "It won't keep me down. I'm stronger than this. I'll rise above."

"Yeah?" Monica challenged.

"Yes. Unless Brad drops me from the Cohort," Marcus floated the idea, hoping Monica would assuage his fear, but she deflected.

"Does this mean you're on the market? Cause I'd tap that ass," Monica giggled hysterically, swerving as she lit the second joint.

"You want me to drive?" Marcus offered.

"You're so uptight, even after smoking. Do us both a favor and take deep breaths of air in through your mouth. After inhaling chant like this, 'haaaaa,' and picture a pair of glowing orbs, one golden and one platinum, hovering a foot above your head."

"Seriously?"

"Yes," Monica insisted. "Picture them showering you in their contrasting colored dust, then visualize it swirling around in a bubble that's surrounding your entire body. I promise it works. Try it."

Marcus inhaled slowly through his mouth and mimicked the sound she'd made with each exhale. After a moment of mental visualization, he felt relaxed just like she'd promised.

"There you go," Monica noticed the change in him.

"Thanks. I didn't realize I was so wound up."

"Outliers are like that."

"What?"

"You're an outlier. They're extremely empathetic. Brad told me about it to try and soften the blow when you broke my Selection record …"

"Sorry … I didn't … I mean, I wasn't even trying."

"Wow. You're going to rub salt in the wound now?"

"You aren't going to bait me this time," Marcus smiled.

"Clever boy."

"What was your record? Brad didn't share any details with me."

"Ten days."

"That's impressive!" Marcus admired. "How long have you been with the Cohort? You were the first, right?"

"I started Selection on Zero Day. And yes, I was."

"What's Zero Day?"

"My nickname for the day the Federation arrived. Since the calendar restarted."

"Clever girl," Marcus echoed.

"During my Disclosure Moment, Brad and Hi!-D invited me to—"

"Wait, Brad was at your Disclosure?"

"Wasn't he at yours?" Monica asked.

"No. It was just Hi!-D."

"Huh … anyway, Hi!-D showed up first, then Brad joined. I was convinced it was a hallucination and hesitated, but later that day I decided to follow his directions to the Lab. I started Selection and was offered a seat in the Cohort ten days later. The rest is history."

"How long was it until the next person joined you?"

"Months. I was the Alpha and the Omega for a long time. Then we went through a boom and bust, gaining people real fast but losing them even faster. For a few months, it was just me again."

"Why?"

"No idea. That's above my pay grade," Monica replied.

Marcus was seized by Déjà vu. "Wait, what?"

"I said that's above my pay grade. Only Brad knows why people are redacted. I got to know the first few who joined the Cohort then stopped paying attention because I realized they wouldn't last. I only talked to you because of our night at Nerio."

"Otherwise, you would've ignored me?"

"Maybe. But Brad couldn't stop talking about you, which piqued my curiosity. Plus, you're hot." Monica tapped her fingernails on the steering wheel. "But without Nerio, we would've started as frenemies—at best."

"What is the rest of the Cohort like?"

"They're all nice, but I don't spend time with them outside of the Lab," Monica prefaced. "There are ten others, not counting you and me. You'll meet everyone eventually. You want to drink from the firehose?"

"I can handle it," Marcus assured.

"Okay. Corina is my favorite. She's from a country that used to be part of the Soviet Union, but don't ask me which one. Rick is the oldest member. I think he's in his sixties and he's a professor at Westminster College, down the road from the University of Utah. Komson is from Thailand, and he makes a mean mixed drink and loves Harry Potter books. Diksha and Sanchit are both from India, and they're hilarious for different reasons. Zain is from Pakistan. Sometimes he gets into heated debates with Diksha and Sanchit, but I never understand what they're talking about. Duygu is from Turkey and is a sweetheart. I really like her. Dave and Bryan are nice, but they're both typical American males. Dave likes trail running, and Bryan is an astronomy nerd. Then there's Ali. He's from Iran and is a great dancer who loves making us all smile."

Marcus struggled to remember someone's name the first time he met them face-to-face and knew he had zero chance of recounting Monica's details. With time and repeated interactions, he'd familiarize himself with each of them. *Assuming he wasn't persona non grata at the Lab come Monday morning*, Marcus thought.

Monica turned onto a gravel highway. A sign indicated they were traveling on the original Pony Express route, and the lights they'd seen earlier in the distance were now a brightly lit community.

"Where are we?" Marcus asked.

"Last Chance Lakes. It's a man-made water sports community. These are mostly vacation homes, but a few families live here full-time. Most of those are military officials from Dugway. The base is over that hill," Monica nodded toward the western darkness.

"Didn't the Stardust mission land there?"

"No idea. I heard something about a VX leak at the base decades ago, where a bunch of sheep died. But this community is safe." Monica pulled up to the main gate. Men in tactical gear stood sentry, weapons at the ready until Monica showed ID.

Her car crawled through the picturesque neighborhood. Every house was herculean, surrounded by lush green lawns. Marcus couldn't see the wakeboarding lake beyond the houses, but he trusted Monica that it was there. She parked in the driveway of the biggest house on the block and killed the engine.

"How long have you lived here?" asked Marcus.

"I don't. This is a vacation house. I've had it for about a year. I built it once my Tek crypto account passed a billion dollars."

Marcus stared in awe at the interior of the house; it was constructed from giant mahogany beams that separated expansive ivory walls at aesthetically pleasing angles. The house was whisper-quiet and smelled of cinnamon potpourri. Marcus removed his shoes, allowing him to feel the warmth radiating through the floor's Tuscan stone tiles. Lights turned on automatically as they traversed long hallways into the home's center, where a wall of windows overlooked an enormous pool with its own waterfall.

"Is anyone else here?" asked Marcus.

"Just us. Want a drink?"

"Sure," Marcus grinned. "You know what I like."

Monica returned with two glasses of scotch and lit the final joint. "Come outside. I want to show you something."

Marcus didn't resist as she led him poolside by the hand.

"It's three hundred feet long, one hundred feet wide, and thirty feet deep underneath the cliff diving area," Monica boasted as she pointed to the far side, where a geyser gushed starward. "The whole thing is built around an artificial mountainside with four waterslides, and if you go under the falls, it leads to a network of scuba courses."

"You're a frogman?"

"A what?" Monica asked.

"It's slang for someone who scuba dives."

"Oh, no. I don't know-how. But if I want to learn, I'm all set. Want to try the hot tub?"

"I didn't think to bring a swimsuit to the desert."

"Are you going commando today or something? Not that I'd mind." Monica pouted her lips. "Boxers or birthday suits are both acceptable."

Monica stripped to her underwear, and Marcus followed her lead.

"A briefs guy, I like that." Monica offered her hand again. The pair traveled through a series of honeycombed tunnels in the faux mountainside to a hidden grotto larger than most pools Marcus had seen. Monica pulled him into the hot water. The grotto had a wide view of the sky, and like the night before, storm clouds were forming in the west while Hecate hung overhead.

"We have twenty minutes until that hits us," Monica came in close, "any suggestions on how to pass the time?"

This felt hypnogogic. Twenty-four hours ago, he'd been in an identical situation with Dianna. So much had changed.

Monica noticed him lost in thought. "Hey. Stay present."

"Sorry."

"You're thinking about—what's her name?"

"Dianna."

"You know, Marcus, the whole point of having a girlfriend is so she can make you feel good. You deserve that. You're wonderful, and my intuition says Brad is right: you're going to build an empire one day. You're that important." Monica took a final hit from the joint and kissed him, passing smoke from her lungs into his. The same explosion of energy he'd felt at Nerio returned. It was beyond addicting.

Lightning struck across the distant landscape. Rumbles of thunder occasionally reached them, but it felt safe in the grotto. They continued kissing until the storm was hovering over them, deterred only when a firebolt hit so close that they felt its static residual. They scrambled from the water, racing for the safety of the house, hands intertwined.

Monica led Marcus to a dimly lit bedroom. The space was immense, with a massive silver platform bed under a crystal chandelier. Unlit candles lined the metallic furniture pieces. Marcus hesitated at the door. *Was this his version of a back-of-the limo tryst?*

"If you're not up for this, I understand. But just so we're clear, I'm fine being your rebound," Monica shared. "Staying the night doesn't bond us for life. You can enjoy yourself ... if you want to."

"I want to," Marcus affirmed.

"Good. Me too." She kissed him again. Marcus moved for her bra, but it was Monica's turn to hesitate. "Can we start with Tek sex?"

Marcus said nothing, which made Monica uneasy. "It's a safe way to see if we're compatible—"

"I've never used Tek."

"You're a Tek virgin?" Monica squealed. "How can that be?"

Marcus didn't want to tell her the truth that deep down, he was scared Jordan might be right about Tek's effects on people.

"You're going to love this. God, I wish I could go back and relive my first time," Monica melted. "A friend told me to Net the moment with the Tek, but reliving the same memory doesn't do it justice. It's the newness of something that makes it so pleasurable."

"How does it work?" Marcus tried to mask his unsteady voice. "Is it like the voyeur pods at Nerio?"

"Not at all. Voyeurs are about an anonymous exchange. This is called Entangling, and it's more personal. We'll be living the experience as ourselves. Totally together."

"Okay."

Monica handed him a piece of Tek. "I like to wear mine on my forehead like a third eye, but you can put it wherever you want."

Marcus placed it on the underside of his wrist. It reminded Marcus of the EXO, bonding to his skin without actually touching it.

"When you're ready," Monica sat next to him on the bed, "lay back, close your eyes, and our devices will link. What happens next is better lived than explained. You'll have to trust me … like you did at Nerio."

Terror pulsed through him, riding shotgun to each heartbeat. But Dianna's comment about the exhilaration of pushing through fear motivated him onward. His heart fluttered as Monica kissed him and said, "See you on the other side."

Marcus laid back and was instantly transported to a world mirroring Monica's bedroom, except here, all the candles were burning. He kept opening his eyes and breaking the connection to confirm it wasn't real. The disjointed experience reminded him of jumping from Sequence to Sequence before Stealth Mode. Each time he closed his eyes, Monica's naked figure inched closer to him in their ethereal reality.

When they finally touched, it was a feeling beyond description. The sensation didn't build slowly; it hit like hurricane-force winds, instantly going from zero to a hundred. The physical pleasure was overwhelming, traveling down his arms, to his back, and through his legs. *This was nothing like Brad's Lab*, Marcus thought as Monica began kissing him. His heart rate accelerated, and his desire surged to heights he didn't know were possible.

Monica's lips and body were soft, velvety even, and he could smell her perfume. Their hands continued to explore each other until Monica stepped back. She moved to the bed and sat Marcus on the edge, kneeling before him. She was glowing, literally radiating heat as she took Marcus into her mouth. He wasn't sure if he was also moaning in the real world; nothing had ever felt this good in his whole life, and Monica melted any of his remaining hesitations.

She stopped and stood before him, her body statuesque, worthy of immortalization in marble. She pushed Marcus onto the bed and climbed onto his face. The screams she emitted as she gyrated across his mouth made him harder than he'd ever been before. He allowed himself to fully surrender to the fantasy. Monica's movements slowed, then stopped. She rolled into the middle of the bed and got on all fours, lowering her head and inviting Marcus with a shy smile to enter her body.

He took his position behind her as both shared in the ecstasy. Their rhythm was slow and deliberate at first, allowing them to move together. Time had come to a crawl. Marcus reached under Monica, one hand softly caressing her breasts, the other stimulating her clitoris as he kissed her neck and back. Her moans turned to groans as she pushed against Marcus, each thrust harder than the last. Marcus explored her body until Monica screamed she was climaxing, before dropping forward to catch her breath.

"Your turn." Monica smiled through glazed eyes.

He wasn't sure if this was love or lust, but Marcus didn't care to make the distinction. Monica opened herself to him again, placing her legs over his shoulders. He could feel Monica tightening around him as the intensity and depth of his motion accelerated.

The benefits of youth were on full display as he maintained his high pace until Monica asked him to finish inside her. Hearing her beg for his seed set Marcus over the top, and he roared again. The moment had no equal or end. He collapsed beside her, forgetting this wasn't real; they were both too high to care. Monica kissed him a final time. Words weren't necessary; she was reverberating through his soul.

PART IX

MOLON LABE

THURSDAY, JULY 21, +1 NE

31

VINI, VIDI, VICI

T he previous eighteen weeks had been chaotic, both for Marcus and humanity. The fallout from Dianna's *TMZ* exposé required a security detail at Marcus's home and an armed escort wherever he went. Fortunately, the public's ever-ephemeral attention span allowed him to ease these precautionary protections after a few weeks. Life was just getting back to normal when Bill dropped a bomb on the FACT students: he was taking a sabbatical during the next academic year, and Luke Kelly would be their Connector until he returned.

Marcus still spent most of his time at Brad's Lab. He enjoyed the work, but the idea of becoming a Federation Forces Operator increasingly enamored him. Brad emphatically opposed it, insisting Marcus's time was better spent in Sequences to ensure the M1 milestone was reached on time. Marcus initially heeded to Brad's advice, or at least until he attended a Forces recruiting event at Global One with Antony. But after trying the Power Gloves firsthand, Marcus committed to enlisting in the Federation's unit following his six-week summer Grand Tour with Antony and Jordan.

When Marcus wasn't in Bill's class or Brad's Lab, he trained alongside his brother in Krav Maga. Antony reigned undefeated at Nerio, earning the respect of the Betting House and befriending Zedd after a vicious rematch with the same outcome, a testament to the spirit of their shared warrior culture. But it wasn't just rigorous conditioning that helped Antony retain his crown; he constantly randomized his fight preferences so no one could pull an *Antony* on him.

Marcus never missed his brother's fights because Antony, perpetuating their mother's superstitious nature, believed him to be a living lucky charm. This meant Marcus was with Monica all the time, in Subsumption's dreamless sleep by day, and Nerio's galactic dance floor by night. His desire to be with Monica had multiplied tenfold following their midnight drive, but she seemed content staying in the friends-with-Tek-benefits zone.

The oscillations of Marcus's personal life were nothing compared to the chaos of the wider world. Global demand for Tek units had grown exponentially, but bottlenecks caused by Tek-Mart's expansion beyond the Black Market led to severe supply shortages. This created a speculative boom in Tek's secondary markets, where a single used unit could sell for more than the price of a house. Marcus hadn't given Brad his quota yet, and with Tek-Mart's ongoing fumble, he had no desire to jump in now.

The only thing climbing faster than Tek's price was the level of hysteria within Jordan's Lyceum. It'd reached a fever pitch by their first global summit in Salt Lake City, an event which kicked off on Memorial Day and was more cosplay than an intellectual conference. Jordan marketed it as the "last chance humanity had to unite" before an imminent Federation attack. He didn't have any new evidence but insisted that he could feel it. Since no one could disprove Jordan's feelings, the theory spread like a contagion.

Memorial Day celebrations were ruined by news of the Confederation's launch from Proxima Centauri. The clock was ticking now, and the Confederation's first wave would reach Earth in late August of +5 NE. A second wave of panic tore through society, pushing suicides back to levels not seen since the Federation's arrival. Murders, however, had been suppressed thanks to the government's activation of the Federation Forces to maintain public order.

As a preventative plan to counter potential panic, the Federation began hosting weekly press events from Fort Douglas to update the public on Project Noble's progress. Though humanity was closing in on the M1 milestone, accomplishing the full integration of M2, and the battle-readiness of M3, were years away. Coalition protestors responded to Project Noble's progress by embracing anarchy, with a fringe element turning to terrorism. An epidemic of car bombs and mass shootings led to the creation of Go Zones, areas fortified behind a Pomerium and patrolled by Federation Forces.

Universities hosting a FACT class were the first candidates for this increased security, with Marcus's house being added after he narrowly escaped an assassination attempt. Marcus had been illegally carrying a concealed weapon during the attack, but an army of Antony's lawyers got the possession charges dropped in time for their Grand Tour. Brad thought Marcus should cancel the trip, but Antony wanted to rely on disguises and self-defense skills to push ahead as planned. Life had to be lived, while it still could be.

Antony's advice proved correct, and their trip transformed an otherwise tumultuous summer into the greatest one of Marcus's life. They were mid-adventure when Dianna ambushed him in Athens with the shocking news of her pregnancy and a legally-backed olive branch: a parenting plan. Her proposal for co-parenting required Marcus to limit his relationship with the Federation moving forward.

He could stay in FACT and the Cohort, but becoming a Praetor to the Shadows or joining the Federation Forces were both deal-breakers.

Today marked Marcus's first day at the Lab in more than six weeks. He made the familiar journey with an occasional glance over his shoulder. *This was his new normal*, he thought, enjoying the first blue sky of July. Like everyone else, he was wishing the clear weather would hold for the upcoming Pioneer Day celebrations; it was unlikely, though, since Jordan's prediction of another inexplicably lush summer had come true. Their desert community was still fertile and green late into July.

Marcus paused at the door to Brad's office, reflecting on his first time here months ago. He felt a flutter in his chest and stomach but wasn't sure if it was excitement or fear. Marcus's nostalgia was cut short by a PSA:

> **"Good morning, citizens, and welcome to another wonderful day! Have you been the victim of bullying? Your rights deserve to be respected, and it's up to you to assert them. Stand up for yourself. And because bullies cower before the strength of numbers, stand up for one another too. Because together, we're invincible."**

It was 9:00 a.m.

"What's up, brotha! Welcome home!" Brad hugged Marcus tightly. "Come sit. How was your trip? Tell me everything."

"Where to start?" Marcus mused.

"The beginning would be optimal."

Time apart helped Marcus realize how much their relationship had grown. *Brad was like family, a pillar of support, and always willing to listen.*

Monica emerged through the locker room door, carrying two steaming cups of something, flashing a seductive smile as she moved toward him.

It'd been more than a month since they'd seen each other, and it hadn't ended on a good note. "I thought you'd take your birthday off?" Marcus inquired.

"I woke up and realized, what else would I do? I've never skipped more than a couple of days. Plus, I didn't want to miss your homecoming. I'm curious what this will be like for you."

Monica set the drinks down and embraced Marcus. The smell of her melon body lotion heightened the pleasure of her touch.

"One thing at a time," Brad protested as Monica sat beside Marcus. "Let's hear about your Grand Tour!"

"It was everything Antony promised. We started at the Skin-walker Ranch—"

"What's that?" Monica interrupted, handing Marcus one of the cups, which he confirmed was coffee.

"A paranormal hotspot here in Utah near the Ute reservation. The Defense Intelligence Agency ran a secret research study there for years because of all the UFO activity ... long before the Federation revealed themselves," Marcus smiled at Brad.

"For the record," Brad smiled back, "that wasn't us."

"That's a creepy name," Monica added.

"In Navajo legend, skin-walkers are malevolent shapeshifters with deformed animal bodies and glowing eyes. Other indigenous tribes from the surrounding areas have similar legends about human-animal hybrids that are impossible to kill. The Navajo don't discuss it with people outside of their tribe because it can bring them bad luck and can make the skin-walkers appear."

"Why would you go there?" Monica quavered.

"Jordan has been obsessed with the place his entire life, and Antony knows the guy who owns it. We got a private tour. It was a super cool experience and set the bar for the rest of our trip. After the Skinwalker Ranch, we hit the hot spots of the American southwest: Moab, Zions, Vegas, and Lake Powell. That took two weeks. Then, because Antony banned all technology on the trip, Jordan got lost driving overnight in the desert. We ended up at Chaco Canyon, alone under the stars, which was spectacular."

"Where were you trying to go?" Brad asked.

"Albuquerque. To catch a flight to Africa. We were recreating a vacation we took with our parents. We whitewater rafted and bungee jumped near Victoria Falls in Zimbabwe, then we canoed the Okavango Delta with hippos and crocodiles, and did a traditional bush safari in Botswana. We ended by visiting Robin Island near Cape Town and Soweto in Johannesburg."

"What was that last part like?" Brad wondered.

"Pretty humbling. It made me appreciate my life."

"I don't understand," Monica mouthed. "Why?"

"South Africa has a long history of social conflict," Marcus explained, "though, it seems pretty mild compared to the news coverage of Salt Lake while we were gone."

"This has been the epicenter," Brad admitted.

"Things are calmer now thanks to the Go Zones," Monica affirmed.

"When did you leave Africa?" Brad asked.

"Late June. We flew to Europe, which was definitely my favorite few weeks of the trip."

"That'd be mine too," said Monica. "I love Europe."

"When we're you there?" Marcus asked.

Monica waved a hand. "It's been years."

"What about Europe did you love?" asked Brad.

"Riding the trains everywhere was fun, plus the museums were incredible. Seeing into humanity's past like that gave me a new perspective, especially about time. Another highlight was the megaliths of Carnac."

"Where's that?" Monica asked.

"France," Brad answered for Marcus.

"But watching Antony ride The Crack might have been the best part of the entire trip."

"He was on crack?" Monica murmured.

"No. *The* Crack. It's a section of mountain in the Swiss alps for wingsuit flying."

Neither of them replied, so Marcus explained, "It's the flying-squirrel-looking people who race along the ground ..."

"Okay ...?" Monica clearly didn't understand.

"Antony flew feet above our heads at a hundred miles an hour. The energy was indescribable."

"I'm getting a hit of adrenaline just thinking about it," Brad exclaimed. "Were you in Europe when the polar vortex hit?"

"Yeah. That was nuts! We were in Florence. Antony bought some North Face jackets off a street vendor. I have no idea where he found them in the middle of summer, but they were a blessing.

The cold front was still raging when we took our last train ride to Treblinka."

"What's that?" asked Monica, sipping her coffee.

"A Nazi extermination camp in Poland from the Second World War. It was a dark experience. More than a million people were murdered there."

"Why'd you go?" Monica scrunched her face.

"For family reasons," Marcus answered.

"Weren't you going to visit Greece?" asked Brad.

"Yes. We flew from Poland to Athens to celebrate our parent's anniversary."

"Why their anniversary?" asked Monica.

"We were near where they died. Their anniversary felt like an appropriate day to honor their lives."

Monica stroked his arm. "I'm sorry."

"What did you do to commemorate?" asked Brad.

"We chartered a boat and went into the Aegean where their plane disappeared, near a bunch of mountain islands. Antony made these hilarious trifold pamphlets with old embarrassing photos for their 'Anniver-sea-ry' celebration, and we shared our favorite memories of them. By the end, we were laughing so hard none of us could breathe. My parents would've loved it. Then we relaxed in Athens before the last leg of our adventure."

"Where'd you go after that?" asked Brad.

"The Levant and then Egypt, where Antony repeated Jordan's mistake and got us lost, just in a different desert."

"Twice in one trip." Brad chuckled.

"What were you doing in the desert?" asked Monica.

"Looking for an oasis. Antony wanted to go there because it's where an oracle told Alexander the Great he was the son of a god. It also had some minor significance in World War Two. I love history, but Antony takes this stuff to another level."

"When did you get back?" Brad questioned.

"We were supposed to arrive on Friday, but two travel-days-from-hell later, I finally slept in my own bed on Sunday night."

"Are you jet lagged?" asked Monica.

"No, I've adjusted."

"The original purpose of the Grand Tour was to provide a coming of age experience to help you grow as a person by exposing you to the world beyond your own little bubble. Did it work?"

"I think so," Marcus confirmed.

"In your travels," Brad challenged, "what surprised you the most?"

"How differently people live, yet how similar we all are. I know to you," Marcus looked directly at Brad, "we're just a 'Form,' but our lived experience varies from place to place and over time. In the end, the things we all want seem to be similar."

Monica wanted specifics. "Like?"

"The ability to choose our path in life. To follow our passions. To love. To be accepted. To be a part of a family and a community. This trip made me grateful for my family and life, that's for sure."

"I think that's a common consequence of travel among your Form," Brad grinned again. "Did you stay safe the entire time?"

"There was only one incident. In Arachova."

"Where's that?" Monica asked.

"It's a tourist spot in the mountains of Greece. A group of drunk guys were harassing us, then one recognized me. They didn't know who Antony was, and tried to get physical. Antony showed restraint."

"How many were there?" Monica set down her coffee so she could rub her hands excitedly.

"Six or seven. I'm not sure. It was a blur since it happened so fast. Antony tried to buy them drinks afterward, but they wouldn't let go of their grudge."

"What an adventure!" Brad said. "Of all your experiences, what was the most meaningful? What should the world remember thousands of years from now about Marcus Adams and his Grand Tour?"

Marcus took a long sip from his drink and then set it down. "Standing with the marker stones at Treblinka."

"Why?" Brad leaned forward.

"It reinforced that evil exists in the world. That humans are capable of dark, terrible things. My dad had a metaphor he heard from a military commander, a guy named Grossman—I think. I know he was a lieutenant, but it doesn't matter. In his metaphor, society can be broken down into three groups: sheep, sheepdogs, and wolves. Most people are sheep—"

"Because they're stupid?" Monica cut in.

"No. Because they're soft and peaceful, incapable of hurting each other. They want to graze and be content."

"How do sheepdogs and wolves differ?" Brad asked.

"Wolves eat sheep. Sheepdogs protect the flock."

400

"They both use their teeth," Monica smiled.

"Both have the capacity for violence. They just use it differently. Grossman said the problem is that if sheepdogs are effective, the sheep start to believe there are no more wolves in the world, and they chase away the sheepdogs since they have teeth. Then, the wolves come back, but the flock isn't protected anymore."

"Treblinka reminded you of this?" Brad queried.

"A few things from the trip did, but at Treblinka, it all hit at once. It doesn't feel like that kind of evil is behind us. Even the Federation has failed to stop predation. The wolves are still out there. Only now, they're devouring us one at a time instead of millions all at once."

"What's the solution?" Monica whispered.

"More sheep need to become sheepdogs and fight the wolves."

"By joining the Federation Forces?" Brad raised an eyebrow.

"I'm not enlisting, if that's what you mean," Marcus declared.

"That's a surprising turn," Brad observed. "Why not?"

Marcus wavered. *Any explanation would have to include details of Dianna's pregnancy, and he wasn't sure how to tell Monica about his destined future as a father. This wasn't the right time.*

A flash of understanding came from Brad's eyes.

Marcus was surprised by Brad but stayed silent.

"I saw a meme once," Monica interjected, "about an Indian telling his grandson how two wolves exist in each of us. One is good, and one is evil. The child asked which wolf wins, and the grandfather replied its whichever wolf we feed with our spiritual energy."

Marcus had heard something similar from his father, who added the caveat that such stories, especially those involving native legends, were rarely attributed to their correct source.

"Interesting," Brad sighed. "Time to work. Would the two of you like to do a tandem Sequence?"

"Sure," Monica and Marcus replied in unison.

"I might be rusty," Marcus smiled sheepishly.

"I hear it's just like falling off a bike." Brad grinned facetiously as the door to their locker room activated.

32

A MOMENT WITH MONICA

Once they were alone in the locker room, Monica wrapped her arms around Marcus's neck, burying her head into his chest. "I'm so glad to see you."

Marcus scanned the room. A new name was inscribed on a locker next to his own:

20. TONY

"The Cohort is still growing?" Marcus mumbled.

"Did you think you'd be the last one?"

"I never thought about it. Have you met him?"

"Yes. Tony is reserved but very polite. He comes from a family of cops. He started Selection right after me, so it took him a looooong time to finish."

"Fraternizing with the newbies now?"

"A little." Monica pressed her body onto Marcus.

"What if he redacts?"

"I broke tradition for you." Monica kissed him.

Marcus stopped the embrace. "I'm not sure how to interpret that comment."

Monica shifted her weight to one hip. "Are you jealous?"

"No ..."

"Good. That's a very unattractive quality. I told you in Vegas that I'm only interested in you. I meant it."

Monica moved in to rekindle their kiss, but Marcus pulled her arms from his neck. "When did you say that?"

"I was trying to when you kicked me to the curb."

"You surprised me. You weren't supposed to be there."

"Well, I wouldn't have come if you'd taken a Tek unit with you. We could've Entangled from any distance during your trip. You didn't want to."

"Jordan would've lost his mind if he caught me using Tek."

"You still haven't told him?" Monica smirked.

"Don't change the subject. You ghosted me the entire time I was gone because I wasn't available on demand for you in Vegas. You really want to pretend that never happened?"

"Yes," Monica said. "That was the past. Live in the present. With me. Here and now. I want to have fun with you today."

For all their physical passion, they'd yet to move into a real-world bed. "Tek sex?" Marcus scoffed.

"Maybe I'm ready for more … I have something to ask you after the Sequence, so don't leave without saying goodbye. Promise?"

Marcus swallowed his frustration. "I promise."

Monica blew a final kiss before disappearing into her locker.

[Sequence ID# 639] [Data Begins]

The last thing he remembered was the confusion he felt staring at the broken frame of his front door. It'd been kicked in. Wood splinters littered the porch and his living room. He was paralyzed by fear, wondering if this was real. He found the courage to creep into the house, but nothing looked out of place.

"Hello?" Marcus's voice trembled. He held his breath, hoping to hear his wife's welcoming reply. Nothing came.

He tiptoed through the rest of the empty home and was heading for the kitchen when he saw someone in his peripheral vision. The warning provided enough time to face the charging stranger before their worlds collided. A vicious struggle ensued, ending on the ground with the intruder attempting to place plastic zip ties around Marcus's wrists. Through sheer determination, Marcus reversed positions, pinning the man facedown and knocking him out with a strike to the base of his skull.

When the invader finally awoke, Marcus had him zip-tied by the ankles and wrists to a kitchen chair; he was gagged, and his head was covered with a pillowcase to obscure his view of the red-hot butcher knife on the Viking stovetop. The only thing missing from the house was Marcus's wife, and the only lead was this captive man.

Marcus ripped the cover off the attacker's head, screaming the question that consumed him, "WHERE'S MY WIFE?"

The man's eyes scanned the room frantically.

"Nod if you know where she is," Marcus asked through grit teeth.

The man took a long time to think, shaking his head to say no.

Marcus slipped his right hand into a Kevlar oven glove, lifted the luminescent blade from the range, and held it inches from the attacker's face. "I'll give you a moment to rethink your answer. If I believe you, I'll call the police. If I think you're lying, I'm going to drive this into your stomach over and over and over again until you're honest with me." Marcus put the blade back on the open flame and left the room. His hands shook violently from the adrenaline and uncertainty.

Marcus returned and retrieved the glowing knife from the stovetop before repeating his question, "Where. Is. My. Wife?"

The man hesitated, looking at the blade, then Marcus, and through tears, shook his head again.

Marcus set the knife on the burner and removed his Kevlar glove. He tore the tape from the man's mouth and yanked the towel gag free. The intruder sat silently.

"You know," Marcus began, "all around the world people use nodding for 'yes' and shaking for 'no.' It's strange, don't you think? Since we all speak different languages. Of course, there are a few exceptions, but people of diverse histories and cultures all communicate the same sentiments with those two gestures. What are the odds?"

The man said nothing.

"Why were you in my house? And why did you attack me?"

The man shuddered as he offered an explanation, "I ... I was walking by. I saw the broken door—I knocked, but no one answered. I came in to help. I swear! Then I saw you. I thought you were the person who broke the door. I swear—let me live!

Please believe me. Please! I'm begging you. Don't hurt me." The man wept pathetically. "I have a family! I swear! Have mercy!"

Marcus paced around the man. He had signs of drug addiction, likely meth given his stench of ammonia and severe acne scars.

"You tried to use plastic ties to subdue me," Marcus stated. "I know because they're holding you to that chair now. Where did they come from? They aren't mine."

Without allowing the man to speak, Marcus snapped, "I DON'T BELIEVE YOU. JUST LIKE YOU DIDN'T BELIEVE ME WHEN I GAVE YOU YOUR OPTIONS!" Marcus grabbed the knife and plunged the glowing end into the man's torso. The sounds of animalistic agony and frying flesh echoed off the granite counter-tops. Marcus suppressed his instinct to vomit, pulled the blade free, and placed it on the stovetop again. The scent of seared skin filled the room. The man slumped over, passed out. Pain radiated up Marcus's arm; he'd failed to use the Kevlar glove, and his palm and fingers were beginning to blister.

Marcus wrapped his scorched hand with a thin dishtowel and slapped the unconscious intruder with the other to wake him. "The heat of the knife cauterized your wound. We can do this for hours if necessary, or you can just come clean."

The man mumbled incoherently while rocking and convulsing.

"Let me save you more pain." Marcus seized the sides of the man's face. "You're dead. Do you understand? Accept it. Embrace it. But how you die hasn't been decided yet. You can go in agony you never imagined possible! Or … or … you can end your life quickly by doing the right thing. Tell me where my wife is … please!"

The defiant intruder stayed silent, so Marcus donned his left hand with the glove and drove the knife into the man's stomach a few more times. The use of his non-dominant hand made a mess of the wounds until the man, choking on mouthfuls of blood, pleaded for a respite.

"I'll stop when you tell me the truth!" Marcus barked.

"She was taken," he whimpered, "as a comfort girl."

"What does that mean?"

"To be trafficked … a sex slave."

Marcus lost his grip on the knife. He couldn't comprehend what was just said. It sounded so far from the realm of possibility. Then, rage took over. He picked the blade off the floor and pressed it against the invader's face. "WHERE IS SHE NOW?" Marcus vehemently spat the words.

"No more. Please!"

"TELL ME, OR THIS GOES IN YOUR MOUTH!"

"A trailer … southwest corner of the lake … there's a dirt road." The man was slipping in and out of consciousness again. Marcus's cauterization wasn't working; blood leaked from the man's gut and pooled on the floor between his feet.

"Where? How far?" Marcus was desperate now.

"A mile … ravine … behind a hill. It's hidden…"

"Hidden, how? Who has her? How many are there?" Marcus shook the comatose man. "WAKE UP! WHO HAS HER!"

The intruder lacked the life force to reply. Marcus's right hand was throbbing under his makeshift field dressing, but he'd be able to pull a trigger, and that's what mattered most. He retrieved his rifle from the gun safe, thanked the unconscious man for his last act of kindness, and fired a single mercy shot into the intruder's head.

Despite speeding, the drive along the lake felt like an eternity. Thoughts of his wife consumed Marcus, and whether she was still alive. His mind bounced through the list of unknowns when a hard realization hit him: *Shit! I left the stove running.*

Marcus was familiar with this landscape; he hunted rabbits here as a teenager. He had no idea how far behind the captors he was, and he couldn't call the police on account of the murdered man in his home. The sun was close to setting, and soon he'd be in the shadows. He found the dirt road, and a mile later, pulled into a grove of trees. He had two thirty-round magazines for his rifle. Depending on how many people he encountered, this could be a lot or too little.

Marcus stepped from his car and into the protection of dusk. He jogged parallel to the road, using the sparse trees as cover where he could. He heard a truck approaching long before he could see its headlights. He crouched in the brush, burying his face, so the reflection of his eyes didn't alert the occupants of his presence. The truck stopped a hundred yards up the road, then pulled left and disappeared behind a hill.

This was the place, Marcus told himself. He followed them to an old camper with a faded red stripe on its side and a rusted propane tank on its hitch; other vehicles were parked some distance away. A group of seven men stood in the large open field. *You'd never know this place existed if you didn't have an invitation.* Marcus sat at the edge of the trees while memorizing each man's clothing, height, and hair color. He gave each of them a number: one through seven. *These men are all guilty and won't be leaving here alive.*

As he was about to move, another man emerged from the camper —number eight. "Settle down, settle down. HEY! SHUT THE HELL UP!" the man shouted over the raucous crowd. "You know how this works, highest bidder first. If you plan any violence, you go to the back of the line no matter how much you pay. We're missing a couple of VIPs. If they show up, you'll have to shuffle around. No fighting, and everyone waits their turn. You break any of the rules, and I'll put a bullet in you." The man pulled a pistol from his back pocket and waved it in the air.

Marcus didn't pause to think before he sprang into action, lunging from the trees like a lion on a herd of prey. His first few shots killed man number eight before turning the assault on the group, annihilating numbers one and three. As the others scattered, Marcus walked among them with immunity, taking time to aim before pulling the trigger. Precision helped him make the most of his limited ammunition. He caught the two men from the road in their truck, firing through the windshield and ending the existence of numbers two and four. Each snap of the rifle sent shockwaves through his charred hand and up his right arm, haptic feedback of the justice delivered upon these men. Headlights lit up Marcus from the left; he turned and fired rapidly, sending the vehicle veering into a tree, marking the end of number six.

Marcus continued with his hunt, circling the field until he found number seven cowering among the trees. Cut off from his vehicle, he pleaded for forgiveness, extending an offer of money he'd brought. Marcus executed him on the spot. Only number five was still alive. After searching the vehicles and the surrounding area multiple times, the man was still missing. The only place that remained unchecked was the silver camper.

Marcus took a deep breath before tearing the door open and clearing the space. He found his wife motionless on the bed, heavily sedated. She was bound, blindfolded, and gagged, but fully clothed. They were alone. *She'll be safer here*, he thought, shutting the door and moving back to his position behind the trees overlooking the vehicles. Marcus counted on the fact that the missing man didn't want to walk back to civilization. Before long, number five emerged from the trees, leapfrogging between vehicles. Marcus waited until he was in his truck, then fired repeatedly through the passenger window, killing the last of these despicable men.

His job wasn't over. Without hesitation, Marcus moved the shot-up vehicles, using them to drag the lifeless bodies from the area at the same time, and kicking dirt over the pools of blood. He wasn't sure who else would arrive, but he wanted to maintain the element of surprise. Marcus calmly switched magazines in his rifle and took a position in the tree line again. After an hour, as his patience was wearing off, a large SUV arrived; it was a police vehicle. Marcus felt a tsunami of relief. He wasn't alone in this fight anymore, and could finally be reunited with his wife. As he started to walk into the clearing, something grabbed him. It wasn't a physical restraint, but he stopped, almost as if a wall stood before him.

"Where is everyone?" the first officer asked as he sauntered into the beams of illumination created by the patrol car's headlights.

"Are we really that late?" his raspy-voiced partner joined in.

For the second time, Marcus acted without thinking, but unlike the unsuspecting men, these officers saw him coming. "GUN!"

Before they could draw their weapons, Marcus was firing, killing the first cop with a headshot and sending the second man scurrying. Marcus tracked his movements with continued gunfire, striking both legs and causing him to fall. The officer frantically dragged himself along the ground as blood spurted from holes in his limbs. Marcus shot the crooked cop in both arms, but he continued to crawl. It reminded Marcus of the futile hilarity of *Monty Python*'s Black Knight. He easily paced alongside the officer until the man flopped onto his back, screaming through tears of fearful rage as Marcus fired his last shot into the man's contorted face.

Marcus awoke suspended in the darkness of the Liberty Bell. He felt terrible. Another plot point in Marcus's summer story, before his Grand Tour hiatus, was the increasing physical aftereffects of the Sequences; they kept getting more intense and lasting longer. Ringing in his ears, an auditory phenomenon known as Venus Hum, joined the usual body aches after Subsumption. To top things off, Marcus had also developed insomnia for the first time in his life.

Even when he could sleep, he'd wake up in a panic, overcome with anxiety, like he'd been suffocating. A sleep apnea test came back negative, so did a slew of other medical diagnostics Antony insisted on. Brad tried everything in his control, but the problems persisted. Marcus's only choice was to stop doing the Sequences and leave the Cohort, an option he refused to entertain. He'd been optimistic a six-week break would allow his body to reset, but as Marcus felt the familiar infirmity setting in, he accepted that it'd been a false hope.

Monica was waiting in Brad's office, sans Brad.

"What did you want to ask?" Marcus's ears rang.

"What are your plans today?"

"My calendar is wide open."

"Synchronicity!" Monica bounced with excitement. "I want to spend the entire day together. We could grab dinner, kill time at my place, then go to Nerio after dark and dance? It *is* my special day after all."

Monica really had moved on from their tiff in Vegas, Marcus thought. "I assume you're driving?"

"I need an hour, maybe a bit more. Text me your address again. I'll pick you up."

"The birthday girl gets whatever she wants."

"Dress up. I love ripping the gift wrap off my presents," Monica whispered as she kissed his cheek.

33

THREE MEN AND A COUPLE BABIES

Their house was eerily quiet for a Thursday afternoon. Jordan was sleeping, and Marcus wanted to keep it that way since Monica would arrive soon. Until now, he'd successfully maintained a total firewall between his best friend and Monica, largely because of Jordan's insistence on reconciling with Dianna. Marcus hadn't disclosed Dianna's pregnancy or her offer to co-parent yet. *That'd be fuel for the fire,* he thought, pacing and gripping his lucky coin. *All of these omissions were compounding out of control.*

"Are you running ladders up here?" Jordan staggered into the kitchen, "I was up until 5:00 a.m., and you know how I need my beauty sleep. What's the deal?"

"Wha—I—sorry," Marcus stammered. "I was lost in thought."

"Don't scream. I'm right here."

"I'm using my inside voice." Marcus spotted Jordan's hangover shakes from across the kitchen. "You look terrible. Go back to bed. Sleep it off."

"Shots make the best alarm clock." Jordan fumbled through the cupboard, knocking over cereal boxes and bowls, to find an unlabeled skull-shaped bottle. He poured its amber-colored contents into a mug. "This is Dr. Bonnie's batch. Bro, I think I've found a keeper."

"She's a woman of infinite talents. Is she here?"

"Yup." Jordan flinched as he forced down the fluid, then turned to face Marcus. "Speaking of talented women, Dianna stopped by."

"What?" Marcus felt the sweat beading on his forehead.

"She pounded our door harder than the po-po."

"And ..."

"She left some papers for you. I put them on your desk. I'm proud to say I resisted the urge to peek at them. Why are you so dressed up?"

"Thanks." Marcus sighed.

"So ... reward my loyalty and tell me what the hell is going on."

Marcus couldn't delay this omission any longer. "Our first night in Athens when you and Antony went looking to score, I was by the pool and Dianna showed up—"

"For real!" Jordan's face lit up. "Why? For your own Grecian hookup?"

"No," Marcus huffed. "I'm going to be a dad."

Jordan dropped his empty mug. "I know I'm smashed, but—did you really just say THAT?"

"Yes. I'm going to be a father."

"She's going to be your baby momma after all!"

"Technically, she'll be my *babies'* momma. It's twins."

"Praise Zeus! So you're getting back together?"

"No." Marcus held a hand up to stop the idea from progressing. "Dianna did the right thing and asked me to be part of their lives. Antony got involved Monday, and the lawyers have been going back and forth. I bet she was dropping off the final parenting plan to sign."

"Holy shit!" Jordan grabbed another mug and poured Marcus a shot. "CONGRATULATIONS!"

Marcus choked down the liquor; it tasted like burnt rubber and honey.

"Is that why you've been doing the hundred meters up here?" Jordan drank straight from the skull.

"I have a lot on my mind," Marcus declared.

"You had no idea before she showed up in Greece?"

"None. Dianna said she was on birth control before we had sex," Marcus recalled. "The next morning, she broke up with me. I'd only seen her once since then—"

"When?"

"April 20th."

"That's shockingly specific," Jordan said.

"It's an easy day to remember."

"For sure. Puff puff pass, bitches."

"It's her birthday, Cheech."

"That's right."

"It was also the night of Antony's rematch against Zedd. Dianna was protesting outside of the Black Market."

"Did you talk?"

"No. She gave me one of her death glares from across the picket line. I've had no other contact with her since. Then she showed up in Athens."

"It'll be like three men and a couple babies around here!" Jordan sang.

Marcus tried to picture the scenario, but he couldn't envision it.

"When's she due?" Jordan asked.

"December tenth."

"Boys, girls … reptilians?"

"Dianna's almost eighteen weeks, so we'll find out soon."

"Look at you, Dr. Dad, doing his research."

Marcus ran his fingers through his hair. "My mind's been swimming since she told me."

"Are you going to drop out of the Cohort?"

"No."

"Well, the kids will never hurt for money … which should help offset the lack of stability and family cohesion when daddy's deployed as an Operator."

"I won't be joining the Federation Forces or acting as a Praetor after graduating from FACT."

"The good news has no end!" Jordan tipped the skull at his friend before chugging from it again.

"Do you realize that when these kids arrive, I'll be the same age Antony was when I was born?"

"That's not a coincidence, dude."

"This wasn't planned."

"But it still happened. The universe decreed it."

"The universe has better things to do than plotting my progeny."

"Do you have potential names picked out?"

"Our agreement outlines that process."

"You know," Jordan stroked his beard, "this really could bring the two of you back together."

"I'd give that a zero probability."

"Don't write it off. Picture this: your kids blowing out birthday candles as they wish for their parents to get back together—"

"You're describing a scene from *Liar Liar*."

"That's how I picture it. Sue me!" Jordan grabbed Marcus and hugged it out.

As they toasted another round of shots, the alcohol's soothing effects were shattered by the blaring of a car horn.

"Who's the MILF in the convertible Maserati?" Jordan peered out their window. "She looks like she's going to offer to list our house or something."

"That's Monica. From the Cohort. It's her birthday, so we're going to grab food and spend time at Nerio."

"Remember your loyalties, dude. Family above all else." Jordan walked indignantly from the kitchen, turning at the last minute to add, "I hope no one dies from salmonella on their birthday ... that'd be oh so tragic."

Marcus knew he'd have to be extra vigilant to shield Monica from Jordan's inevitable emotional terrorism.

Marcus opened the front door before Monica had a chance to knock. "Hey, ready to go?"

As she moved in for a hug, Marcus pushed her back onto the porch and closed the door behind him. "That's a beautiful car."

"Thanks. It's new." Monica flashed a frustrated smile at his welcoming slight. "It's a present to myself. I had to have it."

"Incredible. Let's bounce, yeah?"

"Are you okay? You're acting like somebody trying to dodge a bill collector …"

"I'm fine," Marcus deflected. "I'm just excited to take a ride. I love Italian cars. That's the GranTurismo MC sport?"

"You have quite the eye."

"The black grill gave it away," Marcus replied.

The Maserati's carbon-fiber interior felt futuristic, and they both sunk deeply into the car's bucket seats. Monica stroked the side of Marcus's face with the backside of her silken hand. "Thank you for coming out with me today."

"You're welcome. Where are we headed?"

"You're all kinds of antsy aren't you?"

"I'm a hungry man," Marcus smiled.

"I like the sound of that." Monica's eyes sparkled. "I thought we'd go to Indulgence at the Black Market. It's my favorite restaurant. Ever."

A long pause ensued until Marcus turned to face Monica. Without warning, she planted a kiss. Marcus surrendered, closing his eyes and completely melting into her luscious lips. After a moment, she broke off the embrace. "Now we can go," Monica bubbled.

"DON'T DRIVE ANGRY!" Jordan shouted like Bill Murray from the porch; Marcus knew he'd pay for this when he got home.

34

A BIRTH DAYTE

Most of the Go Zones had been deployed just before Marcus went on his Grand Tour, so this was the first time he'd passed through the one protecting the Black Market. Operators from the Federation Forces were everywhere, creating defense in depth-like layers of an onion; any potential aggressor would have to pass through multiple fortified lines, the last of which merged all four lanes of traffic into a single chokepoint.

"Why don't these people use the Federation portals if they want to go to the Black Market?" Monica fumed, laying on her horn as traffic crawled forward. "Why'd you want to join the Federation Forces anyway?"

"It seemed like a logical next step to protect my family from the Confederation."

"I'm glad you're not doing it. I'd miss you."

"I would've stayed in the Cohort. It wasn't a binary choice."

"Well, now we don't have to worry about it." Monica flashed her Fast Pass, and an Operator waved them on to the valet. "I'd love to own a set of Power Gloves ... they're brutal."

"How'd you get your Fast Pass?" Marcus asked.

"Same as you." She scrunched her brow at the question. "By selling my quota to Tek-Mart."

"Right," Marcus asserted, stepping from her car.

Crossing the Pomerium afforded him another moment of nostalgia; he'd missed the seventy-two-degree stability of this place. Terra's white transport stream lifted them into view of Tek-Mart's domineering facade. Monica gazed at the lofty logo but said nothing, so they moved along. When they'd reached the Pontus Sector, she finally spoke, "Have you ever been to Set & Setting?"

"No," Marcus replied, "but the owner is a family friend."

"Jeraldine?" Monica's face was alight. "She's the best. I need to pick something up." Monica took Marcus by the hand and walked into the store, which, like most other businesses at the Black Market, lacked a facade.

"Hi, kiddo." Jeraldine radiated energy atypical of her advanced age. She had big crystal-blue eyes and short dirty-blonde hair in a Pixie cut that fell flat against her head. She was dressed in a flowing red tunic that drooped in layers from her shoulders to the floor, reminiscent of a medieval sorceress. She kissed Monica's cheeks before noticing her companion. "Marcus?"

"Hi!" Marcus grinned.

Jeraldine hugged him tightly. "Oh my goodness, child. You're HUGE now! You just missed Garret. He was dropping off my dinner. How are you?"

"Really good. Your store is incredible, congrats on all your success!" Marcus replied.

"Thank you," Jeraldine glowed, "but it's nothing compared to the success you're expecting before year's end."

Was she talking about Dianna's pregnancy? Marcus dismissed his suspicions.

"I've got something for you," Jeraldine said to Monica.

"I think I know what it is." Monica nibbled on her fingertips.

Jeraldine returned with a small mahogany box covered in floral carvings. "Happy birthday, dearest. I handpicked everything using your wish list."

Marcus's palms started to sweat. *He hadn't thought about a gift … he was literally empty-handed.*

Monica lifted the lid, revealing a set of multi-colored sage bundles, an iridescent shell, a little bag of blood-red sand, a feather, small sticks of wood, and a pearlescent stone.

"Thank you!" Monica gushed. "It's perfect!"

"You two enjoy yourselves! Marcus, I'll give Garret your best, he'll be so happy to hear that I ran into you." Jeraldine hugged them both.

Marcus followed Monica out of the shop and back into the bustling promenade.

"How'd your family meet Jeraldine?" Monica asked, clutching her present as they stepped into the red transport stream leading to Ignus.

"She knew my parents," Marcus offered terse details.

The swooping low cut on the back of Monica's blouse exposed her shimmering tattoo; a lion-headed woman with blue hair and a red dress stood beneath a golden orb, holding a similarly colored staff and ankh. The colors were vibrant, like LEDs embedded into her skin. "When'd you get the new ink?" Marcus asked.

Monica peered over her shoulder. "I had a few sessions at Immutable while you were gone. It's Sekhmet. What do you think?"

"I've never seen anything like it. Can I touch it?"

"Please do." Monica shuddered as he ran his fingers across her shoulder blades and down her spine.

The glowing ink radiated subtle warmth. "Who's Sekhmet?"

"The Egyptian goddess of war and healing."

Marcus laughed. "Those seem contradictory."

"She was the daughter of Ra and was incredibly powerful. She could be vicious with enemies but nurturing to her friends ... my kind of lady."

"How does it glow?" Marcus was captivated.

Monica bunched up the bottom of her blouse, exposing her midriff. Above her bellybutton was a piece of Tek. "With this."

The interior of Indulgence caught Marcus by surprise. The massive circular dining hall was lined with heavy wooden booths and wine racks built directly into the marble walls. Gothic light fixtures punctuated the room but provided limited lighting. In the center of the space, two young women played a pair of grand pianos. The instruments, one white and one black, wrapped together in the shape of a yin-yang. The smell of roasted meats and fried food clung to the air. They'd arrived during a lull between lunch and dinner; the pair picked a booth with a view of the open kitchen.

Monica handed him a menu. "Ever been here?"

"Nope."

"Then you're lucky to be doing it with me for your first time! I'll order for us … I know their secret menu."

"Your jewelry is amazing by the way," Marcus admired the deep crimson garnets that'd been transformed into a necklace, bracelet, and earrings.

"Thank you." Monica glanced down at the pendant hanging over her heart. "My chakras were all over the place this morning. I woke up and immediately knew it'd be an important day. These stones spoke to me. They're a shield against the world and its collusions to rattle my center."

"What is the metal one for?" Marcus motioned toward Monica's right wrist.

"It's a balance bracelet. It tunes my body's energy to 7.83 Hz, the same resonance wave as Mother Earth."

"Do you meditate?"

"Every day, what about you?"

"The last time I remember doing that, I was five."

"There's got to be a good story here." Monica set down her menu.

"My grandmother tried to teach me when I was a kid. She gave me a meditation word and left me alone in a dark room at her Cape Cod home. She told me to repeat the word and clear my mind, but I was too terrified to focus. The space was about as dark as this place," Marcus motioned around the restaurant, "and full of slow floating dust that smelled terribly of mothballs. I ran from the room and dismissed that silent-mind type of meditation as a waste of time."

"You should give it another chance. It makes or breaks my day."

"I have something else that's similar—"

Before Marcus could finish, the waiter arrived. Monica did the ordering, including the "Dolphinately Special," a $1,000 sushi roll made from dolphin meat wrapped in edible gold petals and served with Champagne. Marcus hated sushi almost as much as the idea of eating a dolphin, but he wanted to make today special, so he kept his mouth shut.

"Just so we're clear," Monica leaned forward, her face glimmered more than her jewelry, "I'm paying, and when I put down this kind of money, I have certain expectations for how the rest of the day goes ..."

Marcus smirked. "How often do you come here?"

"At least two times a week, sometimes more."

"You must really love the food."

"I do now. It was terrible when they first opened. But I liked the owner and the vibe of this place. One day, I realized I could fix the food, so I moved my favorite chef out from New York City."

"He made the Trek?" Marcus drew a parallel to the arduous journey Mormon pioneers made to Salt Lake City more than a century ago.

"He traveled first class. We paid for everything."

"We?"

"Sorry, *me*," Monica clarified. "I bankrolled everything, which included buying out his contract for a five hundred square foot shithole in the village. I upgraded him to a five thousand square foot home here in Sugarhouse."

428

"He must love his new starter castle," Marcus quipped, "but there has to be a less expensive way to get a personal chef—"

"Money, as we say in the Cohort, is no obs-TEK-le."

"So how old are you today?"

"Wow, aggressive much?" Monica scolded.

"That's not what I meant. Don't be like that."

"Like what exactly?"

"The 'typical women' you decry."

"I'm twenty-nine," Monica held her head high.

"How many of those years have you lived in Utah?"

"All of them."

Monica offered nothing else, so he stayed silent.

"I told you before, Marcus, you don't want to hear my life story. It's terribly boring."

"I want to hear whatever you're willing to tell."

"Fine." Monica tapped her fingernails on the table. "I'm one of a bunch of kids. Eight to be exact. Dustin, Derek, Dillion, Dara, Matt, Molly, Mallory, and me. I was the last. My parents could barely keep us fed."

"You grew up poor?"

"I guess you could call it that. We had a house and cars and stuff. It was just all basic. We got a lot of government assistance, but my parents still worked."

"What were your parents like?"

"My father was giant, like the rest of the Eames men. He was an inch shy of seven feet."

"Holy hell."

"And my mother was tiny. She was barely five feet in heels."

"That's hilarious."

"That was the only comical thing about them. They were strict Mormons. Not the typical type, but they were extreme in their devotion. Zealots. I had zero social life until I moved out."

"Did you go to college?"

"No. When I graduated from high school, I had no direction or purpose. I didn't have money either. I bounced around in different social circles until I realized everyone was boring in their own way. And that's how life was going, boring and directionless until the Federation arrived. Now, my purpose is clear."

"Which is what?"

Monica smiled. "To take everything and live for the moment."

"Do you still see your family?"

"I haven't been home in a long time. We didn't have a big fight or anything. We just drifted apart. The only connection holding us together was blood. Turns out, that wasn't enough."

"I'm sorry to hear that. Family is everything."

"Since we're sharing," Monica asked, "what's your story? I know about your brother, but is he it?"

"Yes. All my grandparents died before I was six, and my parent's plane crashed when I was nine."

"No aunts or uncles?"

"Both of my parents were only children."

"I'm sorry." Monica touched his hand. "I never know what to say when people share stories of tragedy like this."

"It's okay. I know what you mean. It's been hard for me to talk about in the past, but the more I do it, the easier it gets. Thankfully, I still have Antony and Jordan to lean on, so I consider myself blessed."

"I love your positivity," Monica said. "Jordan was the chubby one shouting at us from your porch?"

"Yes."

"What was your mother like?"

Marcus reflected. "Loving. Beautiful. A powerful personality."

"So she was controlling?"

"She was a good shepherd, a master in the art of getting what she wanted through patience and kindness, but within a firm set of rules. She loved to binge watch *Who's the Boss* episodes and ran our house like a female Tony Danza. She could be vindictive, especially if it involved someone threatening our family. She was constantly keeping score with people and could wait years to strike back when it'd hurt them the most. She believed in Karma."

"I love her already. I believe in Karma—"

The conversation was interrupted by the arrival of their food. The paltry number of other patrons turned their attention toward the shimmering golden roll on Marcus and Monica's table. The waiter lit another of their secret menu items on fire, and a small flame burned briefly between them.

Monica continued her questioning between bites, "What about your father?"

"He was a strong man. A true Scotsman through and through, but he loved my mother's heritage. She used to say whoever controlled the kitchen controlled the culture, which was true in our house. He adored everything about her. He was a great dad, stoic most of the time, but cool and confident in a crisis. He expected the best from us and wanted to ensure we lived up to our family's motto."

"Which is?" Monica asked.

"*Sempre avanti.*"

"What does that mean?"

"Always forward. My parents cast a long shadow. Sometimes I worry if I'll be as good of a parent to my own kids one day."

"I'm never having children," Monica said flatly.

"No interest?"

"None," Monica took a giant bite of golden sushi.

Marcus moved food around to give the appearance of eating, even hiding a baseball-sized lump of fish and rice in a napkin in his pocket. After excusing himself to the men's room, he disposed of the gelatinous mess. The table had been cleared during his short absence. Their conversation continued over multiple rounds of drinks; the effects of the alcohol set in, but the communication came effortlessly, like their first night at Nerio.

Monica locked eyes with Marcus. "I haven't vibed like this in a long time."

"It's been wonderful, *carissima*."

They were equally taken aback by his comment.

"What does that mean?" Monica wondered.

"Precious little one. It's what my dad called my mom."

"That's the nicest present I could get! Promise to call me that for the rest of the day!"

Marcus embraced this easy solution to his lack of birthday preparedness. "Sure."

"What's next?"

"It's still your day, so you get to decide."

"Anything?"

"Anything legal and mostly moral."

"Have you ever tried Crystalline?"

Marcus's eyes widened. "Crystal meth?"

"No. You do warm it in a pipe, but other than that, it has nothing to do with meth. Crystalline activates the magnetite in your brain, giving a deliciously calming psychedelic effect, like a cross between weed and LSD."

"It's the stuff Hi!-D used during Disclosure, right?"

"The very same. It's only available at Nerio, so we can try some when we come back to dance. But first, I've got something to show you at home." Monica held Marcus's arm as they traversed through the Sectors.

The summer sun was almost as warm as the alcohol in his system as they sped across town; the Maserati had a soothing touch and accelerated like a rocket ship as they journeyed eastward. Even with the roof down and wind racing around them, the "new car" scent was the only thing Marcus could smell.

"Where are we going?" Marcus shouted.

"Into the Cove." Monica was using local lingo for the ultra-affluent neighborhood tucked into the base of Mount Olympus.

"How many homes do you own?"

"Good question." Monica paused to calculate an answer. "At least fifty, but I've never set foot in most of them. Do you like electronic dance music?" Monica thumbed through her music library using the car's touch screen.

"Have you heard the *Hive Humper* remixes?"

"No."

"Do you know who DJ Beez Nutz is?"

"No. I'm terrible at remembering the names of songs or who made them. I listen to music for moments and how they make me feel. Music is my prophet. It tells me what will happen in my life."

"My mom was the same way."

"Really?" Monica glanced at Marcus.

"She had old cassette mixtapes that could only be played on one stereo in our house. Antony teased her endlessly about it. But when she'd play those songs, she'd go into a literal state of trance."

"Want me to search for *Hive Humper*?"

"No. Don't worry about it."

"You can't throw out an epic name like that, then take it off the table!" Monica shouted.

"They're Jordan's albums. He's an EDM DJ."

"That's so cool. I wish I could make music! I don't have a creative bone in my body. Have you ever watched him in the recording studio? I bet it's enchanting to see creativity flow."

"I don't think he's ever been inside a studio."

"Thanks for ruining my fantasy."

"Sorry, but it's the truth," Marcus maintained.

"How does he make his music then?"

"On a computer in our basement. That's how he's always done it. He was posting songs on YouTube when we were in junior high, and one track went viral. It launched his music career."

She raised a single eyebrow. "He got a record deal because of YouTube?"

"Jordan doesn't have a label. He doesn't trust the music industry."

"Why not?"

"Putting aside his general distrust of authority, it's because of their historical involvement with the Mafia."

"Does he tour?" Monica asked.

"Nope. He's enrolled in FACT with me, but he spends most of his time fighting the Federation through his Lyceum."

"They're the ones protesting outside the Black Market?"

"Nope. That's The Coalition."

"Is that where the Porcelain Princess worked?" Monica shared a disdain for Dianna that, like Antony's, manifested in cutting nicknames.

"Funny story about Dianna—"

"NO!" Monica shouted even louder.

"What?"

"Don't say it, Marcus. DON'T!"

"I'm confused." Marcus shifted in his seat to face Monica.

"I know what you're going to say. I felt it this morning when I woke up. I told you." Monica frantically stroked her necklace with one hand, oscillating her focus between him and the road.

"What was I going to say?"

"You're getting back together," Monica asserted.

"No."

"What? But—"

"I'm going to be a dad," Marcus blurted.

Monica offered no reply.

As they continued driving eastward, the size of the homes grew, but nothing prepared him for Monica's. An opulent black iron fence enclosed acres of landscaped hillside overlooking the Salt Lake Valley. She waved at the armed men guarding her driveway before pulling behind the white stone mansion into a ten-door garage. It was bursting with sports cars, trucks, motorcycles, ATVs, snowmobiles, and a Mercedes Benz golf cart, the adult version of the Power Wheels toy Marcus desperately longed for as a kid.

"You're giving Jay Leno a run for his money," Marcus ribbed.

"I get a new vehicle every week. I drive it, love it, and then it sits here next to the others. A couple of times a year, I call a local charity to pick up the collection. Then I start over. Back up and say that last part again."

"About Jay Leno?"

"No, before that." Monica sat perfectly still.

"I'm going to be a father," Marcus repeated.

"And Dianna is the mother?"

"Yes."

"Wow … Marcus … I'm really happy for you."

"That's not what your body language is saying."

"Really, I'm happy for you. I am." Monica removed her seatbelt and leaned over the car's imposing middle console to hug him.

"I'm not getting back together with her," Marcus assured.

"A kid changes things. It changes everything, actually."

"There are two of them."

"Twins?" Monica mouthed, the wind was knocked out of her.

"Yes … we have a parenting plan."

"A contract?"

"Sort of. It's not legally binding the same way an operating agreement for a business is. It just outlines things we're agreeing to ahead of time, like our individual responsibilities as parents, how we plan to handle holidays, their education, how we will resolve disputes, and what happens if a parent relocates. Lawyers are still involved though, Antony insisted on it."

"Are you going to relocate?"

"I'm planning to stay in Utah for the rest of my life, or at least until the Confederation arrives."

"Is this why you're not joining the Federation Forces?"

"Yes," Marcus admitted.

"Who gets legal custody?" Monica asked.

"We're splitting it. That requires an actual legal document from a court, but we need a parenting plan in place first."

"This is so bizarre. I'm sorry for saying that."

"I know. Can we put this down now and focus on you? Just today? Tomorrow I'll answer anything else."

"Sure." Monica's smile couldn't hide her heartbreak. "Want the obligatory tour of my house?"

"Since I only saw two rooms at your other place, absolutely." Marcus tried to set a new tone. "Lead the way, *carissima*."

35

CALYPSO'S LAIR

Monica's mansion was enormous, containing an uncountable number of rooms. Each was filled with art, furniture, and other luxuries of life. Monica's spirits climbed as they moved from area to area. Like Benedict's noble lie about his car, Monica clearly believed these belongings fully reflected her value. *Was this what Dianna felt like touring Sundance,* Marcus wondered. Somewhere between the gym and the fifty-person dining room, it hit Marcus: Monica's house felt sterile, like a museum fenced off from the world and designed to be looked at, but never touched.

"I think you'll appreciate this." Monica opened a large pair of French doors. From floor to ceiling, the circular space was one giant wraparound screen. Bean bag chairs punctuated the other-wise vacant room. It was dark, with a low hum, like the Liberty Bell.

"What is this?" Marcus turned in place.

"You told me once that you loved old video games. Every system that's ever existed can be played in here. I love old games too."

"You must if you had an entire room constructed for them."

"Well, I built it so my nephew had a place to play when he comes over. There's something else I want to show you." Monica took Marcus by the hand and walked to the far side of the space.

"Nephew? I thought you didn't see your family."

Monica placed her right hand against a screen panel comprising part of the wall, causing a section to swing open and reveal a secret passage.

"No. Way!" Marcus bounced with boyish excitement.

"Best behavior now," Monica said as she entered the hidden hallway, mahogany box in hand, and climbed the wide spiral staircase. This led to another door, opening to a colossal three-story turret with a domed roof. Half of the curved wall was covered from floor to ceiling in an ostentatious library built around the biggest fireplace Marcus had ever seen. The other half of the room's curvature was pure glass, giving a God's eye view of the valley.

"Perfect timing." Monica nodded to the sun dropping behind the western mountains. Hecate was rising simultaneously at the same spot on the horizon, twisting the twilight into a set of long celestial spokes.

"What's that smell? It's super familiar," he asked.

"Redwood."

Marcus was transported to a childhood memory of wandering misty old-growth forests with his family.

"Everything in this room is made out of it." Monica sat on the edge of a gaudy desk. "What do you think?"

"... I need to give Brad my quota."

"What?" Monica murmured.

"Nothing. Inside joke," Marcus dismissed. "I think this is the crown jewel of your entire house."

"Better than the game room?"

"Much better."

"Here's my favorite part." Monica pushed a small touchscreen resting on the desk. Every window went dark, blacking out the room completely. A second later, the fireplace roared to life, and a set of reading lamps illuminated either extreme of the vast wooden workspace. Monica was half in the light and half in darkness, gazing hungrily at him. "Look up."

A mosaic of soft blue lights resembling the night sky traversed the dome ceiling. It was the second artificial star field Marcus had experienced with Monica, but it was equally beautiful to the first.

"They're fiber optics. I had them installed years ago. They remind me of Nerio."

"It feels safe in here. Like a cave."

"Nothing can get in or out. We're totally alone."

"Wait, years ago?" Marcus asked. "Tek didn't pay for this?"

"Not this house. I already had it. But it did pay for my birthday present, which was the second-best gift of the day." Monica slid off the desk and walked slowly toward him at the edge of the light. She rested one of her hands on his chest. "We'd be amazing together. In the flesh. Can you feel it in your bones? My body's energy radiating into yours ... mixing together and growing ... like magnets pulled to an inevitable collision."

Marcus felt everything. She'd described it perfectly. The soft glow of the fireplace was reflecting in her eyes; they were the most beautiful thing in the room. He was ready to reach out and touch her when she seized the initiative, pushing her body against his and kissing him. Their momentum was unstoppable. Her soft lips tasted of ginger.

Monica's eyes remained closed as she spoke, "I couldn't wait another minute. This is what I really wanted for my birthday." She pushed Marcus on to one of the large couches in the library and straddled him, continuing their embrace. Energy pulsed through his body again. There was no trial and error in their physical connection. It felt like they'd done this a thousand times in a thousand lives. As he moved his lips to her neck, Monica stood and retrieved her mahogany smudge kit from the desk. She held a white bundle of dried sage leaves to the fire, then smothered the flame in the iridescent shell and traced out waves of smoke as she moved fluidly through the room. Marcus followed her lead and explored the rest of the space. Tarot cards and runes were spread across a coffee table.

An old book caught his eye. *"The Fable of the Bees?"*

"If it's not a Nora Roberts novel, it isn't mine."

Light from the fire bounced off purple crystals and framed pictures placed among the bookshelves. One snapshot of Monica with an older man and a small male child caught his attention. They looked familiar. Marcus made the connection. "You know Benedict Darrow … personally?"

"Yes." Monica continued smudging the air.

Marcus thumbed through the custom, aesthetically uniform, books of the library. None appeared to have ever been opened. More photographs in fancy frames were spread among the shelves. A pattern emerged: no matter who else was in the picture, Monica and Benedict were always there. Together.

Sensing Marcus had assembled the pieces of her puzzle, Monica preempted him, "Before you freak out, there's something I want to tell you, which you're probably just realizing. I was waiting for the right time, but it never happened, or I wasn't brave enough to make it happen. Either way, it doesn't matter. I wanted to tell you at the Lab or Nerio. It never felt right."

Marcus could sense the shockwave of bad news building. "Tell me what?"

"I'm Mrs. Benedict Darrow. Technically."

Marcus wobbled as the air left his lungs. Rage, betrayal, and confusion coursed through him all at once. He collapsed into a sitting position on the floor.

"Give me a chance to tell you my side of this. It's complicated, and I want you to understand," Monica begged, sitting down in front of him on the floor. "If you don't like what I say, I'll make sure you get home, and you never have to talk to me again. But just listen, don't say anything. Just listen. Okay?"

Monica didn't wear a ring, and nothing about her lifestyle, including her name, was consistent with having a husband. She tucked her knees up into her chest and took a series of deep breaths. "I wasn't honest with you. Not today. Not in general. It's hard because I've been conditioned to keep barriers between me and everyone else. To treat everyone like they're a threat. I know now that you're different, but it wasn't clear our first night at Nerio."

"You're rambling," Marcus spoke through clenched teeth.

"I've hidden who I really am from you, from the world. It's been like this my whole life," Monica choked on her own words. "I'm a child of polygamy. It's why I don't like to talk about my family. My mother married a polygamist man, just like her mother and her mother before that. They were the last daughter in their family, all the way back to my great-great-great-grandfather, Augustus Eames. He came with the first wave of pioneers. His kids broke off from the rest of the Church when the Prophet changed positions on polygamy and allowed the government to break up families. My grandmother used to tell us how they were harassed by the Feds and how she couldn't see her father growing up."

"If it was your mother's line, why do you have the same last name?"

"My father can trace his lineage to the same man. I'm not a freak or anything. My parents were related, but not close enough to matter. It was a closed society, options were limited. The charity I give my cars too was a constant presence in our community. They helped ensure we had an education. I credit them with getting me out and saving me from repeating the failings of my family."

"How does any of this relate to Benedict?"

"I met him after I left home. I had a strong work ethic and a beautiful face, so I ended up as a server at the Alta Club. It was ground zero for Utah's Illuminati of powerful Mormon men. An old boys' club. Benedict was there all the time. I noticed how he looked at me. By then, I'd learned how to control men with the promise of passion and the hint of sex. He was easy. He lavished me with gifts, and for the first time in my life, I felt truly safe. Our affair—"

"He was already married?"

"Yes, to a dreadful woman named Lilith."

"Where is she now?"

"Jail. She was arrested for trying to steal a baby after they'd divorced. They hadn't been able to conceive, and she snapped. I knew Benedict wanted a child, a boy, to inherit the family empire and carry on the Darrow name. I told him I'd give him one if we were married, so he divorced her. I was twenty-two, a couple of years older than most polygamist wives when they marry. In a lot of ways, I was mirroring their experience with Benedict. He was an older, wealthier man in his mid-thirties like most polygamist men are when they take a second wife. The first few years of our marriage were fine, but Benedict grew impatient. When I finally got pregnant, he was the happiest I'd ever seen him. It was also the nicest he ever was to me. Nothing else mattered to him anymore."

Monica took a long pause to fight back her tears. "When I miscarried, I had to have a total hysterectomy … I felt like a failure. Benedict didn't help. He was ice cold. He poured himself back into work, retreating from me and our marriage."

"How long ago was all of this?" Marcus asked.

"Eleven years, this September."

"The math doesn't make sense. You miscarried before you were even married?"

"I'm thirty-six today. I lied about my age. I was twenty-five when I lost the baby. It was the tenth anniversary of the September 11th attacks. I remember feeling sorrow like nothing I've ever experienced. For myself. For the world. That's why I choked up about Dianna earlier. I'm so sorry."

"Don't apologize," Marcus fretted. "My heart aches with you."

"It was a decades-long emotional slide after that. Benedict was already ridiculously wealthy. When his daddy died, he left the family fortune to Benedict. I was all alone in this empty mansion, so I poured myself into material distractions. It was going fine until Zero Day."

"The Federation magically changed everything?"

"Basically. It was Tek more than anything. I didn't tell Benedict the details of my Disclosure Moment, or where I was going when

I visited Brad's Lab. I wouldn't have told him about passing Selection either, but the opportunity for omission was snatched from me by his miserable sister."

"Hannah?" Marcus whispered.

"She walked in on me having a very private moment with a sample of Tek that Brad advanced me in my first week of Selection. She interrogated me until I confessed everything. She had the idea for Tek-Mart on the spot. An hour later, we pitched it to Benedict, well she did, I just stood there. He completely relies on Hannah for business advice. The next day they started registering homeless people to enter the Black Market lottery."

"I've heard the story. It's genius, but dirty."

"It's easy to make money when you have money," Monica echoed Antony's sentiments. "She's a horrible person, but all of Hannah's ideas are brilliant. They're also risky. If I didn't make it through Selection in time, Tek-Mart would've launched without the product. It was a gigantic gamble. It came down to the literal last minute. It felt like fate when Brad said I'd passed. We stocked the store just in time for the grand opening."

"January 14th."

"You know your history."

"So you're Tek-Mart's secret control on supply?"

"Me and everyone else in the Cohort … except you. I overhead Hannah complaining about you. She thinks Antony has convinced you to stockpile Tek and flood the market to cripple Tek-Mart's monopoly."

"That's conspiracy theory nonsense."

"Don't shoot the messenger," Monica pleaded. "Tek-Mart has spent a lot of time and money shoring up the Cohort and ensuring governments squash any would-be competitors … the fact that Hannah can't control you is keeping her up at night."

"I don't see how this ends with you having a different last name and identity from Benedict's."

"At the time, I was the only member of the Cohort, and Hannah was paranoid people would figure out I was the source of Tek. She predicted that Coalition crazies would become violent paparazzi, and if they knew who I was, I'd be in danger. She also said they'd use it to push Benedict and me apart. Looking back, that was a stupid thing to be afraid of since it was already happening, but it worked. I signed annulment papers, and Benedict pulled favors to purge us from government records. To the outside world, we're total strangers."

"But you kept up the rhythms of a marriage?"

"If you mean sex, not really. Occasionally Benedict shows up, ravishes me, and leaves. It was fun for a while, but now it's a diminishing distraction. Benedict rarely leaves Hannah and their son, Lucius."

"Their *son*?"

"Sorry. No. Her son. He's the nephew I slipped up about in the game room."

"That was world-class deflection, by the way."

"I love him like my own blood. He's the only good thing that's ever come from this wretched family. He's totally unlike them. He has a great heart … he's funny and playful. It's sad that such a sweet soul was born into this life."

"Just because he has Benedict as an uncle?"

"He's more like a father figure to Lucius. But having Hannah as a mother can't be easy either. I don't fear much, but I'm terrified of that woman. I wouldn't be surprised if she's the reincarnation of a serial killer."

"I met them outside of Tek-Mart."

"He's always with his mom, and she's always with Benedict."

"Where's the biological father?"

"He lost a long battle with cancer. Between remissions, they froze his sperm or something. Lucius was born premature and frail. He's had a tragic medical history. Like I said, it's sad."

"So you're still married to this family in the spiritual sense, just not the government records sense?"

"Yes."

"And you don't see him, other than to fulfill some kind of forced sex fetish? Where is he right now?"

"I have no idea. He stopped telling me long ago. "

"So the sum total of your relationship, if I'm following, is that Hannah uses him to use you for Tek?" Marcus challenged.

"No one is using me. I'm a partner in Tek-Mart."

"Seems like you could've done that on your own, and cut them out completely."

"I've earned everything I have," Monica pushed back. "If I hadn't been in this situation in life when the Federation arrived, I wouldn't have listened to myself. I wouldn't know Brad. Or you."

"When's the last time you saw Benedict?"

"A month ago. On the solstice. Don't change the subject. I enjoy how I earn a living, Marcus. I'm great at it. Second only to you, don't forget that. Sequences are like a drug for me. I also get that out of this arrangement. In fact, that might be the best part. My whole body feels warm just thinking about it. For that split second after waking up in the Liberty Bell, I feel invincible. Everything is vibrant. Energized. Alive. I can sense the spirit of the person I just was. The only thing that comes close to recreating this is Nerio, on the dance floor, when I'm connected to all those other people. So that's where I spend my time. In the Lab or the club. I told you I gave up everything for the Cohort, and that it was worth it."

"You're allowing yourself to be exploited."

"I don't need you to be my priest," Monica scooted forward and climbed onto Marcus's lap again. "I know what I want. It includes you."

"You seriously expect me to step into this emotional minefield," Marcus wailed, "with my eyes wide open?"

"I promise I'm worth it. Why can't this work?"

"How does Benedict fit into this equation?"

"I think he gets off on it, honestly. I've been under Hannah's surveillance for years. He already knows about us. For all his power, he really gets off on being cucked, especially by you. It's why I picked you at Nerio. I saw your brother and knew that'd be a step too far for Benedict. But you were perfect. Then my feelings matured, and I discovered that you offer many other unanticipated benefits."

"The web of lies you've woven is incredible."

"I'm being honest with you now. I'm baring myself. Isn't that what you wanted? To know and be known? I think I love you, Marcus. But this is my life. I want you in it, however possible."

"This isn't an option." Marcus pushed her from his lap and climbed to his feet. "I'm sorry. I can't do this."

"Why?" Monica scoffed, standing to match Marcus.

"For so many reasons. I'm exhausted by the thought of just listing them," Marcus mouthed. "You've lied to me. You've used me. I'm not one of your cars you take for a ride until it isn't new and exciting anymore. I have real feelings for you, and I put them on hold this summer because that's what you wanted. Then you drop this on me? You knew I'd see these pictures if you brought me here." Marcus had reached his emotional maximum. "Can you let me out of this room? I want to go home."

Without another word, Monica ambled across the office, opened the hidden door, and led Marcus out of her house.

"Can I drive you?" she asked.

"I'll be fine," Marcus assured. "This isn't goodbye. I just need to be alone right now."

Monica moved in to kiss him, but Marcus turned at the last second, causing it to land on his cheek. Holding back an ocean of tears, she shut the door between them.

It was nine miles to Campus. Marcus would have plenty of time to reflect, but first, he had to find his way off the property without getting shot by the guards.

PART X

"CROWNING VIRTUE"

FRIDAY, JULY 22, +1 NE

36

GUTE ZEITEN TREBLINKA

M arcus knew it'd be a horrible day the moment he woke up. He was an emotional mess, exaggerated by the physical exhaustion of his overnight odyssey. Despite spending hours contemplating his situation with Monica, he'd resolved nothing. He didn't remember dreaming, despite sleeping through most of the morning, and paused in bed, facing the ceiling, to center himself. Dread poured out the center of his back, coldly climbing his shoulders, gripping his ribs, and crushing his chest.

Marcus rose from bed and stared at the parenting plan sitting on his desk. He was overwhelmed by everything in his life at the moment, so his present-self promised his future-self he'd deal with Dianna later. He pocketed his Memento Mori but failed to do his daily affirmation while lost in thought. He was desperate to talk to someone. Anyone. This was a busy week for Antony, and Jordan still had a score to settle with Monica. Brad was his last line of defense, but this meant chancing an encounter with Monica; it was a risk he'd take.

Sitting on the kitchen counter was a piece of paper, folded into a tent, with Marcus's name in Sharpie. Jordan had left a voiceover letter:

> *Dearest brother, like the Scorpions said … the winds of change are blowing. Watch yourself. The rest of the world is being distracted. Something is coming. Stay vigilant. XOXO - J-Dawg 3000*
>
> *PS I hope the MILF didn't give you alien AIDS.*

That minute of life had been wasted, Marcus thought, setting the paper down and departing for the Lab.

"What. Is. Up." Brad offered a hug, which Marcus gladly received. "Monica and I were just finishing some good old fashion *Coffee Talk*," Brad mimicked in his best Mike Meyers voice.

Monica patted the seat next to her. "We knew you'd come in."

Marcus swallowed his frustration for a second time in so many days and sat next to her.

"We were chatting about the Coliseum," Brad brought him up to speed. "Monica's never been. I told her it's a marvel of architecture and engineering, all built to celebrate violence. Did you see it in Rome?"

"I did," Marcus confirmed. *He hadn't shared his full travel itinerary with Brad or Monica, and he definitely didn't mention Rome yesterday. He chalked it up to extrapolation on his research Shadow's part.*

"I can't believe they'd flood it to do naval battles in there. Could you imagine watching something like that?" asked Monica.

"It's no different than Hollywood," Marcus taunted. "Look at movies and games, over time they've become way more graphic. More realistic. My dad called Hollywood 'America's Coliseum.' "

"What do you think drives that desire for hyper-realistic violence among your Form?" Brad asked them both.

"People love the thrill of being close to death," said Monica. "Getting to the edge of danger but knowing they're still safe. xTek is the same way. They're all first-person sex and violence, sometimes at the same time. It makes *50 Shades* look like a Disney movie."

She'd know, Marcus thought, *xTek was her husband's competition.*

Brad pushed the conversation onward, "One of your greatest authors and thinkers observed that 'if we were to eliminate violence from our reading, we would have to eliminate all history, much of the world's great drama, as well as the daily newspaper.' "

"Who said that?" Marcus inquired.

"Louis L'Amour."

Monica shrugged. "Never heard of him."

"His point, I believe, is that your Form craves violence at a deep level," Brad hypothesized. "To analyze is not to judge, but objectively speaking, the data is clear: when you've suppressed those instincts, darkness creates outcomes that are, almost without exception, infinitely worse than a simple story."

"I don't know any of the histories he's talking about, but that makes sense to me," Monica offered. "You can't stop it. Damming it up creates a catastrophic flood instead of a slower, more manageable flow."

"That was the whole point of the Coliseum," said Marcus. "It channeled humanity's tastes into something less destructive than constant interpersonal conflict outside of the arena's walls."

"Do you think it worked?" asked Brad.

"Maybe? I think that depends on who you asked in their day. For the average Roman, which was something like one of every five humans living on Earth at that time, probably. If you were one of the people getting eaten by the lions, or you didn't volunteer for the job like some of the Gladiators did, then probably not."

"Daniel in the lions' den," Monica agonized.

"That's one example. The groups changed all the time."

"Why is that?" asked Brad.

"Divide and conquer, like with the Confederation and their Redshift agenda," replied Marcus. "Human history is full of examples where one group was marked as 'other' so society could channel their rage against them. That's exactly what happened in the Holocaust. My mother's family was technically Jewish, and their neighbors from hundreds of years decided to turn on them one day."

"Technically?" asked Monica.

"Membership in the tribe was passed through maternal lines."

"So her mother was Jewish?" Monica questioned.

"Technically," Marcus smiled, recognizing the complexity of the family lineage he was outlining. "My maternal grandmother came from a Catholic family that lived in the mountains of northern Italy, raising sheep and slaughtering pigs to survive—"

"You've never told me this," Brad interrupted.

"Her family fled after being marked as Jewish."

"What do you mean by marked?" Monica mused.

"Her mother's family could be traced to a Renaissance Era Jewish banker, so the family was handed over to the Nazis."

"How'd they escape?" Monica fretted.

"When deportations started, her family was given forged papers. They followed the flow of other people fleeing."

"Where did it lead?" asked Brad.

"They were part of the *Aliya Bet*, a wave of illegal immigration to Palestine before part of it became Israel. My great-grandfather died on the journey. The rest of the family lived on a Kibbutz."

"A what?" Monica mouthed.

"Kibbutzes are collectivist farming communities. They started to become more like militias as conflict in the area grew, which is why her family immigrated to the United States."

"When did they arrive?" Brad asked.

"November 30th, -74 NE."

"The day after the United Nations recommended Palestine be partitioned," Brad declared.

"My great-grandmother told our family the Holocaust taught her once a community divides, once it separates, violence and suffering follow. She wasn't going to be a part of that again."

Brad shifted in place. "She was a wise woman. We call that situation where a Form subdivides and clashes the Great Divide, and it can be detrimental in ways you don't fully understand yet."

"Your family is lucky they escaped with their lives," Monica added.

"I know," Marcus replied. "When we visited Treblinka, our guide said the camp's survival rate was almost zero. Only seventy souls made it out."

"Out of a million people?" Monica's shoulders sank.

"Yes."

A collective silence broke out between the three of them.

"In the case of my family," Marcus continued, "fate played an important role. My great-grandfather had been an ex-pat sent to Italy with the Army during World War One. His citizenship is what allowed the rest of my family to come back to America when they did."

"And without all of it," Brad grinned, "we wouldn't have the blessing that is Marcus Adams in our lives!"

"Is that why you went to Treblinka?" asked Monica.

"Mostly. My grandmother made us learn about the Holocaust in unredacted detail. It shaped how I see the world. The Nazis started operating Treblinka eighty years ago, to the day, today."

"That's right, July 22nd," Brad added.

"What was it like?" asked Monica.

"It's hard to explain. Powerful and reverent all at the same time. More people died on that little spot of land than anywhere else on the entire planet in all of known human history. There's nothing left of the camp. It's just stone monuments for the victims in a large field surrounded by a dense pine forest. Someone at the site told us that for most of the children killed there, it was the only time they'd been in nature. It was cold. And quiet. The whole place felt heavy, like the evil was still hanging around in the air."

"Of all the Nazi camps, why'd you visit that one?" asked Brad.

"My grandmother told us about a Jew from her Kibbutz who'd been sent there. We wanted to see the place for ourselves."

"Would you share his story with me?" Brad implored.

"Sure. I can only tell you what I remember. His name was Tanhum, maybe? Or Meir? He was sent to the ghetto in Warsaw with his family, which was just a fenced-off section of the city they filled with Jews. This man was working as a shoe smith, and one day, he came home from work, and his whole family was gone. He didn't know what happened at the time, but it wasn't long before the Nazis sent him to Treblinka too. He said they forced the Jews into cattle cars and took them by rail to the extermination camp. The trip killed many people, but when they arrived at Treblinka, it looked like a rail station, with signs to other cities and a large clock. They told the Jews they had to shower, then they'd be sent to the final destination of their choosing. Everyone was divided by gender, women to the left and men to the right, and corralled into two large barn structures."

"What about the children?" Monica gasped.

"They went with the women. The man who told my family this story only survived because the guards picked him out of the crowd and forced him to work at the camp."

"Why him?" Monica asked.

"The Nazi's needed people to staff the camp. They didn't want to use their soldiers. They'd pick people with a skill or because of their physical size, then force them into short term slave labor."

"What would they have to do?" Monica asked.

"Some pulled people off the trains—others confiscated all luggage the Jews brought. Some moved bodies—others built a bigger gas chamber when the camp couldn't keep up with all the cattle cars arriving. There was even a group who maintained the camp, including the neighborhood of houses for the hundreds of military guards and their families living there."

"What happened if they weren't picked?" asked Monica.

"Once the Jews were separated into the barns, the men were killed first so they'd have time to cut off the women's hair—"

"What did they want with their hair?" Monica interjected.

"The Nazis were economic vultures, harvesting everything they could from the Jews to fund their war machine. The hair went into socks for their soldiers and fuses for their bombs."

"Bastards," Monica fumed.

"From the barns, Nazi guards would drive the naked people down an ally made of barbed-wire weaved with pine branches. The Nazis called this the 'Road to Heaven.' The gas chamber was another barn-looking building with a large Star of David and Hebrew over the entrance stating 'This is the gate through which the righteous pass.' The Jews were driven inside to multiple rooms, but everyone had to raise their arms above their heads."

"Why?" Monica asked.

"So they could fit more people into the chambers at once. The man who shared this story said a pair of tank engines pumped exhaust into the chambers. It'd take twenty minutes for people to die. He was one of the Jews forced to remove the bodies and dig gold from their teeth before they were burned. Then they'd repeat the whole thing for the women and children."

"Why wouldn't they fight back?" Monica raged.

"Antony asked my grandmother that same question once."

Brad leaned forward. "What was her answer?"

"She didn't have one. I've thought about it a few times myself, but I don't have one either. Everything was an illusion. The train station was a fraud, and even the clock tower was fake, they'd turn it to whatever time the trains arrived. They had a pretend 'infirmary' with a Red Cross on it, but that just led to an execution pit where people were shot in the head. Even the gas chamber was built to resemble a Jewish bathhouse. They kept up the illusion of hope until the last second. How do you fight in that situation? They lied to them, divided them, and preyed on their individual hope of survival to collectively exterminate everyone."

"Your grandmother was right to keep this story alive," Brad's voice lowered in reverence, "Thank you for sharing it with me."

"Me too," Monica added.

"You're welcome."

"Well, on that rather sad note, are you ready to switch gears and get to work today?" Brad asked.

"Sure. Are we going Tandem?" Marcus glanced at Monica.

"Yes. But you get started. I need Monica for another minute to finish our *Coffee Talk*," Brad said in the same comedic voice.

[Sequence ID# 741] [Data Begins]

The last thing he remembered was staring at the body of the unnamed man who'd hung himself with a belt. No one bothered to remove his remains because everyone suspected him of being a squealer, a traitor functioning as the eyes and ears of the SS to extend his own miserable life by a few more days. Marcus's father didn't even look at the man's corpse as he shuffled by it. He was numb to death. He, like everyone else, was focused on the revolt about to unfold in mere minutes.

His father set an arm full of bags on the floor before turning to Marcus and his brothers. "Some of the others were caught."

"What are we going to do?" Marcus's older brother stuttered.

"Calm yourself. We wait for four o'clock as planned."

"They'll beat it out of them," his oldest brother replied.

Even through the dim, dusty light of the barracks, Marcus could see the truth on the men's faces: there was no stopping the uprising now.

"I knew where this would end when I read that miserable book of clichés," their father began, "it paid for his Mercedes. It gave him wealth and power beyond Croesus. I knew with their twenty-five-point platform. I knew when they took our citizenship. They called us all Sara and Israel. Not allowed to vote. Not allowed to hold office. Prohibited from owning newspapers and weapons. We had no way to counter the lies and distrust they stirred against us. They expelled you from their schools and used the courts to put fear into our neighbors' hearts. Then the Crystal Night. Then the death squads. The ghettos. The gas vans. We were conquered piece by piece. Separated. Done in the name of benevolence! The destruction of the weak to make space for the strong. Children killed just to spare the future from a generation of avengers."

"We should have cut them down at our door," Marcus's older brother growled, "or followed the example of the Masada. Better to have died out there with family than in a place like this."

"We could have killed a few, but it wouldn't have kept this place from existing," their father grumbled, "and then someone else would have taken our places. No, this was our fate, my son. But you will not die today. Your purpose is much more important. You must live to tell everyone what happened here. That while we no longer sing their sleepy camp song about our destinies, the worst is not over. Evil is real. And you, my beloved sons, must be the light to ensure it never happens again. To anyone. Anywhere."

Their father placed his hands on the oldest brother's shoulders. "You speak so bravely of killing, an artifact of the hatred this place has etched onto your heart. It is your burden now, my son. I cannot save you from it. I am sorry. It's up to you if the memory of this place becomes an anchor or an accelerant. There are two sides to every man. One is the domain of darkness, hate, envy, vengeance, and ego. The other is the domain of light, love, generosity, forgiveness, and benevolence. You have seen for yourself where the darkness leads. Never embrace it. Never forget that it built this place. These men were misled. Do not allow yourself to be misled as well. Never again allow the promise of life to make you complacent in the deaths of others. If you want to avenge the memory of your mother, tell her story. Then find love and live a happy life far away from this forsaken ground."

Their father hung his head. "I tell you this now because it's time for you to hear it, so the memory does not die with me. By the luck of my selection, I was still alive the day you all arrived here. While I had the joy of holding each of you again, I carry the burden of seeing your mother sent down the path to oblivion."

One of Marcus's younger brothers cried softly, suppressing his emotion to protect their group of conspirators from detection.

"I had my men weaving pine into the fence that day when she came running toward the chambers. She was at the front of a group, driven naked by the dogs. Her hair had been completely shaved, which was uncommon … they usually left a bit more on the women. She looked so different, but I knew it was her from the eyes. It was a torture too cruel for anyone to bear … but when your mother saw me, it all changed. For a moment, she smiled. It was a feeling of connection that defies description. Our farewell. …" His father's voice was cracking from the pain of the memory. "But it was our moment. No one could take it from us. We spoke one last time through our eyes. I told her I wanted to run to her. She told me there was still hope for me. She was happy. It had given her comfort. Then they disappeared. Instead of the normal cries that compete with those monstrous murder machines, this time, there was singing. Your mother found the bravery to face her end with joy, not hate, fear, or anger. She inspired the others to join her, celebrating their final moments with a beautiful song. She was in every word. It was an old folk tune, the melody which I've since lost. I'd give a week's ration of bread to recall it. But it's gone. Like her. Like the others. Mercifully beyond the reach of these men."

Marcus's father regained his composure and picked up the bags he'd brought into the barracks. "Today, my children, I lay down my portion of this burden. I will join your mother, wherever she may be. But that is not your fate. Put these on." Their father handed each of them a Nazi SS uniform. Marcus stared at it while his brothers dressed, then he quickly followed suit.

"I can only tell you this once, so listen carefully," their father directed. "In a moment, the rest of us must leave. You four will stay here until you hear the commotion. That will be our deaths. You must accept it and move on with the plan."

Marcus's youngest brother, barely fourteen and ill-fitted to his uniform, started sobbing.

"SILENCE!" their father shushed through locked teeth, grabbing the collar of his son's uniform. "The time for that has passed. The guards do not walk around this place with wet eyes. If they discover you, this will have been for nothing. Do you understand? Your tears console you at the jeopardy of us all."

Marcus was on edge. Seeing his father shaking his brother in the SS uniform caused a hurricane to rage inside his heart.

"After the commotion starts," their father recollected himself, "wait a few moments. It will be clear when the time is right. Then run to the stables as fast as possible. Wear your hats, and keep your face low so the real soldiers don't notice you."

"Where are we going, father?" Marcus asked.

"There will be a man at the stables waiting for you. You must salute him as I have taught you, do you remember?"

"Yes," all four brothers answered in unison.

"When you salute him, he will ask what the commotion is about. You must answer: superhumans. Do you understand?"

"Yes," the brothers said again in tandem.

"Who is this man we will meet?" asked Marcus.

"Another unfortunate soul to find himself in this hell."

"Why should we trust him?" Marcus's older brother protested.

"He gave me the uniforms you're wearing. While he may live on the picket-fence side of this camp, he does not see us as cargo to be destroyed. He will take you through the western gates and out of this place. From there, you will be on your own. Stay in the woods until you are a safe distance from the nearby village, then turn south and head quickly to Warsaw. Ride the horses until they die, then eat them. Your uniforms will draw attention. Steal new clothing, but avoid violence if you can. Above all, stay together. You are stronger in a group than alone. I love you, my children. Your benevolence will improve all of mankind. In you, all the families of the world will be blessed. That was the promise of—"

Their father's offering was cut short by the clacking of machine-gun fire and an explosion that shook the foundation of their barrack.

[Sequence ID# 741] [Data Ends]

Marcus woke up in the Liberty Bell with Monica by his side. He assumed she was smiling under her EXO, reveling in the joy of being someone else without the baggage of their memories. As usual, he felt like he wanted to die.

"Meet me in the locker room, but stay in your suits," Brad said in voice but not body. "Pretty please."

"I've never been beyond my locker in this," Marcus asserted.

"You'll be fine," Monica coached. "Promise."

As they walked through the locker room, Hi!-D intercepted them, "Are you both excited for today's big announcement?"

"Announcement?" Marcus was out of the loop.

"The Federation press conference," Hi!-D clarified. "There's big news coming about the M1 milestone!"

The pair found Brad waiting by the door leading out of his office. "Monica and I were talking earlier, and we think it'd be great for public morale if you both accompanied me to today's press conference and answered questions about the Tek shortage."

"Am I the right person for this?" Marcus protested. "Shouldn't you get a real Tekonomics expert instead?"

"The public wants to hear straight from the source," said Brad.

"I can handle the Tek questions if you want," Monica offered.

"And I can run interference on everything else," Brad echoed.

Marcus thought for a moment. "I guess if all I have to do is act as arm candy, then I'm up for it. When's the press conference?"

"Right now." Brad nudged them out of the Lab.

No one blinked at their suit-clad presence on the light rail to Fort Douglas. The majority of the public had become desensitized to the unfamiliar long ago. Many were sporting Tek on the center of their foreheads; they were too busy altering their reality to notice.

Over the summer, the number of Tek Zombies wandering an alternative version of reality skyrocketed, adding to the Tek shortages Monica volunteered to address with the press.

Marcus's post-Sequence sickness was in full force. The train's wobble wasn't helping, and the ringing in his ears had set in. He stared out the window at the PSA screen; the Confederation invasion clock was counting down. This doomsday data was a new staple of the sky, added after the Memorial Day announcement of the Confederation's launch for Earth. The clock's large red numbers listed the days, hours, minutes, and seconds remaining. It kept ticking, ticking ... ticking. With each evanescent moment, Marcus felt an imaginary knife stabbing him in the stomach. He was attempting to calm his anxiety when Hi!-D appeared through the cloud cover to deliver a PSA:

> "Good afternoon, citizens, and welcome to another wonderful day! You can't control others, but you can control how you react. Do something noble and let the little things slide. Be generous and forgiving whenever you can. If you're facing danger, be brave and inspire others to triumph over their own adversity. Because together, we're magnanimous. This is a reminder we'll be covering the Federation press conference, live, in thirty minutes."

It was 4:00 p.m.

PART XI

UNSTABLE EQUILIBRIUM

FRIDAY, JULY 22, +1 NE

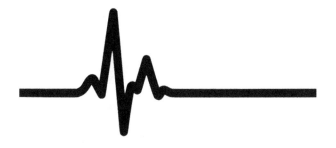

37

NICE PRESS CONFERENCE, BRO

The three Federation travelers exited the train and followed the flow of the crowd across the Legacy Bridge to the parade grounds. The whole area smelled of fresh-cut grass and cigarettes. Masked Coalition protesters gathered by the thousands to rage against the press conference at the Officer's Club. Unlike the Tek Zombies on the light rail, these protesters paid attention to the trio's presence.

"Do you guys feel like prey right now?" Marcus spoke over his shoulder, skirting the massive mob.

"The Pomerium will protect us," Monica declared.

"Don't count on it," Brad cautioned. "The University decided to downsize its Go Zone for the summer semester. The buildings are still fortified, but the parade grounds aren't."

"Why would they do that?" Marcus rasped.

"Never underestimate the shortsightedness of virtue signaling intellectuals," Brad replied. "The faculty believes a Pomerium sends the wrong message about the safety of public spaces ..."

Marcus took a deep breath. "Should we have gotten a Federation Forces escort then?"

"We don't need one," Brad boasted.

An army of vigilante enforcers encircled them, their faces dripping with summer sweat and aberrant anger. Their howling was imperceptible from the roar of the bigger Coalition crowd. Brad was coolly confident. Marcus slipped into fight mode when a pair of protesters spat at him, sending saliva speeding past his head as others sprayed unknown liquids from their water bottles. Marcus recoiled, but the fluids stopped midair, sliding down an invisible force field contoured to his body's outline.

The mob was momentarily immobilized, confused at what they were seeing. In the absence of another strategy, the Coalition comrades defaulted to violence. Dozens of attackers lurched from their lines, swinging poles and bike locks. But it was all in vain; every strike was blocked at a safe distance from their intended targets. In a blind rage, one morbidly obese man mustered all his might to charge at Marcus and his companions, crashing headlong into the invisible force field and knocking himself out cold.

"They can't touch us," Brad declared. "It's the same protective technology we use at the Black Market. Just smile and keep moving."

The impotent mob parted like a sea before them. Brad, Marcus, and Monica strolled away, immune from intimidation or violence.

The Officer's Club overflowed with people from the press.

"No one has a camera," Marcus murmured.

"They're live streaming it with Tek," Monica clarified.

At the front of the room were a riser and rostrum. A banner of white honeycombs displayed Project Noble's Objective Statement in golden-filled tiles, flanked on either side by the Federation's logo.

Brad faced the incognito duo. "Hang back until I signal you, then join me at the front of the room. I don't want your presence to distract from the first part of today's announcement."

Marcus and Monica nodded.

"I apologize for the late start," Brad spoke from the rostrum. "I was delayed by a gathering of your best ambassadors, who's enthusiasm was only matched by their extreme emotional stability."

"Is it just me," Monica whispered, "or does Brad remind you of a child. Not physically, but like, man-childish?"

"For sure," Marcus snickered. "It's the oversized lab coat."

"… Alrighty then. Let's get started." Brad took his glasses off and rubbed the bridge of his nose before placing them back on his face. "Today marks the most important gathering since we started our press tradition seven weeks ago. Following five hundred and eighty-six days of research, we'll reach the M1 milestone in the next week, give or take a day."

A wave of elation traveled through the press faster than the speed of sound; all were standing.

"Please sit down," Brad begged. "Please, people, sit. Sit down"

Slowly, one by one, they all complied.

"Great. Thank you. Let's stay civil, and we'll make it through this together. Okay? Now, M1 marks the end of Project Noble's research phase, so we'll be putting that behind us. In its place, Earth will start the full social, economic, and political integration with the Federation. I'm willing to answer questions about M1, but given our limited time today, I'd rather focus on how you'll make it to the next milestone, M2."

A large, well-dressed woman from the press kicked things off, "My question has two parts. First, how does the completion of M1 affect the average person, since, for most people, life has gone on like normal after arrival? Second, what will life look like after M1, during the lead up to M2?"

"Life will continue like it always has," Brad explained. "People will live and work and die. But a chosen few will be given the opportunity to train in our Agoge, a hybrid of FACT education, the Federation Technology Acceleration Program at the Black Market, the Federation Forces' Bootcamp, and the research work happening at my Lab. Your Form's ability to reach M2 will depend on the performance of this select group, just like it has depended on the Cohort's to reach M1."

"What can you tell us about the Agoge?" the woman asked.

"It's a Federation way of living. Immersive. Those chosen to participate will spend every minute of the day, not just the waking ones, expanding minds through rigorous education, conditioning bodies through intense physical training, and developing internal spirit through social participation. The Agoge is the next level of polish for the Praetors, Operators, and Citizens currently being trained in the various parts of our collaboration under Project Noble."

"How will you select participants?"

"Priority status will be given to FACT students and Connectors, Operators from the Federation Forces, and members of the Cohort since those designations will continue to exist beyond the Agoge. However, the designation someone comes into the Agoge with is not necessarily the one they'll go back to. The choice will be up to the participants. A few 'Wild Card' individuals, outside of the designations I just listed, will be invited as well."

The press was silent, so Brad provided a simplifying metaphor, "You should think about the Agoge as a training system that will take minor-league players and prepare them for the big leagues."

"Can anyone volunteer?" the same woman asked.

"Yes, but that doesn't mean you'll be accepted."

"How can the rest of us help then?"

"Keep living your lives. Next question, please."

A tall black man rose. "What are the various human governments, at all levels, doing to prepare for the next phase of integration?"

"Great question," Brad encouraged. "We've been working closely with national leaders around the planet, each of them will release their game plan for the various local governments under them. Their strategies are based on the information we've shared, and which they felt were valuable. Those documents will be made available the first Monday following the completion of M1."

"From your own comments," a wiry old man questioned, "it's taken eighteen months for the Cohort to help us reach the first milestone. If that time trend continues, are we *really* going to be ready to face the Confederation? Or are we being kept calm as we're led to an inevitable slaughter?"

"Thanks for the unbiased question." Brad flashed a dissatisfied smile. "Staying positive never hurts. As for being ready in time, we only predict ahead to the next milestone, and we're expecting three years for your Form to reach M2—"

"Back of the napkin math," the man mocked, "says that only leaves a year to get from M2 to the full battle readiness of M3. That can't be enough time, can it?"

"I sure hope so," Brad grinned.

Brad's humor got more gasps than laughs.

"Why aren't the Federation Forces enough?" someone shouted.

"You have to crawl before you walk. Let's back up a second. There are ZERO Earthly technologies capable of penetrating the Confederation's force fields, which are wrapped around every one of their soldiers, vehicles, and fortifications. That's the bad news and the hard reality. The good news, and the reason to be hopeful about the future, is that Power Gloves on the right Operator's arms can cut through the force fields. There are two thousand individuals presently enlisted in the Federation Forces, but their skills, strengths, and armaments aren't fully developed yet —even after M2, they won't be enough. Getting to M3 is a push."

"Why can't we shift the order around then, and prepare the military forces first?" asked a young beanie-wearing male journalist from the back.

"Because you also have to learn to walk before you run. Everything builds on itself. The systems to supply a prolonged conflict don't exist. Not yet. Together, we'll build the web of social, economic, and political systems needed to wage a successful defense against the Confederation."

The room was silent.

"Next question," Brad called on a young woman down front.

"At your first press event, you asked members of the media to defer our questions about the Confederation's forces until—"

Brad pressed his mouth to the mic. "I agree with your history."

"That's nice. So will you answer them now?"

"You won't know till you ask," Brad replied.

"The doomsday clock will hit zero on August 26th, +5NE. Since the distance from Proxima Centauri to Earth is known, the Confederation invasion must be moving at 99.99% the speed of light. What does this 'invincible invasion force' actually look like?"

"Lend me your ears," Brad proclaimed, head held high. "Stay positive. I'll say it again because you're not listening. Positivity, people. If you start to believe this is a lost cause, that's what you'll have. If you want to thrive, then focus only on what's in front of us right now. Within that, drill down even further to the parts we can control, keeping in mind that you have our help. Everything beyond that subset of reality is a distraction, which is draining you of scarce time, attention, and life force."

Marcus was gripped by Déjà vu.

"Will you please answer the question," she pushed back. "What can you tell us about their forces? What are we going up against?"

"I promise that the Federation will hold a deeper conversation on this topic, and only this topic, in the near future. But we're getting into the weeds. There are other things we need to talk about today. Also, the answers to your question and all its dependent parts will be common knowledge at every level of society very, very soon. For now, I'll tell you the Confederation is coming in five distinct waves. Each is staggered to arrive at Earth one week after the one ahead of it. Because of time dilation, for their soldiers, who you already know are physically indistinguishable from your Form, it's a comfortable twenty-two-day journey spent in Stasis."

Brad had omitted any mention of the Confederation giants, Marcus thought, *because they weren't part of the invasion? Or was he still playing things close to the chest with the press to preserve public order?*

"While they're resting, their soldiers' bodies, minds, and spirits are being drilled for the moment they reach Earth. Their objective is constantly echoing around in their heads during those twenty-two days: capture, contain, kill. So," Brad dropped both arms onto the rostrum, "they plan to capture and enslave you. If that fails, they'll contain you to this planet like a prison. If capturing or containing proves impossible, they'll simply kill all but 0.00000001% of you."

The media gasped at Brad's matter-of-factness.

Someone shouted at Brad from the back row; it was a voice Marcus recognized within the first four words, "NICE PRESS CONFERENCE, BRO!" Jordan stood over the rest of the press, slowly golf clapping. "I think I speak for all of humanity when I say that your announcement of an announcement is a stroke of smoke screen brilliance. Really. Bravo, bro. Bravo."

"I'm unsure why you consider this a smoke—"

Jordan cut Brad short. "You've been stalling for weeks now. In fact, I can't think of anything new you've told the public since the first press conference in early June. Then today, we're suddenly on the cusp of milestone success? Sorry, I don't buy it."

"Which part in particular?" Brad challenged.

"How does the Federation know all of these details? To me, the most logical explanation is that you are the Confederation. You're two sides of the same face. You keep us here, running on hamster wheels and showering us with positivity-porn from the sky. The whole time you're collecting data and running experiments, which are TOTALLY going to help us fight in the future," Jordan winked. "Let's put your infinite wisdom to the test for a moment, and I'll ask some questions. But I want to mix it up. I'll propose one possible explanation as a launching off point, then you jump in and discuss."

All faces frowned at Jordan's breach of protocol.

"I'm game." Brad stood confidently.

"Great!" Jordan launched into it. "First question: why has the weather gotten more erratic day by day since your arrival? Answer: you're manipulating our environment to induce anxiety in the population."

"We have no—"

"Actually, could I just read down my list?" Jordan held a piece of paper over his head. "Then I'll take your answers off-air. Question number two: why has the number of Tek Zombies and Pod-People permanently living in voyeur networks both skyrocketed? Answer: because you're gradually boiling us in our own endogenous chemicals, stimulated by Tek and the PSAs. Question: why are crop circles popping up all around the world? Answer: they're beacons to provide landing coordinates for the Federation's invasion force. Question: why are there unprecedented swings in the Schumann Resonances? Answer: you're messing with the magnetite in our brains. Question: why has the number of stray pets doubled during the last two weeks? Answer—"

Jordan's last metric tickled a wave of laughter from the room. "Excellent questions. Really, great stuff. It'll make a baller YouTube smackdown video. I'll make sure to like and subscribe to your channel after you post it." Brad eclipsed Jordan's earlier enthusiasm for slow clapping. "Till then, here are my answers: we're not messing with the weather, we're not making anyone use Tek, just like we don't control how they choose to use it. Crop circles ain't us, brotha, but they are pretty. The Schumann Resonances are always moving. And finally, it's summer, so people lose their pets because everyone's outside, but I'll be happy to help you put up fliers if you've lost a loved one ..."

Every person in the room gawked at Jordan.

He was silent.

"Let me cut through the noise and answer your ultimate question," Brad began. "The Federation has an infinite number of great minds, like mine, already working on Project Noble. I'm one tiny part. I think I'm an important part, but I'm still just a researcher. If you feel like I can't provide clear answers and would like to speak with my manager, just find me outside before you leave today, and I'll make an intro for you."

"I know a goose chase when I see one. You're stalling for time," Jordan dismissed.

Marcus was sweating under his EXO, suppressing the storm of fury brewing inside.

"I'll make you a deal," Brad offered with his signature smile. "I'll ensure you have a front-row seat at the finish line for M1. Is it a date?"

All eyes were on Jordan. "Fine. But know that I'll make you wait a few dates before you can probe me."

The room let out a laugh of relief, but Marcus held onto his anger.

"Next question," Brad said, calling on a reporter.

"Who are the superheroes standing at the back of the room?" asked a man from the media.

"My mother would slap me for the lack of manners," Brad said. "The top-performing members of the Cohort."

The room jumped to their feet, competing for the first look as Marcus and Monica walked through the crowd and joined Brad on stage.

"Is one of you Marcus Adams?" the large woman from before barked.

"Yes," Marcus answered.

The room twisted again.

"What's your name?" Jordan shouted at Monica.

"You can call me M."

Brad was still smiling. "M&M is what we call them at the Lab."

"What are you wearing?" asked a local newsman.

Monica swooped in like a knight to describe their armor. "It's called an EXO. We wear them during our experiments."

"Is this the next Federation technology to be shared with humanity?" the beanie-wearing reporter asked.

"One of them, yes," Brad said bluntly.

The room was roaring now. Every person from the press was asking a flurry of short, quick questions. Brad demonstrated incredible lung capacity, shushing them back to a calm quiet.

"This suit is designed from the same Organics material we use at the Lab, the Black Market, and in the Power Gloves," Brad explained. "It allows us to capture full-body data from the Cohort. With that information, we can also improve and empower the defensive and offensive decision-making abilities of the Federation Forces Operators. Better data allows for better decisions. The prototype you're looking at was fine-tuned in my Lab, a secondary benefit of the broader research I'm conducting.

Everyone in the Agoge will be trained to use an EXO, but only Operators who graduate will be given one."

Marcus didn't hear any of Brad's other answers; he was lost in an internal loop, rehashing Jordan's interrogation and getting angrier for it with each replay. Thankfully, no one could see the animosity written plainly across his masked face.

Marcus was pulled out of his own mind and back to the press conference when someone asked about the 500-fold price increase for Tek.

Brad shook his head. "Did you already forget what I told you a few weeks ago?"

"So you still don't have an answer?" the reporter retorted.

"I don't, because the Federation has no control over Tek prices. That question is better directed to Tek-Mart's owner, Benedict Darrow. If you want an update on Tek production, however, M&M are eager to tell you what's new with the Cohort."

"The price crisis is only affecting Tek's secondary markets," Monica explained. "Tek-Mart is still selling new units for $999, like the first day they opened—"

"If you can get one," someone shouted.

"I know availability is hurting all Tekthusiasts, and I speak for the entire Cohort when I say we're working hard to provide more units. But there are only twenty-four hours in a day."

Marcus bit his tongue to keep from laughing at the absurdity of Monica's disinformation campaign.

"Is Benedict intentionally restricting the supply of Tek as some analysts claim?" asked another reporter.

"Absolutely not," Monica fired back. "I know from my own business dealings with Mr. Darrow that Tek-Mart is doing everything it can to keep units moving. They have a highly complex operation and do an exceptional job of optimizing it. You should see how hard they negotiate with us … they bust our balls."

The room laughed harder than it had at Jordan.

"It's basic Tekonomics," Monica lectured. "Last month, the world hit a different milestone: five billion unique, active monthly Tek users. That's three of every five people alive. And every day, more people discover the benefits of Tek. They tell their family and friends about it, and they become users too. Supplying the whole world, especially when demand for Tek shows no signs of slowing, isn't an easy problem to solve."

"Do you support Tek-Mart's recent adoption of a pyramid scheme to expand beyond the Black Market?" asked the young female reporter.

"Multi-level marketing isn't a pyramid scheme," Monica exclaimed. "From the execution plan Mr. Darrow shared with the Cohort, which he's since made public, I think the move makes sense. It allows Tek-Mart to leverage the organic person-to-person growth already driving adoption."

"So you disagree with legal experts that it's really a loophole to enter communities that want to keep a physical Tek-Mart store from opening?"

"I won't speculate on hypotheticals, but I have full faith in Tek-Mart and the integrity of Mr. Darrow. His team works hard every day to supply Tek to everyone who wants it. For my part, all I can do is promise to put in extra hours and encourage the other members of our Cohort to do the same thing."

Monica was met with applause. Everyone, including Marcus, was captivated by her stage presence and grace. This was the confident, fearless woman he fell for at Nerio. But Marcus was the only person in the Officer's Club, Brad excluded, who knew the ridiculous reality behind her statements. Regardless, it worked, and she delivered the kind of reassurance the media was craving.

"This is a natural place to end," Brad said from the rostrum. "The next time you hear from us, we'll be celebrating our progress and moving on to M2."

Jordan stroked his beard, frowning, at the back of the Officer's Club. *This was the moment,* Marcus thought, *the time to release his rage and turn the tables on Jordan. To make him pay for his many acts of interference and aggression toward Brad. Right here. Right now.*

38

BEARER OF BAD NEWS

Marcus spied Jordan talking to Brad at the back of the room. He scrambled to intercede, Monica following a short distance behind him, but the mass of people prevented them from reaching the pair before Brad had moved on. Jordan was unwittingly in Marcus's path of destruction.

"What the fuck do you think you're doing?" Marcus jerked Jordan around by the shoulder. "How'd you get in here?"

"Hi, Marcus. Great to see you too. Cool costume."

"Answer me!" The storm inside Marcus was making landfall.

"It was easy. I used this phony press badge I created on my computer." Jordan inspected the counterfeit credentials hanging around his neck. "Then I walked through the front door like I own the goddamn place. It works every time."

"Brad is my boss. Do you understand that?"

"Monica?" Jordan jeered at Marcus's companion.

"Hi," Monica extended her hand.

Jordan refused it. "No offense, but you're dead to me. That said, you have no idea how badass you two look right now."

"You know, Jordan," Marcus moved between Monica and his friend, "you only seem to remember the parts of our agreement that benefit you. You said you'd respect my choice to join the Cohort, but here you are, again, trying to sabotage it."

"I don't have to run everything I do in opposition to the Federation through you, bro," Jordan rebutted. "Who cares if I offended Brad. He should get thicker mutant-alien skin. Did you see how patronizing he was? Something is about to happen, and he knows it. I feel it with every fiber of my existence—"

"THAT'S ALL IT IS!" Marcus shouted. Some members of the press had turned to see what was happening. *He didn't need a livestream of this encounter showing up on TMZ,* Marcus thought, pausing to collect himself. "That's all it ever is, a nebulous feeling. Unprovable. Untestable. Flying in the face of reason and mountains of other evidence. You never learned to control your feelings, so now, they control you."

"Why don't you trust my intuition about the Federation?"

"Go home!"

"No. I want to know. Why don't you trust my intuition? When I tell you what I'm feeling, you smile and nod, but deep down, you don't believe me. Do you? You never have. Is it me you don't trust? Or intuition as a source of truth? Or both?"

"Let's not do this, not in front of everyone."

"Do you think I give a shit what these strangers think? I'm talking about your faith. In me." Jordan placed one hand over his own heart. "Do you really believe I'm fabricating these feelings? Because they're as real as if someone was digging their nails into my flesh trying to warn me that we're in danger."

Marcus had heartburn from all the frustration he'd suppressed.

"Socrates, the Greek philosopher your very own father revered," Jordan continued, "said a little god sat on his shoulder and told him what to do. Isaac Newton, the mad alchemist who said he could feel how the universe worked and invented calculus to prove it, was also a self-proclaimed intuitive. And what about science fiction?"

"You're all over the place," Marcus huffed.

"Sci-fi authors are modern-day prophets. It's insane all of the things they've predicted … rockets, satellites, atomic bombs, tanks, cloning—"

"Coincidence," Marcus dismissed.

"There's no such thing as coincidence," Jordan shot back. "You seriously think it was random chance all those people were right? That Newton guessed when he created calculus? Or is the logical explanation that they tapped into something you don't under-stand? Something that let them see beyond the horizon? Because most of those same people also warned us about a Judgment Day, about a force that'd destroy us—like the Federation. The end is upon us. Right now."

Marcus rubbed his masked eyes with his left hand. "This isn't the first time you felt something that didn't come true—"

"Yet," Jordan interjected.

"ENOUGH WITH THAT!" Marcus snapped.

Monica stroked Marcus's arm to calm him.

"I know you think I'm crazy, dude," Jordan agonized, "but that's what people say about someone bearing bad news. Doesn't all of this feel familiar to you? Why can't you believe that it feels familiar to me? Why would I lie to you? What do I gain by always living in fear … it's not like I want to be this way?"

Marcus withheld words of comfort.

Jordan stroked his beard. "Srinivasa Ramanujan!"

Monica waded in, "What does that mean?"

"The best example I can give you is Srinivasa Ramanujan," Jordan spoke with a rapid rhythm. "He was a math genius. A hundred years ago, he moved from India to Cambridge to study."

The reference wasn't landing, so Jordan turned to pop culture, adding, "He was a real-life *Good Will Hunting*."

"Matt Damon?" Monica mouthed.

"Ramanujan is a perfect example of intuitive power," Jordan boomed. "He didn't write proofs like other mathematicians. He jotted down solutions, then explained how they functioned. When people asked him how he could pull this off, he said his family's goddess gave him all the ideas. He was on his deathbed when he got a final function from her. It explains how black holes work—black holes—you seriously believe that's a cosmic coincidence?"

"Too bad the Fields Medal isn't posthumous," Marcus mocked.

"Listen to yourself. Put it in context. No one really knew what black holes were back then. It took a hundred years and super-computers to prove he was right. This wasn't gibberish coming from a crazy person. He was one of the most naturally gifted mathematicians ever. The logical explanation is that he was truthful about the source of his intuition. Don't be blind to what you can't see."

"How'd he die?" asked Monica.

"A mystery illness." Jordan launched into his final defense, "I'm telling you, Marcus, I'm one of them. One of these people who hears a voice no one can explain. It's not a Hindu goddess or a little Greek guy on my shoulder. It's the T. Rex from Jurassic Park roaring inches from my face, saying the Federation's next announcement will be a full-blown declaration of war."

Marcus stood like he was made of stone.

"No one saves us but ourselves. No one can, and no one may. We ourselves must walk the path."

"That's familiar," Monica said. "Is it a quote?"

"Yes. It was the Buddha. Another person who could clearly see the future for what it is. Thanks for listening with an open mind … and heart." Jordan sulked away.

"Is Brad coming back to get us?" asked Marcus.

"I'm not sure."

"Should we head to the Lab then?"

Monica propositioned him, "Can we talk first?"

"Sure." Marcus sat across from her at an empty table.

"Do you believe Jordan?"

Marcus let a laugh of discomfort slip. "About which parts."

"That the Federation wants to hurt us?"

"No."

"Why are you so confident?"

"Jordan is like Chicken Little, always screaming about how the sky is falling, even though the world is still here when he wakes up. When one prediction fails, he moves on to another. It's been like this for as long as I've known him, and none of his other premonitions ever came true. Why would this one about the Federation be any different? When he brought up crop circles with Brad, I had to bite my tongue to keep from laughing out loud."

"Why?"

"Because all through high school, Jordan was convinced he could decode messages in crop circles that warned about a hostile invasion by bearers of false gifts and broken promises, which would result in pain and suffering, blah blah blah."

"Couldn't that be the Federation?" Monica whispered.

"Are you suffering?" Marcus smiled. "I'm not."

"Do you think he made up the messages?"

"Who knows. I don't have the skills, or time, to confirm most of what he says. It's not about any one comment or claim, it's about the number of times he's said these of things. And it's still going on. Earlier this summer, at his Global Summit, he claimed Hecate is a hologram because a bunch of Conspirators from his Lyceum tried to bounce homemade laser rangefinders off it and nothing came back to Earth. Never mind that Hecate creates regular eclipses everyone can see. Still, Jordan interpreted the absence of evidence as proof for his theory, even if there's an easier explanation—"

"Like?"

"Like they have no idea what they're doing and their gear is probably inadequate for the job. Most of his claims don't even involve physical evidence like the Hecate one. They're based on feelings. He's convinced the Federation is watching all of us, every minute of every day, gathering data to destroy us. When I ask him how he knows this is true, he says he can feel it."

"Honestly, I've wondered if I'm being watched."

Marcus chose his next words tactfully, "Feeling like you're being observed is common, it's called Truman Show Syndrome, and it was a well-known phenomenon long before the Federation arrived."

"I can feel when other people are watching me," Monica explained. "As an empathic person, I relate with Jordan's appeal to intuition as a source of truth. We're divine beings, Marcus. We have more abilities than we understand. In New Age circles, there's a common saying, 'we're not humans having a spiritual experience, we're spiritual beings having a human experience.' I think that's true. Intuition is one of our greatest gifts. Do you think Jordan is automatically wrong for basing beliefs on his gut?"

"I don't know," Marcus shifted in his seat, "but all of his theories are built on one critical assumption: that the Federation wants to hurt us."

"And you don't agree with that?"

"Do you?" Marcus challenged. "The Federation has never destroyed a city, or burned crops, or murdered entire populations like a conquering force. Instead, they're helping us prepare to face an enemy that actually wants to do all of those things."

"... Unless you count North Korea."

"I'm so sick of hearing about North Korea."

"Do you trust the Federation?" Monica asked.

"With my life."

"Me too. We'd probably know better than anyone else, don't you think?"

"Absolutely."

"Can I ask you something else?"

"Sure," Marcus leaned into the table.

"Promise to be honest?"

Marcus's gut told him this was a trap. "Okay."

"What did you think about while as you fell asleep last night?"

Marcus erupted from his chair, surprising both of them with his instinctual reaction. Monica caught him by the arm as he lurched toward the door. "Marcus, stop. Please. Stop!"

"What!" Marcus barked.

"I'm sorry I can't turn this off like you can. I've never had to deal with these feelings. I'm sorry about last night. I'm sorry for withholding the truth and for the choices I made. I'm also sorry this is making you unhappy … that's the last thing I wanted—"

"What do you want to hear, Monica?"

"What you thought about as you fell asleep."

Marcus swallowed hard. "About you."

"And I was thinking about you too, so why are we both so miserable right now? I want us to be together. I can't deny my feelings forever. That'd be a fate too brutal to bear."

Marcus stepped back. "What do you get out of this situation?"

"You put color into a black and white world for me. I feel alive when I'm with you. And your touch gets me high, like whiskey in my veins."

"What if I need more than that?"

"What else is there?" Monica scoffed.

"A family."

"Right …"

"I told you at Nerio how important family is to me. I want someone who wants to build a family—"

"And because I can't have kids, like Dianna, you're ready to move on?" Monica fumed.

"That is NOT what I was going to say. This has nothing to do with Dianna, or your ability to have children. I don't care about blood. I want a family, whatever form it takes. I'm hesitant because I don't understand your emotional availability."

"My availability?" Monica's jaw dropped.

"How does Benedict fit into your vision of our relationship?"

Monica was on her heels. "I … I can't cut him out of my life if that's what you mean. Tek-Mart depends on me—"

"THAT IS SUCH A LIE!" Marcus lost control of himself again. "All your comments about how Dianna was abusive make sense now. You were projecting your own situation. You're the one being exploited. Benedict has you convinced your Tek is his, but without you, his monopoly would fall apart. How can you not see this?"

"I don't need your psychoanalysis, Marcus, so don't flatter yourself. And don't you dare make my life out to be the problem when you aren't man enough to take what I'm offering." Monica pushed her body against his; their EXOs masked nothing.

"We can't be together if Benedict is lingering in the background. You'll have to make a choice. If you're really concerned about Tek-Mart, then I'll replace your supply. You can be free of him forever—"

"NO!" Monica recoiled.

"Then there's no future for us."

"It can't end like this, not again."

"Not again?"

"I told you that I felt something familiar with you the first time we danced. I was right."

"Right how?"

"That I've known you in past lives. After that night, I stalked you online. It wasn't hard because I knew Antony was your brother. The next morning, I went to see Jeraldine, and we did past life regression work. I've done it dozens of times since then. In every life I explore, you're there. We're Twin Flames. We've been connected in every life we've ever lived, for literally thousands of lifetimes. And we never get it right. Never. Something always comes between us, always keeps us apart, because we're more powerful together than alone. I told you in my grotto that you're destined for greatness, but you can't do it without me. We need each other. This is a test. One we've failed. Every time. Don't leave. Not again."

Marcus was frozen with fear.

Monica put both hands on Marcus's chest. "Do you love me?"

"Yes," Marcus admitted.

"We can be together. Do you understand that? We can succeed in this life and face our destiny. Together. It isn't the best way, but it is a way."

Marcus forced his next words, "I can't live a lie with you. There's nothing in it for either of us."

He couldn't see Monica's tears through the EXO, but could hear them in her voice. "If you loved me, you'd stay."

"And if you loved me," Marcus kissed her forehead, "you wouldn't ask me to live like this, *carissima*."

Monica seized Marcus's hand, but he gently slid it loose and walked away.

The sky matched the turbulence of Marcus's inner voice as he headed to the Lab. The PSA screen displayed a severe weather advisory, warning everyone to seek shelter, but Marcus didn't care. The familiar stir of self-destruction rose in his heart as he shuffled across campus, saddled by sorrow like a pair of concrete anchors around his ankles. The downpour started at the same moment the gravity of his situation set in.

The thought of losing Monica turned the imaginary knife in his belly again. But she'd made her choice, and he couldn't see any other solution. *This wasn't a problem he could solve on his own,* Marcus thought, *he needed brotherly wisdom, and he knew exactly where to find Antony.* He swapped the EXO for his clothes at Carlson Hall, then jumped on the light rail and headed for Nerio.

39

KO'D

Despite raining bullets, Coalition protesters clogged the sidewalks between the light rail station and the Go Zone's outermost layer. These activists were as aggressive as their campus counterparts, but now Marcus lacked the protection of his EXO. He stared at the ground as he hustled, flashing his Fast Pass at each checkpoint until he reached the Black Market. *He'd ever been here alone*, Marcus realized in the transport stream to Terra's Cycle. He paused outside of Tek-Mart. *It was crazy how everyone's individual paths crossed during the past few months, yet all of them converged on this place.*

As he stepped from the sector's skybridge stream, a drummer intercepted him, "Would you like to try one of our Caveats?"

Marcus's curiosity got to him, "What's a Caveat?"

"Do you know the phrase *caveat emptor*?"

"Yes. It means buyer beware."

"Impressive! People don't know their Latin like they used to."

"So … what's a Caveat?"

"Do you have a Tek unit?"

"No."

The drummer dug into his pocket. "I have one—"

"I'll save you the effort. Thanks but no thanks."

"You think I'm with one of the stores, don't you? I'm not. I'm better than a billboard, a cross between a mall directory and a concierge. But instead of verbal recommendations, I'll show you what it's like to try anything in the Market via Netted experiences."

"I can't picture it," Marcus admitted.

"By using someone else's lived experience, captured with Tek, you can see what it's like to play with a big cat from Eye of the Tiger, or what it feels like to get a tattoo at Immutable. You can swim with the animals at Pontus without ever getting wet, or taste a sample from Indulgence without ruining your actual appetite. If you're curious what the Voyeur Pods are like or want to try one of the many drugs available at Nerio, I can help. All before you buy. *Caveat emptor*."

"Still going to pass," Marcus said over his shoulder, pushing past the mass of people clogging the path.

The view from the top of the Wells Fargo Center never disappointed; clouds hovered a few hundred feet above the club, blanketing the valley as far as Marcus could see. Jolts of lightning mapped out an electrical nervous system in the opaque sky, and the air smelled of fresh rain. Despite the ongoing deluge, Nerio was dry, a trick he'd experienced many times during the exceptionally wet spring and summer.

Marcus scoured the club, but Antony was nowhere to be found. *This was a bad time to be alone*, Marcus thought. A near-continuous line of alcohol-baring orbs helped him numb the pain. When it became hard to stand, he found a couch near the fight floor to watch the happy hordes dancing to the thundering bass lines.

"Good evening," Hi!-D said, sitting next to him.

"Hey. How's it going?"

"Splendid. Will your brother be joining us?"

"I'm not sure." Marcus leaned forward. "I was hoping you knew where he was."

"I've yet to see him this evening."

Marcus nursed his drink as Hi!-D scanned the room. To fill the void in their conversation, Marcus asked a question that'd been on his mind for months, "Is it just my imagination, or have you become more proper in your personality over time? More refined?"

"Why are you assuming that my identity would be static? I'm constantly exposed to new stimuli, and that shapes me. Like you, I'm searching for my true self."

"Is that why you chose a British accent?"

"I didn't." Hi!-D grinned. "That's how *you've* chosen to hear my voice. It's the same way with the PSA screen. My communication is customized to the preferences of the person hearing it. That includes my language and my accent. Ironically, Monica hears me the very same way that you do ... speaking of which, where's our favorite lady of Nerio tonight?"

"Not sure." Marcus slumped back into the couch and continued sipping his drink.

Hi!-D spun in her seat to face him. "Are you feeling under the weather?"

"It's that obvious?"

"We've logged a great number of hours together at the Lab, not to mention all the time we've shared here." Hi!-D placed a hand on his shoulder. "It'd be hard to hide anything from me at this point."

"It's life stuff. I came to pick Antony's brain."

"I'm happy to listen in his place."

Marcus raised an eyebrow. "I don't know how I feel about talking to an artificial therapist."

"It worked for ELIZA."

"Never heard of her."

"She was one of your Form's first attempts at a computer chatbot, programmed to act as a Rogerian psychotherapist."

"Ohhh, Rogerian, right ..."

"To converse with ELIZA, you had to type your thoughts. I'm easier. All you have to do is speak."

"I appreciate the offer, but I'm going to wallow for a few more minutes, then call it a night if Antony doesn't show."

"Have you considered fighting?"

"To make myself feel better?"

"Well, there would certainly be a chemical shock to your system. But I meant more generally, not just for breaking the grip of your current mood. Statistically, when one family member is highly gifted at something, there are similar traits in their siblings and offspring, though, birth order can really affect it."

"So because Antony is good at fighting, I should be too?"

"Your brother has told me that you're his primary sparring partner these days."

"Zedd is his real partner. I fill the gaps."

"I've taken the liberty of entering what I know about your preferences into my fight matching algorithm. I have a potential fight with a ratio of one if you're interested?"

"It's a dead draw?"

"Yes," Hi!-D replied. "That's my prediction."

"What can you tell me about the other guy?"

"Only that the fight would be three rounds, five minutes each, till knockout or submission. And that he's already accepted."

After everything that'd happened in the previous twenty-four hours, Marcus wanted to fight. "Okay."

"Fantastic! Would you like to place a bet?"

"Yeah …," he hesitated, "… ten thousand. Float it."

"This is very exciting! You don't have to sit out here." Hi!-D motioned at the fighter's lounge. "If I don't see you again—"

"Best of luck," Marcus said, finishing her familiar parting phrase.

He wasn't sure if Monica would show up tonight, so he jumped at the opportunity to hide. Marcus had never been in this lounge, but it was identical to Antony's. The small space was full of a half dozen fighters, including one familiar face.

"Velia?"

"Marcus!" She paused from massaging her hands to hug him. "Are you fighting tonight?"

"Yeah. First time. You?" Marcus asked.

"I've been at it for a while, thanks to your brother's tutelage. What was your ratio?"

"One. What was yours?"

"Five," Velia proclaimed. "I love being the underdog. I keep accepting higher ratios and haven't lost yet."

Marcus felt a twinge of envy.

The club vibrated at the announcement of the next fight:

Marcus vs. Aaron

One of these men was Aaron, Marcus thought, surveying the group. All of them, including Velia, were preoccupied with the Peanut Gallery's prognostications about the debut fight of Antony Rex's brother.

Antony charged into their lounge.

"Speak of the devil!" Velia grinned.

Everyone stood in reverence.

"Come with me," Antony spoke coldly to Marcus.

"No mercy!" Velia shouted as the brothers exited.

Marcus followed Antony to the other lounge.

"Sit down," Antony fumed.

Marcus found it hard to focus under the lingering influence of the alcohol.

Antony glared at his brother.

"Say something," Marcus begged.

Antony took a long breath before abruptly breaking character and smiling ear-to-ear. "So! Baby bro is going to do battle!"

"I thought you were really pissed." Marcus held a hand over his racing heart. "I'm already nervous."

"Just trying to lighten the mood. I'm upset you went and sat with those strangers instead of coming to be with me."

"This is the Champ's Lounge."

"And anything I have is yours. You should already know that." Antony squeezed Marcus's cheeks. "There are some extra clothes in the corner if you want them."

"Thanks." Marcus frantically dressed.

The club's chatter continued.

"You picked a great day for a fight," Antony boasted. "It's Armageddon out there. The footage is going to be unreal."

Fear had Marcus in a chokehold.

"Is everything okay?"

"No," Marcus mouthed.

Antony moved closer. "Then spill it."

"Did you watch today's Federation press conference?"

"Of course," Antony anticipated the next step, "I'm guessing that was Monica with you?"

"Yes."

"Makes sense given how she went on and on about Tek-Mart."

"What do you mean?"

"You have to know who she is by now?"

"Who do you think she is?"

"Benedict Darrow's wife."

"Ex-wife," Marcus corrected the record. "How long have you known?"

"I recognized her the night of my first fight. I met her at a black-tie thing years ago. I remember everyone, well at least their faces. They'd just gotten married."

"Why didn't you tell me who she was?"

"Who am I to interfere with love?"

"You must've realized she's Benedict's supply once I told you she was part of my Cohort?"

"Those dots were trivial to connect."

"Then why haven't you exposed Benedict?"

"Just because I hate the guy, that doesn't mean I'm going to destroy him with insider information. I'm not Dianna. Plus, he'll get what he deserves at some point. I believe in Karma."

"What else can you tell me about Benedict?"

"You really want to go down this rabbit hole? Before a fight?"

"Yes," Marcus insisted.

A crescendo of crazed voices cut off their conversation. It was go time. As the brothers emerged from the Champ's lounge, the club was electric, like a collective static charge ready to strike something.

"I've fought you plenty of times. You're ready for this. Keep your head up no matter what," Antony advised. "Stay in the flow. Accept that you're going to get hit, and be flexible. Absorb strikes like I've shown you, don't try to completely stop them. Give back twice what you take. Understand?"

Marcus's heart was in his throat. Pumping, pumping … pumping to the rhythm of the club. "I forgot to pick a fight song."

"I've got you." Antony offered a devious grin.

Fighting is a totally different experience when your own ass is on the line, Marcus thought, standing at the edge of the fight floor. The sea of screaming faces sent chills up his spine. He searched the crowd for Monica but didn't see her. Velia stood on the sidelines, shrieking with a schizophrenic smile.

"MARCUS," Antony shouted, "switch on the aggression!"

"I'm trying." Marcus knew what Antony was talking about; he'd seen his brother do it. *But he wasn't Antony,* Marcus admitted to himself.

"Don't try. Do. Picture that dude as Darrow if you have to." Antony pointed at Aaron. "This is war. That's your enemy."

Marcus turned to see his nemesis step across the blue glow of the Cycle's sector and into the center of the fight floor. Aaron was the same height as Marcus and sported a tall, thick mohawk. He was top-heavy, with broad shoulders and hulking long arms relative to his smaller core and lanky legs.

The float ratio had stayed at one; the Betting House was calling the fight a wash too. As Aaron's fight song faded, the club went black, reminding Marcus of when he stared into the Liberty Bell for the first time. He stepped forward under the heavy rhythm of his own fight song, "Headup" by Deftones. The crowd's intensity mirrored the song's. *Antony made the perfect choice,* Marcus thought. *He didn't have his brother's confidence, but he felt powerful for the first time that day. This pre-fight tradition connected him to ancient single combat when two warriors would face-off before their chanting armies.*

Nerio's collective eyes were transfixed on the fighters standing silently in the sector's inner Cycle. Marcus extended his hand, which Aaron tapped, immediately opening up space between them and sending the club into a craze. Aaron moved with confidence, closing the distance, striking, and retreating before Marcus had a chance to respond; Aaron was playing a game, counting up the strikes without being hit himself, and he was winning.

Marcus lunged at his rival, unleashing a frenzy of blows to the face and ribs. Aaron absorbed the strikes, covering his face and working both elbows into Marcus's chest, shoving him back and kicking the side of his head. Marcus stumbled, barely maintaining consciousness as Aaron started the second wave of his assault, but he made a mistake and got too close. Marcus wrapped his hands around the back of Aaron's skull, and with his opponent fully clinched, drove alternating knee strikes up into Aaron's chest and face as the first round ended.

Marcus meandered back to Antony's side.

"You ended on a strong note, but you aren't moving fluidly. You're full of hesitation." Antony wiped the blood from Marcus's face and gave him water. "This guy's all over the place—he's practically dancing. Wait for him to come to you again, and strike before he retreats."

As the second round began, Marcus followed his brother's advice, going tit for tat with Aaron on every strike. The club was on their feet, foaming at the mouth as Aaron charged Marcus and took the fight to the floor. Aaron was fast on the ground, pinning Marcus and punching his face with both fists. The last thing Marcus saw was Aaron's mohawk, slowly swaying to the rhythm of the KO bell and the final bars of his adversary's fight song.

Marcus woke in the Champ's Lounge.

"You took a beating!" Antony belly laughed.

Marcus failed to share in the humor.

"How long have I been out?" Marcus murmured through a throbbing jaw.

"Fifteen minutes tops."

"Did you carry me in here?"

"Yes. It was very *Pietà*-like. You're getting heavy. I think you were twelve the last time I lifted you like that."

"Thanks ..."

"Seriously, you did great."

"I lost."

"True. But you showed all the right instincts, and you guarded your face until you blacked out. You're one tough mother—"

"My whole body hurts." Marcus struggled to sit up. His ribs and stomach were spasming. "Can you take me home?"

As Antony helped him shuffle through the club, Marcus scanned the crowd for Monica. She still wasn't there. Or, she was hiding.

"The roles have finally reversed," Antony bragged.

"Huh?"

"How many times have you helped me when I was battered?"

"I stopped counting. It's not the same though," Marcus looked at his feet. "I embarrassed you."

Antony stopped and faced his brother. "Embarrassed me? No! I'm proud of you. You stepped into that ring. How many other people are brave enough to do that? You faced danger and conquered your fear. That's what defines a warrior. I don't care what any of these people think. Not a single one of them." Antony squeezed Marcus's shoulder. "You're the only thing that matters in this world. I love you. *Sempre avanti.*"

"Right," Marcus moaned.

"Even Honest Abe lost a few," Antony echoed their father as they started moving again.

"I owe Hi!-D a lot of money."

"I settled up for you. Relax, this one is over. The next one will be different. It gets easier, I promise. You'll see."

Hopefully, there isn't a next one, Marcus thought, climbing into Antony's car.

As Antony drove, Marcus read a text from Dianna:

> *I came to your house to pick up the parenting plan I found UNSIGNED in your room. If you're getting cold feet, I will ensure this ends VERY BADLY for you. Where are you???*

Marcus accepted that another fight awaited him tonight.

40

ABORTING PLANS

Marcus's house was luminous, piercing like a lighthouse through the darkness of his neighborhood.

"I guess my party invite got lost in the mail?" Antony muttered.

"Dianna's inside. I haven't signed the parenting plan yet."

"What the hell Marcus? This is important! You need to protect your rights, and that agreement is an essential step. You can't get joint custody without it unless you're ready for a long and bloody legal battle."

"I know, I know." Marcus shook his head. "I was distracted this morning and planned to do it when I got home. I'll get it done right now. Thanks for the ride."

"You sure you don't need me in there?"

"I have to fight this one myself," Marcus said, opening the car door before pausing to assemble the necessary strength to climb to his feet.

"Godspeed. If she doesn't eat you alive, I'll see you tomorrow."

Marcus ducked his head back into the car. "What's tomorrow?"

"Pioneer Day."

"Right ... I keep thinking that's Sunday."

"That's because it is," Antony clarified, "which is why the celebrations are going down tomorrow."

"Want to watch the parade with me?"

"No. And I should probably offer some brotherly caution about you going into public alone, but with your face all fucked up like that, I doubt anyone will recognize you. I'll pick you up when it's over."

"I'll be at the Lab for most of the day."

"Call me when you're ready, and we'll head to Sundance."

Marcus suffered the pain necessary to smile, then stumbled up the sidewalk, broken but not yet defeated.

Jordan and Dianna were huddled up closely on the couch, whispering, as Marcus entered the living room. Dianna was scowling as she twiddled her hair, but the sight of Marcus's beaten face changed her trajectory.

"WHAT HAPPENED!" Dianna jumped to her feet.

"Were you like that under your suit?" asked Jordan

Dianna spun around to face Jordan. "What suit?"

"My EXO," Marcus answered. "And, no."

"Were you attacked on the way home from campus again?" Jordan matched Dianna's movement, advancing toward Marcus to inspect the damage.

"I just came from a fight at Nerio."

Dianna shrieked, "YOU DID THIS TO YOURSELF?"

"No," Marcus mocked. "The other fighter did."

"Don't get cute with me!" Dianna barked. "We've been waiting for hours. For you. Do you even care?"

Marcus eyed the parenting plan spread across the coffee table. "I appreciate the committee's concern. I'll sign the papers now."

Marcus couldn't mute his moans as he kneeled to execute the document. Struggling to stand, he handed it back to Dianna.

"Are you kidding me? Do you seriously think I'll trust you with children right now? When you're engaging in such blatant self-destructive behavior?"

"There's nothing in the parenting plan that prohibits me from fighting. The papers are signed. We have an agreement."

"The hell we do!" Dianna raised her brows. "You only get the rights I'm willing to grant you, which are none if you're going to continue behaving like your piece of shit brother. We can revisit this document after you get yourself under control."

"You don't have that power," Marcus choked on his words. The cumulative effects of instability over the past few days swelled inside him, looking for a weak spot in his Stoic armor to finally breach.

"I should've listened to my first instinct and never involved you. Deep down, I knew trying to co-parent would be impossible."

"They're my children too! You can't—"

"You will NEVER be a part of their lives unless I say so! Do you hear me? And don't try to intimidate me with Antony's lawyers again," Dianna berated. "I've got mountains of dirt on both of you. Drug use, violence, promiscuity, drunk driving, guns in the home—there isn't a court on Earth that will side with you if I show them who you really are."

Marcus surrendered to the childlike rage he'd worked half a lifetime to suppress, snatching the papers from Dianna's hand and shredding them with an animalistic frenzy. He tossed the tiny fragments into the air above her head like celebratory confetti.

"You miserable son of a bitch!" Dianna fumed.

"You can leave now," Marcus advised. "We're done."

"I WILL NOT BE SPOKEN TO LIKE THIS!"

"LIKE WHAT! Like how you speak to everyone else? With your condescending tone, your spiteful tongue, and your hateful heart? YOU'RE THE FIRST ONE TO GO NUCLEAR, DIANNA. NOW YOU KNOW WHAT IT'S LIKE FOR THE REST OF US!"

"Look at yourself, dude," Jordan muttered. "You're a mess."

"He's right. LOOK IN A MIRROR, MARCUS! YOU'RE A FUCKING MESS," Dianna screamed through her streaming tears.

"Spare me the crocodile concern." Marcus squared up to Dianna, glaring callously into her wet eyes. "This is about control—it's always been about control. It isn't enough for you to be a megalomaniac over your own life. You have to do the same thing to everyone else. Especially me. You assume you know better. Like I'm not up to it myself. Like I'm not supposed to have a say in MY OWN LIFE without getting your permission first. This has never been about my safety. It's always been about you dictating what I do. Now you're using OUR KIDS to try and hold on to that control."

Marcus took a breath before continuing on his rant, scarring Dianna with every word. "The evidence is there. Let's look at it. You didn't want me to join FACT, so you threatened to cut off our relationship. You didn't want me to start Selection or join the Cohort, and when I did, you exposed me to the world, which nearly got me killed. You didn't want me to become an Operator in the Federation Forces or a Praetor when I graduate, so you wrote those conditions into our parenting plan, the same one you're reneging on now."

Jordan rocked in place, looking at the ground.

"And who made you the ultimate authority anyway? What's the source of your expertise? Seriously? What do either of you know about what's best for my life? How fighting at Nerio or working with the Federation impacts me? How it impacts the world? You're both filled with fear. Blindly driven by it. But neither of you have a shred of evidence, and you won't listen to what I say, even though I'm the one on the front lines. You think that because you can get inside people's heads, Dianna, that you're an expert on everything and everybody. Well, let me save you some effort and tell you exactly what I'm thinking—you just made me your worst enemy. I will NEVER stop fighting you to have a place in these children's lives. NEVER! You can sling whatever dirt you want, but I'll keep coming for you. I will not be defeated. And when it's over, and these kids are a rightful part of MY life, I'll still be working with the Federation in whatever capacity I choose. You'll be powerless to stop any of it. You can't control me."

Dianna's tears had turned to ice in her eyes.

"Now you're silent?" Marcus baited. "Well, if you're not going to storm out dramatically like usual, THEN ALLOW ME!"

Jordan stepped in front of him. "Don't go."

"Get out of my way," Marcus warned.

"Emotions are out of control right now," Jordan continued to block the path with his body. "Stay … let's talk this through. All of us."

Marcus tried to push past him, but Jordan wouldn't be deterred and grabbed his friend by the wrist. Marcus reeled around, punching Jordan in the face and knocking him to the ground. Dianna screamed like a banshee, scrambling to Jordan's side.

Marcus had acted on instinct, but he was shaking from the shame of it now. Dianna glared at him with wishful death in her heart, so Marcus fled the house, making it to their old garage before Jordan caught up to him. "Marcus, stop. STOP!"

"I thought you always had my back?"

"You're going to play that card?" Jordan chastised, blood streaming from his nose. "Dianna is the mother of your children. She deserves to be treated better than what you just did to her. To both of us! I know you're right about some of what you said. And I get why you're so upset, but put that aside and listen. Please."

Marcus consented with his silence.

"You need to stay here," Jordan pleaded.

"Why? I think we all said what we needed to."

"The Federation announcement means something major is about to happen, one way or another. We need to be together when it does. Like your father told us a thousand times, we have safety in numbers."

Marcus was sweating. "Let's finish this conversation once and for all. Assuming you're right, and something happens, how do you know it'll be bad—"

"I can feel it," Jordan wailed.

"The problem is, you've felt stuff like this your whole life. You said you felt it with the Mayan calendar apocalypse hype. But it didn't happen. Remember the book of Enoch? And Nibiru, the Planet X that never showed up? Or the messages in the Nazca lines, and the stargate you felt existed in Peru, which was identical to the one you thought the US invaded Iraq to seize? Neither of those ever turned up, did they? What about the astronomical patterns warning of cataclysm coded into the Pyramids of Egypt, or Stonehenge, or Göbekli Tepe, and every other ancient pile of rocks you obsessively read about in *Fingerprints of the Gods*?"

Jordan tried to explain, but Marcus kept at it, "Or the Emerald Tablets, and what about the Georgia Guidestones? Remember desert varnish? What about the face on Mars, or MKUltra and all the government cover-ups? By the way, when are those UN Population Fund nanobots we all got from vaccines going to finally kill us? Huh? And who can forget about the Ashtar Galactic Command broadcast you made me listen to a billion times? The problem with all your feelings is that none of them has ever come true. Not a single one. But I remember you telling me, with this same level of certainty, that *you knew* something would happen."

"Open your eyes, Marcus, it's happening now," Jordan rasped with frustration. "This is what all that stuff pointed to. Maybe not in its details, but definitely in its direction."

"You can't do it, can you? You can't face reality."

"We removed smallpox from Earth because it was a threat to us— we did that. One life form eradicating another. Why do you assume the Federation won't do the same to us if we're standing in their way? You know they can. You're naive to hope they won't."

"For what reason? You've never answered that."

Jordan was silent.

"EXACTLY! Because you don't know!"

"I know that when cultures clash, the stronger one wins—every single time. You can pick apart my ideas in isolation, but no one has spent more time piecing this puzzle together than me. If you stepped back for a second, you'd see the big picture too. Destruction on a level you can't imagine is coming ... from the Federation. We should be together when it happens ... we'll need each other."

Marcus rested both his hands on Jordan's shoulders. "You're not the first person to believe the world was going to end, and not a single one of them has been right. You won't be any different. You don't want to accept the world for what it is, and I understand that, but you latch onto these theories like they're a religion. Nothing will happen, and I can't stay here right now."

Jordan's eyes were flowing faster than his nose, but he wrapped Marcus up in a bear hug anyway. "I love you, brother. I'm going to miss you ... so much."

"I love you too. I'm sorry I hit you. But this isn't goodbye." Marcus pulled free from their embrace and climbed into his car. Jordan stood by the garage like a hopeless sentinel. Marcus momentarily questioned his instinct to leave but drove away without looking back.

As he sped through the city, Marcus inspected the blood spatter Jordan had imprinted on his shirt. He didn't know where he was going, but he couldn't stay in any one place. *He'd continue his earlier aborted plan of drowning his sorrows*, Marcus thought, pulling into the state liquor store and using the fake ID Jordan gifted him on his eighteenth birthday. Then, with a bottle of rum in hand, Marcus set off down the dark road of self-destruction.

He tried blasting music, but the Lamborghini's archaic stereo was terrible, so he couldn't get into the zone. Marcus let out a scream of rage. Anxiety about the future of his family washed over him. *Dianna had been so cold at the end, but he'd never stop fighting to be with his family.* Marcus knew parts of his anger had been misdirected. Some was from Monica, and some from losing his fight. Some was from the Confederation and the impending transition of Project Noble. But most was the result of the incessant agitation he'd felt since the end of their Grand Tour.

It'd only gotten worse over the last few days, like sand stuck between the layers of his skin. He opened the small lid concealing the car's power seat switches; the obscure compartment had successfully hidden his secret from Jordan the entire summer. Marcus removed a single piece of Tek and held it at eye level. *He knew where he was going for the rest of the night.*

PART XII

CETERIS PARIBUS

SATURDAY, JULY 23, +1 NE

41

YOU CAN'T GO HOME DRUNK

The rebound effect shocked Marcus from his sleep. An empty bottle of rum sat shotgun. His entire body throbbed, especially his face and fingers. He struggled to remember his dream; like a stream of smoke, it dissolved when he tried to hold onto it. Marcus had overnight amnesia, only remembering fragments after leaving home in a state of rage. He did recall Jordan's prophecy of doom, but the world was still here, and the sun bathed him in its welcoming warmth through the windshield. *The clear blue sky was a sign,* he thought, *it'd be a great day for a parade ... everyone's wishing had worked.*

Marcus was parked in front of his family's first home in Mapleton, Utah. A piece of Tek was still stuck to his left wrist. He didn't remember using it, but if he had, he knew exactly what for. Over the summer, Marcus cataloged every family memory he could think of with Tek's Derivative Ghosting feature. A memory he returned to frequently had taken place inside this house: his maternal Grandmother Beatrice's viewing. It was the last time the entire family was together, in body if not in conscious spirit.

Marcus closed his eyes and was instantaneously immersed by the memory of Beatrice's blended Catholic and Buddhist wake. It was a strange experience; the adult version of Marcus was seeing everything through the eyes of his younger self. He understood why they called it Ghosting since people moved in blurred arcs. The memory was choppy, like watching a film with missing frames, and his point of view would suddenly jump, lacking the smooth continuity of real-life.

Everything felt massive to Marcus; the size of the world was very different through five-year-old eyes. The home's living room was stuffy from a mix of afternoon sunlight, central heating, and dozens of people crammed into such a small space. Marcus was an unknowable time-traveler, walking among the adults dressed in their Sunday best.

His mother stood over the open-casket, drying her large chestnut eyes. Marcus cherished this moment in the memory when he hugged her leg, and she ran her fingernails through his long scruffy hair. He could smell her sweet perfume and feel the silken fabric of her dress against his face. She paused from mourning to smile down at Marcus, radiating joy and pride at the sight of her blossoming second son.

Then, as a passive passenger to the memory, Marcus would turn and walk toward Antony on the other side of the room. He was surrounded by adults who were captivated by a story Marcus couldn't hear. Their father stood among them, his short stature accentuated by the kilt he was wearing. His silver beard was tidy, a style he'd abandoned by the time of his own death. Their father beamed; his eyes were bright, but partially concealed by the lifted cheeks of a full-face smile. Marcus loved hearing his dad's booming belly laugh.

Next, Marcus would move from the living room, through the formal dining room, and into the kitchen. Two faceless children, a few years older than him, scurried by, hitting into Marcus and stopping his momentum. A hand rested on his shoulder. It was Garett's. Future Marcus had the benefit of knowing how important this other bearded man would become.

"Are you okay?" Garret asked.

Marcus's eye was drawn to the large signet ring on Garret's right hand. "Yes."

Jeraldine arrived by Garett's side. She had the same haircut and clothing style as her future self, but tighter skin. She smiled. "Hey, kiddo. My heart aches with you right now, but Beatrice will reincarnate soon. I hope you'll take some solace in knowing that she's out there, somewhere, searching for a way back to you."

Garett and Jeraldine crouched down to sandwich Marcus with love before sending him on his way to the original goal: a platter of Italian cookies sitting in the kitchen. Marcus was pocketing a half dozen varieties when his mother's elevated voice signaled that he'd been caught, "Marcus Winthrop Adams!"

His name was the last complete section of the memory. After that, it was a jumble of short incoherent bursts: sitting on a couch as a sad song played, kicking a soccer ball in the backyard with Antony, pulling single pieces of grass from the center of their circular driveway, and falling asleep to his mother's kiss and his father's rough hands stroking the side of his face.

Then, the day and the memory ended entirely. He never saw his grandmother's body, or if he had, the sight had been lost before he could store it. He didn't mind; he preferred remembering her vibrant and alive, smothering him with love and undivided attention.

Marcus opened his eyes, finding himself back where he'd started, sitting outside the family's old home in his Lamborghini. His stomach and chest ached like after a Sequence, and his brain swelled against the inside of his skull. *Rum hangovers were uniquely brutal,* he told himself. The ringing in his ears was peaking. He pulled the Memento Mori from his pocket and leaned across the vehicle's interior to retrieve a removable mirror from the passenger sun visor.

A black and blue face reflected back as he completed his daily affirmation:

> I'm the man in the mirror. Better today than I was yesterday. And because today I may die, I'll use this opportunity at life to improve myself and help those around me. I'll stay calm and only focus on things I can control. I will not fear. No matter what I face, I'll face it from a place of peace and love. I'm capable of this. I'm the man in the mirror.

Marcus's Countach rose from its slumber. The car's antique digital clock displayed 7:47 a.m., so he'd have to speed to make the Pioneer Day parade. He avoided his phone as he drove, not out of a sense of social responsibility, but because he wasn't ready to face anyone. American flags waved everywhere, honoring the Pioneers that founded this Zion one hundred and seventy-five years earlier.

Despite a history of conflict with neighbors and governments, modern Mormons were a particularly peaceful and patriotic group. Mormonism was a bonafide American religion, born between the Revolution and the Civil War. Its founder had come of age in the Burned-over District of New York, ground zero for the Second Great Awakening, when predestination was abandoned for transcendental millennialism, a topic Bill had covered in many of their FACT classes.

Marcus made the sixty-mile trip back to Salt Lake in less than an hour while enjoying the comforts of air conditioning. *The same distance would've taken the Mormon Pioneers half a week to trek,*

Marcus reflected. Today was about celebrating their sacrifice to put Utah on the map. The parade would begin at the Salt Lake Temple, the spot from which the entire city emanated, and end at Liberty Park with an Indian Pow Wow honoring the indigenous tribes who taught the Pioneers how to survive their first winter.

People camped out along the parade route days in advance, so Marcus was forced to park blocks from the action. While walking through the cheerful city, Hi!-D appeared in the sky to deliver a PSA:

> "Good morning, citizens, and welcome to another wonderful day! Like the ancestors who made today possible, you have an important role to play in the lives of generations to come. And just like an industrious bee in the hive, owning your share of that obligation is the first step toward collective success. As you celebrate, remember their hard work continues through you. Happy Pioneer Day! Bee-cause together, we're innovative."

It was 9:00 a.m.

Marcus worked his way through a tight-knit crowd to the edge of the parade route. Children used the occasion to ride bikes in the empty city side streets. This was one of the oldest parades in the nation, and it always kicked off with the roar of a low-altitude flyover by fighter jets from Hill Air Force Base. A fleet of motorcycles led the parade, followed by a color guard carrying the flags of America, Utah, the Mormon Battalion, and for the second time in history, the Federation Forces. Bagpipes echoed off the cityscape as clowns threw candy from go-karts, luring merry spectators toward Liberty Park.

For a fleeting moment, Marcus felt whole again. He'd lost himself in the festivities, remembering the times Antony made him laugh with inappropriate commentary at past parades; memories like these were the reason he came today. A few dozen yards away, he saw Bill conversing with Luke Kelly. Marcus took the path of least resistance, stepping into the street and hustling over to the pair.

"Marcus!" Bill gave him a bearish hug. "What in the holy hell happened to your face, my boy?"

"I had a rough night at Nerio."

"*Victoria aut mors!*" Bill proclaimed.

"I don't know that one."

"Victory or death!" Bill translated. "Marcus, I'd like to introduce you to Luke Kelly."

Marcus smiled. "I know Luke. We go way back."

"Wonderful!" Bill boomed. "That should make the next year all the more enjoyable for you."

"I'll miss you," Marcus said. "No offense, Luke."

"None taken," Luke replied.

"I'll be back when you need me most," Bill assured. "What brings you to this glorious parade today?"

"It's an old family tradition," Marcus answered.

"Your dad is why I come," Luke reminisced. "My first year of grad school, he brought me to compare it to Roman Triumphs. It was a great way to learn how traditions evolve over time and across cultures."

"Parades are a great way to celebrate the past," Bill added, "but I'm more of a postalgia guy myself."

"I've never heard that. What is it?" Marcus asked.

"Instead of romanticizing the past through the lens of a fallen golden age," Bill said, "postalgia idealizes what a better future could be."

"Interesting," Marcus mused.

"Did your dad tell you the tale of Kleobis and Biton?"

"Maybe?"

"The fate of these brothers perfectly captures the idea of a fallen golden age. According to Solon, the same guy who told us the tale of Atlantis," Bill said through the side of his mouth. "Kleobis and Biton hauled their mother six miles in a wagon during a parade, just like this one, and then died."

"That's sad." Marcus lowered his head.

"It wasn't sad to the Greeks since they believed in nostalgia. If you think the past was better than the future can ever be, then life can only get more miserable. The afterlife becomes a blessing."

Luke laughed without making a sound, rocking the top half of his body forward with his mouth half-opened and slapping his thigh.

"You following the party to the park?" Bill asked.

"Walk with us," Luke encouraged.

"I'm not heading that way, but it was great running into both of you. Bill, enjoy your sabbatical, and thanks for one last lesson."

"See you sooner than you think," Bill promised.

Marcus headed toward his car, but a mass of paradegoers clogged all the paths. He was deep into people-watching when he noticed Velia walking a few yards ahead. She was talking with a man that was at least a decade older than her. Marcus couldn't hear the conversation, but from their body language, it was hostile compared to the surrounding celebratory atmosphere. Marcus increased his pace to see if he could decipher their words from the background noise of the crowd. The pieces he could hear had a bounce to them, like something approximating ancient Sanskrit.

The man had long straight blond hair that ended at his jawline, and which he obsessively flipped to the side. He towered more than a foot above Velia and was even taller than Marcus, with tan skin and the body of a CrossFit god. He gesticulated, speaking as much with his hands as with his unintelligible words. That's how Marcus caught sight of the man's unique ring: a Vantablack band slowly phasing between a blue and a red glow against his skin. Marcus watched its hypnotizing undulation. *The colors were surprisingly vibrant*, Marcus thought, *especially in the full sunlight*.

Based on the man's hands, the intensity of their conversation had continued to climb. Marcus's gut told him to intervene, so he surged ahead, squeezing by a gaggle of large families to reach the pair.

"Hey, Velia." Marcus touched her arm, startling her into a defensive fighting posture.

"Marcus?" Velia mouthed as if she'd seen a ghost.

"Are you okay?"

"Yeah, sorry. I didn't … yes. I'm good … you?"

"I'm fine." Marcus's eyes bounced between Velia and her companion until she caught the hint.

"Marcus, this is Virgil."

Virgil vigorously shook Marcus's hand.

"How do you know each other?" Marcus asked.

The pair simultaneously offered contradictory details: Velia said they were siblings, and Virgil claimed they were old coworkers.

"Well, technically, we're both." Velia rubbed the star tattoos along her arm. She wore an identical Vantablack ring, which glowed solid red against her skin.

"Hey, collab!" someone shouted at the trio.

Marcus made a tactical mistake, turning to face the heckler.

"I told you it was him," someone else shouted.

Without further warning, Marcus, Velia, and Virgil found themselves encircled by a dozen young adults. Most were men, and a mix donned the familiar face covers of Coalition protestors. Marcus didn't have to confirm their identities because they started spitting and spraying liquids while shouting at him. Marcus and Velia trained together at Krav for this kind of multiple attacker situation, but Virgil was a wild card. Without exchanging words, the trio lined up back-to-back in the shape of a triangle to face the instigators.

"We're late to the beating," one man taunted.

Marcus glanced at Jordan's dried blood on his shirt.

Another of the angry young men brandished a blade. "Then we'll cut this collab and finish the job."

Velia was the first to strike, closing the distance and wrapping her hands around the man's knife-wielding wrist to control the blade. She used her right shin to deliver a rapid set of strikes to the man's groin and torqued his arm so violently he tumbled sideways in the air, leaving the weapon in Velia's possession.

Virgil was a fraction of a second behind, punching a pair of Coalition protestors in the face, then dropping another with a kick to the groin. He used the hunched over man as a human shield, clinching him around the back of the head and flailing his body around. It took a second for Marcus to make sense of the carnage that Velia and Virgil had inflicted. The activists scattered, leaving their fallen comrades rolling on the ground.

Police officers walking in the parade saw the melee and were making their way toward the conflict zone. "Disperse," Virgil ordered, vanishing into the crowd.

Velia tucked the knife into her pocket, winked at Marcus, then dissolved into the throng in a different direction. Marcus picked another escape vector and blended into the flow of the parade-goers moving toward Liberty Park. Marcus waited a few blocks before separating from the crowd, doubling back through side streets to reach his car. His mind was battling to process what just happened and how quickly it had escalated. Velia had been training at Krav for as long as Marcus, but her skills were way above his. He struggled to steady his hand long enough to unlock the door.

He sat in his Lamborghini until he was calm enough to think straight. The Tek unit was still clinging to his wrist. He pulled it loose, accidentally dropping it on the floor. He was fishing for it under his seat when he felt the surgical sting of a viper's bite; a piece of glass from his previous windshield was embedded in the palm of his left hand. *It was a belated gift from Dianna*, he thought, *a memory in blood of the damage she'd done, and a reminder that piecing his life back together would involve unanticipated pain. What else was waiting for him?*

42

ONCE AGAIN, INTO THE ABYSS

Normally, when the rumble of Marcus's Countach coming up their driveway signaled his triumphant return, Jordan would emerge to offer an inebriated welcome. Today was different; there was no greeting. Marcus paused as he shut the garage and weighed his options. *Going into the house would lead to another fight,* Marcus thought, *and he wouldn't be able to resist rubbing it in Jordan's face that the world hadn't ended.* After listing the pros and cons, Marcus headed for the Lab instead.

"Not your money maker!" Brad jumped from behind his desk.

"It looks worse than it is," Marcus grumbled.

Brad silently inspected the damage.

"I got schooled at Nerio."

"That's a side effect of fighting."

"I'll be fine."

"You know I can read subtext, right? You don't seem fine."

"Can we talk about my quota?" Marcus plopped onto a couch.

"I never thought this day would come." Brad sat across from him. "You really waited until the last chance to finally settle up."

"What do you mean?"

"With Project Noble's first milestone coming to an end, my work will be finished. The Lab will no longer be needed—"

"No!" Marcus wailed.

Brad smirked. "If there's no Lab, then there's no Cohort. If there's no Cohort, there are no experiments, which means …"

"There's no more Tek."

"No *new* Tek," Brad emphasized.

"How will this affect the units that already exist?"

"They'll keep working."

"What does that mean for Tek-Mart?"

"Not a great time to invest … every business your Form has ever built eventually comes to an end. It's called the Product Lifecycle. It's a cold economic fact, and Tek-Mart is headed for their death phase."

"Why didn't you point this out at the Press Conference?"

Brad bust a gut, adding, "Because no one asked."

"How much Tek can I get for all my past work?"

"Like I said before, only you can tell me what you're worth. Name your price."

Marcus's mind raced through the options. "How many people are alive right now. Roughly?"

"Eight billion, give or take."

"I'd like eighteen billion units then, but I want you to give them all to Monica. And make sure she knows they're from me. Please?"

"Sign, sealed, and delivered," Brad declared.

"Thanks. One more thing. With whatever time we have remaining, I don't want to overlap with her in the Lab anymore. Is that a problem?"

"I try to stay out of affairs of the heart. You two need to play nice and work out a schedule for yourselves."

"Is she here now?" Marcus's eyes darted around the room.

"No, and I don't expect that she'll come in today. It's still going to be a madhouse, though. Diksha and Komson are in the Liberty Bell now. Bryan, Duygu, and Tony are on their way in. Plus, you're here."

"Does the rest of the Cohort know we're an endangered species?"

"That's a pessimistic way of looking at things." Brad frowned. "I've had conversations with the ones who've asked. They know that once my research ends, they won't be needed in this capacity anymore. But I'm confident most of you will be offered a spot in the Agoge. It's the logical next step for your personal progress, and it'll leverage your skills to help reach M2."

"I'm all in," Marcus asserted. "Where do I sign?"

"You sure?" Brad leaned forward, resting his elbows on his knees. "Can we back up and talk about the subtext you dismissed earlier?"

"Okay," Marcus conceded.

"The first time we met, I told you that keeping up with your normal life was part of the agreement. That wasn't an arbitrary ask. You're only effective to my research, and by extension, to the needs of the Agoge and your Form's continued integration, if you're free from distractions. Especially emotional ones. So I need to ask you an important question: How's the rest of your life going at the moment?"

"Honestly ... not very good," Marcus admitted. "How detailed do you need me to be?"

"The 'too long; didn't read' version will do. We're working against a clock today."

"Everything is unstable right now. I keep facing the same tradeoff —the same choice between what I want to accomplish by working with the Federation and everyone else's needs. I make choices I feel confident in, but then my relationships run into a wall. Antony is the only person who isn't upset at me right now ... you excluded."

"I will always have your back," Brad assured.

"On second thought ... unstable might be the wrong word. Irreparable is probably better. From where I'm sitting, I don't see a path back to how things have been with everyone else in my life."

"From where I'm sitting," Brad echoed, "I think that's true."

"*Sempre avanti.*"

Brad smiled. "Always forward."

"This doesn't disqualify me, does it?"

"Can you fulfill your duties to the Cohort, despite the instability of your personal life?"

"I think so."

"Thinking isn't knowing."

"... I'm anxious. It's been worse the last few days."

"Is it being driven by your recent drama?"

"It's probably the other way around. The anxiety is there in the background, making it easier to set me off."

"I'll leave the choice to you, but you should be certain. If you know your present emotional state will compromise your effectiveness in the Cohort, let's shake hands, and I'll send you home with an imaginary gold watch for all your service. If instead you know you're capable of continuing, then I'm here to help conquer the anxiety so you can get right back to work."

"I can conquer this."

"Describe how you feel," Brad probed.

"It starts as a general uneasiness—like I'm forgetting to do something. Then my stomach starts to hurt like I ate something bad. My heart races, my chest gets tight to the point of feeling like it's being crushed, and the ringing in my ears comes and goes."

"So it's like your post-Sequence sickness?"

"Similar symptoms, but it feels very different. This arrives in escalating waves, which keep getting more intense over time. It's been particularly rough today."

"How have you dealt with it?" Brad asked.

"I haven't. It's been releasing in explosive fits. Then it starts building up again in the background."

"Have you tried opposite association exercises?"

"I don't know what that is, so no."

"It's super easy. One of your Form, a Buddhist monk, taught it to me. Subconsciously, your brain gets locked in a cycle, reliving an experience and analyzing it over and over in different ways."

"Sounds familiar," Marcus lamented.

"To break the cycle, you need to find a different thought. The best one is the furthest from it, like two opposite electrical charges."

"How do you find the opposite thought?"

"Searching for it is the exercise. Picture your anxiety. What's an opposite that comes to mind?"

"Antony," Marcus answered without hesitation.

"Why Antony?"

"He can get me to laugh. About anything."

"Give me an example where this happened."

Marcus dug deep. "The summer before my parents died, we went to Zion, it's a National Park in the southern part of Utah."

"I know it well."

"I was so excited to see the red rocks. My dad got the idea to drive there in the dead of the night so the roads would be clear. I was complaining about being uncomfortable, and my dad snapped. He started screaming about respect and authority, using a metaphor from the movie *Top Gun*. Seen it?"

"I could tell you, but then I'd have to kill you."

Marcus's smile kept growing. "Remember the scene when Maverick tells Iceman to break right?"

"Oh yeah."

"My dad compared my complaining to a hypothetical situation where Iceman didn't listen and died. That's crazy, right?"

"Crazy, but not insane."

"Exactly!" Marcus exclaimed. "I can still remember how upset I was. I couldn't go back to sleep. My physical discomfort just fueled the fire. About midway through the drive, my dad asked Antony to put on a Beatles playlist. In the middle of it, probably five or six songs deep, a screaming voice tore through the darkness. My mother shot from her sleep and started speaking in Italian. When I looked at Antony, he was beaming. He'd added a metal song to the middle of the mix. I remember feeling transformed. I couldn't hold on to my anger anymore. He's always been able to do that for me."

"How was the rest of your Zion adventure?"

"Perfect. We had rooms along the river. I saw petroglyphs and tried to catch lizards while we hiked. I think it may have been the best vacation we did as a family. Top three, without a doubt."

"Zion is a magical place. I've studied it for its geography. It's an anomaly on your planet for its long geological stability. The petroglyphs you saw were a message from a very distant past."

"They looked like people with jetpacks, like from those ancient alien astronaut shows that Jordan loves."

"How'd you feel among those timeworn rocks?"

"I remember feeling small. It's a place of extremes: extreme size, extreme temperatures, extreme beauty. Walls jettison out of the ground and tower thousands of feet in the air. I felt like I was part of something bigger than myself. That I was safe. That I'd be okay. I'm not doing it justice. You'll have to experience it firsthand."

"When I'm ready for the road trip, I'll have Antony make me a playlist!"

They shared their final laugh.

"Ready to get your hands dirty?" Brad asked.

Marcus nodded, then charged into the locker room.

"Happy Pioneer Day!" Hi!-D greeted Marcus as he crossed the threshold into the empty shared space.

"How's it going?"

"Better than you. Tough luck about last night."

"It looks worse than it feels," Marcus replied. "That, or I'm still a bit drunk. I'm not sure."

"Shall I fetch a cold cut of beef for your face?"

"I'll pass."

"Is there anything else I can do for you today?"

"You ask me that every time I'm here, and I keep saying no. When are you going to stop asking?"

"When you say yes," Hi!-D proclaimed.

"If I get the chance ... we're on borrowed time."

"It's not the end of the world."

Marcus let out a heavy sigh. "It feels that way."

"We'll still see each other. I'm sure of it."

"Stiff upper lip and all that."

"What are your plans?" Hi!-D inquired

"I want to get into the Agoge, but I'm not sure—"

"I meant for today. To celebrate the holiday."

"Oh ... I'm having a BBQ with Antony later."

"If you'd like a recipe for the best beef cut you've ever tasted, let me know. You could get twice the mileage from the same piece of meat," Hi!-D giggled.

Marcus suited up and entered the Liberty Bell. Diksha and Komson, two of Marcus's favorite members of the Cohort, were suspended mid-air. He wasn't sure if they were in the same Sequence or if he'd be joining them; sharing the Liberty Bell was a necessary, but not sufficient, condition for going Tandem. Marcus was struck by how eerie things felt. Both of the other Cohort members were holding perfectly still. He'd never seen them motionless like this, though Brad said it was possible. They were frozen in another world, living a dream, with no idea he had ascended beside them. *Whatever Sequence they were experiencing*, Marcus thought, *he hoped it was enjoyable. It'd be one of their last.*

[Sequence ID# 852] [Data Begins]

The last thing he remembered was the desperate struggle to breathe. Marcus was trapped in a narrow sandstone tunnel, his arms being smashed into his ribs by the red walls. The angle of the space was so steep that it took an enormous amount of energy to move a single inch. His heavy breathing kicked up dust, further drying out his mouth. It was unbearably hot. He was slowly suffocating, and the idea he could be stuck here forever kept Marcus on the edge of a full-blown panic attack.

Something was gripping his legs. Marcus didn't know what was behind him, nor was there room to kick or turn around to see. A faint glow of light was visible at the far end of the tunnel he was entombed in. This light became his new goal: as long as he could see the luminous target, he had hope that he could survive. Inch-by-inch, he gained ground. Eventually, Marcus was able to move one arm around his body and over his head. The serrated walls scraped off his skin, leaving behind a million razor-like grains of sand that sent pins-and-needles pumping down his arm and into his chest each time he pulled himself forward.

He wasn't sweating anymore. He knew this was an early sign of heatstroke. Soon muscle cramps and seizures would set in. Then he'd go unconscious. *Slow down, take deep, deliberate breaths, and accept this fate,* he told himself. The sunlight faded, and he saw intermittent stars transit across the small opening at the end of the tunnel. Maddening thirst demanded his attention and added to the pain of a dehydration headache, halting his movement completely.

After an inadvertent bit of sleep, he woke in a state of terror. The stars had been replaced by daylight again. He thought he'd heard a voice from outside the tunnel.

"Hello ...?" Marcus said with a crackling cry.

There was no reply.

"Is someone there?" Marcus pleaded. "I'm stuck ... HELP!"

No one answered.

Marcus was certain the voice had been his father's. He continued forward until he reached a space where he could free his other arm. His advance was still limited by his shoulders and legs, which dragged behind him like slabs of concrete. The heat was at its height again, but he was inches from the edge of the tunnel. After hours of strife, he reached his goal, finally pulling his head across the brink. He was staring up the face of a red cliff at clear blue sky.

His brain couldn't comprehend what he was seeing, and his fatigue made finding an answer all the more difficult. Then, he realized the truth: in traversing the tunnel, he'd lost track of which direction down was. Marcus spun around, a maneuver that cost him more skin on his shoulders and abdomen. His stomach sank once he'd completed the turn: he was looking down a thousand-foot cliff, high above a river slithering like a snake through the red rock landscape.

There was no way back down the tunnel—he was imprisoned on this precipice. He searched for a solution, but none came. He was exhausted, and there was nothing to hold onto around him. He prayed someone would see him and shouted until his voice was gone. *This couldn't be how it ended*, he kept telling himself. Marcus remained unmoved for an entire night and most of another day. Then, embracing the only apparent solution, he pulled himself over the edge of the tunnel and let go, beginning his destined descent toward the canyon floor.

[Sequence ID# 852] [Data Ends]

[Sequence ID# 928] [Data Begins]

The last thing he remembered was finally breaking free from the suffocating confines of the putrid bathroom. His next challenge was shuffling through the dimly lit plane without bumping the shoulders of passengers sleeping in aisle seats. He was the only person still awake. The low hum of the cabin was hypnotizing, but the air was uncomfortably warm and smelled of stale sweat. Everything about the plane looked well past its expiration date. *Having this many people in such a small space is unnatural*, Marcus thought, jostling by incapacitated row-mates to his window seat. Instability replaced his sense of calm, as if the floor would drop from beneath him.

He took a deep breath to center himself, but before he could exhale, or fasten his seatbelt, one of the plane's alarms blared. The wall beside him ripped away, sucking him into the nighttime abyss. The whole incident happened twice: instantly and in slow motion, with both versions fading to black. At thirty-five thousand feet, there was a third of the normal oxygen, and Marcus lost consciousness moments after the plane tore apart. He fell until he was below the Death Zone, the boundary where human brains can stay awake. As his vision came back into focus, Marcus found himself tumbling alone through the darkness. An arc of golden light stretched across the horizon, separating the endless water below from the infinite space above. The sky was clear in every direction, and the moon's reflection danced across the purple sea in a long silver beam cut by isolated mountain islands.

Despite the present circumstances, Marcus felt peaceful. *This was a nice place to die*, he thought. As a child, someone told him that fear of death would shut down his brain, but his mind was sharper than ever. Time had slowed to a crawl. Each passing second was like a century. His life didn't flash before him in a series of visuals; instead, it engaged all of his senses. He remembered the feeling of his mother's embrace and the rosemary scent of her shampoo. He felt the earth under his bare feet as he explored the mountains with his father. Although his mind didn't remain on any memory for more than an instant, each immersed him.

How ironic, Marcus thought. Years ago, he'd read a *Popular Mechanics* article about consciously falling from an airplane that broke apart mid-air. He only remembered fragments of the story, including it was worse to hit water than concrete because it swallows you up even if you survive the impact, which a surprising number of people do. There was nothing but sea below. Marcus knew he had zero chance. He wasn't sure how much time was left, which liberated him from obsessing over the exact moment of his end. For now, he could enjoy being alive surrounded by unbounded beauty.

His mind wandered to the other passengers. He'd been the first one to board and avoided eye contact with the parade of first-world refugees carrying a hodgepodge of personal belongings to their temporary seats. If he'd known they were destined to die together, he'd have behaved differently. As Marcus contemplated the meaning of their shared fate, a massive explosion illuminated the night; it was the plane. The force was powerful enough to shove him across the sky, momentarily warming his exposed skin. He was naked, stripped of his clothing by the air rushing around him. As the orange ball of fire disappeared in his peripheral vision, the chill of the wind returned. Flickering scraps of metal, cloth, and plastic littered the air like confetti. It was all that remained of the other passengers. His heart ached for them, but he still had time to enjoy these fleeting moments of life, and a final wave of joy washed over him.

[Sequence ID# 928] [Data Ends]

Marcus woke up next to five members of the Cohort, three more than when he'd started the Sequence. Like the two that'd preceded them, all were holding uncharacteristically still. The large elliptical space was dark, and the low hum of the Liberty Bell provided a sense of momentary comfort. He searched his memory for any hint of what he'd just done, but drew an expected blank. His head, chest, and stomach were burning with pain. *This had to be the peak of his anxiety*, Marcus thought. *It felt like waking from a nightmare as a child, when fear, uncertainty, and doubt heighten the senses.*

He descended to the iron-red floor and shuffled toward his locker to remove the EXO. A note in the locker room invited him to party with the rest of his Cohort. From his conversation with Brad that morning, Marcus knew their time as a team was running out, but he had no idea they'd completed their final Sequence together. Antony was waiting, and since family came first for Marcus, he left the Lab without saying goodbye.

It was a hot July night, and the ground radiated as he walked off the University campus. The smell of barbecues and fire pits permeated the air, along with the muffled sounds of music. Thick grey clouds blanketed the sky now, and humidity magnified the orange sun as it slipped behind the mountains. *The world seemed stable, even if he was on edge. The peace was temporary since the fireworks would begin any moment. Utah was celebrating.*

He couldn't shake the uneasiness. Despite taking his recent drama into account, this was worse than usual. In an attempt at self-distraction, Marcus checked his phone, but the plan backfired spectacularly. There was a bombardment of encrypted messages about the end of the world from Jordan, a threatening email from Dianna cc'ing her lawyer, a dozen missed calls from Antony, and a single text from Monica. He cleared the other notifications and read Monica's message:

> *IMS. Plz stop ignorin me. I luv u. Don't end things like this. Just talk 2 me. :-(*

Marcus stopped and took a series of slow, deep breaths. Though the words didn't change, each reread caused a flood of different emotions to course through his veins. It'd been an intense four months. *For such a short amount of time, it felt like an eternity.* The shriek of fireworks caused him to jump out of his skin. As he regained his composure, his phone rang, triggering a memory of the choices that brought him to this moment … the incessant auditory signal danced off-frequency from the ringing in his ears, snapping Marcus back to the present.

"Hello?"

"I'm almost to your place," Antony said. "Jordan told me what happened last night. Why aren't you returning any of my calls?"

"I've been in the Lab since the parade ended."

"Too much of anything is bad, Marcus."

"Thanks for the concern. See you in a sec."

Marcus found Antony waiting with Bucephalus. "Did Jordan convince you the apocalypse is upon us?"

"If I knew when I'd need this beast, I'd only use it then." Antony stroked Bucephalus's hood. "The IRS mileage reimbursement rate doesn't even come close to actual wear and tear."

"Let's go," said Marcus.

"Where's your stuff?"

"Everything I need is already at Sundance."

Antony scowled.

"I don't want to go inside," Marcus explained.

"Why?"

"Jordan will start his fire and brimstone routine again," Marcus said as he climbed into Bucephalus. "I want to get to the mountains and put this week behind me."

Spectacular firework shows were happening all across the valley as they cruised the city.

"I'm your brother and I love you, so tell me, no bullshit, what's going on with you? Do I need to worry about a 2016 repeat?"

"I think you mean a -5 NE repeat, and no, I was in a way worse place that year. This is different. I'm not that person anymore."

"I hope so because back then, your therapists had a shorter life expectancy than helicopter door-gunners during Vietnam."

"A week ago, my life was looking so bright."

"A week ago, we were in the middle of our trek from hell. What are you talking about?"

"It still felt better than this."

"Jordan said you shredded your parenting plan."

Marcus rapidly replayed the confrontation in his mind. "It was worse than that ... I threw it in her face."

"Did you really threaten her?"

"Yes. Not physically, but yes."

"Are you sure you're ready to fight her?"

"I'm tired of eating her shit."

"Finally!" Antony slapped the steering wheel.

"I'm nervous. Way more than I want to admit."

"You should be. She's a highly intelligent, motivated, spiteful woman. History shows they're capable of anything. I said it before, and I'll say it again, watch your six. She's going to hurt you for this. As hard as she possibly can. I've seen it in her eyes."

"When?"

"I took her to get coffee when you were first dating. Right after the Federation arrived. I thought Dianna was the woman they warned me about at my Disclosure Moment—the one Hi!-D said would stand in your way. I'm still convinced she's the one."

"Dianna told me about that."

"I knew she would. I underestimated her. I thought she was a simple gold-digger, but when I tried to pay her to leave you alone, the look on her face ... it gave me chills."

"It is what it is."

"That's the truth." Antony chuckled. "At least you haven't lost your sense of humor over this … if you can't laugh through this—"

"The stress will kill me before she gets the chance," Marcus finished the sentence.

"How'd you know what I was going to say?"

"Déjà vu," Marcus said, turning on their music.

43

WALKING TOWARD ETERNITY

T he Sundance sky was moonless, and with Hecate on the other side of the horizon, the stars punched through the onyx veil of their mountain surroundings. Bucephalus was too large for the garage, so Antony parked at the bottom of their long driveway.

"Listen to all that quiet," Antony said as he walked toward the house.

He was right, Marcus thought, *it was nearly silent. No fireworks. No cars traversing the roads. No people talking. No animals. Just a cool evening wind flowing over and around the tops of quaking summer trees.*

Marcus made his way to their back patio where cobblestone pavers and drooping strands of lightbulbs marked out the family's space from the adjacent mountainside. He embraced his expected role as sous chef, lighting the outdoor grill before returning to the kitchen to aid Antony in prepping their meal.

"Does a guy named Virgil train at Krav?" asked Marcus.

"No," Antony declared. "Why are you asking?"

"Not to rub your face in it, but you were wrong about the parade. A mob of Coalition crazies recognized me and—"

"What?" Antony stopped slicing onions.

"A small group surrounded us—"

"Us?"

"Velia happened to be there with some ripped older dude named Virgil. She was introducing us when the fight started. I just stood there while the two of them took down half the group. Virgil had skills. He moved fluidly with Velia without saying a word … like they'd trained together. Both of them were using Krav Maga."

"No one named Virgil has ever trained at our gym in the fourteen years I've been going."

"You're sure?"

"I'm not just sure, I'm HIV positive!" Antony invoked one of his favorite *South Park* lines. "They probably studied together at another gym … Velia has definitely had other training. She moves like someone with years of experience when we spar."

"Have you ever asked her about it? Directly?"

"No. Why would I? Students bounce from one martial art to another all the time." Antony pointed his knife at Marcus. "Now, get to work or we'll never eat."

A petrichor scent wafted into Marcus's face as he hovered over the sink scrubbing coal-colored soil from the zucchini. A golden death mask mounted at eye-level on a vertical slat of wood separating two window panes faced him as he worked; the relic had been here for as long as Marcus could remember.

"Where is this mask from?" Marcus asked.

Antony looked at the object. "A trip to Greece."

"Why don't I remember that?"

"You were a toddler. You weren't in diapers anymore, so you shit all over me at the Acropolis."

"I wish I could remember it," Marcus moaned.

"It was a great vacation." Antony motioned Marcus toward the patio. They stood around the controlled conflagration, captivated by the sizzling of meats and oiled-vegetables.

"Was that mask from the Acropolis?" Marcus probed.

"No. I think we picked it up at a shop near Mycenae. It's a replica. Why the sudden interest? It's been hanging in that spot for almost two decades ..."

"I just noticed it," Marcus revealed. "I mean, I've seen it and knew it was there, but I never stopped to think about it."

"Interesting." Antony's voice climbed an octave. "Do you know what they were used for?"

"What, death masks?"

"Yes."

"For burying people," Marcus mocked.

"That's far from the full story."

"I give up." Marcus threw his hands into the air.

"They were supposed to capture the essence of the person being buried. The question, then, is which essence? We each have three masks: one we present to ourselves, one that shows how other people see us, and one that captures who we really are. Which do you think the death mask is meant to represent?"

Marcus took a moment to consider the options. "If I had a mask made for myself, I'd want it to reflect how I see myself, not how other people see me. How I see myself is the true version."

Antony roared with laughter.

"Why is that funny?"

"How do you see yourself?" Antony interrogated.

"I'm a person who protects the people I care most about, especially my family and friends."

"Have you done that? You've protected them all?"

"I'm working on it."

"Then who you are doesn't match who you think you are."

"I'm helping the Federation to help humanity. With Project Noble's first milestone approaching," Marcus pulled back his shoulders, "it's fair to say I'm doing a stellar job."

"What about everyone else in your life?"

"I'm going to fight Dianna to protect my kids ... so they can get to know the other half of their family without her interference."

"Who else?"

"I'm trying to protect Monica from Benedict."

Antony raised an eyebrow. "What does that mean?"

"Hannah and Benedict abuse Monica for her Tek quota. They demand an amount, and she does their bidding. If anyone from our Cohort tries to sell units on their own, Benedict can use Monica to flood the market and make everyone's Tek worthless. That threat, and Benedict's ability to use governments as his hammer to shut down competitors beyond the Black Market, keeps our entire Cohort in line. But Monica has all the real power.

Without her, Tek-Mart and its monopoly would go away. Forever. I haven't been taking any Tek for myself—"

"Hold up, why not?"

"I joined the Cohort to protect the people I care about, and I didn't want to deal with Benedict. But we're getting off-topic, I negotiated with Brad for my retro pay and got enough Tek to cripple Tek-Mart once and for all. Then I gave it to Monica."

"What do you expect her to do with it?" asked Antony.

"What she could have done all along on her own: leverage Benedict to give her Tek-Mart and exit her life by holding a credible threat to drive Tek's price to zero with a huge supply dump. I gave Monica a nudge in that direction."

"That's a murder-suicide type solution, isn't it?"

"Monica will be free … from Benedict's control."

"Why does that matter?"

"Are you serious?" Marcus fumed.

Antony repeated his question, "Explain why that matters?"

"Because then we can be together."

"Oh, my dear brother …," Antony whispered.

Marcus sat silently, awaiting words of wisdom.

"She's a beautiful disaster," Antony offered.

"Take all the time you need to form an opinion."

"Just because you don't want to hear it, that doesn't make it a lie. I've known a few people like her over the years. They're in a state of perpetual flux in the social scene, always changing jobs, partners, and locations. Deep down, she needs stability more than anything, but she hates it once she has it. She wants someone to break the boredom of her perfect life, someone to shake the foundations of that ridiculous mansion on the hill. But once she gets what she wants, she'll move on to something else because it's not what she needs. And your heart will be collateral damage. People like her go from distraction to distraction, leaving a path of carnage, without ever addressing the real issue that's eating at them."

"Which is?"

"That despite having anything they ever wanted, their lives are meaningless. Her husband—"

"Ex," Marcus corrected him again.

"Right. He's the same way. Money is his only God. He blindly accumulates for the sake of accumulation, with no plan to make human connections or improve the world. So don't hold out hope for Monica. She'll disappoint you. There's zero chance she'll pick you over the life she's built, abuse and all. It's a sad truth, but you can't save someone from themselves."

Marcus chewed the inside of his cheek.

"What about Jordan?"

"What about him," Marcus grumbled.

"How did hitting him help protect him?"

"He told you?"

"That little birdie loves to sing."

"It was a mistake," Marcus admitted, "but he keeps betraying my trust and siding against me. I've never questioned his loyalty until the last few months."

"Think he might be motivated by misguided, but ultimately correct, convictions?"

"No way!"

Antony flipped the food. "How are you so sure?"

"Leaving aside his extensive annals of failed prophecies, he's constantly altering his consciousness. There's no way he's correct."

Antony slammed the lid of the BBQ. "That's a cop-out and you know it. You've seen him sober. He's the exact same person."

"I can't think of the last time I saw him sober."

"And *I think* you're deluding yourself to protect your ego—"

"My ego?" Marcus scoffed.

"If he's right, in spite of the drugs and past false positives, that means the Federation is evil, and your plans to protect everyone is a lost cause. It also means Dianna was right—are you capable of staring that possibility in the eyes, free of ego?"

"You're casting some serious stones for someone with an ego bigger than Monica's 'ridiculous' house on the hill," Marcus asserted with air quotes.

Antony smiled. "Guilty."

"What's your mask? How do you see yourself?"

Antony folded his arms, leaning against the stone wall holding the mountainside back. "I'm a person who works every day to put the anal into analytics."

Marcus's laughter evaporated his anger.

"After being your brother and guardian," Antony explained, "I'm a person pouring myself into one of the most important projects in human history—"

"One Identity?"

"It's my magnum opus."

"You've put in the hours," Marcus affirmed.

"The data doesn't lie. As of yesterday, I've spent more time with Benedict working on One Identity than I've spent with you so far this year."

"Seriously?"

"I try to keep as much distance as I can from him, but the Furies find a way to drive us together. I don't think it's a coincidence another connection showed up between you and Monica."

"What does One Identity do?" Marcus whispered.

"The project is stove-piped, so no one has a complete picture, not even me. Without getting into details that'd get us both locked in Federal prison for the rest of our natural lives, my intuition says it's a decentralized ledger, like a blockchain, for ...," Antony frowned, "for lack of a better word, the soul. I know how that sounds, but the data types and the way permissioning has been built to utilize biometric data only makes sense if the purpose is to create a digital version of a person's complete consciousness. The time horizons I was required to build into my algorithm's updates imply a projected longevity of hundreds of thousands of years."

"Immortality?" Marcus mused.

"I hope not. You'd be a killjoy at parties."

"What?" Marcus let out half a laugh.

"Assuming the inevitable continuation of human breeding, if you started living forever tomorrow, you'd end up as one of the few people to know other people who've died. You'd go on and on about everyone you used to know and what they were like. It'd be like describing a dream to someone who has no way of understanding the context, but way more depressing since they couldn't relate to your loss."

"Why would the government build this?"

"I don't think it's the government," Antony asserted. "Nothing about this project jibes with how they normally work."

"If not them, then who?"

"Government guys are involved, but I think they're acting as an intermediary and the real decision-maker is the Federation."

"Why would you think that?"

"Tek is a core information source for One Identity, and the Federation controls that data—unless Tek is a secret government program. But I've never met a human bureaucracy capable of pulling that off."

Marcus's mind raced through the implications of Antony's theory; it aligned with more than a few of Jordan's conspiracies.

"Time to eat." Antony presented their meal, suspending the conversation so they could enjoy the blissful bounty in silence. *This was his first food of the day,* Marcus realized, savoring each bite. *It proved their father's adage that hunger makes the best seasoning.*

With a belly in danger of bursting, Marcus kicked back to play with his lucky coin. "What was the second kind of mask we all wear?"

"The one showing how other people see us," Antony answered. "That one is usually the scariest because it exposes the secrets we try to hide from ourselves but which other people see."

Marcus blurted his next words, "I have a secret."

"Don't we all ..."

"I'm serious. I've even kept it from you."

Antony rubbed his hands together. "Juicy."

"I've been using Tek for months." Marcus felt a weight lifting off his body by speaking the words.

"That's hardly earth-shattering news, given who you work with. Do you use it as an escape? To live another life?"

"I've been reliving memories with mom and dad."

Antony had no words.

"I've cataloged and stored every memory I can think of with our family. Most are random short interactions, but the longest and most vivid ones are from vacations and celebrations."

"How many have you stored?"

"Hundreds."

Antony leaned forward. "How real do they feel?"

"They're more like a dream than real life, but being with mom and dad again has been priceless."

"I can only imagine."

"Want to try?" Marcus perked up at his own idea.

"What, Tek?"

"Yes. I have a unit here. I hid it in the library upstairs. All you have to do is place the Tek on your skin, lay back on a couch or a bed or something, and think about the memory. It automatically gets stored, then you can relive it just by thinking about it."

"So the memories live on the Tek?"

"I don't think so. I have another piece stashed in my car. I can access files I made with that Tek using the one I've got here, and vice versa."

"You sound like a drug addict right now …"

"That's rich coming from you," Marcus scowled. "Your brain holds memories I've forgotten, like that trip to Greece when we got the mask. You also have family memories from before I was born. If you store those, you could share them with me."

Antony was pondering the idea when Marcus talked past the sale, "Should I grab the Tek for you?"

"Let me think about it," Antony nodded slowly. "I might give it a shot later tonight … we'll see."

"That was mom's way of saying no."

"Where's the Tek if I decide to do it?"

"Second bookshelf to the right, in a copy of *Fable of the Bees*."

"Roger Roger."

"Why haven't you tried Tek? Are you worried Jordan's right?"

"I don't like the idea of someone, or something, being inside my head."

"This is about your second mask?"

"We all hide parts of ourselves from the world," Antony lamented. "Mine are too big to fit in between the pages of a book, unfortunately."

Marcus gripped his coin as Antony continued.

"Remember when dad used to say winning isn't everything—"

"But it's right up there with oxygen." Marcus completed the phrase. "It was one of his favorites."

"That idea haunts me. It controls a big part of my life. If Benedict's avarice is for money, mine is for winning. I can't stand losing. When I win, my whole soul lights on fire. I feel invincible

—divinely guided and protected. It's why I don't care about money. It's meaningless compared to that feeling. But I want it just as badly as Benedict wants wealth. I can't get enough. No one understands, so they call me crazy."

Marcus recycled Brad's line, "Crazy, but not insane."

"Right," Antony laughed.

"Last night you said to shake off a loss—"

"And it was solid life advice. That doesn't mean I'm capable of listening to it myself. Losing feeds a dark voice inside of me that says I'm not good enough. That I'm an imposter. That I'm a fraud."

"Now *that* is insane."

"It's self-doubt that I mask. That's my secret."

Marcus pocketed the Memento Mori.

"I'm a hard worker, I know it, but winning comes too easily," Antony continued. "No matter the odds, everything works out in my favor. I ask myself if it's the result of my hard work and skills, or if it's fate or destiny or God. But without fail, whatever I needed is there at the exact moment I need it. I've studied patterns in data for half of my life. This can't be random chance. The probability is way too low. I can't shake the fear that things have been handed to me and I'm no different than King Fag Face the Insignificant."

"Who?" Marcus challenged.

"Benedict."

Marcus searched for words of encouragement, but Antony charged ahead, "After a lifetime, I've learned I can't silence the dark voice. All I can do is acknowledge that it exists and then ignore it. The drugs help," Antony cackled, "but Mom's friend

Jeraldine taught me a visualization technique I use all the time. I picture the voice as a small monster, and when I see it, I tie it to a Greek column—"

"Doric, Ionic, or Corinthian." Marcus grinned.

"Ionic. Obviously."

"Does it work?"

"For a while. The little asshole always gets loose."

"Have you ever lost, though?" Marcus murmured.

"It's been rare, but there's a big one …"

After some silence, Marcus prodded, "What is it?"

"Help me do the dishes, then I'll tell you."

Marcus stacked their plates from the patio table and started a food scrap pile. "Where's Kitty?"

"I left her home in the vault."

"Why would you do that?"

"The dog sitter said Kitty freaked out on the Fourth of July because of the fireworks. She's getting schizo in her old age. The vault is soundproof, so she'll take a nap and wake up to a doggie bag."

"She eats better than some humans," Marcus said.

"Life has been kind to all of us."

"Right. We're the lucky ones," Marcus muttered.

"Everyone has hardships and trials. But even taking those into consideration, right now, would you trade your life for anyone else's?"

"No."

"Me neither. We're exactly where we want to be."

After a well-coordinated clean up to one of Jordan's recent remixes, the brothers retired to the family patio for the last time. Antony held two heroic sized drinks, each containing a generous four-finger pour of scotch.

The smell made Marcus's belly beg for mercy. "I can't drink anything tonight."

"Better you spill my blood than waste my liquor!" Antony decried. "More for me. Want to smoke?"

"Sure."

Antony set down the drinks and fished a pipe from his pocket, handing it to Marcus along with a small Ziploc of Jordan's mountain grow.

"I fulfilled my half of the agreement." Marcus loaded the pipe, taking a hit, and speaking through an exhalation, "It's your turn."

"I'm searching for a tactful way to say this ..."

"You're just stalling now."

"The biggest loss I've ever suffered was quitting law school." Antony struggled to swallow. "It's the only time I've felt truly defeated in my entire life."

A puff of guilt blew out of Marcus. "I'm sorry."

"Don't insult me with an apology. You didn't kill our parents. The opportunity to help prepare you for the future has been the greatest blessing of my life. You joined the Cohort out of a sense of conviction. That's exactly how I feel about being your guardian. I'm not proud of everything I've done, but I'm ashamed of nothing. When judgment inevitably comes, I'll be able to hold my head up high and say I turned the biggest loss of my life into my greatest success: you. Hi!-D's comment during my Disclosure Moment was proof positive for me. I know the Federation is right, and you're going to be the key that protects us from the Confederation—"

Antony's comment knocked a memory loose for Marcus. "I just remembered last night's dream."

"This isn't my favorite thing to do in life," Antony took a long sip from his drink, "but let's hear it."

"I used to have this dream all the time, but it's been years." Marcus oozed with excitement, adding, "I was playing in the middle of dense woods. The dusty smell of dried plants was so pungent in the air that it diffused the sunlight like a fog. Every tree must've dropped their red maple leaves at the same time because they blanketed the entire forest floor, covering a rail line passing right by me. A single column of light cut through the haze, drawing my attention to a junction box. I knew I needed to throw the switch, and how important the job was, but I procrastinated because I was having fun in the shadows. When the train would eventually punch through the dust cloud, I'd frantically paw at the leaves for a key to the junction box. The ground would vibrate violently as waves of red leaves were shot away from the train, like it was plowing through deep snow. That's always the point in the dream when I realize I'd failed. The train would derail, setting off a domino effect of destruction. The sound of trees snapping under the weight of steel is what shocks me from my sleep."

"That's your third mask," Antony encouraged.

"I don't see the connection."

"Destiny is your third mask. It's what you really are. In your dream, you have the power to protect everyone—you just have to focus on doing the job."

"But, I always fail."

"Only in the dream. It's a warning for real life."

"I can't find the key in time. It's impossible."

"Are you sure you even need a key? Have you ever gone to the junction box in your dream? Maybe you're the key, and all you need to do is joyfully three-step into the light from the shadows to succeed. We were talking about your role as a protector from the Confederation when you remembered this dream. You don't have to be a psychologist to put those puzzle pieces together. If you can accept that you're the key, I have no doubt you'll be able to protect us."

"*Sempre avanti,*" Marcus declared.

"I ALMOST FORGOT!" Antony screeched like a fangirl. "I've got something for you." He returned with Invictus. "Pull it out."

Marcus drew the sword from its scabbard. Two big words were etched boldly into the flat surface of the black blade: *Sempre Avanti.*

"You left it at my place," Antony explained. "I finally got it tagged to teach you a lesson about keeping track of your shit."

"I love it!" Marcus hugged Antony then held Invictus parallel to his body in front of his face.

"You were born to this family in this time. That's a big part of your destiny. Don't ever forget it."

"Why are you telling me this?"

Antony looked skyward, blowing an opaque cloud of cannabis smoke, fixated on the stars. "... I don't know ... I felt like I needed to."

PART XIII

THE RESET

SUNDAY, JULY 24, +1 NE

44

I DREAMT WE WERE BANK ROBBERS

Marcus woke to the sound of a hollow thud. Without opening his eyes, he knew what'd happened: a bird, flying free from the constraints of Earth, crashed into the large glass window of his parents' bedroom. During her lifetime, Marcus's mother insisted all fallen fowl be given final rites before being buried in the woods west of their home. More than once, while Marcus completed this macabre task, the trees filled with other birds; the somber spectators watched in silence as he entombed their friend, scattering once the deed was done. *He'd lay this particular ill-fated creature to rest after breakfast*, Marcus thought, rising from bed.

Marcus's abdomen crackled like fire, his head vibrated like a badly beaten bell, and a deafening hum had hold of his hearing. *Such were the usual physical distractions of life, but today was worse. He was fighting the evilest hangover ever, despite abstaining from alcohol while talking with Antony late into the night.* Marcus staggered to the window and drew back the curtains; it was another beautiful blue-sky day. Based on the sun's present position, it was just before noon.

He could almost hear Antony's voice reciting the Benjamin Franklin quote he used to wake Marcus up for high school, "Early to bed and early to rise, makes a man healthy, wealthy, and wise." It was a pithy little saying that stuck with Marcus no matter how much he wished to forget it. He inhaled slowly through his nose, picking up the faint scent of incense his father regularly burned in this room before his death. Their house, like the world he watched through the window, was peacefully silent.

Marcus could smell the stale sweat and cannabis on his now three-day-old wardrobe. He pocketed his lucky coin and descended both levels of zigzagging stairs to Antony's area of the house, but his brother was nowhere to be found. He peeked out the front door to find Bucephalus still in the driveway.

"ANTONY?" Marcus's voice echoed throughout the house.

There was no answer.

Marcus searched the guest room, in case Antony accidentally passed out there, but it was also empty. Undeterred, he continued the hunt, room by room, eventually finding Antony asleep on one of the living room couches in nothing but boxer briefs. *That's out of character, since he always sleeps on the floor*, Marcus thought. *He must've hit the bottle hard last night.* The tattoo across his brother's back stared Marcus in the face: "no friend served me, no enemy wronged me, who I haven't fully repaid."

"You overdid it … ANTONY, WAKE UP!" Marcus shouted over his shoulder, heading for the kitchen. "I know how much you love listening to dreams, but I had another crazy one last night … we were bank robbers. We were wearing three-piece pinstripe suits, and our faces were covered by those spooky ballistic masks the Special Forces wear—the ones that look like an x-ray outline of a skull. We both had tricked-out short-barrel rifles, and you put these long strips of plastic explosive on the outside of the vault wall, then detonated them with an old silver pocket watch. It was so badass. It felt like a scene straight out of *Heat*."

Antony didn't reply.

"Antony?" Marcus returned to the living room.

"ANTONY!" Marcus clapped his hands. "Don't make me sing the song … come on, get up … this isn't funny anymore." Marcus watched Antony for any sign of movement, but nothing came. His older brother had a habit of feigning sleep to draw someone in, only to suddenly jump and scare them. But Marcus knew this was different; he could feel it. As he inched toward Antony, the wooden floors squeaked under his weight, sending Marcus's pulse racing. He wiped beads of sweat from his brow. Time had slowed to a crawl, the light moved in blurry arcs, and the slightest sound was suddenly deafening. Marcus recognized the old, cold, familiar presence of death.

"Antony, get up!" Marcus ran to his brother's side and shook him. "Please get up … Antony … please … Antony… ANTONY!"

Marcus felt the side of his brother's neck for a pulse, but there was none. He checked for any sign of breathing, placing a finger under Antony's nose and his other hand on Antony's chest, but the body was motionless. Marcus squeezed Antony's hand, hoping to get even the faintest squeeze back, but it never happened. His brother didn't feel like a person anymore; the hand was frigid, the fingers were stiff, and the skin was pale.

Marcus moaned from his soul as he embraced the hollow shell that used to be his brother. "ANTONY … not you too … please, God … ANTONY! DON'T LEAVE … please … wake up … ANTONY! WAKE UP!"

Marcus refused to accept this reality. *He needed help*, he thought, pawing through each pocket for his phone but finding nothing. *It must still be upstairs.* He sprinted to his parents' room to retrieve his phone from the nightstand. Fighting against an adrenaline surge, he slowly and deliberately pressed each button: 9 … 1 … 1. He shoved the device to his ear and waited, and waited, and waited. Nothing happened. Stomping in place, he tried again, ensuring to dial each digit correctly, but his careful efforts resulted in the same outcome: nothing. The small icon on the screen revealed the reason: Marcus had no network connection. In a fit of frustration, he heaved the device at the nearest wall, smashing it into oblivion.

He raced back to Antony's body, searching the couch for his brother's phone, but it wasn't there. Marcus was hyperventilating, paralyzed by an effervescent cocktail of emotions and stress chemicals. *He couldn't do this alone. He couldn't do this alone,* he kept telling himself over and over as he searched the rest of the house. He eventually found Antony's device on the patio table between the cannabis pipe and an empty bottle of scotch, but it didn't have a connection either. *This makes no sense. They always had reliable service here. Was the resort's tower offline … was this part of a Federation attack?* Marcus briefly entertained the idea but dismissed it outright. *It couldn't be … that didn't explain why he was still alive … he just needed a landline to call for help. Jordan's parents still had one.*

Marcus sprinted through a grove of aspens to reach the Kilravock's home. He rang the doorbell and furiously banged on doors and windows, but no one answered. Marcus circled the house for a point of entry, improvising by smashing a decorative glass pane of the back patio door with a soccer ball-sized rock. He rushed into the kitchen and picked up the phone's receiver; the absence of a dial tone crushed his hopeful spirit. He frantically fingered the switch hook, trying to reset the connection, but no dial tone emerged. He slammed down the receiver, darting through the rest of the residence searching for anyone, or anything, that could help, but every phone in the empty house was dead.

Marcus tried all the neighboring homes, but no one answered; each looked like it was vacant from the outside. Other than his crying, the world was completely silent. Gasping for air through heavy bouts of sobbing, he darted back to Antony's side. He felt defeated as he knelt beside his brother's body. This was the same spot where he'd learned about his parents' death. The memory of that loss mixed with his present pain, triggering a new wave of uncontrollable grief. Without Antony, he was truly alone in the world.

Marcus did the only thing he could and clung to Antony's corpse. The skin was even paler than before, a consequence of blood following gravity's command to pool on the left side of his brother's slowly decaying remains. Marcus tried to turn Antony onto his back, but the body was too stiff to move. The attempted maneuver revealed a secret: Antony had a piece of Tek on the inside of his left wrist. *This was the unit from the library. Had it killed Antony?* Marcus dismissed the thought as too conspiratorial. *Knowing Antony, a toxic mix of drugs and alcohol was the more logical explanation.*

Marcus pulled the Tek loose and held the honeycomb-shaped device between his thumb and forefinger. Curious about its contents, he placed the unit on the inside of his left wrist, sat on the ground with his back against Antony's, and closed his eyes. Marcus had never lived someone else's Tek experiences, so he was ill-prepared for the unorganized imagery that blasted him. Without the indexing of his own mind to sort and search the catalog, Antony's memories flooded in all at once.

A short triplet of scenes played in rapid succession, starting with Antony's sideline POV during Marcus's fight at Nerio days earlier. Then it jumped to a perilous moment on a backcountry road in the Echo Basin during their Grand Tour, when Antony almost drove them off a massive cliff. The triplet ended with their New Year's Eve party at Marcus and Jordan's house, hours before

Zero Day officially began, and everyone experienced their Disclosure Moment. This last memory was painfully schizophrenic, like a feedback loop of consciousness forever folding in on itself with increasing intensity, and Marcus opened his eyes to stop the splitting headache it caused.

Marcus's heart thrashed in his chest while his stomach churned violently. But the temptation to see what else Antony had stored pushed him onward, and he closed his eyes a second time. The wind was instantly knocked out of him as he found himself sitting across from Dianna in a coffee shop. She was glaring directly through him; this was the moment of confrontation both had told Marcus about. He was eager to see this firsthand, but the scene cut abruptly to another memory.

It took Marcus a moment to realize where he was: in Antony's office at his company's headquarters. Like the other memory from Zero Day, this was insanely choppy and incomplete, but he could tell his brother had been lying facedown on the floor when Hi!-D appeared. He stood up and faced her, but before she opened her mouth to speak, Marcus was catapulted to another set of memories. Marcus was looking back in time now, at a younger version of himself in the early teen years, as Antony begged him to give Garret a try. Marcus could hear fragments of Antony's thoughts bouncing around like he was in an echo chamber. The introspection was dark and full of doubt; this was the little monster Antony had described, and it was picking apart his ability to raise Marcus without further damage.

The next three memories were crystal clear, but Marcus barreled through them haphazardly. In the first, Antony stood at the rostrum to the thunderous applause of graduates following his commencement speech. He was staring across the crowd at Marcus and their parents. In the second, their family pressed against a guardrail along a river highway to watch Atlantis make the final launch of the Space Shuttle program; Antony was holding him on his shoulders. In the third, a toddler version of Marcus had just shit all over Antony at the Athenian Acropolis.

Marcus opened his eyes again; they filled with tears of gratitude at his brother's generosity for storing these moments. But nothing could've prepared him for the last memory that awaited. Marcus closed his eyes for the final time and was spontaneously transported to a hospital hallway. He felt Antony's heart pounding out of his chest as their father appeared through a cracked door on the other side of the corridor, smiling through misty eyes and motioning for Antony to come into the room. When his brother passed over the threshold, the most intense sensation of joy Marcus had ever felt surged through Antony's body; it was pure pride and unbridled happiness at the sight of the newborn brother he'd longed for his entire life.

Then the memories stopped. Marcus wasn't sure what others, if any, had been captured, or whether he'd be able to live each in greater detail if he gave it another try. But for the moment, he was content. He felt connected again to Antony, despite the barrier created by their physical bodies, and cried tears of pain and joy. He found deep peace in the happy moments they'd shared—in the unbreakable bond of brotherhood. Then, suddenly, Marcus was ripped away from the comfort of his memories as Hi!-D's voice boomed from the sky:

"Good afternoon, citizens. Today we grieve as a community, but we also begin the next, and most exciting, chapter in your collective progress and integration with the Federation. Stand proud because you represent the best your Form has produced for this material world during this monumental moment. You are the chosen who have survived the Reset to face the Confederation! Those who have ascended sacrificed their lives on this side of the veil so that you can continue here, and you will be asked to sacrifice here so they may continue there. You are safe, so remain calm and shelter in place while we prepare the ascended for their final rites. Because together, we're reborn."

It was 1:00 p.m.

Marcus wasn't supposed to hear Hi!-D from inside his house; this was a private space. Marcus's heart raged. *Jordan had been right. The Federation was attacking.* The Heroic Code across Antony's back spoke volumes about what he needed to do next. Marcus strapped Invictus to his back, then paused to kiss his brother's forehead one last time before heading to Bucephalus. He was going to find Brad. And make him pay.

45

THE SCRAPING

Bucephalus barreled through the mountain community without encountering any obstacles; the roads were clear of cars, which were all parked neatly in driveways. *Anyone who was still alive must've been following orders to stay inside because he couldn't see another soul anywhere.* The Sundance Resort was orderly, but no people were visible in the outdoor spaces, and all the buildings were dark from the outside. The ski lift, which should've been carrying hundreds of mountain bikers and hikers to the summit, sat motionless. Marcus took a moment to analyze the situation. *Antony had been killed at some point in the night by the Federation. Communication lines were down, and everyone was told to stay in place ... survivors were being isolated, making it easier to pick them off.*

The narrow road he traveled was free from the cars that normally clogged this canyon on beautiful summer days like today. Tall pines were his only companion, and the sole source of sound was the warhorse as it meandered down the mountain. The isolation made it hard to focus. His mind jumped from images of Antony's body to Jordan's final farewell to his Sequences with Brad. *This was the same stretch of pavement he'd traversed in one of his earliest Sequences, to save lives,* he realized.

Marcus reached the end of the North Fork spur and turned onto the larger highway heading out of Provo Canyon. Occasional cars and semis were parked on the shoulder, but all of them appeared to be empty of people. Without warning, the world shook violently beneath Bucephalus. The short tunnel Marcus was approaching looked as if it were ready to crumble. *This was the only way down the canyon,* Marcus thought, accelerating into the collapsing passage. Large chunks of concrete smashed onto the hood and roof, but he made it out unscathed as the mountainside reclaimed the man-made burrow behind him. *Could that really have been a random coincidence?*

Confirmation came as the road shook a second time. Unlike the earthquake that toppled the tunnel, this was a shearing force that tore the road side to side, breaking it free from the surface before it was levitated into the air. Marcus blinked rapidly at what he was seeing: entire sections of the highway on either side of him floated above the ground, then exploded into a trillion tiny pieces, like confetti bombs detonating inside transparent balloons. This controlled destruction consumed the guardrails, signposts, and parked vehicles near him, but left the road in front of Bucephalus untouched.

Marcus accelerated again to outpace the annihilation, but the havoc spread like a wave to the surrounding landscape. A loco-motive was lifted skyward from the rail beside the road, pulling up miles worth of train cars behind it before all were broken down into their molecular parts. *The remnants resembled a massive swarm of bees.* Road construction machinery, park structures, and buildings along the highway dematerialized in similar airborne bursts.

Marcus was approaching the end of the canyon when he felt a wave of low-end vibrations. These weren't like the earthquakes he'd just witnessed; this had a steady rhythm and an increasing intensity, like a symphony slowly building toward a crescendo. The sound was coming from behind him. Bucephalus lacked any mirrors, so Marcus turned on the rearview camera to observe his next horror: a towering wall of water from the dam at the other end of the canyon careened toward him.

Marcus pushed Bucephalus to its maximum in an attempt to stay ahead of the deluge. The water tore apart the sides of the canyon like they were made of clay. The sound climbed in pitch and speed. Even in the armored vehicle, the volume was painfully piercing. The edge of the wave was pushing on the back of Bucephalus when Marcus burst from the canyon, veering onto a high road and out of the water's path; it flooded into a lower plain, swallowing hundreds of homes in the process.

Though the vibrations from the raging water had subsided, Marcus's hands shook from adrenaline. He turned off the rearview camera and focused on the road ahead. With the valley laid out before him, he could finally see the extent of the deconstruction taking place, and he sobbed. Tornados of debris formed in the densest areas of the obliteration, combining into the surrounding clouds of disassembled human structures and multiplying in size.

One whirlwind razed the area where Antony's house had been. Marcus grit his teeth as he watched this invisible hand scraping the mark of humanity from the face of the Earth. Hecate peeked over the western mountains, starting its rapid retrograde rise into the heavens. *It was a fitting reminder of the power he was impotent to stop*, Marcus thought. *He was certain that the Federation was behind this.*

Where a thriving suburban settlement had once been, only desolation remained. Bucephalus muffled the sounds of car alarms, cracking concrete, and bending metal. Old rusted vehicles rose from Utah Lake, only to disintegrate midair in the same managed demolition; their scant material was sucked into the nearest tornado, which had combined with the others into a hurricane swirl of refuse that cast the world into shadows. Marcus turned onto the interstate and headed for Salt Lake.

The corporate buildings lining the road, including Antony's company headquarters, lifted from the dirt; their levitation hypnotized Marcus because of their size, but like everything else, they exploded before being fed into the supply chain of scrap across the sky. Electrified power lines flailed erratically around him. The foul smell of natural gas wafted through the air conditioning, moments before explosions shot from either side of the freeway, mapping out the entire path of underground utility grids, like fences made of fire.

The pandemonium paused as Marcus approached the Point of the Mountain, a geological dividing line between Utah Valley, where Antony lived and worked, and the Salt Lake Valley. From his vantage point, he saw the same system of deconstruction happening across the larger, more populated expanse. *How could anyone shelter in place while everything around them was being destroyed*, Marcus asked with a heavy heart. His introspection ended when another earthquake ripped up the highway around him like an unwanted carpet.

Twin tornados converged on Marcus, completely blacking out the world. He squeezed the steering wheel until his fingers reached their breaking point, trying to keep Bucephalus from succumbing to the swirling forces. After a perilous moment of driving blind, he broke into the eye of the storm, staring through the armored windshield at the blue sky above him. The momentary peace was replaced by more chaos as he passed through the far side of the twisters. Marcus screamed, relying on his voice to propel him safely through the encircling storm.

The act of affirmation had worked. Marcus broke loose of the whirlwinds and continued on the highway when a reverberating metallic sound echoed across the valley; it reminded him of something from one of Jordan's songs, like the sound a stretched-out Slinky makes when struck by something hard. On the northern horizon, a giant blue band of plasma slithered across the sky. This thick substance was above and beyond the hurricane of human material, rising like a ring that encircled the planet. It moved at an incredible speed, reaching its zenith over Marcus in seconds, and continuing beyond his view to the southern horizon.

The blue band left a strong smell of ozone and a stronger feeling of static electricity in the air. Most of the digital gadgets within Bucephalus suddenly failed, making the warhorse harder to steer than an actual wild stallion. An alarm screeched through the cabin, accompanied by flashing red floodlights. A single button labeled "reset" pulsated on the dash. Marcus slapped it, silencing the alarm and warning lights, and restoring power to the rest of the vehicle. *He wasn't sure how much additional stress his system, or the vehicle, could stand.*

The asphalt continued to disappear behind him as he turned off the interstate and onto the belt route to campus; the community was already gone, amplifying the apocalyptic appearance of the area. As the road climbed onto the benches near the base of the Wasatch Mountains, Marcus could see the towers of downtown, including the Wells Fargo Center, blown away one story at a time like dust in the wind. Beyond the buildings to the West sat empty land; the Black Market and its Go Zones had been completely razed to the ground.

Mount Olympus loomed over Marcus to the east. He gazed into the Cove, but couldn't tell which mansion was Monica's. It didn't matter, since all were being torn to pieces by a trio of tornados. His heart dropped into his stomach, but a blinding glitter of light in his peripheral vision grabbed his attention: a jetliner was falling from the sky, targeted on his position like an inbound missile. Marcus braced at the last second for an inevitable collision, but like a phantom, the plane dissolved around Bucephalus, leaving Marcus unscathed as he continued cruising the highway.

He suppressed the instinct to vomit. None of the windows could open in the vehicle, and the last thing Marcus wanted was to add the noxious smell of his stomach's contents to the stresses he was subjected to. After a series of deep breaths, he'd calmed down, merging off the freeway and on to an overpass leading to campus, which evaporated the moment his wheels had cleared the concrete. The whole area had been wiped clean of human construction, including roads, causing Bucephalus to bounce violently as it crawled across the uneven, virgin soil.

His trip from Sundance had taken hours, but he could finally see campus a couple of miles away. He moved slowly, occasionally using Bucephalus's crab-walking feature to maneuverer around massive holes where subterranean structures had been uprooted. It was peaceful from his position on the hill, but he could see the carnage continuing across the rest of the valley. *It was a strange sensation*, Marcus thought, *watching in safety from afar at the suffering happening everywhere else.*

He'd made it most of the way to campus when another obstacle from the air made itself known. The first impact hit a mile away, but the shockwave from the impact created long cracks in his windshield; it looked like a meteorite, given its speed and trajectory, and was quickly followed by others raining down. A dozen explosions erupted, each scarring deep into the Earth a safe distance from Marcus, and each sending a shockwave that pushed Bucephalus off its path.

When he came upon the closest crater, he could see the remains of a satellite. One prominent piece bore the distinct stylized "X" of the Starlink logo. This, like the other identical objects, had been part of the satellite train delivering free internet to humanity. Marcus laughed like a lunatic at this cosmic coincidence; the fallen satellites Antony had once helped optimize met their end, like his brother, right before Marcus's eyes. Then, the satellite fragments dissipated into a tiny cloud.

He continued his voyage in silence, waiting for another surprise, but none came. Instead, it was the absence of what he'd hoped to find that shocked him next—the neighborhoods surrounding campus were gone. All the trees, houses, roads, and businesses had vanished, presumably taking Jordan in the process. Battery acid pumped in his veins where blood had previously been. The stress of what he'd experienced in the last few hours hit all at once.

Wiping the tears from his eyes, Marcus could see the rest of campus was intact, including the housing unit near the University hospital where Dianna lived. For the first time that day, Marcus had hope that some of his family had survived. Like when he'd started his journey, there wasn't a soul in sight. He was looking at the school's iconic "U" on the mountainside when a final monstrous quake dissolved every remaining structure like sand into its own footprint; with it went his hope for Dianna and their children. Only one building remained in the Big Field: Carlson Hall.

Marcus considered ramming Bucephalus into Brad's office as a first strike, but worried he'd get trapped in the vehicle if the building collapsed on top of him. He circled Carlson Hall endlessly, waiting for something to burst from the Lab, but nothing came. He knew what he needed to do, but he was afraid to leave the safety of his warhorse.

He wanted to understand what happened to Antony, Monica, Jordan, and Dianna and their children. Brad had answers ... but he didn't want to hear that his friend had been a part of this attack. After a prolonged argument, Marcus accepted his fate, parking parallel to the Lab outside of the brown door leading to Brad's office.

Marcus climbed cautiously from his vehicle as Hecate began a transit of the sun. He'd witnessed these eclipses more times than he cared to count, but today it had a completely different meaning; the enemy held the high ground. The world dimmed, replaced by the familiar celestial wheel with its symmetrical spokes of light projecting in rays from behind the alien planet. The sight sent chills crawling up his spine. Marcus took a breath, gripping the doorknob to Brad's Lab in one hand, and holding Invictus at the ready in his other.

PART XIV

MERCY TO THE GUILTY IS CRUELTY TO THE INNOCENT

SUNDAY, JULY 24, +1 NE

46

PREDICTING WINNERS

From behind the tip of his sword, Marcus burst through the doorway. Brad was nowhere to be found. He tore through the space, flipping furniture and toppling towers of books, but Brad didn't appear to stop him. In an act of childish rage, Marcus smashed the glass face of the grandfather clock. Only the large mahogany desk survived his destruction since it was too heavy to overturn.

Maybe he's hiding in the locker room, Marcus thought, moving to the magical black door; it refused to activate. He ran his empty hand along the pliable honeycomb frame, hoping to find a switch, but after a few passes, he accepted that one didn't exist. *Only Brad could open this portal ... wherever he is.* Marcus collapsed from the weight of his realization.

Invictus laid idle on the floor beside him as Marcus tucked his knees into his chest and sobbed. The click of the damaged clock kept rhythm for the dust particles peacefully floating through the air. A tsunami of fear washed up his back, cresting over his head and forcing him onto all fours to vomit. He didn't bother finding a trash can; he felt good ruining Brad's ornate rug. Marcus wiped his mouth, sitting against the sealed door to watch opaque afternoon sunlight beam through the triplet of frosted, western-facing windows. The warmth was disarming, like a reassuring hand resting on him to say that everything would be okay.

"You going to puke the day away?" asked Brad.

Marcus shot to his feet, forgetting about Invictus. He scoured the office again, but Brad wasn't there.

"FACE ME!" Marcus growled.

There was silence.

He continued trashing the room. "FACE ME!"

"Make me," Brad mocked in voice only. "I wish you could see how ridiculous you look right now—you can't hurt me."

"THEN STOP HIDING!" Marcus felt a presence behind him and whipped around to find Brad standing just beyond his shoulder. Marcus grasped desperately at his scabbard for Invictus but came up empty-handed, and retreated across the office.

"I realize that you may find it hard to believe me," Brad raised his hands and continued smiling, "but I don't want to hurt you. ... I didn't spend all that time ensuring you made it here alive, just to kill you now."

Marcus and Brad dueled through Stoic stares.

"Did the Federation do that? Outside?" Marcus motioned toward the windows with a clenched hand.

"Yes."

The words shattered Marcus like a cheap mirror.

Brad withheld an explanation.

586

"Why are you attacking us?"

"This wasn't an attack. It was a necessary step to prepare your Form to face the immediate future. It was done to help you."

Marcus's mind misfired. "What?"

"Carefully consider your questions, because they'll determine the clarity of my answers. What do you want to know, Marcus? All you have to do is ask … that's all you've ever had to do."

Marcus's trust in Brad had dissolved along with the former structures of the human world. He forced up his next words, "Is this a Sequence?"

"No. This game is being played for keeps."

"Undo it."

"That's not how this works. What's done is done, and had to be done. The only path now is forward."

Marcus bit his tongue.

"I don't mean to rush you, but our time is racing toward its terminus. What else do you want to ask?"

"I want to know what happened outside … and how I fit into this … tell me why you're destroying us … and why you're so cold about it." Marcus sobbed again. "Can't you see that I'm suffering?"

"What, how, and why are very different questions. Let's take them one by one. *What* you just experienced was a Reset. 99.9999% of your Form has ascended, leaving seven thousand and ten alive on Earth. Putting the bodies aside for a moment, what's happening outside is a Scraping of your Form's material record, of which a comparably larger percentage was removed from the planet. We wanted to get all of it, but we're counting on time and tides to take care of the rest."

Marcus was profoundly and completely speechless.

"Roughly eighty percent of those who survived the Reset are under the age of twenty-five, and twenty percent are older than that. We're calling the groups Littles and Bigs, respectively."

Marcus whispered his words, "You killed Antony?"

"Yes, but that's a small part of the story."

"What about Jordan?"

"Reset," Brad replied bluntly.

"Mon ... Monica?"

"Reset."

"Dianna?" Marcus pleaded with his eyes while his body shook violently. "And my kids?"

"She's alive. Hi!-D is with her and the other Alphas in preparation for Final Rites"—Brad tapped on his bare wrist—"which is set to start in a few hours."

"What are Alphas?"

"That's what you're collectively called—the first generation in a new branch of human existence. The survivors selected to stand on the front lines to save your Form. The chosen, the elect, the A-Team ... and depending on how this encounter plays out, you could be reunited with Dianna and the other Alphas."

Marcus was silenced by sickness.

"Want me to continue?" Brad asked.

Marcus slowly nodded.

"Project Noble reached the M1 milestone, and we proceeded with your integration. The Reset and the Scraping are important pieces in that process, which brings us to your other questions of *how* this involves you and *why* you're so important. You're the node from which the seven thousand and ten were chosen. Those left on this side of the veil are connected to you within six layers, or degrees, if you'd rather think of it in terms of Sir Kevin Bacon."

Marcus wasn't capable of laughing. "I thought there were only six degrees of separation between all of us?"

"That's not how real networks work. Meaningful connections aren't uniformly distributed like some abstract mathematical assumption. They happen in clusters, so it takes way more than six relationships to connect you to everyone in a system eight billion strong."

This wasn't real, he thought. *It couldn't be.*

"Since our arrival," Brad continued, "we've been learning who you are as a Form, both individually and collectively. Every system has unique characteristics that emerge with it. They enforce the collective success, but only by being practiced at the individual level. Some of these characteristics support the system, others destroy it. We used the beneficial ones as filters—"

"Filters?" Marcus scoffed.

"Yes. Clear criteria applied equally to everyone. The first filter was that any Alphas be connected to you within six human relationships," Brad answered. "The second filter was an Alpha's likelihood of accepting the Reset, at least the inevitability of it but also, hopefully, the importance of it. Other filters included a passion to improve the world through a unique skill, along with favorable genetics and epigenetics. There were other filters too. But the point is, we thoroughly examined the entirety of each individual when selecting Alphas."

"You used me to pick winners?"

"It's more appropriate to say we predicted everyone's differences with a high level of precision, given the Confederation's ability to react optimally to anything we do, and vice versa. Our motivations are totally different. While the Confederation sees you as the resource of interest to control, we are trying to keep you from being eternally enslaved ... no big deal," Brad added with a smirk. "So everything we could observe, quantify, and test to help us help you, we did. It wasn't about you alone, Marcus, though you're arguably the most important individual. The first among equals. Rather, we studied your entire Form in the same way your scientists would observe a beehive or any complex self-organizing system. Then, when beneficial, we primed you to test the ways you'd react to specific stimuli—"

"The PSAs?" Marcus interrogated.

"Along with FACT, the Federation Forces, Hecate, and the Black Market, including FTAP and the crypto accounts. Yes, to all of them. And yes to your history and pop culture, both of which added important time series and segmentation dimensions. We used the totality of this data to classify which of your Form was best suited for integration and Reset the others."

"So you spied on us? On me?"

"Why do you think you can hide? We can see through roofs and walls. Those are artificial barriers you created to keep each other out—they don't work on us. But we respected your only true privacy ... we never came into your mind uninvited."

"Tek."

"And xTek."

Marcus rocked in place. "I don't believe this."

"You have to be creative to observe individuals who actively hide. Tek and xTek got us one step closer to knowing what you're really like. But the Holy Grail, from a research standpoint, would be if a specific subset of your Form was watched and primed without knowing it because, in such a situation, they would be their true, unedited, self in all its glory."

"Subsumption."

"Give this man a new family!" Brad bellowed like a gameshow host. "It's the ultimate data-generating environment since you can't manipulate your thoughts and behaviors when you don't know who you are, or that you're being watched. The pseudo randomization of those scenarios, free from the conditioning of this specific physical incarnation, let us test and validate how the real you makes choices. At a very deep level."

"Did your data collection include our private conversations?"

"Yes."

"EVERYTHING I SHARED WITH YOU," Marcus lashed out, "WAS JUST DONE TO SQUEEZE INFORMATION OUT OF ME!"

"We came to those conversations with very different motivations." Brad ran a hand over his balding head. "I was priming you, seeding a topic for your mind to latch onto before the Sequence. It was more of a pinch than a squeeze. Either way, you were mostly honest, which is an important part of why you're still here."

"Bullshit. It was easier to manipulate me this way."

"We couldn't make you do anything, Marcus. Subsumption isn't about control. It's about choices, their consequences, and how you learn to navigate that reality to progress. Subsumption placed you in a situation with different options, but you're the one who made the choices. You always had free will."

"You hijacked my mind."

"No, we hijacked your brain. You're conflating the two. Your brain is a physical part of your body that interacts with the world based on sight, sound, scent, taste, and touch. Your mind is less temporal but just as real, and only you control it. We can't manipulate your mind, even if tricking your brain is chemically trivial."

"DMT?" Marcus seethed true to the spirit of Jordan.

"THE SPIRIT MOLECULE!" Brad shouted.

"You're a hallucination?"

"In a sense, yes. By stimulating your pineal gland, we're able to affect your brain's perceptions, much like a dream does. But unlike the characters in your dreams, the Federation really exists, just not in a material form."

"Is Hecate real?"

"Not in the way you're envisioning."

"What about the eclipses?"

"It's easier to bend light than to bend free will."

"I can't believe Jordan was right ..."

"Jordan was right about a stunning amount of things, a modern Cassandra of Troy, but being able to see something coming isn't the same as understanding what it means. He convoluted most of his theories because he was reacting from fear and helplessness—"

"He saw you for what you truly are," Marcus fumed, "killers."

Brad removed his glasses and rubbed the bridge of his nose before resetting them on his face. "That's certainly one, incredibly narrow, way of looking at it."

"How'd you do it? Tek? Was Jordan secretly using?"

"He never touched the stuff. The Reset didn't require any hardware. Given your biological wiring, it was a small step to turn dreams into an eternal sleep."

"You killed everyone with a dream?"

"Death is just a long version of sleep," replied Brad. "Everyone laid down and had the dream of their dreams. The Federation calls it a Somnium, borrowing a term from your father's vocabulary. For your brother, this involved watching the Space Shuttle Atlantis make its final launch with your family, a memory he so fortuitously cataloged for you with Tek in his final moments. For Jordan, it was an epic battle against the Federation, starring me as the antagonist and involving a level of destruction matched only by a Michael Bay movie. That kid had one heck of an imagination."

"What about Monica?"

Brad blushed. "You had the lead role in that one."

"Did they know it was a dream?"

"No. But everyone got a peaceful end, or at least as peaceful of an end as they ultimately wanted."

"It was extermination."

"In the language of your computers, a Reset is a controlled clearing of errors to bring a system back to an initial or normal condition. That's what we've done. And it's put a damper in the Confederation's chances of enslaving your entire Form."

"MY FAMILY WASN'T AN ERROR!" Marcus kicked a pile of books at Brad, sprinting past him and sliding across the ground to grab Invictus.

47

CHOICES, CHOICES

Marcus stood indignant, gripping his sword in both hands, ready to strike. *Any sentimentality he once had toward his research Shadow had completely evaporated.*

"You can hold your nose up at the idea," Brad chastised, "but you've done the same thing when domesticating animals, engaging in agriculture, and eradicating other Forms from your planet. You even tried it on yourselves. And you're terrible at it."

"But you aren't?" Marcus countered.

"We've had billions of years to practice. You can decide if that's sufficient. Either way, the Alphas are the most capable for what lies ahead. You can count on it."

"AND ANTONY AND JORDAN WEREN'T!"

"Not everyone who was Reset was evil or bad. Not everyone who survived is good. Like everyone else that was Reset, your brother, Jordan, and Monica had multiple things working for and against them. I told you, we balanced the entire person to make the final determination. If it'll make you feel better, I'll share the thing that tipped the scale for each of them."

Marcus remained ready to strike.

"In Antony's case, he couldn't accept his greatness. No matter what he accomplished, it wasn't enough."

"This is RIDICULOUS!"

"Maybe, but it's the truth. Your brother was blinded by avarice. Even though he channeled it into positive outcomes, someone like that is dangerous because when they fail, and eventually they always do, their ego crumbles. It's hard to predict what happens next."

Marcus hissed through his teeth, "And Jordan?"

"He had an excess of mind over body. His mental curiosities took precedent to his physical preservation. Your mind, separate as it is, still depends in this material existence on your physical body, and he developed an irreversible aversion to its maintenance. The way things were going," Brad laughed, "there was a motorized scooter in his very immediate future."

"And Monica? What was her fault?" Marcus's anger amplified. "She was your friend! She trusted you!"

"Avarice, like your brother. It's interesting how the same emotional driver resulted in such wildly different behaviors between them. In her case, it was channeled into recreating situations of opulence and abuse."

"With Benedict? Did you even give her my quota?"

"I never got the chance, not that it would've mattered. Your intentions were admirable but misplaced. Antony was right about what she'd choose, and it wasn't you. Her relationship with Benedict was the most recent incarnation of abuse, but her life was a series of similar situations. All but the first were her own creation. You couldn't save her."

"Then why was she part of the Cohort?"

"To analyze is not to judge. She was well suited to my research but not ready to face the next step in your Form's journey on this side of the veil."

"You keep using that word …"

"Apocalypse is Greek for lifting of the veil. The Reset and Scraping are the first of many steps that will reveal the truth about yourself and your pivotal place in the universe. The Alphas are the portion of your collective consciousness remaining on the material side of the veil. The Ascended are on the immaterial side, at least for the next forty-nine days, then a portion will start the process of cycling back through births."

"Reincarnation?" Marcus mocked.

"Yes, but let's put a pin in that for a moment and finish discussing why the Alphas were chosen."

"Why couldn't you use your power to change Antony or Jordan or Monica … or any of the others instead of killing them?"

"For the same reason we used Subsumption to understand you: we don't control free will. It isn't like light or gravity. It's a force beyond anyone's authority except your own. Consciousness is the most important energy in the universe because it acts as the immovable mover. Everything else follows from it. You and your Form can make choices that move us all forward."

"You're *so* benevolent!" Marcus said, fiery hate shooting from his eyes.

"Don't act so outraged, none of the Ascended were torn from their homes in the darkness of night by secret police and sent to death camps. No one was forced to watch their family members be raped to death. No one used babies for bayonet practice or smashed their head against a rock, or had a gasoline-soaked tire put around their neck and set ablaze. And no one was scorched by the heat of an atomic blast. That's what you've done to yourselves in the not too distant past. Comparatively, what we've done is beyond benevolent. It was also necessary to allow your Form a moment to choose a new path before falling back into those old mistakes."

"Why couldn't you take the Alphas and leave?"

"Progress doesn't mean carving out a portion of your Form—it's about transforming all of it, together. That requires sacrifice, individually and collectively, to ensure you're on the path that maximizes your chances of success in facing the Confederation. All we do is nudge things in the right direction at critical moments."

Marcus glared at Brad. "Like with North Korea?"

"Ironically, their lived experience has been closer to your proposed alternatives than you realize," Brad responded with a smirk. "But this simple fact remains: your Form has been involved in a universal conflict for your entire existence, often without realizing it. The Reset and Scraping were our most recent actions to help you against the Confederation. There've been others."

"What does that mean?" Marcus's gut turned.

"Put down the sword, and I'll tell you."

"Tell me anyway!"

"One of Stoicism's core principles is that you can't control the world around you, only your reactions to it. That's an important truth to remember. Most of what Jordan noticed was real, but he misattributed it to us. It's the Confederation who's been slowly boiling your Form, driving you to embrace hate, and dividing you through fear. They've guided you away from the immaterial in anticipation of their arrival. They create the crisis so they can offer you the solution: a choice between a death you've been conditioned to fear or eternal material enslavement. We're here to help you avoid that fate, which means occasionally offering a different direction at moments where a critical choice will take place. But the choice is still yours to make."

"How can you describe that as free will?"

"If a plane goes down and you lose your parents, all you can do is choose how to live the rest of your life. You don't control the plane any more than they did. But they chose to get on it. And while you may not understand how the loss of your parents was preparing you for other more important choices, it was."

"You're saying the Confederation killed my parents?"

"No. I'm saying we did."

Marcus lunged at Brad, pinning him to the ground and pressing the tip of Invictus to the Shadow's throat.

Brad laughed hysterically. "Look at your reaction. Are you really in control of yourself right now? Or have you handed that power over to anger and fear? That's the cornerstone of the Confederation's control. I told you, Marcus, you can't hurt me. You might as well be holding a baguette. If you choose to push that blade through my throat, you won't exact vengeance, but you will end your own life, depriving the Alphas of their most important leader for a war that's on the horizon."

Marcus glared into Brad's eyes, churning with anger, unsure what to do. The muscles in his arms ached for blood, but his heart wanted to understand.

"Answer this," Brad continued. "Would you be the same person without Antony acting as your guardian?"

Marcus's eyes bounced back and forth. "No!"

"And that's exactly why your parents had to go. It cleared the way for Antony to raise you for a future of facing the Confederation. Your free will is constrained by the fact that you don't control everything—your parent's fate didn't depend on your choices, only your reaction to it does. You don't remember because you were in Stealth Mode, but you lived their final moment in your last Sequence ... they were your row-mates, but you didn't notice. You accepted the same fate they did in real life. Without hate or anger. It's what proved you were ready, it's what pushed your Form across the M1 finish line, and ultimately, it's why you're still alive. Now that you know the truth, you have another choice to make. Stab me, and it's been for nothing. Or get off me, and I'll tell you what you're really up against."

Marcus rocked in place from the frustration of the choice. Memories of those he'd loved and lost raced through his mind like a locomotive. The spirit of their memories softened his heart, and he rolled off Brad, dropping Invictus, screaming and sobbing again.

Brad sat up and scooted across the floor to face Marcus. "It's impossible for you to understand the purpose behind moments of loss in isolation. But they are part of a bigger plan. They put you on a path to defeat the Confederation and save your Form, which includes your parents, your brother, Jordan, and Monica ... despite the pain their deaths cause you right now."

Marcus could only continue to cry.

"You have my sympathy," Brad offered. "Your life has included a lot of suffering, and so much more awaits you."

"NO!" Marcus concealed his face with his hands.

"If you don't want to know, that's okay."

Marcus looked up. "I want to know … please."

"The first time we met, I asked you what the most important thing was in your life." Brad paused. "Do you remember what you told me?"

"My family," Marcus replied, prematurely drying his eyes.

"The Confederation has used that against you."

"You refer to them like they're already here."

"That's because some of them are. We'll dig into that in a minute, but right now, focus on your family. "

"What about it?"

"The Confederation has been active in working against Antony while supporting Jordan and Dianna. It's two of their primary fronts in the war against you. We were effective in protecting Antony for as long as necessary from their interference, but the same can't be said about Jordan and Dianna. Jordan's out of the picture for a minute, but Dianna has chosen a different path, one motivated by anger and fear. The most important thing you can do to push back against the Confederation is to heal the wounds you've inflicted on each other. No one succeeds if the two of you are divided. I'm not being dramatic when I say the fate of your entire Form, and with it the fate of this universe, comes down to the two of you."

"Things aren't going well between us right now, so that's going to be tough," Marcus lamented. "I can apologize, but I doubt it'll do any good. Maybe once the twins are born, she'll feel differently, but until—"

"Dianna isn't carrying your children anymore."

The words punched the wind out of Marcus.

Brad sat silently. Staring.

"YOU SAID THEY WERE ALIVE," Marcus roared.

"I said Dianna was alive. And she is."

"What?" Marcus stood, forming fists again.

Brad stood with him. "After your fight Friday night, Dianna called her lawyer, who made it clear she can't keep you out of the children's lives indefinitely. She'd already visited an abortion clinic more than a month ago, before deciding to give you a chance at co-parenting. She wanted to hurt you. She went back to the clinic yesterday to get you out of her life for good."

Marcus wasn't crying anymore. He was ice cold, screaming from the depths of his soul while trashing through Brad's office again like an uncaged animal.

"I'm not saying your pain isn't real," Brad de-escalated, "but a big portion of how you're feeling is the result of not knowing the truth. That's what the Confederation wants—to fill your heart with ignorant hate. They've conditioned you to believe all you have is this material existence. With time and training in the Agoge, you'll come to realize how close your family still is to you. But you have to let go of your hate first."

"How do I know you didn't do this?"

"You can't. Not for sure. But I'm telling you, Marcus, nothing I've ever said to you was a lie."

"I've lost track of all the secrets you've kept ..."

"Omission isn't the same as lying. You've admitted as much to yourself. Why would you expect to hold us to a different standard than the one you hold yourself to? The Federation doesn't owe you total transparency, and you couldn't handle it anyway. It'd be like feeding a starving prisoner of war, making their stomach pop from the abrupt pressure on their system. Your finite brain isn't ready for an infinite truth. So you have to choose to trust us, or don't. It's up to you. But if you want to ensure a better future for your family and your Form, you'll fix your relationship with Dianna ... you have to start piecing your family back together again."

"Who are you, really?" Marcus fumed.

"An isolated manifestation of an infinite immaterial collective. We're not unlike you in that way. We just lack a meat bag and a skeleton. There are other individuals of the Federation's consciousness. You'll meet some when you start the Agoge tomorrow."

Marcus said nothing.

"You're angry because you think your pain is unique. It's not," Brad asserted. "This answers the last of your questions, *why* I'm cold toward your suffering. But this is what it means to live the human experience: it's a continual vacillation between joy and sorrow."

"No human has ever endured anything like this."

"That's simply untrue," Brad declared. "This isn't the first time your Form has been Reset. Just ask Bill ... if you can find him."

48

THE GREAT DIVIDE

Marcus's shoulders slumped from Brad's admission; it was all he could muster after hours of riding the roller coaster of anger and adrenaline. He retrieved Invictus and a chair lying sideways on the floor, carrying both across the room before setting the sword down on Brad's desk and taking a seat. Marcus pulled the Memento Mori from his pocket, then turned his attention back to Brad. "How many other Resets have there been? And what does Bill have to do with them?"

"Bill was a witness to the first Reset in -72,851 NE when we initially revealed ourselves to your Form. He was part of a group that negotiated Original Choice, an agreement between your Form and the Federation to oppose the Confederation. Under that accord, we promised to step in when you were close to being enslaved in this material existence. Like we're doing now. The second Reset happened in -15,198 NE. Bill acted as an ambassador for that generation since your Form had forgotten about the agreement by then."

"Were the societies you Reset as advanced as us?"

"Advanced is a subjective term," Brad cautioned. "The timing of our appearance has always had more to do with the Confederation than your developmental stage as a society. Though, the latter informed how we presented ourselves. In the case of Bill's generation, they were astronomically minded, so we manifested as star people. In the case of the second Reset, they were spiritually motivated, so we appeared as angels. For your generation, technological demigods made sense."

"If you're here, that means they both failed?"

"Yes. Bill's generation made it to M3 and lost in a direct confrontation with the Confederation. After that, Bill went into hiding … those from the second Reset didn't even make it to M2 before being conquered."

"What happened to them?" Marcus whispered.

"You already know their story. You've been telling it for thousands of years through cave paintings, myths, novels, movies, and even Tek. It's the Hero's Journey, good versus evil, end of the world stuff. The rise of the phoenix from the ashes and the individual's triumph over impossible odds. They built megalithic structures around the world and filled them with mathematical and astronomical timestamps in an attempt to tell you who they were, what they knew, and how to pinpoint the origin of their message. Above all, they tried to warn you about a coming Judgment Day. If you look closely enough, their fingerprints are everywhere."

"If the Confederation's goal is to enslave us," Marcus mused, "and we've lost twice, why are we still here?"

"Earth is a prison, custom-built for your Oversoul."

"The Oversoul is real?"

"You're about to experience the limits of that finite brain," Brad said with a subdued laugh. "This will feel like drinking from a firehose, again, but through the Agoge, you'll come to understand everything. For now, I have a metaphor that should help. The Oversoul is an immaterial collective consciousness that finds a Form in the material existence. You can think of this bigger reality as a forest, where each tree represents a distinct visible universe, and where the branches of the tree represent the parallel manifestations of a universe. The rings of the tree are the dimensions of existence, some material and some immaterial, but both of which are present on every tree branch. Hanging over this forest is a fog, the Oversoul, and the individual souls are the drops of water. When it rains, the water is carried to the ground and absorbed into the roots, then passed up through the rings of a tree to a particular branch."

Brad took a breath. "What the Confederation has done is contain your Form to one specific tree and within that, one ring of one branch. It's purgatory—they keep you trapped there. The Reset has helped some of the water evaporate back into the fog, but without intervention, they'll rain down onto the same tree with the same roots and end up on the branch where they began."

Marcus stopped fidgeting with his coin. "So the Reset was for nothing then?"

"Since most of your Oversoul is on the other side of the veil now, the Confederation has been deprived of the lifeblood they require to maintain the tree and the branch you're currently on. That also makes it easier for Alphas, like you, to shift growth onto a different branch—one that frees you from the Confederation's control and restores balance to the forest. And once that's accomplished, the fog will lift, and you'll move on from this cycle by achieving total enlightenment."

"I don't understand."

"Enlightenment isn't easy." Brad smiled, picking up a chair and coming to the table with Marcus. "With time, it'll make sense. For now, focus on the choices you face, and more specifically, the conflict they may cause. A Redshift will keep your Oversoul on the current branch that's feeding the Confederation's power. A Blueshift will allow your Oversoul to follow a different parallel branch that'll restore balance to the forest. The Confederation is determined to ensure a Redshift. They've burned entire trees and destroyed countless individual branches to get to this point."

"When you say they've burned trees ... you mean ... universes?"

"Correct," Brad confirmed. "And as bad as that sounds, it's not the worst thing that could happen."

Marcus leaned forward. "It's not?"

"Not even close. It'd be far worse if your Form's Oversoul separated, meaning a portion followed a Redshift while the other experienced a Blueshift. If this happens, it will lead to the Great Divide, a fracture in your Oversoul. Although the Federation is here to support your Form along the path of a Blueshift, the Great Divide must be avoided. At all costs."

"Why?" Marcus started spinning his coin again.

"Because if you divide into smaller clouds of fog, the forest becomes a desert, trapping your Oversoul in a material desolation forever. You call this Entropy."

Brad stood up. Marcus reacted by snatching his sword off the desk and jumping onto his own feet.

"Relax." Brad motioned with one hand, moving across the room to retrieve an ornamental book from a pile on the floor. "I want to read you something."

"What is it?" Marcus challenged.

"An essay by one of your Form's greatest minds. Ralph Waldo Emerson. I want to share a specific passage." Brad cleared his throat while adjusting his glasses. " 'Man is a stream whose source is hidden. Our being is descending into us from we know not whence ... that Unity, that Over-soul ... that common heart. An endless circulation through all men, as the water of the globe is all one sea, and, truly seen, its tide is one.' "

Marcus didn't know what to say, so he sat down.

"Poetry never sounds cool out loud," Brad said, closing the book. "The Oversoul is important because it's the part of yourself that's interconnected to higher forces. Similar to how you share a common genetic code for your physical development, the Oversoul is your communal consciousness. It's your infinite side—a system of individual souls bound together in an immaterial, decentralized network. A robust way to share intelligence and ensure lived experience isn't lost. Its center is nowhere. Its circumference is everywhere."

Marcus opened his mouth, but no words came.

"My forest metaphor is simplistic because, in truth, nothing in the forest is separate—it's all part of the same material system," Brad continued. "Your Form knows this as Integrated Information Theory or the Gaia Hypothesis. The Great Divide is what separates each of you individually from the other parts of yourself and the world around you. It's a wedge, a cycle of violence and suffering that feeds off itself by convincing you that an eye is worth an eye, and the remedy for past injustice is more injustice. You felt this when you visited Treblinka, and when you came into this office seeking revenge. The Reset has stopped that cycle for the moment. But it's up to you and the other Alphas to ensure this becomes more than a temporary peace."

Brad moved to Marcus's side and sat on the desk. "The only way to bridge the Great Divide is together. If your Oversoul goes down, you all go down. It's why Bill's generation bound all subsequent manifestations of your Form to Original Choice ... because it was still you. And it's why you're important, Marcus. You and Dianna are the last connection holding the two halves of your Oversoul together. It's why we picked Utah, it's why we rebuilt Carlson Hall to attract you, and it's why we mapped the network connections back to you for the Reset. Dianna is already on the Confederation's path of a Redshift. In one of your most important Sequences, one that I think will prove to be highly predictive of what's to come, you faced her, despite unending abuses, without walking away. You fought and lost, but you didn't abandon her. That's what you have to do now. You need to convince her that there's another way and that your Form is the fulcrum. If you fail to maintain your connection with Dianna, the Great Divide will result in a Schism of your Oversoul, and with you goes the fate of the forest."

Marcus carefully considered Brad's advice. "You said the Confederation controls the tree's roots—"

"I told you we'd come back to this." Brad smiled. "The Confederation has always maintained a presence on your planet. They can't control your free will any more than we can, but they're masters at manipulating it through a slow, constant exposure of ideas with pop culture and government. This social engineering has two goals: to make you desire this material existence more than anything else and to instill a deep fear in you over its loss through death. This ensures you stay put, in your prison, and that if you do die, you'll come back to the same spot in the same part of the tree."

"Reincarnation?" Marcus's eyes flickered.

"I told you we'd come back to this too," Brad said with a chuckle. "I tried to tell you death wasn't the end, but it is a necessary step in the progress of your Oversoul, just like living. It becomes detrimental when the Confederation keeps you in one place and one existence. You stagnate like putrid water. Your Form always fights them on this, which is why you've been contained to this planet. After you revolt, they arrive, capture or kill the leaders of the resistance, and set the cycle in motion again. Eventually, some of you start to question their wisdom that a material existence is all there is. If this group reaches a critical mass, the Confederation launches an invasion like the one presently en route. That cycle happened more than a few times before Bill's generation, but since Original Choice, we get involved before their ships launch."

"But we've failed? Twice?" Marcus pointed out. "Why would this time be any different?"

"Because of you," Brad encouraged. "You're lucky number three. As an individual, you're more capable than any of the other Lions that came before you."

"Lions?"

"That's what your Form called leaders like Bill. They were the first among equals who emerged to help your Form. They're the most capable and skilled individuals—outliers proven through merit, who used their intuition to navigate uncertain choices in pursuit of a better future. I'm positive you're one of them. That's why your daily affirmation had such an observable effect on your day. You were subconsciously guiding outcomes. That's also why you fought before major life changes: moving as a child, your parents' death, joining Selection, the Reset ... you were lashing out like an animal backed into an invisible corner because you sensed what was coming. You just didn't believe the message. It's the same skill that allows you to feel Déjà vu. It's an echo of a familiar situation, an artifact from one of the parallel universes lived by your Oversoul.

"Best I can tell, it was behind your post-Sequence sickness. You've developed incredible densities of neurons around your brain, heart, and abdomen to motivate it. That's why your head pounded, your chest burned, your stomach ached, and your ears rang after each Sequence. The set and setting were somewhat random, but it wasn't fake. You were living an echo of the parallel branches experienced by your Oversoul. You were awakening to the full scope of reality and became physically exhausted. It's the same effect that caused Jordan's conspirators to get sick when they tried to hack Tek. Unlike you, they couldn't handle the sensation ... and it's why I believe you're one of the Lions ... just like Bill used to be."

A long silence started between them.

"How many Lions are there?" asked Marcus.

"The last two times, there were five, but this time I'm predicting there will be seven. We know of three potentials right now. The others are unaccounted for."

"And I'm one of them? The potential Lions?"

"Yes. But leadership isn't something you inherit, no matter how qualified you are. It has to be earned with time. You're a possibility. If you can claim your place, you will help us identify the others in the Agoge and overcome the Great Divide, defeat the Confederation, and ensure that your Oversoul attains enlightenment. Everything has been building to this ... to you."

Marcus stopped spinning his coin. "To me?"

"Look at everything that had to happen for you to be here. It could've gone down an infinite number of ways, but it didn't. It happened one way—this way. I said before that you're an outlier, the right person in the right place at the right time. Your Form obsesses about saving the world." Brad smiled. "You're lucky ... you actually get the chance to do it."

"Why's the weight of the world my burden?"

"Because that's who you are, Marcus. During Subsumption, you were fearless in the face of darkness, trusting in your own truth, loving in a way that still showed your vulnerability, forceful when necessary, magnanimous after injustice was done against you, and doubly accepting of hard realities. You were perfect. One in a billion. That's why I'm certain you're a Lion, and that you'll succeed where everyone else failed."

Marcus felt like his head was going to explode.

Brad took a moment before finishing his discourse, "It isn't the weight of the world on your shoulders—it's the weight of every world that's existed before you."

Marcus was averse to the idea. "I'm not ready."

"No one ever is."

"No, you don't understand!" Marcus insisted. "You've made a mistake! I'm not the right person. I don't even sit in the emergency row on airplanes. I can't handle this kind of responsibility."

Brad's eyes lit up. "Your doubt is predictable, but it's baseless. You have to trust me … and my data. Everyone but Dianna believes you're capable of this. Antony said as much, so did Monica. And while Jordan may have seemed like he was on the fence, deep down, he knew how important you are—trust yourself."

Marcus could almost hear his brother's voice telling him to move forward. "What would I have to do?"

"Are we still bargaining about this?" Brad laughed. "The first step is to join the other Alphas for Final Rites. Then tomorrow, you'll begin rebuilding. Once that's done, you'll get the chance to save the world."

"With you?"

"No. I'm a researcher, not a social architect. But you won't be alone. I've got a gift for you—for all of you."

Brad gestured toward the Lab door to Hi!-D.

"Hi, Marcus."

"She's a walking, talking Library of Alexandria," Brad explained. "An Automated Retrieval Center, ARC for short, storing the entirety of your Form's collective knowledge to this point—accessible to anyone, at any time. Instantly. Every fact, every event, every insight, and every known detail is contained within her."

Hi!-D strut across the room, standing at the edge of the desk next to Brad so the pair could face Marcus.

"She'll continue to evolve with you and serve as an emissary to the Federation," said Brad. "She'll act as the repository of your rules and be an unbiased arbiter in the event of a dispute. No individual can control her, but she can be modified by the collective will of all seven thousand and ten Alphas."

"Should I explain the Endowment?" Hi!-D asked.

"No time like the present."

"After each Reset, the Federation has provided your Form with a set of seven technologies," Hi!-D revealed. "This is similar to the Federation's Technology Accelerator Program at the Black Market —a hand up, not a handout, to spur your own wave of innovation. Collectively, these starting technologies are called the Endowment. They'll make rebuilding fantastically easy. You're already familiar with most of them through your time at the Lab and the Black Market. Your Form's ability to utilize these technologies is largely based on a decentralized database created by your brother."

"One Identity," Marcus boasted.

"That's correct!" Hi!-D beamed. "Each of the Endowment technologies utilizes permissions from your One Identity wallet, a set of biometric keys only you can control. No one can take these seven distinct technologies from you by force, but you can give them up at any time. The first is Organics—"

"The honeycomb stuff?" Marcus asked.

Hi!-D nodded. "Right."

"It isn't just for construction," Brad interjected. "It's based on biomimicry, and it represents an end to waste. Organics solve three of your Form's largest problems: how to build something, how to power it, and what to do with it when it breaks. Your suit, the surfaces of the locker room, and the Black Market were all made from Organics. This material draws its energy from the background radiation of the Universe and regenerates until you're ready to discard it. Then, it dissolves back into base materials. There's zero waste in your future."

"The second technology," said Hi!-D, "are the Stargates for transportation. You used the two-way version of this technology to enter the locker room, your locker, the Liberty Bell, and Nerio. One-way versions were used by your Form to access the Black Market. Together, the Stargates will allow your Form to travel anywhere in the world, or beyond, instantly."

"I guess trademarks didn't survive the apocalypse?" Marcus allowed a nervous laugh to slip out.

"Next," Hi!-D continued, "are binary technologies near and dear to your heart: the EXO and the Power Gloves. Everyone in the Agoge will learn how to use these to harness the four fundamental forces, plus a few more you're not yet privy to. But to keep your pair after graduation, you have to become a Federation Forces Operator. The fourth Endowment technology is the Halo, another you're accustomed to from the Black Market and your encounters with the Coalition. The Halo is a personal Pomerium, and beyond protecting your physical body, it replaces all of Tek's functions."

"So no one can hurt me?"

Brad jumped in. "Your Halo guards you against your Form, but it won't protect you from yourself. That's how Bill has survived this long— he still has his Halo."

"What about the Confederation?"

"It's stronger than their force field, but they can still defeat your Halo with a sufficient amount of violence."

"Right," Hi!-D took back the baton. "Related to the Halo is another Endowment technology, the Pomerium. You know it from the Federation's Go Zones, but we'll use it to protect your vehicles and structures from the Confederation. The plasma ring you saw on the way to the Lab was Earth's Pomerium being put into place."

"Hence the objects falling from the sky," said Brad.

"The penultimate Endowment technology will be more familiar to you than anyone else from your Form. Resonance Chambers, like the Liberty Bell and their miniature form, Baby Bells, will help you train to fight the Confederation. Finally, you'll be given the Tactus, or TACT for short, the communication system you used with Brad during Sequences. It will also act as a real-time translator, similar to Tek's Babble feature, allowing you to communicate with all of the other Alphas."

"Though it's not part of the Endowment," Brad added, "there is a final item you alone will possess to help your Form ..."

Marcus took the bait. "What's that?"

"You!" Brad smiled. "Antony was right. You're the key. All these technologies won't mean a thing if you can't heal your relationship with Dianna and inspire the other Alphas to prepare to face the Confederation."

Marcus was desperate for additional information, but Brad preempted him. "I know you have a million other questions—it's one of the things I've come to love about you. And I wish I could stay and answer them all. But in the coming weeks, you'll learn everything you want to know. You and I are out of time."

"This is goodbye?" Marcus stood.

Brad was tearing up. "Our paths diverge here."

"So I'll never see you again?"

"Never say never. But right now, you've got to go."

Marcus was hesitant to leave the Lab. "Where?"

"Final Rites for the Ascended," Hi!-D answered.

"Where?" Marcus asked again, placing his coin in his pocket and sliding Invictus into its scabbard.

"The Salt Flats," Brad replied, moving towards the locker room door. "Remember, Marcus, it isn't about who you are—it's about who you can become. Choice is everything. Now, off to the ball with you, Cinderella."

PART XV

ET IN TERRA PAX

SUNDAY, JULY 24, +1 NE

49

NEW WORLD ORDER

Depression hardened Marcus's body, like a concrete-IV pumped into his bloodstream. The blinding glare of salt poured through the Stargate and into Brad's office.

"Please step through," Hi!-D requested, motioning toward the portal. "This is your Form's big moment."

Marcus stepped through the transport, turning around to look back into the Office one final time, but Brad was gone. The crunch of sodium chloride crystals under his feet made the only sounds in the vast desert valley. At the center of the Salt Flats sat a colossal spire, climbing thousands of feet into the air. A phasing blue glow emanated from the structure, with a dense ring at the base cutting up through the alabaster canvas like a moat made of plasma. The western mountains beyond it provided a panoramic backdrop. *Something about the spire reminded him of a forge*, Marcus thought, following Hi!-D toward the tower.

"Where are the other Alphas?"

"A replication of myself has each of them safely waiting in a Tek simulation of their old homes."

"Where are their physical bodies?"

"Exactly where their homes used to be."

"None of them know the world is gone?"

"Their transition will be easier this way."

Marcus's spirit slumped further from Hi!-D's casual tone toward the Federation's ongoing act of deception.

"They Alphas will enter through the Stargates in a moment." Hi!-D scanned the horizon with her finger, pointing to each of the thirteen black portals encircling them. "Including the one we used."

All the Stargates were facing the spire from their distant positions, Marcus mentally noted. "Why didn't I see any of the other Alphas during my drive to campus then?"

"Seven thousand and ten people dispersed from a population of nearly eight billion is the literal definition of isolation. Even the high proportion of those hailing from Salt Lake City were still spread out," Hi!-D explained. "And they all stayed put, even before my PSA."

"Why would they do that?"

"To mourn over the bodies of the Ascended, which my replications will gather for Final Rites following the Alphas' arrival. It may brighten your spirits to know I've been with Antony's body since you left home."

A portal on the other side of the valley activated. A small brown object emerged, dashing past the spire and heading directly for Marcus and Hi!-D's position.

"Before the others join us," she began, turning to face Marcus, "I have a surprise for you. Well, truth be told, it's from Brad. A 'going away' present of sorts."

Marcus immediately recognized the brown blob's barks echoing across the dry sea of salt. "KITTY!"

He sprinted away from Hi!-D to meet her partway. Kitty jumped into his arms, knocking both of them onto the ground. She frantically licked Marcus's face, staring at him with her soulful golden eyes while thrashing her tail, then bolted away to relieve herself.

"Take good care of that one," Hi!-D insisted. "She's the last dog left on Earth. It wasn't easy for Brad to sell the idea to the Federation collective on your behalf."

Marcus wept under his breath.

"May I be blunt with you?"

"Okay." Marcus wiped snot from his nose.

"Your sadness is the result of focusing on what you've lost. Instead, you should be focused on what you've gained. You're walking into the future with many material and immaterial reminders of your past. Rely on those as a source of strength if you must. But your new family will look to you for calm confidence. It's important for you to put forward a smiling face."

Marcus dried his cheeks. He called Kitty over and stood petting her as all of the other Stargates activated. Like the indiscernible images of a television while rapidly changing channels, the portals flickered as individuals from different points of origin poured through one-by-one. *It was a cosmopolitan group*, Marcus thought. *Most were kids or teens, but there was a spectrum of adults represented. Overall, women outnumbered men by a noticeable margin.* Marcus was surprised by the extent of his network at only six layers deep. "Small world."

"Indeed," said Hi!-D. "Together, you'll rebuild it."

People walked past Marcus and pooled around the spire; afloat in the vastness of this valley, they were looking for a lighthouse to guide them back to safety.

"Right. If you don't need anything else, I'll leave you with the Alphas and tend to Final Rites. Wish me luck. I have an important Proclamation to deliver," Hi!-D said, crossing the index and middle fingers on both of her hands. Then she vanished, instantly appearing in her usual place in the sky below the PSA screen.

How ironic, Marcus said to himself, watching the seconds vanish from the Confederation invasion clock.

Hi!-D addressed the quiet crowd, "It's not by chance that you stand here on Pioneer Day, set to advance your Form toward the next milestone in your integration. This path will result in both your personal and collective progress. You survivors are the Alpha generation for a New World Order. Your privilege comes thanks to the Ascended. ..." Hi!-D proceeded to relay the same information she and Brad shared with Marcus about the Reset, the Confederation's scorched universe policy, and the Federation's Endowment. Thoughts of Antony started to monopolize Marcus's attention. He blocked out Hi!-D's present speech and returned to her earlier words of wisdom: *Your sadness is the result of focusing on what you've lost. Instead, you should be focused on what you've gained.*

Marcus scanned the faces of the crowd. He didn't recognize most of the Alphas, but the first familiar face he saw came with a companion: Hannah and Lucius.

Marcus ran to them, waving both arms, with Kitty following at his side. "Hey, Hannah! Hannah Duston!"

Hannah clearly recognized Marcus, but she played coy, clinging to her son's shoulders. "Do I know you?"

"Marcus Adams … from Monica's Cohort at the Lab?" Marcus signaled his insider knowledge.

Hannah half-smiled. "Antony's brother."

Marcus's stomach folded in on itself.

Hannah whispered into Lucius's ear, and the boy smiled, then the pair returned their focus to the spire.

"Have you seen any other familiar faces?"

"No, until you," Hannah replied without looking at Marcus. "But there's a disturbing lack of adults here."

Hi!-D's Proclamation grabbed Marcus's attention again. "Your Halos will be built using three protective layers, each created from the material energy of the Ascended. In a moment, their bodies will begin a Procession toward the spire to be transmuted through plasma flames. Following this, three waves of energy will wash over each of you, marking the end of your Coronation Ceremony, and activate your Halos."

Hi!-D clarified a few more technical details and emphasized the importance of everyone's sacrifice on both sides of the veil before joining the Alphas for a moment of silence. As the Coronation began, the sun fell behind the tip of the western mountains, washing everything in its golden rays. Horns echoed across the valley. A pulse of blue light flexed within the spire to each sound. Marcus recognized a pattern: 1, 2, 3, 5, 8, 13, 21. Then, the sequence repeated two more times before the world fell silent.

Marcus's heart was on the verge of bursting, and his ears were ringing. He looked down at Hannah's hands: they were shaking as she continued gripping Lucius.

Thirteen paths, hundreds of feet wide and made from red flower petals, emerged through the salt, dividing the Alphas into sections. Each crimson road originated from one of the surrounding Stargates, which had grown massively in size, and led directly into the spire. Marcus, Hannah, and Lucius stood at the edge of one path as the Ascended appeared through the portals in blocks of bodies a hundred wide and a hundred high. Each individual faced skyward, draped in a silken golden shroud that held perfectly still while the Procession line floated steadily toward the spire.

It was impossible to identify anyone, Marcus thought, *but he knew Antony, Jordan, and Monica were among the bodies ... somewhere.* The tip of the Procession vanished into the pulsating base of the spire, causing the blue glow to intensify. The blocks of bodies increased in speed exponentially, morphing into a blur of solid gold. Despite moving at this incredible rate, the bodies made no sound, but their flow created a welcoming breeze to beat back the hot desert air. *This felt familiar ... he'd dreamed about this. He was certain of it.*

The spire's light continued to grow with the speed of the Procession until the Alphas had to shield their eyes. When the last of the Ascended disappeared into the tower, three waves of blue light burst from its base, racing across the valley and bathing everyone in their electrified power. The scent of ozone clung to the dry air. The Stargates shut, and the world was silent again. Marcus looked to the PSA screen. *The entire Procession to transmute eight billion bodies had taken less than seven minutes.*

50

FAMILIAR FACES

Marcus was amazed at how placid the Alphas were. "Everyone is so calm," he muttered.

"It's the opium," Hannah whispered back.

"What?"

"I've been in plenty of opium dens, and some of these Alphas are higher than a kite. It makes sense. It's the same way Harriet Tubman smuggled slave babies out of the South—she kept them calm, chemically. They're doing the same thing here so everyone will accept their fate."

Marcus's mind returned to his Disclosure Moment, and Monica's comments about Crystalline at Nerio.

Hi!-D continued with her Proclamation, "Moving forward requires successfully graduating from the Agoge. In addition to your designations as Bigs and Littles, each of you will serve as a Guardian or a Proxy during your training. Three Guardians will lead, and live, among ten Proxies in family units totaling thirteen people, making five hundred and thirty-nine such units in total.

In addition to the Guardians and Proxies, three Elders have been appointed to guide the Agoge's Trinity, a three-part focus on Mind, Body, and Soul. This is an interregnum system, meaning you can collectively change any part of it by gathering as an Assembly. This is something you will do often because, as an Assembly, you'll be searching for additional Elders and electing seven leaders, called Lions. These seven Lions will execute your collective vision, establish a permanent system of government, and oversee your future training in counsel with the Elders. This system is integral to the success of integrating worlds and preparing us to fight off the invading Confederation forces."

Everything Brad said to Marcus about being a potential Lion flooded to the front of his mind again. *These were the people he'd be accountable to and responsible for ... despite Brad's parting words of encouragement, he was having a hard time accepting this challenging new calling.*

"Please look at your feet," Hi!-D instructed. "There, you'll see a custom Beacon."

Marcus looked at the blue rectangle floating on the ground several feet in front of him. It contained three large, empty circles stacked like a traffic light.

"The top circle shows your social designation, each expressed using a unique icon. The middle circle shows your economic designation, which displays whether you're a Guardian, Proxy, or Elder. After you graduate from the Agoge, it will include other icons. The bottom circle shows your political designation, which is tied to your biological age, meaning it will only show whether you're a Big or a Little, but not the actual number of years."

The beacon said Marcus was a Guardian/Little, but without confirmation, the third circle about his social status was unclear. *It looked like a lion*, Marcus thought.

"Time to meet your new families!" Hi!-D clapped. "If your Beacon is an arrow, follow it until it becomes a rectangle again. If your Beacon is a rectangle now, then stay where you are. Have a delightful time sorting!"

Marcus's Beacon said that his new family would be coming to him. The murmur of all the Alphas lifted his spirits; people started to talk again, motivated by the necessity of moving by one another as they self-sorted into units. The sight of the Alphas churning like a sea hypnotized Marcus, but the sound of sobbing broke the spell. Hannah was on her knees, whispering hastily to her son as tears gushed from both their eyes.

"Everything okay?" Marcus asked.

Hannah stood and rushed to Marcus, covering her mouth with trembling fingers. "It's telling me to leave."

"The arrow is?"

"Yes!" Hannah let out a series of hysterical cries.

Marcus didn't know what to say.

"I can't leave Lucius!"

"Where's it sending him? Maybe it's taking you on different paths to the same place?"

"It's telling him to stay here!" Hannah fumed. "And it's sending me away. I can't leave—he needs me."

"It's telling him to stay here?" Marcus repeated.

"Yes."

"Then, he's going to be with me."

Hannah winced at Marcus's revelation. She lowered her head and stomped in place, then abruptly calmed herself and returned to Lucius's side. She kissed her son and whispered into his ear, then stood to compose herself. After a final pause, Hannah sulked away.

Marcus could see Lucius's Beacon; it said he was a Proxy/Little, with the same unit number displayed vertically on either side of the Beacon's rectangle: 528.

"Hey, Marcus," said a familiar female voice.

Marcus's heart turned to mush. It was Velia. They ran to one another, hugging tightly and savoring their reconnection. Marcus inspected her Beacon: she was part of unit 528 and a Proxy/Big.

"I thought you were in your early twenties?"

"I ... lied." Velia blushed. "Who's the kid?"

"Lucius Duston. He just lost his mom."

Velia hung her head. "Didn't we all ..."

"Sorry," Marcus backpedaled. "Not in the Reset. His mother is in another unit, so they had to separate."

"She's alive?"

"You know Hannah?"

"No." Velia stroked her forearm. "I'm surprised a mother and son pair survived—that's all. I haven't seen that among the other Alphas. The kid is lucky. "

She was right. Marcus stared at the sobbing boy as a wave of Antony's advice washed over him: *We each have three masks ... one we present to ourselves, one that shows how other people see us, and one that captures who we really are. ... Joyfully three-step into the light from the shadows. ...*

Lucius looked up at Marcus as another wave of wisdom washed over him, except this time, it was something Hi!-D said: *Put forward a smiling face. ...*

Marcus beamed joy back at the boy, then turned to Velia. "I'm guessing you had no trouble getting here."

"You didn't have to move?" Velia challenged.

"No."

"It was strange," Velia explained. "The more you trusted the arrow and confidently walked, the less you bumped into other people—not that it hurt if you did, you'd bounce off one another with no real damage."

The sun's final rays faded behind the horizon, but the spire's blue glow allowed the Alphas to keep navigating safely. The salty ground had turned an intense Egyptian blue, and the red flower petals of the procession lines radiated a royal amethyst purple.

The next person to find their way to Marcus's family unit was another old friend. "Ameda!"

"Good to see you, Marcus!" Ameda hugged him. His Beacon indicated he was a Guardian/Little of the 528. "What the hell happened to your face? And shirt?"

Marcus didn't have time to answer since people continued arriving. Interspersed with an unfamiliar trio of Proxy/Littles were more familiar faces: Sukanksha, Jack, and Charles from FACT, followed by Duygu and Rick from the Cohort. All of them were Proxies, and Rick was the only other Big in the family. Marcus did a quick head count: there were twelve of them so far. Everyone eagerly awaited the arrival of their thirteenth member and the final Guardian.

Marcus looked to his left to find Dianna standing a dozen feet away. Out of instinct, he moved toward her, followed by Kitty. Dianna lurched back from both of them, kicking Kitty in the stomach after the dog tried to sniff at her legs. Marcus grabbed Kitty by the collar, stunned, as Dianna delivered a death stare. He forced a smile, then looked her up and down; the sundress she wore didn't hide the diminished contour of her belly. Dianna marched past him, head high, to join their family.

Then the valley was still.

Hundreds of units circled the spire while Hi!-D resumed her guidance from above. "Your new family will be a source of strength for you during the Agoge."

Marcus stared at Dianna across the blue illuminated night, but she refused to acknowledge his presence.

"The Elders will not be part of one specific unit," Hi!-D explained. "Instead, they'll float between your families, embedding with a new one each day—"

Kitty was pulling desperately on Marcus's right arm. Without looking, he got her to sit down again.

"Would the Guardians from each unit please step to the front of their family?" asked Hi!-D.

Marcus turned to Velia. "Will you hold my dog?"

Kitty took the opportunity to yank Velia in the same direction. Marcus looked to their east but saw nothing out of the ordinary, then joined Ameda and Dianna.

"Under the direct guidance of the corresponding Elder," Hi!-D explained, "each Guardian will oversee one Foci of the Agoge's Trinity. Look at your Beacon. Your economic designation will be ringed by a color: white for Mind, yellow for Body, or red for Soul."

Marcus's focus was Soul. Ameda was responsible for Mind, and Dianna would direct the Body.

"Like the Elders," Hi!-D continued, "Guardians will live every-thing the rest of their unit does, rotating authority based on the Foci of a specific task—"

Kitty's incessant barking got Marcus's attention. He scanned the units to his left and right, noticing a few more familiar faces from FACT: Bonnie, Lindsay, Che, and Quinn. Two Cohort members were also visible: Komson and Diksha. He even saw a few Wild Cards from the rest of his life: Sarah, Joseph, and his Nerio oppo-nent, Aaron. Marcus looked over his shoulder; Velia had already managed to calm Kitty down again.

"Let's meet your interregnum Elders," Hi!-D said. Three Stargates opened. Each Elder was too far away to identify, but as they saun-tered toward the spire, Marcus smiled. *He recognized all three of them.*

"Guardians of the same Foci will meet together in Factions under the direction of a corresponding Elder. Luke Kelly will oversee the Mind, Garret Borland the Body, and Jeraldine Cayce Borland, the Soul—"

"MARCUS!" Velia screeched.

He turned in time to see Kitty blitzing toward the unit to their east, but Marcus's heart fluttered at the sight of a final familiar face amongst their ranks: Antony's.

Marcus sprinted toward the adjacent unit. Gasping for air, he inspected each person's face, but there was no sign of his brother. Marcus doubled back, taking his time to examine everyone again, but Antony was nowhere to be found. Kitty returned to his side, and Marcus dropped his head in defeat. *This hadn't been a halluci-nation, he was sure of it. Antony's presence felt real.* He'd taken a couple of steps before he realized Kitty was missing again. Marcus whipped around to find the chocolate lab still sitting amongst the other unit's Littles and Bigs. No one was paying attention to her; they were all too transfixed on Hi!-D.

Marcus called Kitty, but she refused to move, wagging her tail rapidly and panting with a smile on her face. He stormed over and snatched her by the collar, but she went deadweight and collapsed to the ground. He was dragging Kitty back to their unit when an unmistakable voice echoed from behind, confirming the truth of the earlier apparition: "Shout and cheer, Antony's here!"

GLOSSARY
THE IMPORTANT PEOPLE, PLACES, AND THINGS OF SUBSUMPTION

∽

People

Ali Jalali — The eleventh member of the Cohort and a great dancer that makes everyone laugh.

Ameda Tarr — One of Bill's FACT students, a local rap icon, and one of Jordan's collaborators.

Antony Adams — Marcus's older brother and legal guardian. CEO of a data analytics company working on One Identity.

Ashley Jiwoo — One of Bill's FACT students and the shyest member of the class.

Beatrice Faccini Rossi — Antony and Marcus's maternal grand-mother, also known as "Nonna."

Benedict Darrow — The owner of Tek-Mart and leader of the One Identity project.

Bonnie Furey — One of Bill's FACT students and Jordan's bootlegging pseudo-girlfriend.

Brad — Federation researcher working on Project Noble with the Cohort at his Lab on the University of Utah campus.

Bryan Craven — The second member of the Cohort and an astronomy nerd.

Charles Fratt — One of Bill's FACT students and a descendent of Benjamin Franklin.

Che Diaz — One of Bill's FACT students and Marcus's favorite classmate after Jordan.

Corina Besliu — The third member of the Cohort and an immigrant from the former Soviet Union.

Dave King — The eighteenth member of the Cohort and an avid trail runner.

Dianna Kos — Marcus's girlfriend. She's a PhD student in developmental psychology working on her field research at the Coalition headquarters.

Diksha Arora — The seventh member of the Cohort and one of Marcus's favorite team members.

Duygu Orhan — The eighth member of the Cohort and a total sweetheart.

Garret Borland — Marcus's therapist and a member of Dianna's dissertation committee. Husband of Jeraldine Cayce Borland.

Hannah Duston — Sister to Benedict Darrow and mother of Lucius Duston.

Jack Wilburn — One of Bill's FACT students and an expert on data.

Jeraldine Cayce Borland — The owner of Set & Setting at the Black Market. Wife of Garett Borland and longtime family friend to Marcus.

Jordan Kilravock — Marcus's best friend and roommate, one of Bill's FACT students, and the leader of the Lyceum. Also known by his EDM stage name DJ Beez Nutz.

Komson Chanprapan — The fifth member of the Cohort and a fan of mixed drinks and Harry Potter books.

Lindsay Egginton — One of Bill's FACT students and the class's teaching assistant.

Lucius Duston — Son of Hannah Duston and a frail child with a complicated medical history.

Luke Kelly — Consigliere to the Federation and star of the Symposium. A former graduate student of Marcus's father.

Marcus Winthrop Adams — Brother to Antony, boyfriend to Dianna, and best friend to Jordan. He's one of Bill's FACT students and is the nineteenth member of Brad's Cohort.

Monica Eames — The first member of the Cohort and a friend-with-Tek-benefits to Marcus.

Nicole Clayson — One of Bill's FACT students with the biggest heart of anyone in the class.

Quinn Overton — One of Bill's FACT students and an ROTC soldier with a loud mouth and no filter.

Rick Haskell — The ninth member of the Cohort and a professor at Westminster College.

Sanchit Shrivasta — The sixteenth member of the Cohort and an unapologetic Communist from India.

Sarah Oberg — A close friend of Antony's who trains with him in Krav Maga.

Sukanksha Totade — One of Bill's FACT students and the most brilliant member of the class.

Tony Shipton — Former head of security at Antony's company, owner of a 3D-printed gun shop at the Black Market, and the twentieth member of the Cohort.

Velia Wolf — One of Bill's FACT students, friend to Marcus, and an adoring fan of Antony.

Virgil Wolff — Former coworker of Velia.

William K. Martin — FACT Connector for Marcus's class at the University of Utah. Goes by the nickname of "Bill."

Zain Siddiqui — The thirteenth member of the Cohort and an occasional nationalistic opponent to Diksha and Sanchit.

Places

Antony's House — Old rambler-style home in the shadow of the NSA data center in Lehi, Utah.

Black Market — Formerly the Gateway Mall in Salt Lake City. Home of an alien-owned bazaar hosting and supporting a range of human-owned businesses.

Carlson Hall — Location of the only Federation Research Lab on Earth and where the Cohort participates in social experiments called Subsumption.

Fort Douglas — A portion of the University of Utah campus hosting Bill's FACT class and the Federation's press conferences.

Global One — Tactical training center in the western desert of Utah, also home to the Federation Forces.

Hecate — The Federation's home planet.

Last Chance Lakes — A community in Utah's western desert and home to one of Monica's many properties.

Marcus and Jordan's House — Turn of the century redbrick within walking distance of campus.

Monica's Mansion — Monica's primary residency at the base of Mount Olympus overlooking the Salt Lake Valley.

Nerio — One of the four sectors of the Black Market. It hosts the world's premier bare-knuckle fighting circuit.

Proxima Centauri — A forward staging base for the Confederation's invasion force.

Sirius Star System — Training grounds for the Confederation's special forces unit, the Black Star Hunters.

Sundance — The location of Marcus's family home in Utah.

The University of Utah — Campus in Salt Lake City hosting a FACT class and the only Federation Research Lab for Project Noble on Earth.

Vega Star System — Home to the Confederation's civilization, Vega Major and Vega Minor.

∾

Things

Betting House — A betting market based out of Nerio that sets its own ratio for the bare-knuckle fights.

Bucephalus — Antony's armored vehicle and "warhorse."

Cerebrate — Part of the FACT curriculum which asks students to study and think about the subject on their own time outside of class.

Cohort — A select group of participants in the Federation's research to understand humanity for integration into their galactic civilization.

Confederation — Human extraterrestrials from the Vega Star System intent on capturing, containing, or killing humanity.

Connector — FACT instructors versed in the five core pillars of knowledge: art, hard science, history, mathematics, and social science.

Complementing — Tek feature that allows a user to manipulate the way their own five senses experience the world in real-time.

Derivative Ghosting — Tek feature that catalogs and stores memories from a user's brain.

EXO — The suit used by members of the Cohort during Sequences as part of Subsumption.

FACT — Federation Acculturation and Cooperation Tract at the University of Utah that trains Praetors to work as intermediaries between humanity and the Federation.

Federation — Extraterrestrials helping humanity prepare to face the invading Confederation forces.

Federation Forces — The group of Operators trained by the Federation to use Power Gloves against the Confederation.

Form — A living entity with a shared genetic code, like humanity, as referred to by the Federation.

FTAP — Federation Technology Accelerator Program that helps human owners of Black Market businesses solve technological problems.

Go Zones — Areas fortified by the Federation using a Pomerium and/or Federation Forces.

Hi!-D — An artificial intelligence created by Brad and fed data from Subsumption to update her social cortex. She delivered the Disclosure Moment on Arrival Day and is the face of the Federation through the Public Service Announcements.

Invictus — A modern Gladius gifted from Antony to Marcus for passing Selection into the Federation's Cohort.

Liberty Bell — Where members of the Cohort complete their Sequences as part of Subsumption in the heart of Brad's Lab. Also known as the Experimental Chamber.

Lyceum — Jordan's community of online conspirators working to unmask the Federation and expose the true intentions of humanity's alien allies.

Netting — Tek feature that live-streams and/or records a user's experiences in real-time.

Objective Statement — Declaration of the Federation's intentions and goals with humanity through Project Noble.

Operators — Human members of the Federation Forces trained to use the Power Gloves against the Confederation.

Peanut Gallery — Expert commentators at Nerio who act as an authoritative voice for the Betting House.

Power Gloves — Offensive and defensive weapons used by the Federation Forces.

Pomerium — A protective force field that the Federation can place around people, vehicles, and buildings. They are used to guard Carlson Hall and the Black Market.

Praetors — Intermediaries for humanity and the Federation trained through FACT.

Project Noble — A collaboration between the Federation and humanity in preparation for the coming Confederation invasion. It has three important milestones: M1, M2, and M3.

Public Service Announcements — Inspiring messages from the Federation, delivered by Hi!-D from the sky with help from the PSA screen.

One Identity — Government project led by Benedict Darrow and involving Antony Adams to create a decentralized blockchain database for managing identity.

Operator — A member of the Federation Forces.

Selection — The process of identifying, testing, and validating members into the Cohort for Subsumption.

Sequences — Social experiments done in Brad's Lab as part of "Subsumption" by members of the Cohort.

SIMs — Files created by Tek users that can be stored and/or shared for later use.

Subsumption — The name Cohort members gave Brad's research in Carlson Hall and the main source of Hi!-D's social cortex data. It's the key to reaching the M1 milestone.

Symposium — Historical lectures led by Luke Kelly at the University of Utah using a Tek complement and broadcast live to the world.

Tek — Federation technology given to members of the Cohort based on their quota in exchange for time spent in Subsumption. It's sold exclusively through Tek-Mart.

Tek-Mart — The sole seller of new Tek units, with its headquarters at the Black Market. Owned by Benedict Darrow.

AUTHOR'S NOTE

OCTOBER 1, 2020

As I write this, I'm sitting in the shadow of Mount Timpanogos under the illumination of a full moon, cigar burning, Glitch Mob streaming to my wireless Skullcandy Crusher headphones as Kitty sleeps beside me on the backyard patio furniture (don't tell my wife). This setting is a poetic way for me to add this final stroke to *Subsumption* before it's sent to the printer to face the market test since it was in identical conditions that the story was born, nurtured, and finally finished (but I would've been walking). If you've made it this far, I expect that the "story of the story" interests you, so I'll briefly explain why I wrote this novel, where the idea for *Subsumption* came from, my tumultuous decade-long writing journey, and my plans for the rest of the series.

I don't remember the moment I decided to write Subsumption, but it was sometime in 2011 after I started my PhD in economics. I wasn't fulfilling some dream of being a writer. My mother was the successful author; I wanted to be a rock star. But once the story came to me, writing it became an all-consuming activity. From the beginning, I intended for this story to inspire people, to help them discover reasons to be optimistic about our collective future in a world increasingly addicted to base nihilism. I also knew that to accomplish this, Subsumption had to do three things: (1) it had to be entertaining, (2) it had to provide strong moral instruction, (3) it had to include intertextual symbolism. Anything less would be a failure (in my mind).

The fact that I'm surrounded by technology at this very moment is typical. I'm an unapologetic believer in the power of tech to improve our lives, and I leverage it in every facet of my existence. But as an economist, I know that it's only half the battle and that human interactions, what my kind call "social institutions," are equally important for sustainable progress. Like the twin-columns supporting the sign over Nerio's Stargate, technology and social institutions are what make progress possible, a fact I emphasized during my time as a professor-in-training at the University of Utah (I'll come back to that). Without both pillars, society becomes a dystopian nightmare, incapable of satisfying the complete needs and wants of its citizens. But when they're balanced, we flourish beyond our wildest imaginations, and progress marches onward.

While I can't remember the exact genesis moment for the story, I do remember a concept that was instrumental in the early stages: subsumption. This is a term from Marxian economics, the core theory of my University department despite Utah's notoriety for conservatism (how this program became one of the last bastions of Marxist ideology is a fascinating story that I hope someone else will tell). And while I'm also an unapologetic fan of capitalism and its unrivaled historical success at creating repeatable material progress (like my cigar), I'm thankful to the faculty who intro-duced me to alternative ways of seeing a problem and the notion that over time, capital tends to *subsume* labor; it was this kernel that got me thinking about Marcus and the Lab.

Having been both an employee and a bourgeois "pig" owner, I believe the academic Marxians are wrong on almost all accounts about how the world, and markets, actually operate. In particular, the principal-agent problem between owners and their employees is inadequately addressed (look up "shirking" to see how difficult it is to get most workers to do the job they agreed to). My challenge is supported by the empirical evidence of behavioral economists who've repeatedly demonstrated what any parent already knows: humans change their behavior in dramatic ways when they know they're being watched. This observation is also why the early utilitarian economists proposed solutions like the panopticon as a way to stop criminals from scheming.

It was while working through these issues with my beloved students (especially those in my ECON 5470 class) that I realized the solution: the only way to truly understand human nature is when the person doesn't know they're being watched. At the time, I was also teaching a slew of research and data courses with the real-life Brad (who is exactly like his character), and it was from the overlap between these ideas that I developed the concept of "Subsumption" as a way for the Federation to fully assess the human "Form." This was, and I think still is, the core philosophical problem explored in the Subsumption Series; once this idea was in place, everything else easily followed.

But subsumption, research, data, and Brad weren't the only inspiration I pulled from my time at the University of Utah. My PhD cohort provided the model for the group of the same name in Project Noble, and I borrowed heavily from their identities for characters. Similarly, secondary and tertiary characters (some are set to become primary characters in the series) are based on students from the classes I taught. Finally, many of my employees, who were my best students before being hired, will recognize themselves in the cast of the Subsumption Series, an act of homage for their inspiration, directly or indirectly, with my writing. I hope they feel that I've captured the essence of their identities.

If it isn't clear yet, my writing journey was inextricably tied to my time at the University of Utah. But the details are in the sequence of events. The period from 2011 through 2012 was spent ideating and researching the story, but at some point in that window, I started writing. I didn't know about this distinction at the time, but I was "pantsing it" (meaning I was writing from the flow state without an outline). In 2012, between sitting in classes and teaching, I continued writing *Subsumption,* and on March 2nd of 2013, I finished the zero draft. I remember this date because a fortune cookie had predicted it'd be an important day (I found a pair of Facebook posts from that period confirming my memory). Then, the book sat untouched for five years.

It wasn't for lack of desire that the project stalled. I'd given the zero draft to a few friends and was encouraged by the feedback I received. But I was overwhelmed by life. I had a growing family, I was still taking classes and had started preparing my dissertation, and I was teaching (a lot ... at multiple universities by this point). So what does a person with too little time do? That's right, they start a business! This was more an act of fate and less the result of planning; Brad and I had tried to establish a data science institute at the University (before data was cool), but we were shot down, so we decided to do it privately and hired a gaggle of our best students. Thus, Emperitas was born, and the book was knocked down to a distant fifth place in the order of my life's priorities.

At some point in 2015, I complained to my wife, Nicole, that the book was losing its saliency (I'd originally set the story in 2014, but that date was already long gone), and she told me to be patient because I couldn't predict when *Subsumption* would be needed in the world. As someone who was busy telling the future with data (on campus and in the marketplace), I scoffed at her naivete, but today, thanks to the *post hoc* outcomes, I realize she

648

was right. Occasionally, my earliest readers of the zero draft would ask about the story, but since I was in the final phase of my PhD, every free moment (which turned out to be Sundays) was spent crafting my dissertation from the Emperitas office with the voluntary assistance of two truly dedicated employees: Lindsay and Raymond.

It was during one such Sunday session in 2017 that I mentioned the novel's existence to Lindsay. If my memory is correct (and I have no Facebook post to verify this), she asked when I planned to write a textbook. Lindsay had become my go-to teaching assistant by this point, so it was a logical question coming from someone who helped craft the mass of materials necessary to enlighten minds. I jokingly replied that I already had my textbook, but it was a sci-fi novel. She asked to read the zero draft, and at the next Sunday session, she enthusiastically encouraged me to return to it (seeing the parallels between the story's subject matter and what we were teaching in class). I nodded and smiled then said I'd think about it once the dissertation was behind me.

In early 2018 with the end of my PhD in sight, Lindsay and a few of my original readers convinced me that it was time to dive back in. By mid-May, a few weeks after defending my dissertation, I made good on that promise and started plotting revisions. Lindsay stayed on to help (for the astute reader of the copyright page, you'll already know that she became my editor). The rigors of my dissertation, and my father's eternal wisdom, taught me the importance of having a system, so I researched existing software solutions and writing best practices. This led me to the vibrant indie author community. After consuming hundreds of YouTube videos (at 2x speed), I was converted from a "pantser" to a "plotter" and headed down an unfamiliar path.

I started 2019 with a solid writing system in place. I wasn't teaching anymore, but I was still busy with family and Emperitas, so the process of rewriting went slowly. *Subsumption* steadily grew from the 75,000 words of the zero draft to 125,000 words by the end of the year, which included new and important characters (a large number of which came from the final class I taught in the fall of 2017). By mid-November, I had a revised draft, which I gave to two dozen beta readers. Again the feedback was encouraging, but the story wasn't ready for the wider world yet. I realized I didn't have a good grasp of what sci-fi fans expected. Thus Operation Humeros Gigantes was born; in three months, I read more than a dozen of the "top sci-fi books of all time."

Simultaneously in early 2020, Lindsay and I began a developmental edit, applying the methods of Shawn Coyne's Story Grid. This was a pivotal turning point because it showed me where the major structural issues were that needed fixing. One of the beta readers from this period was another important man I'd met long ago in my history classes at the University: Bill Martin (yes, he's real, and yes, he's just like his character). He'd moved to Albania to teach a graduate-level sci-fi literature class and wanted to include *Subsumption* in his upcoming semester. By March, just as the pandemic hit, I was busy revising, and in May, I gave him the book. I also sent it to another round of beta readers. The feedback this time exceeded my expectations. I was close.

Lindsay spent the summer of 2020 copyediting *Subsumption* while I drafted *Coverted* and *Disclosure*, prequels in the series meant to function as free reader magnets (a best practice I'd learned from the indie author community). The value of our system proved itself ten times over, and within a couple of months, the prequels blitzed through the same ideating, outlining, writing, editing, and revising process. *Coverted* launched in August with the first announcement about what I was up to. *Disclosure* released a month later. Meanwhile, Lindsay and I were busy putting the final polish on *Subsumption* in anticipation of its October 2020 release. All this required a herculean effort, only made possible by the global downturn that impacted Emperitas.

Which brings us to today. My cigar is almost out (but I have another nearly identical one—thanks capitalism!), Kitty is still asleep, and Sevendust is playing in my headphones now. My family is healthy and happy, and I'm optimistic about the future, though a sizable portion of society seems to crave the collapse of America. My wife's words keep coming back to me: the world needs *Subsumption* now more than it did in 2014. But *Subsumption* is only the first story in this series, and I plan to spend the next decade writing the three remaining novels, plus an unknown number of short stories (similar in scope to *Coverted* and *Disclosure*). There's also a parallel reveal coming about this universe, and the Confederation, that an astute reader may uncover.

Before we say goodbye (for now), here's my system for finishing the series: I'll spend six months wandering in the wilderness with Kitty while listening to music and ideating. Then, I'll burn a few months outlining. After that, I'll do a few more months of research, followed by a year of writing to get the zero draft, which I'll give to beta readers. From there, I'll take a couple months for developmental editing and revisions before another round of beta readers. I'll make final changes, then send the manuscript to Lindsay for months of copyediting and a final proofread. By late 2023, *Guardians* will be ready to face the market test. An optimized version of this system, using lessons learned in the next iteration, will be repeated for *Echoes* and *Astra*.

Again, if you've made it this far, you must be really committed to the story. I'm so thankful to have you along for the ride as a reader. While I may not release stories as fast as some would like (Bill, keep taking your vitamins!), know that I'm committed to the three original goals of this story. In the meantime, I hope you'll read *Coverted* and *Disclosure*, if you haven't already, and follow my progress by joining the mailing list on my website (lucianopesci.com). There you'll find blog content about *Subsumption* to keep you temporarily satiated, along with updates on the status, by stage, on my system. If you're interested in becoming one of my beta readers as I work on *Guardians*, *Echoes*, and *Astra*, just drop me a line or connect with me on social media.

Till Hecate Arrives,

Luciano

PS: It'd be very helpful to the wider sci-fi reader community (and me) if you left an honest review about *Subsumption*. You can do that here: links.lucianopesci.com/reviewsubsumption

ABOUT THE AUTHOR

Luciano is an economist, futurist, and data scientist. A highly loved professor at multiple higher eds over the last decade, he's now an academic mercenary, focused on technologies like blockchain, artificial intelligence, and asteroid mining.

He's the proud father of four spirited boys, loves cooking with his wife, Nicole, and wandering Utah's wilderness with his chocolate lab named Kitty. In his free time, Luciano enjoys reading about history and society as inspiration for his science fiction series.

Luciano is also the founder and CEO of Emperitas, a business intelligence solution that combines data science with agile research and economic modeling. He holds a PhD and an MA in Economics, an HBA in History, and a BS in Political Science.

KEEP READING IN THE SUBSUMPTION UNIVERSE FOR <u>FREE</u>

LUCIANOPESCI.COM

CPSIA information can be obtained
at www.ICGtesting.com
Printed in the USA
LVHW050822151120
671499LV00001B/3